WHY YOU WILL LOVE THIS ...
by Michael Mor...

This is a tender and deep ... story of the love
of a young girl, for a c ... .y old wooden horse
discovered in a junk shop. Both horse and girl are
sad and lonely, and both find the friend they so
need in one another. But it is how they find it that
is truly magical, and when a magical story is made
utterly believable, then you know you have a rare
story. This is one of those.

Quite unputdownable, and quite unforgettable.

Michael Morpurgo

Michael Morpurgo OBE is one of Britain's best
loved writers for children. He has written over
100 books and won many prizes, including the
Whitbread Award and the Blue Peter Book
Award for his novel *Private Peaceful* and the
Smarties Prize and the Writer's Guild Award
for *The Butterfly Lion*. Michael was Children's
Laureate from 2003 to 2005, a role which took
him all over the country to inspire children
with the joy of reading stories.

Also by Magdalen Nabb

Twilight Ghost

MAGDALEN NABB

The
Enchanted
Horse

Illustrated by Julek Heller

HarperCollins *Children's Books*

First published in Great Britain by Collins in 1992
This edition published by HarperCollins *Children's Books* in 2009
HarperCollins *Children's Books* is a division of HarperCollins*Publishers* Ltd,
77-85 Fulham Palace Road, Hammersmith, London W6 8JB

The HarperCollins website address is
www.harpercollins.co.uk

2

ISBN-13 978 0 00 731733 2

Printed and bound in England by
Clays Ltd, St Ives plc

This book is dedicated to
Maestro Nino di Fazio
with admiration for his boundless knowledge of horses

～∞ *One* ∞～

It was Christmas Eve, and the afternoon had frozen as hard and milky as a pearl. The sun was as thin and pale as a disc of ice in a sky as white as the snowy ground.

Irina walked in front of her mother and father along the lane that led across the fields to the village. She was dressed in a sheepskin coat and boots and mittens and a sheepskin hat. Her long fair plait hung down beside her. The cold pinched her thin cheeks, and the trees that grew on each side of the lane poked their black fingers through the freezing fog as if they were trying to clutch at her as she went by.

Even before they reached the first houses at the edge of the village, Irina heard the faint sound of a band playing Christmas carols. But she didn't look up and smile or turn to say "Listen!" to her mother and father. She only walked quietly on, looking down at her thick boots as they trod the hardened snow. Irina didn't like Christmas.

When they reached the village, all the shop windows were already lit, making haloes of light in the fog. The snow-covered square where the band was playing round the Christmas tree was hung around with coloured bulbs. But Irina and her parents didn't stop to listen to the carols because they had so much to do. They lived on a farm and at Christmas everyone wants more cream and eggs and milk, and besides, they had to be back home in time to feed the animals. So her father stopped to talk to the dairyman at the corner and Irina went ahead with her mother to help with the shopping.

They went to the baker's to buy bread and flour and had to wait in a long queue. At the front of the queue a girl who was smaller than Irina reached up and pointed at the cakes and little pies sprinkled with icing sugar.

"And some of those," she shouted, "for Grandma! And the big cake! Grandpa likes cakes! The big cake!"

Irina watched her and listened to every word, but when it was her mother's turn she didn't ask for anything. She was thin and never had much appetite and there was no Grandpa or Grandma coming for Christmas dinner.

They went to the greengrocer's and waited in the long queue. A fat little boy with a red scarf wound round and round his neck was quarrelling with his older sister.

"I like *dates* best!" he protested.

"No you don't," his sister said, "you only like the box with the picture on it, and we're going to buy figs and nuts and tangerines, so there." And their mother winked at the greengrocer's wife and bought figs and nuts and tangerines and dates.

Irina watched them and listened to every word, but when it was her mother's turn she didn't ask for anything. She had no brothers or sisters to quarrel with.

The band in the square began to play "O come, all ye faithful" and the fat little boy in the red scarf and his sister joined in the singing as they went out.

It was getting dark, and the coloured lights twinkled brighter now against the shadowy snow. On the corner outside the greengrocer's shop a fat lady with a long apron and thick gloves was selling

Christmas trees. A thin boy, taller than Irina, was choosing one with his father. "This one! No, this one, no, that one, *that* one, it's the biggest!" and his father laughed and said, "And how do you think we'll get it home?" But he bought it, even so, and the fat lady wound some thick string round it to help them carry it. Irina watched and listened but she didn't ask for anything. Years ago her mother had said, "You're too old to be bothering about a Christmas tree. It's a waste of money. You can choose a nice present instead."

So they walked past the Christmas trees and crossed to the other side of the square. There was a toy shop there, and next to that a gloomy junk shop with a bunch of dusty mistletoe hanging in the window, and next to that a shop that sold pretty frocks with full velvet skirts. Irina stood beside her mother and stared at the shop windows with bright eyes but she didn't ask for anything. What was the use of a party frock when she lived so far from the village that she never went to a party? And what was the use of toys when there were no children near enough to play with?

"Have you thought what you'd like?" her mother asked. "You know we mustn't be long, we've a lot to do."

Irina tried to think. It's nice to be able to choose anything you want but it's nicer still when your present is a surprise. So she stared at the big dolls in boxes and then at the dresses and then at the tinsel and the silver bells decorating the window. She wanted to choose something that would please her mother. Then she remembered the fat little boy and his cheerful red scarf and so as not to keep her mother waiting and make her angry she said, "I like the red velvet frock…"

"And where do you think you'll go in it?" said her mother impatiently.

"I don't know…" It's hard to please your Mother when you don't know exactly what she wants you to say. Then she turned and saw her father coming.

"Well?" he said. "Have you finished shopping? It's about time we were getting back."

"Irina hasn't chosen her present," said her mother crossly. "And to look at her face you'd think it was a punishment instead of a treat."

Irina wanted to say, "I don't want anything. I'm not asking for anything. I'd rather go home." But she didn't dare.

Then her father said, "Come on, let's have a look in that toy shop. There must be something you'd like."

"She's spoilt, that's what she is," her mother said. "She doesn't know what it means to want for anything."

The band in the square was playing "Silent Night" very quietly. The sadness of the music, the growing darkness, and the cheerfulness of all the other families made Irina want to cry.

"I don't want anything," she said to herself fiercely, "I don't—" But just as they were coming to the toy shop she stopped.

"Come on," said her father, "you're not going to find anything there."

But Irina didn't move. She was staring in through the window of the junk shop, trying to make something out in the gloom.

"Irina!" said her mother. "For goodness' sake, we have to get home."

But Irina, always so quiet and obedient, for once took no notice.

"The horse…" she said, "look at the poor horse."

"What horse?" said her father.

"I can't see any horse," said her mother. And they both peered into the gloomy junk shop. Beneath a jumble of dusty broken furniture they could just make out the head and tattered mane of what was probably a rocking horse.

"I see it now," her father said. "Well, come on, let's get on. You don't want that old thing for Christmas."

"I should hope not," her mother said. "It looks filthy."

But Irina stared up at them bright-eyed, and the tears that had started with the sad carol and the growing darkness and the cheerfulness of all the other families spilled over and ran down her cheeks.

"It's being crushed," she cried. "It's lonely and frightened and being crushed under all those things!" And before her parents could stop her, she had run inside the shop and all they could do was to follow her.

～ *Two* ～

Once inside, Irina stood still, wondering what to do. She'd never seen such confusion in a shop before. It didn't really look like a shop at all, more like the untidiest house in the world. The piles of old furniture reached right up to the ceiling and it was difficult to pass between them. There were ornaments, too, and brass buckets and lampstands and old stoves and typewriters and objects you couldn't tell the use of, and everything was thickly coated with dust, including the one bare light bulb which left most of the room in shadow.

"What can I do for you?" asked a voice in the gloom.

Irina looked about but she could see no one. She felt frightened, but she stood where she was and waited.

"Anyone at home?" said her father's voice behind her.

A voice chuckled. "I am," it said, "if you want to call this home. Past the big dresser on your left."

Irina looked round. At first she could make nothing out but then she noticed a huge armchair with carvings on it as big as a throne, and the profile of a man's head just visible.

"See me now?" But the head didn't turn and the eyes were shut. "I suppose it's getting dark, but I can't see and I don't know why I should pay out good money so that others can see. There's nothing much worth looking at, though I make a living after a fashion. What was it you wanted?"

"The rocking horse," Irina said, as loudly as she dared, and she went closer to the huge carved chair. The man seated there was almost as small and slight as herself, and his closed eyes were sunk in his white face so that he seemed to have no eyes at all. He wore a black overall and his pale hands rested on his knees as quietly as mice.

"Irina...!" protested her mother in an angry whisper. Irina stood where she was, her fists clenched in fear and determination.

"She saw the horse in the window…" Irina's father began, but the blind man took no notice of him.

"What's your name?" he asked, his face lifted towards Irina.

"Irina."

"Irina," he whispered. "Come closer to me."

Irina was frightened of the blind man, but she had to rescue the horse. She went closer. The blind man lifted his mouse-like hands and touched her face, feeling her eyes, her thin cheeks, her mouth and her chin in turn.

"Irina," he said again, and he patted her face gently. "You're a very sad little girl. Why don't you play and be happy?"

"Because there's nobody to play with," Irina said.

"And that's why you want Bella? To play with?"

At first Irina didn't answer because she didn't know who Bella was, but then she thought and said, "Is Bella the name of the horse in the window?"

"That's right," said the blind man.

"Then I don't want her to play with," said Irina boldly. "I want to look after her because she's dirty and lonely and crushed under all those heavy things in your window."

"In that case," said the blind man, "you'd better take her home with you."

Irina stood still and waited, wondering if her mother would say she couldn't, but nobody spoke until the blind man said, "Would you like to know why I call her Bella?"

"Yes," said Irina. "Did she belong to another girl who called her that?"

"I don't rightly know," the blind man said, "who she belonged to, but I'll tell you her story, such as it is. Do you remember a wicked farmer who used to live hereabouts who was known as Black Jack?"

"No," said Irina, "I don't."

"Well, well," said the blind man, "you're very young and it was all before your time."

"I remember him," said Irina's father, coming closer. "He kept horses."

"He did," said the blind man. "And the most beautiful one of all was named Bella because Bella means beautiful. But he was an evil man and treated his animals badly, very badly. They never got more than a handful of oats a day, barely enough to keep them alive, and Bella, who was as finely bred and elegant as a racehorse, was forced to pull him around in that dirty old cart of his. They say he whipped her until she bled. No one knew where he got her, but some said he captured her himself from a wild herd that sometimes passes by this way."

"And what happened to her?" Irina asked.

"I don't know," the blind man said. "But I can tell you what happened to Black Jack. He died."

"I remember," said Irina's father. "I went to the auction when his farm was sold. My old father was still alive then and he kept a pony and trap himself. It was he who talked me into going, but there was little enough worth buying and the horses were only fit for the knacker's yard."

"Even Bella?" asked Irina.

"Bella wasn't there," the blind man said, "Bella wasn't there. I asked about and I spoke to the auctioneer himself but there was no horse of that description on his list. Poor creature. Poor beautiful creature…"

The blind man fell silent with his thoughts as if he'd forgotten there was anyone there.

"Was she dead, then…?" whispered Irina after a while.

"I bought all that stuff in the window from Black Jack's place," the blind man said, without giving her an answer, "and there it's been ever since, including the horse."

"Now what would Black Jack have wanted a rocking horse for?" wondered Irina's father. "He had neither wife nor child."

"But that's just it," said the blind man very softly, just as if he were talking to himself. "It's not a rocking horse."

Then he spoke more loudly, turning his face up towards Irina's father's voice.

"Take the horse home for your little Irina," he said. "If it will make her happy I don't want anything for it. Only perhaps you'll have to come for it another day when the boy who helps me is here. You understand. I can't move all that stuff to get at it."

"That's very nice of you," said Irina's father. "We'll call another time."

He took Irina by the shoulder, but Irina, who never asked for anything, cried, "Please! Please can we wait in case he comes?" And she touched the blind man's arm, no longer afraid of him. "*Please* let us wait! You can tell us more stories about Bella."

"Come on now," said her father, and he led her to the door. "You know we have to get home."

"And don't imagine we're coming back," warned her mother as they went. "That filthy thing must be a mass of woodworm and it's not coming into the house."

Outside on the snowy pavement Irina began to cry. The band was still playing under the Christmas tree and the people had finished their shopping and were starting for home loaded with parcels and calling to each other under the winking lights.

"Merry Christmas! Merry Christmas to you!"

Before her parents could take her away, Irina turned her tearful face for a last look at Bella's poor head, crushed under all that junk, and then from inside the shop the blind man's voice called out, "Stop!"

It was as if he had given an order that had to be obeyed. Irina's parents hesitated and looked at each other.

"Come back a moment, if you will."

Irina's father shrugged. "I suppose we'd better see what the old chap wants."

They went back inside the gloomy shop and Irina ran straight to the blind man's chair. He was sitting just as they'd left him, with his hands resting quietly on his knees.

"I never mistake a footstep," he said. "When you can't see you learn to recognize people in other ways." Then he lifted his face up and called, "Hurry up now! We have customers waiting!"

Irina turned round, and saw a tall cheerful boy come in from behind where her parents stood watching.

"I came to wish you a Merry Christmas, Grandad!"

The grinning boy spoke at the top of his voice as though the man were deaf rather than blind.

"And just as well you did," said the blind man, "there's a job for you to do. This is Irina, and she wants to take Bella home with her, so you'll have to get her out from under all that stuff in the window."

"Right you are, Grandad!" said the boy.

"I don't think…" began Irina's mother, but the boy had already climbed into the window and was heaving the broken furniture about. "I'll have her out of here in two minutes!"

"Is he your grandson?" asked Irina shyly.

"No," said the blind man, "but that's what he likes to call me."

"I haven't got a grandad," Irina said, and she stared at the blind man, wishing he were her grandad, because he could make her parents do what he told them.

"Here you are!" said the boy, and he set Bella down on the floor by Irina. She touched the dirty tangled mane timidly.

"Your father will carry her home for you," the blind man said. "She's too heavy for you."

And sure enough, without a word of protest, Irina's father came and picked up Bella.

"She's a fair weight," he said, "but I'll manage."

"I'll help you," Irina said.

"You help your mother carry the shopping," said her father. Irina followed him to the door, holding her breath because she could hardly believe they were really taking Bella away. But once they were back outside she remembered something and ran back.

"Thank you," she said to the blind man. "And thank you for getting Bella out for me," she said to the cheerful boy who was perched on the arm of the huge chair, swinging his long legs.

"Goodbye, Irina, and Merry Christmas," said the old man, and he lifted his small white hands towards her. She went closer, understanding now that he needed to touch her because he couldn't see her. "Be happy," he said gently and patted her cheek.

"I will be happy," Irina promised, "and I'll

look after Bella – and can I… can I come back and see you one day?" She would have liked to ask him if she could call him Grandad like the boy, but she didn't dare.

"Come whenever you like," said the blind man, "I'm always here."

"Merry Christmas!" she whispered, her eyes shining, and she ran outside.

~ *Three* ~

All the long way home, Irina's mother had a lot to say about moths and woodworm and dirt not coming into her clean house, but Irina hardly heard her she was so happy, and by the time they reached the farm it had been settled that Bella should be put in the old barn which in any case was already half full of junk, where she would dirty nothing and be in nobody's way.

"Can we put straw down for her?" Irina asked as Bella was carried in.

"You can do as you like," her father said. "But you'd better change into your old clothes first, or you'll have your mother after you." And he stood Bella in a corner of the barn just inside the door.

"Let me just look at her first," said Irina. "I won't touch her, I just want to look."

They both looked. It was a sorry sight. There was no telling what colour the horse was meant to be because she was so thickly coated with dirt. Her mane and tail seemed to be of real horsehair, matted, tangled and filthy. It was difficult to tell just what she was made of but it was true, as the blind man had said, that she wasn't a rocking horse. She stood square on her four hooves and there was nothing to suggest that she had ever had rockers. Her head drooped a little and her eyes under the tattered fringe were squeezed almost shut, as though she were crying.

"Poor creature…" whispered Irina, imitating the blind man's words.

"Come on, we've got work to do," her father said, slapping the dust from his hands and coat. "Get changed and start collecting the eggs. We're late with the milking."

Irina was used to working hard on the farm, and since there were no children around to play with she never minded it. But that evening she worked twice as hard as usual so that she would have time to visit Bella before supper.

She ran so fast with the heavy baskets of eggs that if she didn't break any it was only because she was lucky not to slip on the icy stones of the farmyard, and it was a wonder that she didn't give the hens calf nuts to eat by mistake.

Even so, by the time she had finished all her jobs there was only time to lay down some fresh straw for Bella before her mother called.

"Irina! Come and lay the table, supper's ready!"

"I have to go in," Irina whispered to Bella, stroking the poor tangled head. "But tomorrow I'll come and see you before we go to church and afterwards I'll brush and comb you and talk to you so you won't be lonely."

"Irina!"

She turned off the light and went into the house. Because there was some extra cooking and baking to help with for the next day, it was late when Irina went up to bed. In her nightdress, she sat on the bed and parcelled up the little presents she had made at school for her mother and father. She was so happy that they had let her have Bella that she would have liked to give them something bigger and better, but there was nothing she could do about it now. Perhaps she could think of an extra job tomorrow to help her father. And if she said she was hungry and ate more than usual her mother would be pleased. She always looked worried and cross when Irina left food on her plate.

When the parcels were tied and ready, Irina put them on the chair by the bed. But she felt too excited to go to sleep, and went to look out of her window where one of the apple trees that grew in the yard almost touched the panes with its bare branches. It was too dark to see the old barn properly, but Irina stood there a long time with her head pressed against the glass, thinking of Bella and listening to faint noises of the cold night.

And in the darkness of the barn with the clean straw spread around her, Bella stood with her head lowered and her eyes half closed as though she, too, were listening.

⌒ *Four* ⌒

Irina was the first to wake on Christmas morning. Dawn hadn't broken, and the house was hushed and dark. She wrapped herself up warmly and tiptoed down the stairs and out across the icy yard to the old barn.

"Bella!" she called softly, as she pulled the big door open and switched on the light, "Bella! It's Christmas..."

Her eyes shone with pleasure as she approached the horse and reached out to touch its stiff ears and tangled mane.

"Don't be sad," she said gently, "you won't be lonely any more now because I'll come every day and talk to you and brush you and give you clean straw."

She knelt beside Bella and lifted the matted fringe from her sad eyes.

"I'll find you an old blanket, too, if I can, because the nights are so cold. And then in the spring I'll take you outside in the meadow where there'll be grass and flowers and a stream for you to drink from. Will you like it? Will you, Bella?"

She would have liked to put her arms round Bella's neck and hug her tight to make her sadness go away, but she was still shy of her. Instead she promised: "After Christmas dinner I'll be able to stay with you all afternoon and I'll wash and comb you so you'll look beautiful."

Then she got to her feet and tiptoed to the door. Before she switched the light off she said: "Merry Christmas, Bella."

Out in the yard it was still dark. Irina mixed some mash ready for the hens as a surprise for her father. Then she washed her hands in the dairy and pulled off her boots to go in and lay the table for breakfast as a surprise for her mother. They were surprised, but not because she'd done the extra work. Her father gave her a pat on the head and said "Well! You look as bright and cheery as a robin this morning. What's come over you?"

Her mother, watching her eat her breakfast

quickly, looked puzzled and said: "You've got an appetite all of a sudden. What's come over you?"

By the time they were ready to go to church, the day was bright and clear. The freezing fog had vanished in the night and the big winter sun made the icicles shine like glass and the snowy fields sparkle like Christmas glitter. All the way along the lane that led to the village, Irina looked happily about her at the blue shadows on the snow, the few crinkly brown leaves and stalks poking out of the frozen ditch, and the darting black shapes of birds looking for berries, and she thought to herself, "I love Christmas!"

Inside the church it was dark after the dazzling snow, but the crib in the corner was lit by glimmering candles. After the mass Irina went and knelt there, looking at the still figures kneeling in the hay. The Baby in the manger held out his stiff arms towards her, and Irina wished they were alone so that she could explain all about Bella, but more and more people were queuing up behind her. She smiled at the donkey on his pile of straw and then dropped her coins into the box and lit a candle, liking the warm smell of the wax.

And after the cold tramp home there was the warm smell of Christmas dinner.

"I'm hungry!" Irina said, and again her parents looked surprised but they didn't say anything.

After dinner her mother and father admired their little presents and then settled in their armchairs, their faces rosy with sleep after the long morning. Before their eyes were quite closed, Irina said, "Can I go out to the barn?"

"Mmmm…" was all her mother said, and her father gave a little startled grunt as if wondering who had spoken. So Irina wrapped herself up and went out.

She ran first to the barn to stroke Bella and then she began fetching and carrying things across the yard. She fetched two heavy buckets of warm water, a cake of soap, an old sponge from under the sink in the dairy and two old towels that hung behind the door of the cowshed. Then she crept back into the house and went upstairs to get her own comb. She needed a brush too but she didn't dare take her own hairbrush in case it got spoiled and her mother found out. As long as she didn't break the comb she could wash it afterwards and no one would know. Then she was ready to start work.

First, she washed Bella's mane and tail, being as careful as she could not to let the soapy water get into the horse's eyes. She washed and rinsed and washed and rinsed but the hair still felt coarse and greasy and she had to fetch two more buckets of clean warm water and do it all again.

"I think it's clean now," she said, "but I'll need more water for your coat and your feet." And off she went again with the buckets. But when she started to wash Bella's coat she got a surprise. She had thought that Bella would be made of painted wood like a rocking horse, but she wasn't.

"Your coat's real," she said, "just like your mane and tail…"

She soaped it all over very carefully and rinsed away the dirty suds with the sponge. It was a real coat all right, and though it was still wet it looked as if it would be quite a pale colour. Irina washed the horse's feet, and then used the last bucket of clean water to sponge her face and ears very gently. Then she rubbed her all over with the towels, and started work with her comb. She combed the tail first and then the mane, holding the long hair and starting from the ends the way she did with he own hair, because that way it didn't hurt. It took a long time.

"There," she said at last, "all finished."

Then she remembered something.

She remembered her grandfather. At least, she didn't remember him exactly because he had died when she was only a baby, but she remembered her father talking about him and how he had kept a pony and trap all his life. Irina went to the far end of the barn where her father kept what he called "Things that might come in useful" and her mother called "Junk that wants throwing out". She began to look at everything carefully. She didn't know exactly what she was looking for, but if her grandfather had kept a pony then there might be something useful for Bella. She was right. It took her a long time and she bumped and scratched herself climbing over bits of old farm implements, and almost choked on the clouds of dust that flew up as she pulled at pieces of torn sacking. But right at the back in the corner, weighed down by what looked like part of a plough, she discovered a wooden trunk with a broken metal lock. The box was hemmed in by so many other things that she had no hope of getting it out, but she did manage to drag away the heavy piece of plough from the top and open it. It was impossible in the dark corner to see properly what the box contained, but Irina felt inside and pulled the things out. One by one she climbed out with them to where she could see.

"Bella! Look!" she cried, examining her treasure. "There's everything for you, even a blanket!" And there was.

The blanket was old and far too big for Bella, but still it would keep her warm. And there were combs and brushes and bits of harnesses and reins whose leather had rotted away. Irina didn't know the use of half the things, but she put everything in a tidy pile in the corner behind Bella except for the blanket.

The blanket she put carefully over Bella, who was still very wet. It was so big that she folded it double and even then it covered the horse completely from head to tail.

"It doesn't look very nice," Irina explained, "but we have to keep you warm."

She stroked Bella's nose, which was all that was visible under the heavy blanket, and said, "Now you can have a long long sleep until tomorrow."

When she came out of the barn the winter sun was setting, huge and red, and all the snow was lit with a pink light.

Irina thought, "It's almost the end of Christmas Day." But she didn't feel sad, she felt excited as if instead of the end of something it was the beginning of something. And it was.

∾ *Five* ∾

"Irina!" called her mother from the dairy. "Are you supposed to be helping or not? Irina!"

The sun glittered on the snow in the yard, but no answer came, and no Irina came either.

"Irina!" called her father like an echo, "Irina! Your mother's calling you."

But still Irina didn't come.

The broken door of the big barn stood open and the morning sun beamed in low, its light glittering with reflections from the snow. Inside the door, Irina stood holding the old blanket, her face as bright as the sunshine as she gazed in astonishment at the result of her work. She had hoped, when she took off the blanket that morning, that Bella would look clean and pretty but she hadn't hoped for this.

Bella was beautiful. She stood there in the broad beam of sunlight and her coat was smooth and fine, the colour of the palest sand. Her mane and tail were as blonde as Irina's long hair, glowing with gold and silver lights picked out by the morning sun. She no longer looked sad, she looked so sleek and elegant that Irina felt all her shyness come back, and she felt afraid to touch such a beautiful creature. Very timidly, still clutching the blanket, she went closer, and saw that something was wrong. Bella was not perfect. Across her back there were marks, reddish marks like stripes. Irina forgot her shyness. She dropped the blankets and went closer still. Those marks were the marks of a whip!

"Oh no…" whispered Irina. She remembered the frightening story of Black Jack, who whipped and starved his horses. Had he been so cruel and stupid that he even whipped a horse that wasn't real, and could do no work for him?

"Poor Bella." She knelt beside the horse and put her arms round its neck, feeling the thick silky mane against her cheek. "It must have hurt when I scrubbed and scrubbed at you but I didn't know. I couldn't see under all that dirt. And now I don't know what to do. I could fetch some ointment for you, the sort we use if the cows hurt themselves out in the pasture – but I don't know if real ointment will work on a pretend horse…"

"Irina! I won't tell you again!"

Irina scrambled to her feet.

"I have to go and help my mother – and I will bring some real ointment and try it."

She ran to the dairy and started working hard without a word, thinking all the time of Black Jack and his whip as though she were afraid he might come back to life.

"I don't know what's the matter with you," her mother said, after she'd told her to do something three times without getting an answer. "You look as though you're in a dream. There's no time for dreaming when there's work to be done."

Irina hardly heard her. All day she watched for the chance to get the ointment from the cowshed without anyone seeing. At last, when it was almost supper time, she managed it. She ran to the barn with the big jar hidden under her coat. The ointment was thick and had a strong smell. Very carefully she smoothed it over each of the angry red weals on Bella's back. Then she put her own clean handkerchief over the worst part. It wasn't really big enough but it would help to protect the sore parts from the rough heavy blanket. She tidied the straw around Bella's feet and gave her a little kiss on the nose that was as soft and smooth as velvet. Then she said Goodnight.

For three days Irina put ointment on Bella's sore back, and each time she had to sneak the jar out of the cowshed without anyone seeing her and sneak it back in afterwards. On the fourth day the marks were gone. On the fifth day she brought scissors and trimmed Bella's fringe so that it didn't fall in her eyes so much. Every morning and every evening she brushed Bella's sandy yellow coat and combed her silvery mane and tail, and on the sixth day, when Bella was quite perfect, she had an idea.

"I'll bring you some of the cows' hay," she said. "They won't mind." Her father would mind if he found out, she knew that. He'd let her have a bit of straw, but hay was much more expensive. Still, she would only take a little bit, and since Bella could only pretend to eat it she wouldn't ever have to take any more.

So that night, when Irina said Goodnight to her, Bella had clean straw around her feet, a thick blanket to keep her warm and a small heap of sweet-smelling hay in front of her.

Irina went to bed at nine o'clock. At first she couldn't get to sleep although she had worked hard and was tired. A terrible blizzard had begun during supper. The wind howled and whined in the chimneys and flung the branches of the apple tree against her bedroom window where snowflakes whirled and flew so thickly that they made her dizzy as she lay watching them. Irina liked the snow when it fell softly, but the screaming wind frightened her and made her think again of Black Jack the evil farmer. Even though she was warm and snug under her thick quilt, she shivered at the noise of the blizzard and hoped that Bella would be warm enough under her blanket. And at last, thinking of Bella, her eyes closed and she fell asleep.

She slept heavily for a long time, and what it was that woke her she didn't know. One minute she was fast asleep, and the next minute she was sitting bolt upright in her bed, wide awake and staring at the window. It seemed to her that a sudden noise, like a door banging, had woken her, but now everything was silent. The blizzard had stopped, as blizzards do, as suddenly as it had begun, and now the full moon was shining in at her window, bright and silvery in a starry sky. Irina gazed at the moon, her body tense and her heart beating loud and fast. Something must have woken her but now it was all quiet, too quiet. The black boughs of the apple tree were still, and yet something out there was moving, she was sure of it. A soft swishing noise – there *was* something! Then a muffled pattering noise!

Irina jumped out of bed and ran to the window. She pressed her forehead to the cold glass and looked down, her heart beating so loudly that it hurt. Down in the yard the big door of the barn stood open, and a beautiful horse, its mane flowing like quicksilver in the moonlight, was trotting swiftly round in wide circles in the snow.

⌒ *Six* ⌒

"Bella!" called Irina softly. The beautiful horse stopped and tossed up her head. Then she spun round on her hind legs and trotted towards the sound of Irina's voice. Right beneath the window she stopped again and looked up, her whole body quivering. She stretched her head forward towards the ground and started to paw at it with her front hoof, striking the icy stones and shaking her silvery mane.

"I'm coming!" cried Irina, and she ran out of her room and down the stairs, swift and silent in her bare feet.

"Bella!" As soon as she saw Irina the horse began trotting in circles again, her head turning this way and that as though she were looking for something. Suddenly, she stopped beside the stump of a tree where Irina's father always chopped wood. She settled there, standing square on her four hooves, and turned her head towards Irina, waiting.

Irina understood at once. Without stopping to think of her bare feet and thin nightdress, without wondering whether she shouldn't feel afraid, she ran to the tree stump and climbed on to it and in a moment she was on Bella's back and holding the streaming silver mane. With a soft whinny of pleasure, Bella turned and cantered towards the farmyard gate. She checked and gathered herself and then leapt. Irina hardly felt the jump. It felt more like flying. Her cold bare feet clung to Bella's smooth warm sides, and her fingers entwined themselves in the thick mane, and they were off like the wind across the wide snowy fields.

The snow was so deep after the blizzard that Bella's hoof beats were almost silent, and the moon was so big and bright that they could see for miles and miles. On and on they went, flying over hedges, fences and ditches, speeding through copses where Irina had to rest her cheek on Bella's mane to avoid the snow-laden branches, then out again across the white fields in the moonlight. Irina didn't think to wonder where Bella was taking her. She didn't think of being frightened. She didn't think of being cold.

She didn't think of anything. She felt the warmth of Bella's galloping body, the strong thick mane in her fingers, the ever-increasing speed that lifted her long hair and made it stream out behind like the horse's tail. More than anything else she felt happy.

At last, Bella began to turn in a wide circle. She jumped a low fence and galloped for home, and all too soon they were over the gate and back in the farmyard. Bella halted, and then walked quietly to the tree stump to let Irina slide down from her back. She was panting, and her breath was steamy in the night air. Irina got down from the tree stump and went to stroke Bella's neck. Bella lowered her head and turned to nuzzle Irina's hair with her warm velvety nose, then she trotted off into the barn and stood quietly in her corner on the straw. Irina hurried after her.

"I have to put your blanket on you. You're so hot with galloping and now you'll be cold." She picked up the heavy blanket but no matter how she tried she couldn't lift it on to Bella's back. She could only reach up to her shoulder. Bella turned to look at her, with big, gentle eyes, waiting patiently. Irina didn't know what to do. She tried again but the blanket was so heavy and Bella was so tall that it was impossible.

"I can't reach you," she told Bella. "You were only small before and now I can't reach."

Bella must have understood, then. She began turning round and round in her corner, pawing and scraping at the straw beneath her feet. When it was smooth and flat she knelt down very carefully and then lowered her hindquarters. Irina covered her with the blanket and Bella at once sat up, straightened her front legs and sprang upright, shaking herself. Irina ran to fetch a bucket of water and some hay – "In case you get hungry and thirsty," she said, placing these in front of Bella. "Goodnight." She reached up to stroke Bella's cheek, but the horse didn't lower her head and nuzzle her as Irina would have liked. She stood very still and straight, looking very serious, and slowly raised her left front hoof.

"What is it, Bella? I don't understand. Have you hurt it?" Bella went on standing with her foot raised for a long time. Then, seeing that Irina did nothing, she put it down and lifted the right one, still looking straight ahead and waiting. She lifted each of her four feet in turn. Perhaps, in the end, she understood that Irina didn't know what to do, so she bent to nuzzle her as if to say Goodnight.

Irina ran into the house and climbed the stairs. As she crept past her parents' bedroom she heard her father snoring. She ran to her own room and jumped into bed, snuggling down under the quilt. She was so happy that she fell asleep at once to dream of riding over the snowy fields with Bella.

"Irina? Irina!"

Irina opened her eyes and sat up. It was morning and her mother was calling her.

"Irina! I've been calling you for the last half hour!"

But Irina didn't move at once. She was trying to remember something. Something had happened. She felt different today. Then she remembered her dream of riding over the snow. Could a dream make her feel so happy and so different? She got up and dressed quickly. The dream was still whirling around in her head, making her feel confused. She ran downstairs and through the kitchen towards the back door.

"Irina!" her mother said, "where do you think you're going? You're already too late to help me with the hens, and now breakfast's ready."

"I just want to go out for one minute, please—"

"Sit down," her mother said. "Your father's already in from milking."

Her father walked into the kitchen and Irina sat down at the table. They didn't usually talk much at breakfast. A lot of work had already been done, and a lot more was waiting to be done, and so they ate in a hurry. But this morning Irina's father had something to tell them.

"That was a fair blizzard we had last night," he began. "There are some drifts as high as a man in some parts." He chewed in silence for a moment, then gulped at his drink, frowning. "It's a funny thing, but all over the yard there are prints in the fresh snow."

Irina's mother put down the plate she was about to carry away.

"Don't tell me a fox—"

"No. You don't need to start fretting about your hens. There's nothing missing, and besides, they weren't a fox's prints."

"What then?"

Irina stared at her plate as they talked, her heart beating faster and faster, her face growing redder and redder.

"A horse, I reckon."

It wasn't a dream. It *wasn't*.

"Are you sure?" her mother said. "I don't see how a horse could have got in with the five-barred gate shut."

"Jumped it," her father said, getting up to go out with a full steaming mug still in his hand. "There's a wild herd passes this way twice a year, but it's early days for them yet. The streams are still frozen. there were some other prints as well, but I couldn't make them out."

"It was Bella!" said Irina, suddenly breaking her silence.

"And who's Bella?" asked her father, standing his mug on the end of the dresser near the door and sitting down to pull on his boots.

"My horse. She... last night I..." Her voice tailed off and she looked down at her plate again, wishing she hadn't said anything.

"Irina, clear the table," her mother said.

"But it *was* Bella," Irina insisted quietly.

"You listen to me, young lady," said her mother sharply. "Making up stories at your age means telling lies. You're not a two-year-old. Clear that table. And I've had enough of your messing in that barn half the day when there's work to be done. If there's any more of it, I'll pitch that worm-eaten old thing out."

"Now, now," interrupted her father mildly, "leave her be. It's something for her to play with. She'll forget about it when school starts." And he went out.

Irina helped clear the table and wash the dishes in silence. And all the time she was thinking to herself, "It's not a lie. If they go in the barn, they'll see! They'll *see*…"

But first she had to see for herself. She had to escape from her mother's watchful eyes. It was a long time before she managed it, but at last she got out into the yard and ran to open the door of the old barn.

"Bella…?"

She was there in her corner, small and still, almost buried in the blanket that was far too big for her. Irina's heart was filled with confusion and disappointment. She knelt beside the little horse, and turned back the big blanket to stroke her mane. Then she saw that the hay was gone and the water bucket was empty.

∽ *Seven* ∽

Bella was real. Whatever happened to her in the daytime, at night she was real. Dreams don't eat hay and drink water. Dreams don't leave hoof prints in the snow.

Every night, Irina went to bed as early as she could and slept happily until Bella came to wake her, knowing that when the moon was high she would hear the noise of hooves striking on the icy stones in the yard. Then she would run to the window and see Bella waiting for her out in the white moonlit world of night.

They rode far and fast, as free as birds, and during their journeys Irina never spoke a word. She clung to Bella with her toes and fingers, her eyes bright and her hair streaming behind her as they flew across the snowy fields like the wind.

She never tried again to tell her parents the truth. She knew it would only make them angry. And yet she had to tell somebody – not just for the sake of telling, because Irina was an only child and used to keeping her secrets to herself, but because she was worried about something. Each night after their ride, when Bella trotted back into the barn, she continued to lift up each of her feet in turn, waiting. Irina had to ask someone what it meant.

Then she remembered the blind man. He knew all about Bella and he had said Irina could go back and see him whenever she wanted. Her chance came when school started. One day a week, Irina's mother came to school to meet her and they did some shopping. Irina waited until they were in a long queue in the grocer's which was only a step away from the blind man's junk shop.

"Can I go out and look in the shop windows?" Irina asked.

"If you like – but stay on this side of the square where I can find you."

"I will!" Irina ran as fast as she could and then paused at the gloomy entrance to the junk shop. Would the blind man recognize her footsteps and call out the way he did with that boy on Christmas Eve? No sound came from inside.

"Can I come in?" asked Irina timidly, taking a step forward.

"Of course you can," came the voice of the blind man.

Irina knocked the snow from her boots and went towards the big carved armchair. The blind man was sitting there just as before, as if he had never moved since Irina last saw him.

"And how is little Irina?" he asked.

"Did you recognize my steps?"

"No," said the blind man, "you haven't been to see me often enough for that, but I never forget a voice. And are you now with Bella?"

"Yes, I am," Irina said, and then she hesitated, wondering if he would believe her if she told the truth.

After a moment's silence the blind man said, "You might as well tell me, now you've come." Just as though, blind as he was, he could see into her thoughts. So Irina told him the truth about her night rides.

"So Bella *must* be a real horse," she said at the end. "And she's mine, all mine, and that's why

I'm happy, only what am I to do about her feet? There's nobody else I can ask except you."

"Give me your hand," the blind man said, lifting his own pale, mouse-like hands towards her. Irina gave him her hand.

"What you say is not true," he said gravely.

"But she is real, she *is*!" protested Irina, tears of disappointment filling her eyes. "I thought you would understand. I thought you knew about Bella."

"Bella is God's creature," the blind man said sternly.

"You don't believe me!"

"Many people believe what you believe," the blind man said, "and all of them are unhappy just as you will be unhappy if you go on believing what is false." He lifted his hands to her cheek. "You're crying, but you'll shed bitter tears before long if you don't listen to what I tell you. Never say what is false. Never say that any creature on this earth is yours. Now, go behind my chair to where there's a big chest and take the parcel that's lying there. It's for you. You see, I was expecting you."

Irina went to the big chest, and took the parcel that was lying on its dusty surface.

"Thank you," she said, but she was still crying tears of disappointment because he didn't believe her. She tried to dry her eyes on the back of her glove and had one last try.

"Couldn't a spell have been put on Bella to stop her being real, to save her from Black Jack so that he couldn't hurt her any ore? Couldn't that be what happened?"

"There's a book in that parcel," the blind man said, without answering her. "Read it carefully. And if you want to go on being happy, remember my words. Never deceive yourself into believing something that isn't true."

Irina ran out of the junk shop and said to herself that she would never, *never* go there again. Grown-ups were all as bad and it was useless to tell them anything. It was better to talk just to Bella. Even if she couldn't answer, she always understood. And as soon as they got home she did talk to Bella for as long as she could before supper.

"I don't care any more if nobody believes me," she told Bella, stroking her mane. "From now on, I'm only going to tell my secrets to you."

She quite forgot about the parcel until she was going up to bed. She saw it lying on the chair where she had dropped it when she came in, and though she hated the blind man now she couldn't help being curious about what was in it.

Upstairs, she settled down in bed and untied the string on the parcel. It was a book, as the blind man had said, and not a nice-looking book either, it was old and its hard red cover had faded to a greyish pink. Its spine was broken and some of the pages had come loose. One of these slipped out and fell from the bed to the floor, but not before Irina had noticed that there was a picture on it. A picture of a horse. She reached down to pick it up. The horse in the picture was standing with one foot raised, and a man was bending over the foot with what looked like a paintbrush in his hand. Quickly, Irina opened the book at its title page and read *Feeding, Grooming and Training Your Horse*.

Then the blind man must have believed her, in spite of everything he'd said. He must have believed her if he gave her a book that would help her look after Bella! Irina wasted no time wondering why he should have behaved so strangely. She started to read the book as fast as she could. It had been written for adults, not for anyone as young as Irina, and there were many words in it that she couldn't understand. Even so, there were plenty of pictures to help her, and she recognized a lot of the things she had found in her grandfather's trunk.

Later that night, when they had ridden as far as they felt like riding over the snow and were back in the barn, Irina knew what she had to do when Bella stood patiently holding up her foot. At least, she thought she did. She was ready with all the right implements from the pile of her grandfather's things in the corner, and she knew she had to scrape the stones and dirt from under Bella's hoof and wipe it clean and then paint hoof grease on it with a brush. But learning practical things from a book by yourself is not the best way of learning, and it was lucky for Irina that she had a teacher on hand: Bella. Bella might not know how to speak, but she knew just what had to be done and how it should be done. She gave Irina her left front foot and turned to watch her as she worked, nuzzling her back every so often to encourage her. Irina's first attempt was slow, but at last she straightened up and said, "There, that's one finished." She went round to Bella's right and waited for the right foot to be offered to her but nothing happened.

"You have to give me your right foot now, Bella."

Bella stood still. What could be wrong? Every night Bella had offered her feet one by one, first at the front, then at the back.

"Bella?" Irina looked up at her, stroking her neck. "What is it?" But Bella only stood there, tall and pale and elegant, gazing straight ahead, blinking her big soft eyes. At last, Irina remembered that the pictures in the book showed the man always working from the horse's left side. She went back to where she had stood before and Bella at once lifted her right foot and passed it to her behind the left. Irina got to work again, and Bella turned and nuzzled her back to tell her she was doing it right. When all four hooves were clean and shiny, Bella knelt to have her blanket put on and Irina brought her hay and water and said Goodnight.

Just before she fell asleep in her warm bed, Irina thought, "Perhaps one day, when she feels well and safe again, Bella will be a real horse all the time."

And she was right.

～ *Eight* ～

There was a time, before she had Bella, when Irina always walked sadly home after school, knowing that all the other children would be running in and out of each other's houses in the village or perhaps skating on the big pond nearby. Irina had never been allowed to stay and play. The winters were so long, and darkness came down so quickly, that her mother had always made her come straight home. And so she had always gone sadly on her way, looking back sometimes when she heard the others calling to each other and laughing.

But now it was different. Irina was always first out of the school gate, her long plait bobbing and swinging as she ran towards the long lane that led towards home and Bella. She would arrive red-cheeked and out of breath, and hurry straight into the big barn, calling, "Bella! I'm home!"

Then she would brush Bella's coat and comb her mane and chatter to her about everything that had happened at school that day, sure that the little horse was listening to every word. Then, at night, when Bella was her real tall beautiful self, they would ride.

One night, when the ice was creaking on the roofs and the streams bubbling under the snow, Bella galloped much farther away than usual. Instead of making a big circle and then heading for home, she went on, faster and faster over the flat snowy fields towards the horizon. Then, very suddenly, she stopped dead, her head lifted and her whole body tense and quivering.

"What is it?" Irina asked. "Bella, what is it?"

Bella remained rigid, her ears pricked. Had she heard something? Smelt something? Irina clung to Bella's quivering body and looked about her at the miles of snowy fields, the velvety sky dotted thickly with stars, the silver moon. She could see no danger. Then she wondered if they were near Black Jack's old farm. She had no idea where it was but then, they had come so far that she didn't recognize anything.

"Bella," she whispered, shivering and clutching tighter at the long mane, "let's go home. I'm frightened."

But Bella didn't hear or turn to nuzzle Irina's toes. She didn't move and Irina could feel the horse's great heart beating so fast and loudly that it seemed as if it must burst. Still Bella stared, her eyes fixed on the horizon. She whinnied, almost under her breath, then she relaxed. Whatever she had heard or smelt was gone. She turned her head to nuzzle Irina's cold toes with her warm nose and then took off at a gallop for home.

The next night the same thing happened, but it was even more frightening. When she saw that Bella was galloping on towards the horizon instead of turning for home, Irina called to her over the noise of the wind their galloping made, "Don't go so far away, Bella! Please don't!"

But Bella galloped on until she came to the same spot where she had stopped the night before. Again she stood rigid and trembling, with her big eyes fixed on the horizon and her big heart beating faster and faster. Her breath came in sharp snorts.

"Bella! You're frightening me! Bella!"

But Bella seemed to have forgotten that anyone was riding her at all. She spun round suddenly, then back again. She ran to the left, swung herself round on her hindquarters and ran to the right, then swung round again, and always with her eyes fixed on the horizon. Irina clung on as well as she could, but she slid sideways at each violent run and only Bella's long mane saved her from falling. She surely would have fallen sooner or later but, just like the night before, Bella suddenly relaxed, breathed normally and turned to gallop for home.

The third night, Irina was almost afraid to go out. But when she looked down from her window and saw Bella waiting patiently by the tree stump, quiet and composed as if nothing had happened, she summoned the courage to go down and mount her.

When they reached the field where they always used to turn for home, Irina said, "Let's go back now, Bella! Please let's go back." But Bella only galloped faster until she reached the same spot and stopped. She trembled so much that Irina started to tremble too, and again she ran back and forth, back and forth, watching the horizon, her ears pricked, snorting sharply.

"What can you hear, Bella, *what*?"

Then she too heard. At first it was a distant, muted rumbling, like a thunderstorm far away. It came closer and closer, and Bella's heart beat faster and louder. Then Irina understood. Hoof beats. Hundreds and hundreds of hoof beats, and on the horizon she saw the wild horses streaming along at full gallop, their manes as white as the snow.

Bella threw up her head and neighed; a long, high desperate call that was almost a scream. From far away came an answering call. Bella reared, pawing the air, then she plunged. Irina felt herself thrown into space with the snow and the sky spinning upside down and then the white ground hit her hard and everything turned black and silent.

When she opened her eyes again she felt sick and dizzy and her mouth and ears were full of snow. She got to her feet very slowly, staring at the empty horizon, her ears buzzing in the silence. Then she turned and started walking home. Her feet were bare in the snow but she didn't notice the cold. She knew that one of her hands was hurt badly but she didn't feel the pain, she just knew in her head that it was there.

She was very far from home but she felt no fear of getting lost. She knew that she must go on putting one foot in front of the other but she felt nothing at all. And she never once turned to look back after the wild horses who had taken Bella away.

∽ *Nine* ∾

Irina lay very still in her bed. Her face was white except for a reddish purple bruise on her forehead. Her right arm rested outside the quilt with a stiff bandage round the wrist. She wasn't asleep, her eyes were wide open. Outside the door of her bedroom her parents were talking to the doctor in low voices.

"It's just the shock… You'll see that in a few days… no serious injury…"

"Sleepwalking… she must have… we found her early in the morning on a pile of straw in the barn…"

"Just keep her quiet, and don't worry…"

Irina could hear them but she didn't listen. Inside her head, everything was empty and silent. The sun was shining outside the window, and the snow was melting and dripping from the black boughs of the apple tree. Irina closed her eyes and slept.

After a while, Irina was sent back to school. She was very quiet and well-behaved as usual, but she didn't learn anything. At home, she answered when she was spoken to but if no one spoke to her she was silent. Her parents looked at her and then at each other. They called the doctor. The doctor looked in Irina's eyes and throat and squeezed her neck behind her ears. He said perhaps she was growing too much and gave her some bitter medicine. But Irina wasn't growing.

She didn't grow one inch taller and her hair didn't grow one inch longer. The doctor said perhaps she was studying too much. But Irina wasn't studying at all. Every evening she took her books and sat by the window. The black boughs of the apple tree grew buds that opened into tiny leaves of the palest green. Irina watched the leaves unfold and inside her head everything was empty and silent.

The sun grew warmer and the cows were turned out into the pasture. In the evenings, Irina was sent to drive them home to be milked. Afterwards she sat by the open window with her book and watched the thick white apple blossom ruffled by the warm breeze that filled her room with its perfume, and inside her head everything was empty and silent.

The tree grew small green apples. By the time they were big and red the air turned bright and cold. Irina helped her father pick the apples. They had always picked the apples together, even when Irina was so small that she could only stand at the foot of the tree with the basket. When he remembered how she used to enjoy it and saw how pale and thin she looked now, her father felt sorry for her and said:

"How would you like it if I bought you a little dog? It would be company for you, something to play with."

"No thank you," Irina said, "I don't want a dog."

"But it might cheer you up," her father said. "It would be your very own dog and you could look after it yourself."

"No!" cried Irina. "I don't want one."

"But why?"

"Because it would run away! I'd look after it and love it and then it would run away!" And she scrambled down from the apple tree and went to shut herself in her bedroom.

Soon the apple tree was bare and its branches tapped and rattled at Irina's window, shaken by the first winter wind. Irina sat watching as she had watched through all the other seasons. Inside her head everything was empty and silent, and never once in all that time, even in her deepest most secret thoughts, had she said or thought the name, Bella. Never once had she shed a single tear.

One night, Irina and her parents were having supper in the kitchen. Over the noise of the roaring wood stove a faint moan could be heard in the chimney pots.

"That's a north wind," Irina's father said. "Next thing you know, it'll start snowing. Once the wild horses have gone through you can count on the snow starting, like clockwork."

"Wild horses?" Irina's fork clattered on to her plate. Her face had turned red.

"They come by this way in the spring, as soon as the snow begins to melt," her father said, "but you've never seen them. They pass too far away from here – but don't you remember once that one of them got into the yard and I found hoof prints in the snow? They'll be on their way back to their winter pastures any day now, mark my words, and the minute they've gone it'll start snowing."

Every night, after her father's words, Irina watched by her window. She no longer pretended to read. There was no book in her lap. She sat there rigid and still, her eyes fixed on the horizon, the emptiness in her head beating to one repeating rhythm: "Don't let it snow yet. Don't let it snow yet." Sometimes, exhausted by the waiting, she fell asleep with her forehead against the cold window pane.

Each night she waited and each day the sky grew duller and greyer and heavier. Then, one evening, as she sat there in the twilight, she saw something twirl slowly down between the branches of the apple tree. It was a snowflake. Another fell and another, and as the evening darkened into night the silent snow fell faster and thicker until there was nothing but whirling snowflakes to be seen.

Then the empty silence in Irina's head was flooded with memories of snowy rides and moonlit fields, of a flowing mane and a warm velvety nose that nuzzled her feet, of the thunder of hooves and her fall through the air to the hard cold ground.

"Bella!" It was the first time since that night that she had said Bella's name. Now she wrenched open the window, calling and calling as though her heart would break, "Bella! Bella! Bella!"

The north wind whirled the snowflakes into the room, touching her face with icy kisses, and Irina began to cry in loud broken sobs as she understood at last what the blind man had told her.

"Never say that any creature on this earth is yours, or you'll shed bitter tears."

⮀ *Ten* ⮂

It was a hard winter that year, hard for the fox who prowled around the locked chicken sheds at night, his ribs showing through his tattered fur. Hard for the small birds who fell frozen from their branches into the snow. Hard, too, for Irina. She had cried until she had no more tears left to shed, and then decided that if she couldn't be happy she could try to be good. She tried to talk more to her mother and keep her company during her long hours of work, and when her father made little jokes to cheer her up she smiled. At school she worked twice as hard as the others to make up for being so behind. But as she walked home alone each afternoon, leaving the shouting and laughter of the village children behind, her heart was as heavy as the grey, snow-burdened sky and it seemed to her that the winter would never end.

But winter always does end, and one night, as Irina slept, the ice on the roof creaked and slid, slid and creaked, until, towards dawn, a great slice of it thundered down into the yard.

Irina opened her eyes. The room was lit with a cold pink light. The sun was only just over the horizon, and the melting snow was reflecting its light. She heard a thin trickle of water in the eaves and another patch of ice dislodged itself and began to slide. Then she heard hooves striking on the icy stones in the yard.

Irina got up and went cautiously to the window, almost afraid to look down. Bella was there. She was standing very still now, watching and listening, her coat and mane reflecting the same cool pink light as the snow. Irina went downstairs. She put her thick coat over her nightdress and pushed her feet into her warm boots. She was trying to keep calm but her heart was thumping loudly.

"Bella…"

Bella allowed Irina to stroke her neck but then she broke away and trotted swiftly to the old barn. The broken door was ajar. Irina started to follow her.

"Bella? Have you come home?"

But before Irina could follow her inside the barn, Bella burst out again, trotted straight towards her, nuzzled her chest, then spun round, jumped the five-barred gate and galloped at a desperate speed towards the horizon.

"Bella! No! Bella!" Irina ran as far as the gate and then stood watching until the galloping form was no longer visible. Bella was gone.

"What's going on? What's all this noise?" Irina's father came out of the kitchen door, half dressed, his hair hanging over his eyes. "Irina!"

Irina turned, but her father was no longer looking at her, he was looking down at the hoof prints in the melting snow. And now he followed them into the barn.

"Well! I never… Irina! Irina! Come and look!"

Irina looked back once more at the sun rising over the flat empty fields. Then she went to her father.

He was standing just inside the barn door near the corner where Bella used to live. Irina had never been in there since, and she didn't want to go in there now, but her father insisted. He took her by the shoulders. "Look, Irina!"

The straw she had put down for Bella last year
was still there. And standing on the straw was a
foal, a tiny perfect replica of Bella.

"It's a female, and a little beauty," said her father
quietly. The foal was too weak and exhausted to
look up at them. It took all the little energy it had
just to stay on its wobbling legs, and one of them,
its right hind leg, was lifted slightly off the floor.

"Why, it's lame," her father said, bending to look closer. Got tangled up in some wire..." He untwisted the wire carefully. "It'll leave a scar, but it should mend. That's why its mother abandoned it, but why she brought it here is a mystery."

Irina stood where she was, her face hard and angry.

"Why did she leave it? She should have looked after it if it was lame. Why?"

"They have to keep up," her father said. "If they can't keep up, the mothers are forced to leave them by the rest of the herd. She must have had a desperate run to get it here and then catch them up... if she did catch them up." He patted the little blonde mane. "Well, I don't think you've much of a chance, little one, unless Irina wants to try giving you some milk from a bottle..."

"No! I won't love it! I won't look after it! I won't!"

"Well, please yourself," her father said, "I thought you might like to have a horse that would be your very own."

Irina ran out of the barn and shut herself in her bedroom. When she came down to breakfast her face was still pale and angry. Her father was talking about the foal, and her mother said,

"There's the baby's bottle we use when there's a weak calf born, I suppose…"

But Irina didn't say anything.

Her father finished his breakfast and put his boots back on. "It'll be dead by the end of the day," he said, and went out.

It wasn't a school day. Irina helped her mother in the house and then in the dairy. They were skimming cream and filling little tubs with it. Irina's mother glanced at the shelf where they kept the baby's bottle for the calves and said, "There's no understanding you, Irina. Last year you spent every hour god sends messing that barn with a toy horse and now there's that poor creature in there and you won't even look at it…"

Irina went on working in silence but her face got paler and paler and her father's words kept repeating themselves in her head: "It'll be dead by the end of the day."

She saw Bella galloping desperately, her brave heart bursting with the effort to save her foal and her own life, felt Bella nuzzling her chest, trusting her to help…

Suddenly the little tub fell from her hand and rolled across the dairy floor. She ran to get the baby's bottle and clutched at her mother's arm.

"Some milk for it! Give me some milk for it!"

"We'll take it warm from the cow," her mother said. "That might help."

The foal had given up its struggle to stand on three legs. It was lying on the straw, its eyes almost closed. Irina knelt down beside it and held the teat of the bottle near its lips, but it was too weak to lift its head. She squeezed a few warm drops into its mouth.

"Don't die," she pleaded, "please don't die! I'll look after you and love you. I'll take you out in the meadow where there'll be grass and flowers and a stream to cool your feet. And when you're big and strong enough you'll be free, you'll be your own self. I'll never say you're mine, but please don't die."

She slid her hand beneath the little head and lifted it gently to cradle it against herself. Feeling the warmth, the foal pushed its soft nose against her breast and opened its eyes. It looked dazed, as though wondering where it was, but when Irina pushed the teat near its mouth it began to suck.

∽ *Eleven* ∽

Loved and cared for by Irina, the foal grew and the lame leg mended. Her pale sandy coat and silvery mane were so exactly like her mother's that, almost without thinking about it, Irina called her Bella. When the last of the snow had melted and the sun warmed the new grass, she led Bella out into the meadow. Bella looked about her at the fresh green world, and her velvet nose twitched at all the scents coming to her on the warm breeze. With a little whinny of happiness, she began to run up and down the meadow, jumping and kicking and sometimes tumbling over on her too-long legs. Then she ran to Irina to nuzzle her.

"Do you like it, Bella? Do you?"

But Bella whirled round and was away again, galloping round the meadow until she had no breath to gallop any more, and she settled to crop the sweet grass near Irina's feet.

Irina was growing, too. Once she was old enough to please herself, she began to call at the blind man's shop after school sometimes. Now that they understood each other, he was the person she most liked to talk to about Bella and how she was growing tall and beautiful and strong. She called on him so often that he soon learned to recognize her footsteps. One day he lifted his small, mouse-like hand to touch Irina's smiling face and say, "I think you're growing tall and beautiful, too, Irina, just like your Bella." But Irina saw the little smile on his blind face and said, "Bella is God's creature, not mine."

The years passed and Bella grew big and strong enough to carry Irina. One afternoon in autumn, when they had ridden far from home and it was time to turn back, Bella suddenly stopped cropping the grass and lifted her head, her ears pricked.

"What is it, Bella?" Irina asked gently, stroking her neck. But she knew what it was and she slid down from the saddle and stood beside the horse's quivering body, waiting.

She heard the thunder of hooves and then the herd came into view, streaming across the horizon in the autumn mist. "Let her be with them and safe," she thought, and then she looked up at Bella's tense body. She didn't speak to her to try to turn her away, she only watched and waited. Bella's head was thrown high and still, her ears picking up every sound, her nostrils every scent. She was excited and her heartbeat was loud and

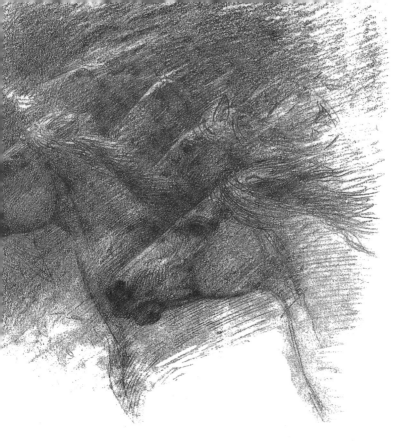

fast, but her big eyes looked puzzled, as though she were trying to connect the thundering hooves and the scent of the herd with a distant memory, a memory of a world that was all white, a terrible pain, a terrifying flight across the emptiness and a warm nuzzle urging her on. But it was all so long ago that the memory faded with the fading of the hoofbeats. Bella relaxed and lowered her head to go on cropping the grass.

"Let's go home," Irina said, stroking her long smooth neck gently, "it's going to snow."

It was the same day that Irina's mother and father settled an argument that had been going on between them for years. They put on their oldest clothes and rolled up their sleeves and went into the old barn to decide once and for all what were the "Things that might come in useful" and what was "Junk that ought to be thrown out". They were still in there, arguing over part of a rusty old plough, when Irina and Bella came back from their ride.

Perhaps it was all that dusty junk that reminded him of the blind man's shop, or perhaps it was the sound of the horse's hooves coming into the yard, but Irina's father suddenly laughed and said, "Do you remember that Christmas when Irina insisted on having a moth-eaten old toy horse for a present?"

"She was a strange one at that age," her mother said.

"She was, but she turned out all right in the end. I was just wondering, though, whatever happened to that horse."

"I forget," her mother said. "She probably got bored with it in the end and threw it out."

MORE THAN A STORY

CONTENTS

Strange but True

Did you know?

People have ridden horses for thousands of years. Even further back, about 60 million years ago, a horse-like mammal called Eohippus, which means *Dawn Horse*, was grazing on the shores of warm seas in what was to become England.

Horses are full grown at 5 years old. They live about 25-30 years but the oldest recorded horse in history, Old Billy, lived to the grand old age of 62!

A stallion is a male horse and a female is a mare. A colt is a young male horse and a filly is a young female. A baby horse is called a foal.

Horses can sleep standing up or lying down.

Horses are measured in 'hands' and one hand is 10cm. You measure from the ground to the 'withers' which is where the horse's neck joins its back. The largest horse ever recorded was probably Sampson, a Shire horse, who was 22 ½ hands!

Which Way Home?

Bella and Irina have to find the way home by jumping over the gates. Can you find the quickest way, starting at Gate 1?

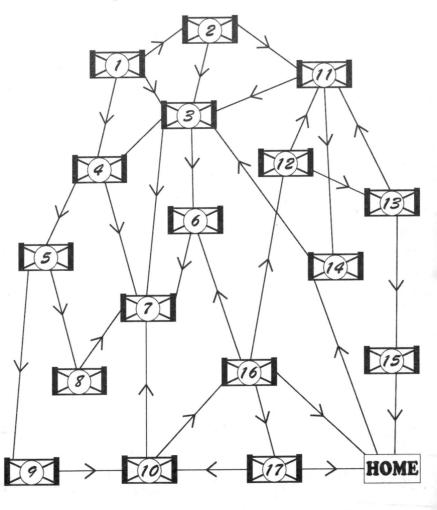

Are you a crack rider?
Could you look after a horse?

 Try this quiz and find out.

1 What is a bit?
   a) A nice snack for your horse.
   b) A piece of metal in a horse's mouth which helps a rider to control him.
   c) A tool for taking stones out of horses' hooves.

2 What do you do when you're 'tacking up'? Are you:
   a) Looking smart in your riding clothes.
   b) Putting on your horse's saddle and bridle.
   c) Walking the horse through a lot of mud.

3 Do you wear a helmet when riding:
   a) When you feel like it.
   b) Always.
   c) When you are on the road.

4 When you come back from a ride, do you:
   a) Jump off and leave the horse. You're tired now.
   b) Take off saddle and bridle and wipe your horse down carefully with a damp sponge.
   c) He's hot so give him a bucket of ice-cold water.

5 Do you make your horse gallop:
   a) Anywhere. It's exciting, especially if you don't know where you're going.
   b) Only when you know that the ground is safe for your horse.
   c) Uphill. So much better than having to walk!

6. **Your horse seems to be limping. Do you:**

   a) Decide to gallop a bit because he'll soon be better. Horses are strong.

   b) Get off and look at his hooves to see what the problem is. Walk home if necessary.

   c) Ride home as fast as you can.

Mostly **a's:**	**Mostly** **b's:**	**Mostly** **c's:**
Don't ever go near a horse! Except in a book.	You know what you are doing and you respect your horse.	You're trying, but you've got a lot to learn.

Wild horses live in many countries. They are usually tame horses that have escaped. They live in small herds of mares and young horses, with a leader, often a mare, and a stallion. When the young colts grow up and become stallions, they leave the herd and go off and find a new group of their own.

Snow Storm

Make your own snowstorm indoors.

What you need:

1 glass (or clear plastic) bottle with a screw top

Some glycerine from the chemists

Some silver glitter

Paper and felt tips OR a picture from a magazine

Sticky tape

What you do:

1. Draw a picture of galloping wild horses (or any thing you like!), smaller than the bottle. (Or, you could cut out a colour picture from a magazine.)

2. Stick the picture on the side of the bottle, so that it faces into the bottle.

3. Put enough glitter in the bottle to cover the bottom.

4. Pour glycerine into the bottle until it is half full. Now, fill up the bottle with water and screw the top on tightly.

5. Shake the bottle and look through it at your horses, which will be galloping through a glittering snowstorm.

Help Irina to look after Bella

Irina spent many hours mending and cleaning the things she needed to look after Bella. Can you help her unscramble some of the words to get them ready for her favourite pet?

MBOC

RUBSH

KETBLAN

TBKUCE

'Grey' horses

Grey horses are born black or dark grey and become paler as they get older until they can look almost white.

Horse Sense

Do you know what these pieces of equipment
are used for? See if you can match each word
to its use.

1. CURRY COMB

A. A tool for cleaning stones
and mud out of a horse's hoof

2. BRIDLE

B. For the rider to sit on

3. REINS

C. For cleaning the horse's coat

4. SADDLE

D. For the rider to put his feet in

5. STIRRUPS

E. Part of the bridle, attached to
the bit in the horse's mouth, for
the rider to hold

6. HOOF PICK

F. For helping the rider to
control the horse

Now copy out this wordsearch puzzle and find these words.
(Tip: CURRYCOMB and HOOF PICK both appear as
one word – CURRYCOMB and HOOFPICK.)

E	K	P	O	T	X	E	U	C
L	Y	C	Y	S	L	S	U	G
D	X	J	I	D	H	R	J	R
I	Z	U	D	P	R	A	J	E
R	W	A	S	Y	F	S	F	I
B	S	A	C	C	J	O	J	N
B	P	O	U	H	M	A	O	S
Q	M	P	E	O	N	S	B	H
B	S	P	U	R	R	I	T	S

What colour is your horse?

Did you know that a horse that is:

skewbald is brown and white

piebald is black and white

dun is pale brown with a darker mane and tail

chestnut is golden brown with the same colour
mane and tail

palomino is pale honey with a white mane and tail

bay is brown with a black mane and tail.
This is the most common colour

appaloosa is spotted

grey is actually pale grey or white.
Mane and tail are grey

Footprints in the Snow

'It's a funny thing, but all over the yard there
are prints in the fresh snow.'
Irina's father knows that a horse has been in their yard
because of the shape of the prints.

Can you match these prints to the animals?

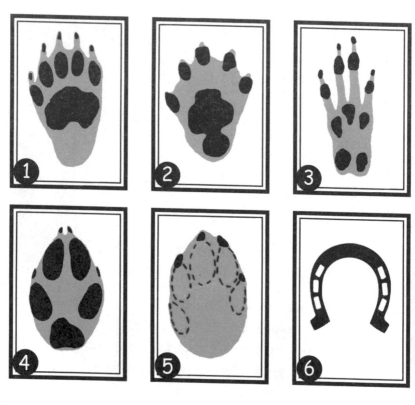

Fox   Horse

Badger   Squirrel

Rabbit   Otter

Lucky horse shoes

Horse shoes are supposed to be lucky – but only if you hang them up so they look like a 'u'. If they are upside down, it's said that all your luck will drain away.

Fox and Geese

This is a good game for playing
when it has just snowed.
You need at least four players.

What you do:

1. Stamp out a big circle in the snow. Now stamp out two
   paths across the circle that join in the middle. It should
   look like a circle with an x in it. In the middle of the x
   is the 'safe' area.

2. Choose one person to be 'Fox'. All the others are 'Geese'.

3. Everyone can only run on the paths and the Fox can't
   catch the Geese when they are in the safe area.

4. The Fox now tries to catch a Goose. No more than 2
   people can stay in the safe area at once, and the Fox is
   not allowed to wait outside the safe area for longer
   than 5 seconds.

5. As soon as the Fox catches a Goose,
   then that person is the Fox.

Snowflakes

Every snowflake has a different pattern.
Try making your own snowflakes.

What you need:

Sheet of white paper
Scissors

What you do:

1. Fold a sheet of paper in half and cut little
   shapes into the edges.

2. Now fold the paper in half again, and cut out more
   shapes. (Don't cut out too much or the paper will
   fall apart.)

3. Unfold the paper. You will have made your own
   snowflake.

4. Lick the paper and stick the snowflake to the window.
   (It will stick without glue. Try it and see.)

Snowballs

These are yummy and especially good after a game of Fox and Geese. Try them and see!

What you need:

100g cream cheese
2 teaspoons of honey
100g plain sweet biscuits
a few drops of milk
icing sugar sprinkled on a plate

What you do:

1. Put the cream cheese, honey and milk into a bowl and mash together until smooth.
2. Put the biscuits into a plastic bag and crush them.
3. Now add the biscuit crumbs to the mixture.
4. Make spoonfuls of the mixture into balls and roll them in the icing sugar.
5. Heap them on the plate and put them in the fridge.

Secret Message

Irina writes a message to Bella on her steamed-up bedroom window. From the outside, it looks like this:

Please come back,
Bella. I miss you.

Can you read what it says?

ANSWERS

Which Way Home?

Gates 1 ➤ 4 ➤ 5 ➤ 9 ➤ 10 ➤ 16 ➤ 12 ➤ 13 ➤ 15 ➤ HOME

Help Irina to look after Bella

COMB   BLANKET   BRUSH   BUCKET

Horse Sense

1 = C, 2 = F, 3 = E, 4 = B, 5 = D, 6 = A

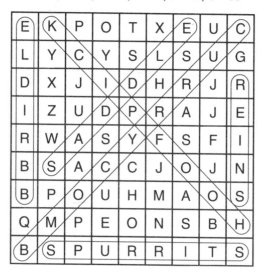

Footprints in the Snow

Fox – 4   Horse – 6

Badger – 1   Squirrel – 3

Rabbit – 5   Otter – 2

Animal tracks taken from www.bbc.co.uk/nature/animals/wildbritain
(except horse)

Secret Message

Hold the message up to a mirror.

About the Author

James E Mack was born in Scotland but ......uch of his childhood abroad, gaining a love of ....he outdoors and wildlife. He became a Comman...... ...ate 1980s and a member of a Special Operations ...... a 22-year career serving in many of the world's ....d hotspots. James subsequently specialised as a Counter-Terrorism adviser and assisted in capacity building operations in support of UK and US Government initiatives.

His passion for wildlife led James to assist in the development of counter-poaching programs in Africa. This passion remains and James spends much of his leisure time photographing the very animals that he strives to protect.

When time allowed, James began writing novels based upon his experiences in Special Operations and conflict zones around the globe. His first novel, *Only the Dead*, was very well-received and attracted interest from several screenwriters.

James lives in Northern Scotland where he enjoys the surfing and the mountains nearby.

Published by Achnacarry Press

ISBN: 9798653119767

Sins

of the

Fathers

A P

ACHNACARRY
PRESS

JAMES E MACK

A lot of thanks go out once again to everyone who continues to support my books and writing. From the readers and fans who humble me with their commitment and loyalty, to my wonderful friends and family. And as always, to my amazing partner for her help and encouragement on this incredible journey.

James E Mack

Also by James E Mack:

Only the Dead
Fear of the Dark
The Killing Agent

'There's no such thing as history in Northern Ireland; just a 300-year battle that started with cannons and muskets and progressed to Semtex, SLRs and Armalites.'

Major, Intelligence Corps, 1990

CHAPTER 1

BELFAST, 1973

Mary Devlin smiled as she watched the pretty blonde girl walking down her path, the grin on her face a real antidote to the greyness of the damp day. The girl saw Mary watching through the window and gave a cheery wave with her free hand as she jostled the bag of laundry over her shoulder. Dropping the curtain and making her way to the door, Mary reflected on what a godsend it was to have the wee girl's laundry services helping her out. With four kids and Sean's work clothes, she had little enough time and energy to run the household, let alone wash and dry all the laundry in this rain-drenched month they'd had.

Opening the door, Mary held her hands out towards the diminutive girl. 'Here now, you wee thing, give me that bloody big bag before you do yourself some harm.'

The girl laughed and swung the heavy white bag from her shoulder and into Mary's waiting arms. 'Tell you what

Mrs Devlin, it's either getting heavier every week or I'm needing to be eating more bleeding Weetabix!'

Mary took the bag with little effort and smiled at the English accent and expressions. 'You're a lot stronger than you look for a slip of a thing but here, come in for a cup of tea and warm yerself up for five minutes.'

The small blonde leaned against the wall and shook her head. 'I would love to Mrs Devlin, but we've got another twenty houses to get done before we start the collections up in Clonard.' She gave a glance behind her and leaned in closer. 'Besides, you know what George is like when we start running late.' She laughed at her own remark and Mary joined her.

'Well, doesn't always do to let the man think he's the big boss in the household and I daresay it's the same at the laundry.' Mary pulled the bag into the doorway and fished in her apron before thrusting her fist out and dropping an object into the girl's own apron pocket. 'Now that's the payment and a wee bit on top. I know it's not much, but you keep that to yourself and don't be showing that man what I've given you.' As the girl opened her mouth to object, Mary laid a maternal hand on her arm. 'Don't say anything. It's a grand service you provide to people round these parts and I'm grateful for it. You stay safe now and here; find yourself a good man and have yourself some babies.'

The girl threw her head back and laughed aloud. 'Babies? Good lord Mrs D, I've got to get married first!'

Mary laughed and waved as the blonde English woman turned and made her way back down the path and out of the gate, closing the black metal barrier behind her. Mary shook her head and smiled again at the cheerful nature of the lass, never without a smile or a skip in her step. She watched as the girl paused to allow a red car to pass before stepping out on the road and making her way back to the big brown van.

Julie waited for the car to drive past before crossing the road and making her way into the passenger seat at the front of the van. As she jumped in, George put the vehicle in gear and slowly pulled away before speaking.

'Any problems?'

Julie shook her head. 'Nah, same as usual. Even gave us a tip.'

George laughed as he negotiated the van around a corner. 'A tip? Geez, if only they knew, eh?'

Julie didn't join in the laughter. She had no issues with the work she was carrying out as an operator with the MRF, the Military Reaction Force. Understood the value and the necessity behind it. But she wouldn't celebrate the deceptions they carried out on a daily basis against the wives and girlfriends of IRA suspects throughout greater Belfast. She knew that a lot of these women while well aware of their husbands' membership of the IRA, were more than likely in the dark regarding the extent of their involvement and details of their activities.

The Four-Square Laundry service that Julie and her team operated in Belfast was a new, secret, intelligence-gathering initiative. The laundry that the team collected from the republican houses and estates wasn't just washed and dried: Prior to the domestic treatments, the clothing was forensically analysed for any traces of gunshot residue or explosives. This enabled Military Intelligence to start identifying active IRA volunteers and plot their homes and addresses. And it was working: The giant map in the MRF Operations' Room had a colour coding allocated to households in the Greater Belfast area according to the evidence that the laundry front had collected. Red for those households where regular traces were picked up during the screenings and amber for irregular. Every day seemed to show an increase in the creeping of red spots across the city. The IRA was upping its game. But so was MRF.

It was dangerous work. IRA checkpoints across the city were a regular fact of life and Julie and her team were no stranger to balaclava-clad men carrying Armalites, conducting checkpoints in republican areas. Her cover was her protection. She portrayed fully the young, bubbly laundry girl picking up and dropping off the white bags of clothing across the city. As most of the republican community used the Four-Square laundry service, their presence in these areas was rarely questioned. And even then, they looked nothing like the soldiers they actually were. The men on the team with their long hair and beards a far cry from the crop-haired squaddies patrolling the streets around them.

She looked up as George accelerated to cross a junction and listened as he spoke.

'Frankie, that's us on Bombay Street now pal.'

From the covered roof-space above her, Julie heard the muffled reply.

'Roger George, we're on task. Keep it as slow as you can mucker.'

She watched as George nodded and slowed the van down, then joined him in the charade of pretending to look for an address while Frankie and Bill took their photographs from the secret compartment in the roof of the vehicle. There had been some unsubstantiated reports from dubious RUC sources that Brendy Hughes was back in Bombay Street. Hughes had been hiding out south of the border for the last year after he had commanded the ambush and killing of three young soldiers from 3 Para. If he was back in Belfast, he was either stupid or very confident as, being designated as an Arrest On Sight, he would know that he was a target. The killing of the paratroopers had only been the latest atrocity for which Hughes had been responsible. Along with Dara McMullin, he had also orchestrated the bombing campaign that was bringing Belfast City centre to its knees and undermining the public confidence in the government.

At their briefing that morning, Julie and the rest of the team had been given the house number that Hughes was apparently staying in. The intent was to mount a covert operation to gain access to the dwelling and place listening devices in it. Their team had been tasked to conduct the first recce of the house and get some close-up images of the approach, the door, and lock types. As the van made its way along the street, George spoke again.

'That's it five doors down on left, black door between two blue ones Frankie.'

The muffled reply: 'Got it mate.'

Julie knew that Frankie and Bill had probably identified the target building themselves but also knew that they sometimes suffered blind spots when engaging the cameras and so George's commentary was useful in ensuring they got an accurate lock-on. George slowed even more as they approached the house and Julie turned to face him, concern on her face that they were showing too much inter- est. Her worry faded as she saw that George had pulled over slightly to let an oncoming car pass them on the narrow street, the driver in the small, red saloon giving a friendly wave of acknowledgement. As George built up the speed again, Julie heard Frankie's muffled voice from above them.

'George, we're good mate. What's next?'

As George shifted through the gears, he replied. 'Few laundry drop-offs pal then some pick-ups in Poleglass on the way back. I'll give you the shout when we get to Pole-glass for a vehicle sweep.'

Julie nodded and relaxed a little, the rest of the trip now straightforward: A few bags picked up and dropped off while the camera crew took images of all the vehicles in the Poleglass estate so that they could check them for owner's details once they returned to HQ. She chewed on the side of a fingernail as she thought about the private meeting she'd had earlier in the week with the Boss. It had taken a lot for her to pluck up the courage to bring the matter to his attention, but she knew she'd had no choice. She'd demanded his utter discretion before speaking on the matter and, even though he'd had a bemused look on his face, he'd given her his word. Which she'd needed. *How could she possibly work in such a small team if they found out she was going behind their backs to the Boss*?

She hadn't wanted to. But what she'd seen and heard just hadn't made sense. The Boss had reassured her that whatever she thought she'd witnessed would turn out to have a simple explanation. She'd challenged him on this, and he'd held up his hand and told her in no uncertain terms that she was not to mention the matter any further. He would look into it personally and get back to her at the end of the week with his own findings. He emphasised that he'd given her his word and that she should trust him to do his job. So, she had. She wondered what he would find out. *Could* she have been mistaken? Misunderstood what she had seen in such a short moment? As the memory returned to her, she was pulled from her concentration by George speaking.

'Sorry, what?' She looked at him as he grinned, white teeth in contrast against the thick, black beard.

'I was saying, it's quiet today isn't it?'

She nodded, stretching her lower back as she felt the Browning pistol digging into her spine. Looking through the windscreen she saw that George was right; it *was* quiet. Something was niggling at the back of her mind as she wondered why the streets were so empty. Thinking about it more, Julie realised that they'd only seen one vehicle since they entered the street and that was a little red...Her eyes widened, and she turned to face George who was now leaning forward and squinting at something in the road ahead.

'What the fuck is that?'

She followed his gaze and saw what appeared to be a car crash; two vehicles close together and blocking the street. Looking in the side mirror, she saw a small, red car following them along the road. Julie felt her pulse quicken and thrust her hand behind her, drawing the pistol from the small of her back. George caught the movement and raised his eyebrows in puzzlement. Julie opened her mouth to explain just as a giant explosion erupted and the van was hurled across the street and into the garden of one of the houses, tumbling over onto its side. Smoke and steam billowed out of the engine as oil and fuel spilled onto the pavement, dark puddles colonising the pale slabs below.

Julie shook her head to clear the ringing in her ears and was immediately confused, her body crumpled and hunched with all the weight on her back and neck. She realised she was upside-down in the footwell of the van and turned herself around so that she was sitting upright. As the memory of the explosion returned to her, she realised she'd dropped the Browning. Thrusting her hand around the floor and beneath the seat, she scrabbled to find the pistol and gave a small exclamation of triumph as her fingers closed on the barrel of the weapon. She twisted her body around so that she was facing the windscreen and felt a jolt of adrenaline as she saw two men marching towards her, black balaclavas covering their faces as they advanced with their Armalite rifles in the shoulder, aiming at the van.

Julie raised the pistol and shot straight through the windscreen, closing her eyes for a brief moment as the glass shattered around her. She saw the man on the left drop to the ground just as the right-hand figure fired a burst of automatic into the van. From the corner of her eye she could see George's body jerking as the bullets slammed into his unprotected chest. She turned the Browning towards the rifleman and fired a quick burst of rounds to get his attention, before taking careful aim and firing off a double tap into the man's chest. He dropped like a stone, the dull, black Armalite clattering on to the tarmac of the road. With the immediate threat neutralised, Julie risked a glance at George but could see from the torn throat gushing blood that he was dead. *Fuck*! She looked into the back of the van but could only see a jumble of laundry bags.

'FRANKIE. BILL. YOU GUYS OKAY?'

A moment later she heard movement and Frankie's voice.

'I'm good Jules, bleeding but okay. Bill's out cold. What the fuck's going on?'

Julie kept watching through the windscreen as she changed the magazine in the Browning for a fresh one, racking the slide forward so the pistol was once again loaded and made ready. 'We've been hit Frankie. George is gone.'

She heard Frankie scrambling about behind her. 'Shit. Okay, can you get to the radio?'

As she looked over at George's side of the van where the radio was concealed in a hidden compartment, the van came under fire from behind, bullets tearing through the soft shell of the vehicle. She heard Frankie scream in agony.

'Fuck, I'm hit, I'M HIT! Jules, I've taken one in the guts. Oh, fuck me....'

Julie knew she had to get to the radio. Stretching upwards, she fired half a dozen rounds blindly through the back of the van as she leaned across George's body and grabbed the handset under the steering column. She pulled the small, black device to her mouth and keyed the pressel.

'Zero this is Echo. Contact. Bombay Street. At least three gunmen and one RPG. We are immobile with one dead, and two wounded. Request QRF and immediate extraction, over.'

To her amazement, the call was answered immediately but interrupted with a large burst of static. Frustrated, she repeated her call, following the format and staying calm to make sure the message came across clearly. Dropping the handset, she accessed the large cover over the centre console and removed the Sterling sub-machine gun and magazines from the compartment. Just as she was loading one of the magazines on to the stubby weapon, another burst of gunfire from behind hammered into the van and she heard Frankie scream again. Julie fired a couple of rounds from the Browning through the back doors and yelled Frankie's name. With no answer she tried again and when the silence remained, she knew her colleague was dead. A further hail of bullets shredded through the back of the van and she crouched down as low as she could. *This van's a fucking bullet magnet.* If she was to survive, she had to get out. With a final look at George's lifeless corpse, Julie fired three rounds through the back door then kicked her way out through the windscreen.

She felt the broken glass on her bare forearms as she rolled away from the front of the vehicle. In a fluid movement, she sprang on to one knee, cocked and readied the Sterling. Ramming the Browning into the waistband of her jeans, she brought the Sterling up, pointing back down the street. Her breathing was ragged, hands shaking as she peered around the side of the van. A figure in a black jacket and balaclava brought an Armalite up on aim as soon as he saw her, but she was faster, getting a burst of rounds down before he could react. She watched with disappointment as the figure darted off into the cover of a garden, clearly unhurt. Julie didn't dwell on her failure to hit the man but used the distraction to turn and sprint away from the van, towards the two vehicles that blocked the road. Her legs seemed far heavier than they should have, and the centre of her back felt hot as she anticipated a bullet ripping through her at any moment.

She leapt over the bodies of the two men she had shot earlier, barely giving them a glance as she continued with her sprint. When she approached the vehicles, she gave a shout of relief as she saw the keys dangling in the ignition of the Ford Cortina with the driver's door open. Giving a quick glance over her shoulder, she threw herself into the driver's seat, slinging the Sterling onto the passenger seat and turning the key in the ignition. The engine caught first time and she yelled in triumph as she reached for the gearstick. An almighty bang filled her world and she was slammed against the door, stunned and winded. She looked across the passenger seat and saw that she had been rammed by a red vehicle. Struggling to find her breath and her focus, she watched as two men alighted from the car, no balaclavas covering their faces but armed with rifles of some sort. She looked for the Sterling, but it was down in the passenger footwell, completely beyond her reach. With her right hand, Julie opened her door while with her left she drew the Browning and brought it up on aim.

She felt a huge kick to her chest and tumbled out of the door, spilling onto the road below. Confused, she tried to stand but found she was struggling to breathe. Looking down, she saw a scarlet stain start to blossom on the white of her laundry apron and realised with an odd sense of detachment, that she'd been shot. From the corner of her eye she could see a man walking around the car towards her and watched as he kicked the Browning away from her side where it had fallen. Julie could hear her own breathing now; wet, heavy, rasping, and knew she was dying. She didn't want to die. She really didn't want to die *here*, in this street, in this city. Tears flowed down her face as she thought about what they'd tell Marcus. What could they tell him that he'd understand? All he would know was that his mother was gone. Never coming back. Had left him. As the greyness began creeping in at the edge of her vision, Julie moaned and dropped her bloodied hand into her lap, fishing for the secret pocket in her apron. She felt the object, smiled as she pulled it out and brought it up to where she could see it. Julie wanted his perfect face to be the last image she left this earth with. She looked at the photograph for a moment before closing her eyes, her hand dropping to her side just as the man spoke.

'She's gone JC. You get yourself to the van and make sure the driver and the two camera boys are done, then get it torched. We've got about three minutes before the QRF are deployed so get moving big lad.'

Even as she drifted into unconsciousness, Julie frowned, confused not just by the terms and the knowledge her killer was displaying but also by his English accent. She strained to open her eyes but there was a heavy weight on the lids and she found it impossible even as the man kneeled beside her and spoke softly.

'This is not what I would call a good day's work for me by any means, but you stirred the hornet's nest. Poked your nose in where it didn't belong. We couldn't have that. You couldn't understand what you saw, and neither would many people and that's why we are where we are. Go on now, go to sleep, let it take you to a better place.'

The man's voice was soothing and calm, almost comforting and as she struggled to place where she had heard it before, Corporal Julie Myers BEM, Women's Royal Army Corps, gave a final guttural breath and died in a pool of her own blood in a deserted street in republican West Belfast.

CHAPTER 2

CAMP BRACKEN, ENGLAND 1995

His lungs were burning, mouth wide open as he struggled to suck in as much oxygen as he could to replenish them. The weight of the guy he was carrying on his shoulders really telling now, his legs starting to buckle as the lactic acid built up. The screaming of the Physical Training Instructor running alongside him a mere sideshow to the physical agony. Raising his head, he could see the finish line at the top of the hill where another PTI stood with a stopwatch and a clipboard. *Fifty metres, c'mon, only fifty more metres.* He shook his head as the sweat rolled into his eyes and drove his legs forward, ignoring their agonised protests. Grabbing a tighter hold of his partner with one hand, he pumped hard with his free arm and despite his exhaustion, opened up his pace on the final part of the hill. As he reached the PTI, he heard his time called out and staggered past, his partner rolling off his shoulders and standing beside him, slapping his back and congratulating him. But Marcus didn't really hear him, bent over and taking in huge gulps of air to feed the oxygen-depleted muscles. His only solace was that he was first. He saw a pair of legs stumble past him and heard a sob of relief as another pair finished the test.

Marcus raised his head and looked back down the forest track where another ten pairs were staggering with their partners on their backs, the steepness of the hill robbing their legs of any power. Two hours into this particular beasting and the course was thinning dramatically. A whistle blew and the PTI with the clipboard looked down the hill at his colleague and drew his hand across his throat: Those who hadn't made it past him had failed. The PTI below them screamed at those around him to drop their partners and get their useless arses back down the hill. The PTI with the clipboard turned to Marcus and his group, addressing them in his deep baritone.

'Well done. Some good effort there. Follow me and don't fall behind.'

With that they were off, wide strides as they sought to keep pace with the fitness machine leading them through the warren of undulating forest paths, his blue tracksuit-top the beacon they followed. Occasionally the sprint would be stopped, and they would be 'rested' with a set of burpees, squat thrusts, or leopard crawls before leaping to their feet and racing after the blue streak to their front. On the third circuit they lost another individual, his leg buckling during another fireman's carry and twisting underneath him, the crack of the femur breaking drowned out only by the shriek of agony that followed. The PTIs screamed at them again.

Don't fucking stop! You're not a surgeon, there's nothing you can do. You want to join him? Vicious, blue-jerseyed collies, snapping at them, cajoling them, nipping at them to stay with the herd.

The rest of the thrashing was a blur of sprints, crawls, carries and press-ups to Marcus, but eventually the six remaining students staggered back into camp still trailing the chief PTI. He led them to the large grassy area in the centre of the camp and had them walk in a circle to get their heartbeats and respirations back to normal. After five minutes he called them to a halt and asked them to provide him with the three times for their physical exertions in the forest. The big Geordie to Marcus' left had forgotten his time for the woods' loop and was told to piss off and go pack his kit. They were now down to five.

～

The figure-eleven targets popped up just as their car crossed the junction. In the passenger seat Marcus lifted an MP5K up, pointed it at the windscreen and opened fire on full-automatic. The windscreen's laminate stopped the glass from shattering completely as the bullets tore their way through it and into the wooden targets beyond. The driver was already out of the vehicle, crouched behind the door and firing his G3, the loud booming of the 7.62 rounds the signal for Marcus to bug out. Dropping the MP5 in the footwell, Marcus scooped up his own G3 as he exited the car and ran straight to a small rise of dirt off to one side. He brought the rifle up on aim and began engaging the targets, screaming for Dave to move. From his peripheral vision he saw Dave lob a smoke grenade towards the targets before sprinting back in line with Marcus then providing covering fire of his own while Marcus moved. They repeated this fire and manoeuvre drill until Marcus screamed to Dave to rally behind the big dune. Together for the first time since the contact, they changed magazines, checked for injuries and sent a SITREP to Zero requesting support and extraction. A voice behind them bellowed.

'STOP. Unload weapons and show clear.'

Both men followed the directive and raised their hands to show that the weapons were fully unloaded and cleared. The voice boomed again.

'Ease springs.'

Marcus and Dave allowed the working parts of the weapons to go forward, fired off the actions and applied the safety catches before standing up and turning to face the voice. The man before them took another drag of his cigarette before speaking.

'Not bad, not bad. Nice slick drills, good cover and a decent rally point. Not much more to say fellas. Go get the car and take it back up for the next lot.' With that, the SAS instructor turned and began walking back up the hill to where the other three students were waiting. Marcus flashed Dave a quick grin as he jogged past him to retrieve the vehicle. Nick, the chief SAS instructor, was notoriously difficult to please and his faint praise was all the more rewarding for that.

As they were cleaning weapons later that evening, Nick came into the cold hangar and addressed them.

'You're down to four now. Fielding fucked up the shoot.' With that, he turned on his heel and left the building. Nobody said anything. There was nothing really to say. Fielding had seemed a decent guy, but they all knew the score; keep up or go home. Marcus looked at the other three guys around him as they ran rods through barrels and scrubbed gas parts. *Four left out of fifty and it's not over yet.*

⁓

The blow to his kidney dropped him to his knees as the Irish voice screamed in his ear.

'Talk ya fucken Brit bastard or it'll be a knife next time.'

Marcus gritted his teeth and felt sick from the pain. He was also freezing, naked since they'd taken him and tied him to...whatever the hell he was tied to, the hood over his head allowing him no vision whatsoever.

The four of them had been deployed out on an exercise to conduct a Dead Letter Box drop, or DLB, for an agent. As Marcus had turned the corner of an estate in St Albans, he'd been accosted by a dozen balaclava-clad individuals who attacked him with punches and kicks. He'd fought back hard with strikes of his own, but their sheer number had overwhelmed him. They'd ripped his pistol and body comms from him before binding his hands and feet, gagging him then hooding him. He'd been manhandled into a van of some sort then brought to a building where the rough treatment had begun.

On his first interrogation, he'd given them nothing and had suffered the consequences. On the second, he'd admitted he was a soldier, little point in denying this as they had his weapons, radio and ID card. On the third, he pretended to crack a little and hinted that he performed unconventional duties. This bought him some time as they dug into his activities. Drawing on his recollections of their role when he had been a young Royal Marine deployed in South Armagh, Marcus drip-fed the interrogators a story about being a Signals courier. He could speak with some confidence on this, having seen how these guys worked. But it also held the added benefit of going at least some way to explaining why he had been carrying covert comms and unconventional weapons. Marcus knew that there was a fine line to be trod between saying nothing and getting killed for being of no use and saying too much that guaranteed maximum torture and violence before death. He knew he had to provide his captors with enough information to keep them interested and have to check on. This bought Marcus time. Time during which his colleagues and the dedicated Special Forces team could find him. He lost count of the interrogations he'd undergone until eventually his hood was ripped off and the face of the course officer was in front of him.

'Marcus, do you know who I am?' He nodded.

'Good. I'm pleased to tell you that the exercise is over, and you've passed. Any serious injuries?' He had none, bar bruising and cuts.

'Excellent. Get yourself away and have a pint or two and some sleep. No training today. First Parade 0630 tomorrow.' Marcus limped away, stunned that it was over, and he'd passed. He was also amazed that he had a whole day off, although, with the state his aching body was in, he would need it.

❧

On a grey Tuesday afternoon, Marcus drove into the compound having completed the surveillance of a target through Luton. After he'd unloaded and secured his weapons, he'd walked into the Ops Room to see what was next on the agenda. He was exhausted, the past fourteen days of the final exercise a blur of agent meetings, surveillance, counter-surveillance and DLBs. Out and about in South-East England for nineteen, and twenty-hour days, eating next to nothing as he and the other two remaining students on the course were tested to the extreme by the Directing Staff. As he entered the Ops Room, he saw Dave grinning up at him from the desk.

'Bloody hell Marcus, it's over. ENDEX mate, the Boss just called ENDEX!'

ENDEX: End of Exercise. The sweetest words in any soldier's lexicon. And with ENDEX, Marcus realised, was the end of the course. The end of four and a half months of mental and physical hell. And there were only three from an initial course of fifty. And they didn't even know if they'd passed yet. Only that they'd finished.

Marcus walked into the course office with a throbbing headache, the result of a large night of celebrating with Dave. Only he and Marcus had passed. Mitch being assessed as not quite coming up to scratch. He and Dave had hung one on, the pints and shots going straight to their heads after the four and a half months of being starved, exhausted, and practically alcohol-free. His appointment with the Boss had been arranged for ten that morning which, while civilised, was still way too early for Marcus in his fragile state. He took a deep breath, knocked on the internal door and obeyed the command to enter.

The Boss smiled at him and asked Marcus how his head was. Grinning sheepishly, Marcus stated he felt a little woolly, truth be told. The Boss congratulated him on passing the course and told him he'd given a strong performance throughout the entire duration. The subject turned to the future and the Boss informed Marcus that he was booked on a flight to Belfast in three days' time. He would be met at the airport and taken to HQNI in Lisburn where he would be given a week of continuation training from the SAS instructors attached to the Unit. After that he would join his Operational Detachment in Belfast where he would take up the role that the course had qualified him for:

A Covert Intelligence Operator.

CHAPTER 3

SPECIAL INTELLIGENCE GROUP, (SIG)
BELFAST DETACHMENT, 1995

Marcus took the final items from the bottom of the bag and placed them in the tall metal locker. As he was moving into a Safe House in the north of the city, he had to secure all military and personal items in his locker for safekeeping. The theory being that if the Safe House was ever broken into by criminals, they would find nothing that would link it to the military or intelligence operations. He paused when he lifted out the final item; a framed photograph. Smiled as he looked at the washed-out colours that dated the image to the 1970s. His Dad; skinny with ridiculously long hair and a suit that had flared trouser legs. Him; a scrawny six-year old with black curly hair and a smile showing a missing tooth. Then her. *Mum*. Short, blonde hair, big smile, Army dress uniform. Holding a medal in a box up for the camera. The three of them, arms around each other outside Buckingham Palace just after his mum had been presented with the British Empire Medal.

Marcus hadn't really understood it back then, just knew his mum was a hero and they were going to London to meet the Queen. It was one of the last times that he remembered them all being happy.

She had been killed a matter of months after the photo was taken. A car crash in Northern Ireland. A terrible accident according to the report his Dad was given. Marcus barely remembered the funeral other than the presence of so many soldiers. His dad started going downhill after that. The drinking that initially took the edge off, now taking full days off. He lost his job, spent what little money he had on the drink, forgot that he had a son who needed him. Social Services stepped in and Marcus found himself on the carousel of foster homes and carers for the duration of his childhood. He was fifteen when he was told that his dad had died but he hadn't felt anything. He'd spent longer without a dad than he had with one and Terry, his foster parent for the past year, had acted like a *real* dad.

He'd missed his mum though. Young as he had been when she'd been killed, he still remembered how much fun she was, how much fun they'd *all* been, when she was around. She was always smiling. Smiling and singing. That's what he remembered. And now all he had left was the photo and the medal sitting in its dusty, velvet-covered box. Marcus took another look at the image before placing it on the top shelf of the locker. He closed and locked the door then made his way upstairs to the kitchen to grab a quick cup of coffee. The room was empty, and he munched on a couple of bourbon creams as he made his drink and shook the sadness from his thoughts.

Walking past the Boss's office, Marcus heard his name called and looked in and saw the Boss beckoning him. Stepping into the office, Marcus took the chair he was offered as the Boss closed the door. He'd met the Boss several times in the last month and found him to be a decent guy. A Major in the Intelligence Corps, he had a lot of experience with the Unit, having started his first tour back in the eighties as an Operator, just as Marcus now was. The Boss cleared his throat.

'Marcus, how are you settling in?'

'Okay I think Boss. Still got a lot to learn but really enjoying it.'

The Boss nodded and smiled. 'Good, good. That's pretty much the impression I'm getting. And you're moving into OXFORD I understand?'

Marcus nodded, OXFORD being the code name of the Safe House he would be living in. 'Yes Boss. Been up there quite a few times and Al has given me the full brief on the security system and actions-on.'

'Good, because it's vital you fully understand the systems and what to do if something goes wrong. It's a lot of responsibility living in a Safe House, but I wouldn't have asked you if I didn't think you were capable.'

'I appreciate that Boss and won't let you down.'

'I know you won't Marcus. There's something else I want to talk to you about while I have you here. You've obviously heard that Iain is leaving us, and that GRANITE will be needing a new Handler? Well, I'd like you to take that on.'

Marcus raised his eyebrows in surprise. GRANITE was the code name for a very reliable Agent who had been working for Belfast Det for over twenty years. He was one of the Unit's best assets and Marcus was surprised to be offered the position and said as much. The Boss raised a hand to silence him.

'Look, not blowing smoke up your arse Marcus, but you arrived with a very strong course report and you've already made a bit of a name for yourself as someone determined to do well here. That's why I'm giving you this opportunity. Don't fuck it up.'

Although the last statement was uttered with a grin, Marcus had no doubt that if he did fuck it up, he wouldn't be given another chance like this. He left the Boss's office elated, the sadness he'd felt going over old memories, all but forgotten.

～

Marcus pulled his hood up against the driving rain and stepped into the small alley that ran between the Crown Bar and the small scattering of shops behind. The man twenty metres in front of him turned left and Marcus pressed a concealed button in his pocket and spoke quietly. 'He's now left, left, left and unsighted to me.' A muted reply came through his covert earpiece informing him that one of the other Operators had 'eyes on,' could physically see, the target. In this case the target was one of theirs; an Agent codenamed VORTEX. Marcus and his team were putting VORTEX through a Counter-Surveillance, or CS route to ensure their Agent wasn't being followed. VORTEX believed he was under suspicion from his superiors in the IRA as a result of one too many operations being thwarted. This was nothing unusual for the Unit to deal with. The Agents that the Unit ran provided real-time intelligence on IRA activities and, where there was a threat to life or extreme damage, the Unit had to act. This obviously put the Agents in a vulnerable position. The IRA had their own security team, referred to as 'The Nutting Squad'. They investigated, interrogated and executed, or 'nutted', suspected informers. Informers were usually referred to as 'touts' and when the time came, after being bled dry of information from the torture and interrogations, they were dispatched with a bullet to the head, or 'nut' as the Irish called it.

The Nutting Squad were the most trusted members of the IRA; all from staunch republican families and with comprehensive experience in torture and killing. Their reputations were unimpeachable due to their utter dedication to their task. For VORTEX to believe he was under suspicion was enough for his Handler Brian, to take all necessary measures to confirm or refute this. A CS route was always the first step that the Unit used to identify if their Agents were under IRA surveillance. Usually a long walking or driving route with changes of direction, stops, and switches from busy to quiet areas. The sole aim of the CS route was to positively identify anyone following the Agent. And Brian would not go anywhere near VORTEX until the team were convinced that VORTEX was clean.

Marcus turned the corner and saw an individual in a large anorak taking long strides across the pedestrian precinct. The man's behaviour immediately set Marcus' antennae off. *This isn't right.* He called it on the radio and gave the individual's location and description. Losing sight of the man for a brief moment, he picked him up again as the man skidded to a halt as he joined the main road. The man looked both ways before striding out again to his right. *The same direction as VORTEX.* Marcus called it in again and heard Neil confirm that he had eyes-on the individual. Marcus, as briefed, did not follow VORTEX's route but crossed the road and continued along Castle Street to make sure he would be ahead of VORTEX by the time the Agent arrived at the rear of the Castle Court shopping centre. Another call came through his earpiece to let the team know that the individual following VORTEX had given a nod to another man who seemed to be loitering on the corner of Donegal Square for no good reason, particularly when the rain was still teeming down.

Marcus felt his adrenaline building. It looked like VORTEX was right; he *was* under suspicion and an IRA surveillance team was now following him to gain evidence of this. Brian came on the net and directed the team to continue with the follow, but he wouldn't be going near

VORTEX. VORTEX knew what to do in the event that he wasn't met by his Handler, to carry out a natural act that would cover his reason for walking the CS route. As Marcus turned down the shabby street that bordered the rear of the shopping centre, he saw VORTEX coming out through the glass doors and walk to the left and towards the traffic lights. A brief moment later the tall individual that Neil reported exited the shopping centre in a manner that suggested he was in a hurry. The moment he saw VORTEX however, he slowed to a stop and relaxed his gait, ambling along behind the Agent at a much-reduced pace. Marcus smiled at the amateur mistake. He called it on the radio and Brian responded, directing the Team to abort the Op and return to base. Marcus waited his turn on the net and acknowledged, taking a route back through the city centre that allowed him to clean himself down, making sure he hadn't picked up a tail. After a few changes of direction and a couple of stops to pick up some milk and a newspaper, Marcus was happy he was clean and gave the call to Zero that this was the case. In his earpiece he could hear the rest of the Team giving their status before returning to their vehicles. As Marcus reached his, he felt an enormous sense of satisfaction at having identified the surveillance. He'd been with the Unit for over three months

now and this was definitely one of his high points of an already rewarding role.

There was some consternation back at the Unit regarding VORTEX's situation and personal safety but again, this was not unfamiliar territory. A disinformation operation was put into play where it was discreetly 'leaked' that a Police technical operation had picked up details of IRA activities over the past six months. Within the fortnight, all suspicion and surveillance that VORTEX had been under, disappeared. For Marcus, the taking on of his new Agent, GRANITE, became the main focus of his efforts.

GRANITE had been running as an Agent with the Unit for over twenty years. Marcus learned that GRANITE had been recruited as a young IRA volunteer when he was caught carrying weapons from a house in the Turf Lodge. The military patrol who stopped him also had a member of the Unit with them, masquerading as just another squaddie. He had immediately seized the opportunity to turn the normal arrest of a not-so significant individual into something much more beneficial and had, in a blitzkrieg approach, recruited the young GRANITE as an Agent, saving him from a good stretch in 'the Kesh'. Over the years, with the Unit's guidance and development, GRANITE had risen through the ranks to his current position on the IRA's Executive Ops team. Tasked directly through the IRA's Army Council, this small team carried out the more sensitive operations on behalf of the movement, each man selected and trusted for his commitment to the cause. SIG had been careful through the years that GRANITE was never used as a gunman or explosives officer but always within the intelligence and planning departments. This allowed him a longevity that was rare among Agents who reported from within terrorist groups. It also explained how his reporting was so good it had netted the Unit some of the biggest intelligence successes against the IRA. The list was impressive, and Marcus knew he was fortunate to be given such a case as a relatively new Operator.

He'd hit it off with GRANITE from the start. They shared an irreverent sense of humour and a respect for the role that each man carried out. GRANITE seemed impressed that Marcus knew so much about the identities, activities and intentions of Belfast Brigade Provisional Irish Republican Army: PIRA to Marcus, and *the 'RA*, or *the Bhoys* to GRANITE. Marcus was pleased that he'd impressed GRANITE but knew that it hadn't been an onerous task for him; he'd been fascinated by this new world and had been reading voraciously, soaking up all available information to prepare him as best he could.

Every meeting with GRANITE was a revelation to Marcus. It still astounded him when he listened to GRANITE discussing a meeting he had attended with members of the republican leadership and what they'd been talking about. Being one of the key members of the Executive Ops team gave GRANITE an automatic 'in' with the members of the PAC, the IRA's Provisional Army Council: The men who ran the entire republican movement. Some of them household names claiming political status and denying any role in past violence, others happy to bask in the renown they'd accrued over twenty years of murder and killing.

But this also meant that Marcus had to be hyper-aware every time he met with GRANITE. Even when they weren't under suspicion, the IRA would routinely place their members under surveillance, looking to see if they met with unknown individuals or were travelling to areas that they had no real reason to be seen in. Throughout his tenure as an Agent, GRANITE had come under suspicion on several occasions when one too many IRA operations had been thwarted by the security forces. But GRANITE was tough, even by IRA standards. He was also trained well by the Unit, who provided him with means and methods for enduring interrogations and distancing himself from blame. The combination of his defiant rebuttals and this training had seen him survive and his reputation remain clear for the remainder of his involvement with PIRA.

But Marcus left nothing to chance. Each time he planned a meeting with GRANITE, he laboured over every possible eventuality that could go wrong and what he could do to address them. GRANITE appreciated the new routes he was given. The occasional Counter Surveillance drive he would be directed to follow, and the enhanced contact procedures that Marcus put in place. Some of his fellow Operators felt that Marcus was being overcautious, but mostly accepted his directives for meeting with GRANITE with good-natured jibes.

Which stopped the day that his countermeasures saved their lives.

CHAPTER 4

TASKING AND COORDINATION GROUP, BELFAST

Colin Woods rubbed his eyes, a vain attempt to wipe away the physical exhaustion he felt. Twenty years of being at the sharp end of Special Branch operations and he still found himself surprised by some of the situations they found themselves in. As the Operations Officer for the Tasking and Coordination Group, TCG, his role was never a dull one. The deconfliction and balancing act of mounting covert operations against the IRA always a challenge. So many moving parts and entities to consider. There was his own organisation, the RUC; the police force of Northern Ireland. Within that body were the specialist elements that were coordinated through TCG; Special Branch, the 'door-kickers' from HMSU and the MSUs, E3A the Agent Handlers, and E4A the covert surveillance unit. Then there was the Army side. The SAS and SBS, the executive strike option for the big jobs. Special Intelligence Group aka SIG or 'the Unit,' the Army's covert intelligence gatherers. Joint Communications Unit aka JCU or 'The Det,' the Army's covert surveillance unit. What made it more confusing was the Army's bloody ridiculous naming conventions. JCU was a unit but called itself the Det, and SIG was a group but called itself a Unit with operational Dets. Then there were the spooks: The Security Service or MI5 and, occasionally where there was a foreign element to the operation, MI6. MI5, or Box as everyone in the intelligence community referred to them, were probably the least popular with TCG, their disdain of the police and the military plain to see. When he'd first taken over Operations two years before it had been a steep learning curve for him, despite coming from his HMSU and Special Branch background. But he'd got there. And with no major fuck-ups on his watch. *So far...*

He looked again at the report in the folder in front of him and sighed as he could already foresee the headaches coming his way. Box, who in his experience did not work or play well with others, had a situation rapidly approaching that they needed to deal with. And when they said *they,* what they actually meant was TCG. One of their top assets, codenamed RED LANCE, had warned them that the IRA had identified an informer working for the police and that very soon, they were going to kidnap and torture the individual with a view to setting up his Handlers. A further IRA team would then ambush the intelligence officers in a capture or kill operation. Colin ran his hand through his greying hair and sighed. In the old days this would have been an easy fix with no paper trail to be concerned about. Now, however, the RUC had to be squeaky clean, the republican bandwagon of Sinn Fein starting to wield serious political clout. One sniff of foul play or dirty tricks from any element of the security forces would be enough to set off the Sinn Fein propaganda machine. Pulling in the gullible Yanks and the British Government, the latter keen to secure a political solution to the Northern Irish problem and be rid of it once and for all. And that meant, publicly at least, coming down hard on any perceived slights to the republican movement. It stuck in the craw of many an experienced officer to see the murderers of their friends and colleagues being elevated to legitimacy by a regime so keen to get out of the political quagmire that they would pander to the grievances, real or imagined, that Sinn Fein threw their way.

The information in the folder was good. Very good. Everything TCG would need in order to stop the kidnap and killing of the informer and the subsequent attack on the Handlers. But that wasn't the problem; The problem was that TCG was being directed by Box *not* to act on the information. Well, not yet anyway. Their concern being that if TCG gave the informer the heads-up that he was about to be scooped and sat on a cooker in County Monaghan until he squealed, he would run and highlight the fact that the security forces knew about the information. Or, as they were now legally obliged to do, issue the threat formally to the informer and have him resettled on the mainland. Colin couldn't even tell the Special Branch Handler that his informer was under threat as Box had also told him that this course of action was not to be pursued. He was also prohibited from mentioning anything to SIG, in case the information somehow leaked from their organisation to Special Branch. Colin understood the concerns; some Handlers had built up very personal relationships with their Agents over the years. *Too* personal in some cases. Box were aware of this and consequently unwilling to put their own Agents at risk of being compromised. And looking at the folder in front of him, Colin could see that RED LANCE was a very high-level Agent indeed.

While Box had provided no details whatsoever on the identity of RED LANCE, Colin's considerable experience in intelligence operations provided him with the knowledge to interpret the level at which RED LANCE operated. The specific nature of the information regarding the IRA operation was of the sort where RED LANCE was clearly one of a very tight, trusted, circle. An operation to lift a tout and get him over the border was usually the responsibility of the Nutting Squad, although sometimes the Executive Ops guys might be co-opted into it. Even at that, it meant no more than four or five people at the most would be in the loop with something like this. Which in turn meant that RED LANCE was, if not one of these four or five individuals, close to them. *Very* close.

The request from Box was for TCG to let the IRA operation run and have TCG put together an interdiction that could be viewed as purely chance. TCG had done many of these operations in the past in order to protect Agents from being compromised. It was usually because the information that the Agent provided was only known by a small group of people, termed the *Circle of Knowledge* by intelligence agencies. The IRA were very good at internal security and every time one of their operations was thwarted, they conducted a thorough investigation. This included harsh debriefs of everyone who knew about the operation, analysing all of their movements and activities in the lead up to the attack and verifying these with family, friends and associates to determine the truth. This meant that there were times when an IRA operation had to be allowed to run but then encounter an obstacle that would cause them to call it off. It could be as simple as raiding a house close to that of the IRA's target, the increased security presence deterring armed terrorists from entering the area while supplying a credible reason for troops to be in the area in the first place. While this might only delay the activity, it gave the security forces some breathing space with which to concoct an initiative of their own to take out the key players in the IRA's team under the guise of an alternative operation.

This one however, was going to be tough. The Nutting Squad and Executive Ops guys were the trusted top tier of the entire republican movement. The mere fact that RED LANCE had such specific information at this level was a surprise to Colin. Names, vehicles, communications, timings. Phenomenal stuff really. According to RED LANCE, the informer was known to be having an affair with a woman in Lurgan who he visited, as regular as clockwork, every Thursday night. The Nutting Squad's plan was to grab him on his way into the woman's estate and get him away over the border and into a farm complex somewhere in the Republic where they could take their time getting the information out of him. The team would consist of three vehicles; two cars and a van. One car would lead, going ahead and acting as a scout, looking for any roadblocks or check points. They would warn the backing vehicles to either take an alternative route or stop and turn around. The van would have the informer and his captors, while the rear vehicle looked for any indications they were being followed or tracked. The rear vehicle would also act as the extraction for the men in the van in the event that something went wrong. In this case the tout would be shot, the van torched, and the team spirited away over the border to lay low for a few months. Standard procedures that they'd used before to good effect.

Who the hell is RED LANCE? Colin stroked his chin as he pondered his own question. This level of information was top drawer stuff and could only have come from someone close to one of the key players. The problem with that of course, was that these key players were very violent men, accustomed to rooting out informers and collaborators. As well as that, the Nutting Squad and Executive Ops boys were the two remaining active IRA departments that didn't adhere to the ceasefire. These boys were *current*. Still, it was Box's baby and as long as TCG could put together a plan to stop the lift of the tout while keeping RED LANCE out of the spotlight of suspicion, everything should work out all right.

Colin looked at his watch and raised his eyebrows in surprise when he noted the late hour, although he really shouldn't have. Twenty-odd years of long days and late nights really meant that it was the norm rather than the exception. As he replaced the RED LANCE folder into the safe and checked that it was securely locked, he reflected that the RED LANCE issue was really nothing that they hadn't experienced before, just a few more moving parts to take into consideration. As he locked his door and zipped up his jacket, he allowed himself a small nod of confidence that whatever route they chose to deal with the issues, it would be fairly routine.

He hoped.

CHAPTER 5

SIG, BELFAST

Marcus leaned back in his chair and studied the Boss tapping on the keyboard of the computer before him. The furrowed brow and tight-lipped grimace showing the man's concern over the information that Marcus had just given him. At a meeting with GRANITE earlier that day, the Agent had told Marcus that there was something going on within the Executive Ops team that he wasn't privy to. This concerned Marcus initially as GRANITE was trusted by the highest level of the IRA and being excluded from anything should raise a red flag as far as Marcus was concerned. GRANITE, while wary of the situation, wasn't as concerned, stating that this happened from time to time. It usually meant a very sensitive operation was underway and wouldn't be briefed to those carrying out the operation until absolutely necessary. GRANITE was sure that this was one of those occasions.

According to GRANITE, Blackie Donnelly, the head of the Executive Ops team had disappeared for over a week.

On his return he had set up a small cell consisting of himself, Declan Burns and, surprisingly, Big Joe Carluccio, head of the Nutting Squad. Carluccio's presence obviously raised GRANITE's hackles as it could really only mean that whatever operation was underfoot, it was related to a tout. In typical black humour, GRANITE had said that he hoped it wasn't him as he had a holiday booked to Tenerife later that year.

With his knowledge of the IRA and its operational methods, Marcus recognised the gravity of the situation. This setting up of such a small cell of key individuals had been done before and usually preceded a brutal killing of an agent. The names of these unfortunates, sad milestones in the ongoing intelligence war. Eamon Collins, Paddy Flood, Frankie Hegarty. Naked bodies, hooded and bound, displaying the burns, scars and wounds of the heinous torture they had undergone prior to getting the final bullet in the 'nut'. The bodies dumped on public roads where they would be found quickly, the message a simple one; deterrence. Even if you were just thinking about it, don't become a tout.

And Dom, Marcus' Boss, was even more aware that the cell formation was very bad news for the intelligence agencies, and it would now be a race to identify the target before the IRA operation was carried out. GRANITE had tried where he could to gain as much information as possible about why the small cell had been set up. But beyond being told something big was in the wings, he couldn't get anything else without arousing suspicion. GRANITE was sure however, that it was an operation against an agent or informer in light of the fact that the Nutting Squad was involved. He'd been told by Burns that it was a high-risk operation that would be briefed to the select few who needed to know in order to protect the IRA men involved. The republican movement had long memories and the death of their martyrs at Loughgall and Gibraltar in years past were as fresh as though the incidents had happened the week before. The general consensus being that all these operations had been compromised by a high-level informer in their midst. As a consequence of this, greater care was taken on sensitive operations to keep the information secure.

As the Boss finished off his typing, he looked up and met Marcus's gaze.

'Okay Marcus, I've got that all down and I'll brief it to the Ops Officer. So, GRANITE doesn't have a clue yet as to the target, but does he think he'll be included on the Op?'

Marcus leaned forward in his seat. 'He thinks so Boss but can't guarantee it. If he does, he'll ring in the minute he gets the info.'

'Mmm...not ideal but I guess we can only work with what we've got. Problem is, this is so tight, we can't even task the other agents to keep their ears to the ground.'

'Yep, that's pretty much the size of it Boss, but GRANITE is bloody good at what he does so if there's anything that's going to help us, he'll get it.'

'I know, I know. Let's just hope it's not after the fact'.

Later that afternoon, Marcus finished writing his own report and drove to Belvoir Park for a run. As he pounded the leaf- strewn paths, his mind was still on GRANITE and the situation. Their best hope was that GRANITE would be brought into the operation in time to give them a heads-up on it. That way they could figure out how to stop it without compromising GRANITE in the process. Back in the safe house, he had just come out of the shower when the telephone rang. He answered it and the Boss spoke immediately.

'You need to come in. We're on.'

CHAPTER 6

SINN FEIN OFFICE, FALLS ROAD, WEST BELFAST

Blackie Donnelly took another drag on his cigarette and watched as Declan Burns pulled down the steel roller shutters over the doors and windows of the Sinn Fein office, closing up for the day. Declan stood, dropped some keys into his jacket pocket and nodded his head. Both men walked along the road in silence for several seconds before Declan spoke.

'What does Big Joe say?'

Blackie looked behind him briefly before replying. 'He's going to take Frankie Vallely with him on the scoop and they'll both do the interrogation.'

Declan nodded. 'What about our boys?'

Blackie thought for a moment before replying. 'You, Kieran and Vincent. You lead, Kieran drives and Vincent's protection. Kieran will have a pistol, Vincent an M16 with some spare mags just in case youse need it.'

'Where's the safest place to get the weapons from?'

'I'll get them from the Lenadoon cache. The quartermaster's a good spud and knows to keep his trap shut when it's me that's doing the asking.'

'How does he get them to us?'

Blackie blew a plume of smoke into the cold air. 'I've got Mairead Connolly bringing them out. I've used her before and she's a good 'un. Asks no questions and there's not much that frightens her.'

'She the one we used for the Canary Wharf deliveries?'

'Aye, the same. Like I said, a safe pair of hands Declan. The M16 will be broken down and in the pram with her wee niece. She'll stow them under the paving slab behind The Slieve, and Vincent'll get them from there. Joe and Frankie will bring their own so that's not our problem.'

Declan nodded, the temporary hide behind the Slieve Bar a tried and tested location that the team had used before. It was very difficult for a stranger to loiter in that area for any length of time without being challenged by a local. The Slieve was republican territory and all strangers were challenged as a matter of course. Between the police and the military, there was always an intelligence operation underway against the IRA and its members. The local population were well aware of this and did not hold back in their willingness to approach someone they knew wasn't from the area. This made it extremely difficult for any undercover police or soldiers to operate there. Over the years there had been many occasions where these clandestine operators had been compromised by little more than a nosy housewife or cheeky teenager. Old or young, every republican saw it as their duty to assist in the protection of their areas. And this was what made the temporary hide behind The Slieve Bar such a good location for their use. The area was staunch republican and the bar itself the haunt of IRA members, their friends, families and supporters.

Blackie took a final draw on his cigarette then flicked the butt into the road. 'When we're done, Pat McCusker and his boys in Monaghan will take the weapons and get them back over the border under their own steam.'

Declan was happy with the plan. It was solid, had a strong team and he felt a ripple of excitement pass through him at the anticipation of scooping a tout. And this tout in particular was well known to Declan, having been under his command back in the eighties. Denis O'Callaghan, or 'Doc' as his name was abbreviated to, hadn't been a particularly good Volunteer, more interested in boozing and womanising than his commitment to the republican struggle. He'd been disciplined by Declan a couple of times for minor offences but then seemed to get his shit together and started to behave like a true volunteer. *Probably the same time he was recruited as a fucking tout. Taking direction from his RUC handlers.* He felt the anger rise as it had done on every other occasion when an informer had been identified. The betrayal of friends, family and community. Declan couldn't understand it; according to the Nutting Squad, none of the touts they had tortured had been paid any significant money for their efforts. *So what the hell made a man turn his back on everything just to give information to the enemy?*

From what they knew about Doc, both he and Blackie agreed that the tout would squeal as soon as he saw his predicament. In the past, the Nutting Squad would just keep torturing a tout until he had nothing more to tell them, then end his misery and dump him where he'd be found quickly. But with Doc, they wanted him to arrange a meeting with his handlers so that they could hit them and either capture or kill them. Doc had to be kept alive until he'd arranged this, so his torture would have to be carefully applied in case the fat bastard had a heart attack on them.

In that case, the whole effort and risk of the operation would have been for nothing. Well, not nothing exactly. A burned, bloodied and naked corpse on a public road still worth the strong deterrent it provided. But successfully capturing or killing a couple of handlers? Priceless for the intelligence value the IRA would gain as well as a huge propaganda coup for the movement. There would, of course, be the biggest investigation and manhunt that the security forces could muster to find the men who had carried out the operation. All hell would be let loose and the gloves would be off as far as the peelers and the British State were concerned. But it would be worth it. And with a bit of smoke and mirrors the blame could be laid at the door of those republicans who weren't following the party line; the Dissidents. A rag-tag army of has-beens and wannabes that, frankly, were nothing more than a pain in the arse to the Provisional movement. But now, possibly a useful pain...

Blackie tapped his shoulder to get his attention. 'Will you brief the boys for me? Tell Kieran that there'll be a maroon Ford Sierra left for him at the back of McCullough's shop, keys behind the visor. It's an old couple's from Twinbrook who will report it stolen the morning after the job. It will stand up to a number plate check but that's about it. You and Vincent have got a wee Vauxhall that will be parked and good to go outside the Bombay Chipper. Again, an older couple from Divis will ring the peelers the morning after the job and tell them their car's been nicked. Joe and Frankie will source their own van, so we don't need to worry about that. Again, Pat's boys will deal with the vehicles once you're in Monaghan.'

Declan nodded, the brief containing nothing that he could see as being a problem. As the men approached a junction they stopped, Declan intending to go one way and Blackie the other. Declan smiled at his superior.

'Well, I guess the only question left is when? When do we go?'

Blackie lit another cigarette before looking at his colleague and returning the grin of excitement. 'Day after tomorrow Dec. Thursday night.'

Declan nodded, hunched himself tighter inside his jacket in a vain attempt to keep out the cold. 'Good. Never been great at hanging around once the order's given.'

Blackie gave him a smile and patted his shoulder. 'Well, there's no waiting on this one Declan. We go Thursday night and scoop Doc. Plan's simple, and the people are good. It's a strong one.'

Declan had to agree. He felt very confident that this was going to be an operation that would be remembered in the republican clubs, bars and pubs for decades to come. He indicated with his head in the direction of the road. 'Okay, this is me. If I don't hear anything from you, I'll see you in a few days with the details of how we're gonna take out a couple of Branch men.'

They didn't shake hands, well aware that a tout could be watching, or a camera trained on them from a secret observation post somewhere. With a final goodbye, they parted ways and Blackie opened up his stride, the anticipation of a few pints in The Slieve a pleasant prospect. He had a meeting the next day with the PAC and was looking forward to briefing them on the progress of the Op, but for tonight, a few glasses of the black and a couple of swift chasers would see him right. He reached The Slieve and pulled on the handle of the main door, instantly enveloped in a fug of cigarette smoke, warmth, stale beer, and body odour. The din of raised voices competing for dominance assailed his ears, but he showed no signs of discomfort. Pushing his way through the throng of men, acknowledging the greetings and good wishes from those he passed, he made his way to the bar where a space was immediately made for him in accordance with his status. A pint of Guinness and a chaser of Powers was slammed down on the worktop without him having to open his mouth. There was, of course, no question of payment. Blackie couldn't actually remember the last time he'd paid for a drink in The Slieve. He looked into the mirror behind the bar and smiled at the reflection of the crowd behind him, republicans to a man.

This was home.

CHAPTER 7

SIG, BELFAST

Marcus waited for the Ops Officer to break the silence. He was reading Marcus' report from GRANITE after their meeting earlier that day. GRANITE would be driving as part of an Executive Ops' kidnap operation against a suspected police informer. Declan Burns was in charge and Vincent Devine, or *the clap* as he was jokingly called after the unfortunate abbreviation of his name, was the muscle. Burns had contacted GRANITE that morning and briefed him at the Agent's house. The bare details about the operation and what GRANITE would be required to do.

GRANITE would be the driver for the job but hadn't been told the target or location. Burns had told him that this information would be briefed to the team once they were in the cars and moving. Again, GRANITE was not concerned by this as, on sensitive operations, this security measure was the norm. This way, no member of the cell could provide the police or the army with anything except their individual roles in the Op. If the police swooped down and arrested everyone, nobody could provide all the information bar the trusted individual running the job, in this case Declan Burns.

Marcus felt the excitement rising in him. GRANITE was now the only person who could provide the information that was going to save this RUC Agent's life. It was, however, also a great risk to GRANITE. The IRA had learned some lessons the hard way and operational security, or OpSec as it was referred to, was one of them. Whenever the PAC cleared an IRA operation, OpSec was always at the forefront of their minds. That was why whoever was involved in an operation was always only given the information relevant to their role. A driver would be told where to pick up a car and where to go to pick someone up. That passenger would have been told where to tell the driver to go but not the driver's identity. Weapons and explosives were taken from dumps by the quartermasters and moved to short-term caches where another individual would be given the location and where they would be taken to. This cell structure insulated the individual from the threat of compromise from other members of the group.

GRANITE would be given the target details very soon. He'd already been told where he would be picking up his vehicle and was now on immediate notice to move, ready to go as soon as he was called. SIG had liaised with The Det, giving them all the details of the car that GRANITE had been allocated and its location. The usual routine would be for The Det to mount a covert operation and insert a beacon to monitor the movements of the vehicle, and internal audio so that the Agent could talk directly to his Handler. Surprisingly, they had called back earlier that morning and informed SIG that they couldn't get near the car due to the exposed location. They'd made a couple of approaches but had been challenged by locals asking who they were. Fortunately, one of the Team was a soldier originally from Belfast and he'd talked their way out of it. They suggested putting a surveillance team on the car but SIG forbade this, unwilling to risk compromising GRANITE if the IRA identified The Det team. A flurry of meetings in the top corridor eventually concluded that their only course of action would be to wait for GRANITE to call Marcus and tell him where the target location was. Special Branch were also on tenterhooks, waiting to see whose Agent was in trouble and what they would do about it.

Marcus looked across the Ops Room at the door of the soundproofed booth that contained the dedicated telephones that they used to communicate with their Agents. The Boss's voice beside him interrupted his vigil.

'You know what they say Marcus; a watched kettle never boils.'

'I know Boss, just never been good at waiting.'

'Me neither. He'll come through. Can always rely on GRANITE to produce the goods.'

Marcus nodded and stared into the distance as he thought about the situation. GRANITE was due to ring any minute with the details of the target that his team and the Nutting Squad were going after. A whole operation was being ramped up on this information with TCG taking the lead on the exploitation. The SIG Ops Officer was co-located with his Police colleagues in anticipation of GRANITE's call.

A shrill ringing of bells startled Marcus and roused him from his thoughts. *GRANITE*. He sprang from his perch on the desk and jogged over to the booth, entering then closing the sound-proofed door behind him. Picking up the receiver, he said nothing but could hear the excited breathing before the familiar Belfast voice spoke. Marcus let GRANITE talk, taking notes on the pad beside the phone as his Agent relayed the information in a quick, staccato delivery before hanging up. Marcus checked his notes and took the pad with him, making his way to the Boss's office. The Boss, alerted by the sound of the bells, was waiting for him, sat behind his desk with his own notepad ready. Marcus stood before him and read from his own notes.

'Okay Boss, short but sweet as he literally had thirty-seconds to brief me. Target is a Denis O'Callaghan, AKA 'Doc,' a PIRA Volunteer. GRANITE is scout car and trigger for Doc's arriving at an estate in Lurgan. He's leading a van with Joe Carluccio and Frankie Vallely from the Nutting Squad and rear car is Declan Burns and VD. GRANITE has a Colt .45 and assumes others will be armed also.'

He paused as he watched his officer scribble down the details and gave him a few moments before continuing.

'Apparently Doc is having an affair with a woman who lives in Connolly Place and has a regular routine where he visits her. GRANITE and team *en route* now to intercept Doc as he enters the road and facilitate the scoop by the Nutting Squad.'

The Boss looked up at him. 'Anything else? Details of the other vehicles? Communications?'

'No more details on the other vehicles, he hasn't seen them. As for comms, he has a radio that he'll use to talk with the van and backing car. That's it Boss, he had to go.'

Marcus watched as his Boss picked up the secure telephone and relayed the information to the Ops Officer. He answered a couple of questions before saying his goodbyes and terminating the call. He looked up at Marcus.

'Well, that's it. Really out of our hands now. TCG will do what they do, and we'll just have to be ready to prepare GRANITE for another round of interrogations when this kidnap doesn't succeed. What's the Circle of Knowledge on the location?'

'He was called directly by Joe and told.'

The Boss frowned. 'Isn't that unusual? The head of the Nutting Squad ringing GRANITE?'

'I asked, and GRANITE said that as this is a Nutting Squad Op with his team just assisting, it was for Joe to call the shots. Probably exercising good OpSec as well; not giving the location to the scout until the last possible moment.'

'Yeah, unfortunately that will point the finger of suspicion back at GRANITE once this thing is stopped. That worries me, particularly when it's Carluccio's operation. He's going to be a very angry man.'

Marcus fully understood his Boss's concerns. Big Joe Carluccio was probably the most feared member of the republican movement. As head of the Nutting Squad, he was responsible for keeping house for the IRA, torturing and killing dozens of individuals over the years. Even the photos that the security forces kept on file seemed to portray a cold, hard individual. Dark tousled hair, swarthy complexion that hinted at his Italian ancestry and a dark stare that burned hostility and hate. In a conversation with GRANITE a month or so before, Marcus had asked the Agent how well he knew Carluccio. GRANITE had thought about the question, before replying that no one really knew Joe Carluccio well. The man didn't socialise or keep company with anyone. Not for him the mandatory attendances at gatherings, protests and marches. He would, however, attend the funerals of IRA members killed in the line of duty. On those occasions, according to GRANITE, it was apparent that even the IRA leadership gave the man his space. GRANITE remarked that there was something about Carluccio that made you feel uncomfortable. His prolonged silences and predatory gaze an unsettling combination. Despite his lack of engagement Carluccio had for some years now, sat as Head of Security for the IRA's General Headquarters, or GHQ as it was referred to. It made sense for the movement's executioner general to oversee his own operational issues, but GRANITE believed it also sent the message to those at the top of the tree that no one was above Carluccio's scrutiny. GRANITE had laughed and stated that, on the few occasions he had seen Carluccio in a republican bar, the man had literally created a ripple of silence as he move through the establishment, nothing short of a miracle when considering the gregarious nature of drunken Belfast men.

Marcus looked at his watch. 'Right Boss, I'll get the report done and wait in the Ops Room in case he calls again.'

The Boss waved his hand in a dismissive gesture. 'Yep. Go on then, get your paperwork done and I'll do the same here for the Ops Officer.' He looked up just as Marcus was turning away. 'Oh, and Marcus? Bloody good work mate. Well done.'

As Marcus left the office, he felt his cheeks redden at the unexpected praise. Making his way into the Ops Room, he reflected that while he had done well to this point, he would only really be happy with his work once GRANITE was safe and free of suspicion. Until then, anything could happen that would endanger his Agent's life.

Anything.

CHAPTER 8

DUNDROD, NORTHERN IRELAND

Joe Carluccio stared out the window as the dark shapes of houses and buildings flashed by. The van slowed and he looked through the windscreen, frowning as he saw the small herd of cattle plodding along the side of the road, their eyes catching the glow of the headlights and reflecting back at them. Frankie edged the van past the beasts before accelerating again and making progress along the dark, country road. They'd decided on using the back roads to Lurgan to avoid any Army or Police checkpoints and were making good time. He'd been keeping an eye on the road behind them since they'd picked the van up, but he'd seen no other traffic since they left Belfast, the grim weather keeping the good folk inside where it was warm and dry. At regular intervals he would wind down his window and poke his head out, staring upwards and looking for the tell-tale lights of any helicopters that might be shadowing them. But he'd seen nothing to indicate there was any aerial surveillance.

He looked at Frankie, the man's face a study in concentration, made all the more menacing by the muted yellow glow from the instrument panel. He'd brought Frankie along not only because he was reliable, but also because the man was quiet. Wasn't a gobshite. The one thing Joe hated on a job more than anything else was a gobshite. He liked to get the job done with the minimum of talking, leaving his brain the peace to consolidate the information and concentrate on the operation. And Frankie Vallely was one of the few volunteers that Joe knew who wasn't big on talking. And that suited Joe just fine. Frankie was also a strong man and good with his fists. As there was only him and Joe doing the scoop, Joe knew that this would come in handy. While Joe was sure that the stun-gun and the anaesthetic would do the job, he always prepared for contingencies. That's how you stayed out of jail; planning for the best but preparing for the worst. He looked up as the streetlights on the outskirts of Lurgan came into view. Just then the radio he had sat between his legs cackled into life.

That's Car One in position, Over.

Joe raised the device closer to his face and replied. 'Okay Car One, this is Van entering town now.'

Another cackle of static preceded the acknowledgement. *Okay.*

Joe leaned back as Frankie reduced their speed when they entered the thirty zone. The last thing they needed would be to get pulled for speeding. The peelers would have

Joe and Frankie on their list of bad boys, and they could expect, as a minimum, to be searched and have the van thoroughly inspected by a professional team. And with weapons, a radio, stun-gun and anaesthetic in their possession, both men could expect to say goodbye to their freedom for quite some time.

He thought about the scoop and the transfer of the tout down to Monaghan. It was a good plan and the Executive Ops boys were a reliable bunch, much like his own, so he could foresee no real problems. But, as always, Joe was ready if there was. The moment they sensed any trouble, Joe would call the Op off. It would then be every man for himself, but he and Frankie would part ways, ditching the kit as they ran. Frankie would draw the security forces away from the area while Joe got picked up by the backing car and scooted away from the scene. It was another thing Joe liked about Frankie; the man was loyal to the core and more than willing to sacrifice his own freedom to help Joe escape. He looked in the side mirror and saw a car's headlights behind them. It only followed as far as the next junction then turned off, leaving the road behind them clear. He knew that VD and Declan weren't far behind but were keeping a discreet distance in order not to be associated as travelling together to any observer. He looked to his right as Frankie cleared his throat.

'That's the road there, Joe.'

Joe nodded as they turned into Connolly Place, the small road quiet in the rainy evening. They passed a Red Sierra parked up past the junction and their headlights highlighted the driver who turned his head away to avoid the glare. Joe's radio cackled again.

Yeah, you've just passed me, Over.

Without lifting his own radio above the door level, he replied. 'Yeah, got you visual. Now heading to position.'

The quiet descended once again as Frankie turned the van around at the end of the cul-de-sac and drove back the way they came, slowing down and stopping outside a small block of flats. He turned the engine and headlights off and looked outside for any signs that they had attracted attention. Seeing none, he indicated with his head towards the end of the road.

'That's good; we can see the scout from here. When he gives the heads-up, we should see the tout about the same time.'

Joe followed his colleague's directions and could see, in the near distance, the rear of the scout car, parked up and watching the entrance to the estate. His radio squawked again.

Car Two in position, Over.

Joe acknowledged Declan's call and nodded to himself. Everyone was now in place. The rear car was positioned outside of the estate, something Joe had factored into the plan. While, for vehicles at least, there was only one road in and out of the estate, someone on foot could make their way between the houses and out through the paths on the other side. From there, it was a short distance back to the main road. Joe's plan was that if they were caught trying to scoop the tout, he and Frankie would abandon the vehicle and escape through the avenues and passages of the estate where the rear car would pick them up and get them away.

The estate was quiet. The damp weather and dark night probably the best conditions that Joe could have hoped for. No curtain-twitchers wondering who the strange men parked outside were. No curious kids kicking around a football and trying to see who was sitting in the van. He studied the street in front of him as he ran through the lift in his mind for the final time. Once the scout clocked Doc driving into the estate, Joe would jump into the back of the van, open the sliding door slightly, and get the stun-gun ready. They'd positioned the van in such a manner that Doc would have to park in front of them and make his way on foot, past the van to his lover's house. Frankie would open his door just as Doc passed him and draw the tout's attention as Joe leaned out, hit him with the stun-gun and dragged him into the van. Frankie would shut the doors and get the van moving as Joe administered the anaesthetic, rendering the tout unconscious. Frankie would let the rest of the team know they'd been successful, and they'd make their way to the border. With the tout secured, Joe would take command again and get in touch with Pat and his boys to get them across into Monaghan. Once there, Pat's boys would guide them to the farm where the interrogation of Denis 'Doc' O'Callaghan would take place. It was a good a place as any for Joe to carry out his work. There was no Garda presence whatsoever and anyone approaching the isolated farm-house would be visible for miles. He looked down at the luminous dial of his watch and saw that, if everything went according to plan, the tout would be arriving within the next ten minutes or so. Joe stretched his neck and reflected that he was quite pleased with his operation. It wasn't easy putting something this dangerous together, but he'd always adhered to the mantra taught to him by an American Marine that PIRA had hired in the late eighties to give them military training: *Fail to plan, plan to fail.* He'd liked the expression as soon as he'd heard it. More PIRA men had been killed or locked in the Kesh as a result of piss-poor planning than of anything else and Joe had always sworn, even as a younger man, that if he ever went down, this wouldn't be the reason for it.

Glancing at his watch once again, he saw that they could expect Doc's arrival at any moment. He looked up in surprise as Frankie spoke.

'Who the fuck is that?'

CHAPTER 9

TCG, BELFAST

Colin Woods leaned back, arms folded across his chest as another call came through the radio.

Plate Check: Bravo Charlie Zulu One Eight Three Four. Red Ford Sierra. Over

He watched as the collator sat beside the radio operator typed the vehicle registration into the computer and turned the screen towards the operator. The operator relayed the information to the ground callsign.

'Roger, Echo. That is a Red Ford Sierra, registered to a Mr Sean Murphy, Glasvey Gardens, Twinbrook. Over.'

Roger, vehicle is static, one-up, at junction of Green One. Over.

Colin cleared his throat. 'Disregard vehicle.'

The radio operator relayed Colin's instructions across the net and the ground callsigns acknowledged. They didn't need to know that the Sierra contained one of SIG's best Agents; all they needed to know was that it didn't concern them. Echo continued her updates as she made her way into the estate. Colin could imagine her; damp and cold, cursing as she pushed her pram along the soaking streets. She was the lead foot callsign that would conduct the walk-past of the target address and look to confirm any activity. There were two cars in support of her, looping around the general area but remaining out of sight so as not to blow the fact that there were undercover troops operating. While Connolly Place wasn't anywhere close to being the hardest estate in Northern Ireland, if word got around that covert soldiers were in the area, the IRA would soon mobilise a crowd. Not for the first time, Colin reflected on the courage of The Det's Operators who, day in and day out, were carrying out these high-risk activities throughout the province.

Another call came through from Echo.

Zero, Echo. I have a dark van 300 to my front, plates unsighted but vehicle occupied by at least one. Over.

The desk operator acknowledged and one of the support cars gave a transmission stating their intention to enter the estate and provide close support to Echo. The desk operator suggested that the road was too small to cover another vehicle and that a foot callsign was preferable. Colin nodded as the car teams coordinated one of them deploying on foot in support. Colin recognised the individual's callsign as that of an SAS Corporal who had been sent over on attachment to The Det only the week before. Colin had initially questioned the justification for putting someone so recently arrived on an operation like this. He'd learned however, that the SAS soldier had operated in the area before, and as such, had been loaded on the Op due to his familiarity with the lay of the land.

He wondered again at the change of heart from Box. Just as he'd been getting to grips with a plan of how to keep RED LANCE safe without getting the RUC informer killed, Box had informed him of their change of plan. TCG could now proceed with protecting the RUC informer as Box no longer needed RED LANCE to be insulated from the operation. In truth, Colin hadn't a clue why they'd changed their minds, but it certainly made his job a lot easier. The teams from The Det were now looking for the vehicles that SIG's Agent GRANITE had said would be involved; his Red Sierra, another car and a van. Now Echo had spotted a van near the bottom of the estate with passengers inside, it looked like GRANITE was earning his keep. Another radio transmission came through the speakers, this time from the HMSU teams waiting to pile into the estate and conduct the arrests. Colin gave a silent chuckle to himself as he thought of the two vanloads of large, aggressive, heavily armed coppers just itching to get their hands on a couple of players. *Patience lads, patience.*

The SAS soldier was now on foot and informed them that he was entering the estate and could see the Red Sierra parked up at the entrance. He confirmed it was still occupied by a sole individual and was informed by the radio operator to continue to disregard the vehicle. He acknowledged this and the radio was silent once again as the covert team made their way deeper into the estate. There was quiet on the net for several moments before Echo's voice broke the silence.

Standby, standby. That's the van moving and towards me. Over.

CHAPTER 10

CONNOLLY PLACE, LURGAN

Frankie Vallely watched the woman with the pram bump the buggy up the kerb. Her hood was up, and he could see little of her features in the dark. He didn't want to put the windscreen wipers on either as it would give her a clear view into the van. Frankie wasn't happy. Something just didn't add up. Big Joe spoke quietly beside him.

'What is it? What are you thinking Frankie?'

Frankie thought for a moment before answering. 'This woman. Look, she's coming all the way into the estate from the main road. Where's she come from? The buses drop off the other way and if she'd been in a car or taxi, she would have got dropped at the door surely?'

Joe stared through the rain-dappled windscreen at the figure of the woman as she alternated between the dark and light of the pools of streetlights. His mind raced as he took in Frankie's words. Frankie was a shrewd operator, very good instincts and rarely wrong about anything operational. His thoughts were interrupted again by Frankie's observation. 'Look. She's got no bags. No shopping or anything. I don't know Joe, she just doesn't feel right.'

Joe was about to reply when some movement caught his eye. 'Shit!'

Frankie turned to face him. 'What is it?'

'There's a fucking guy just come into the estate, opposite side of the road, hood up, hands in pockets, approaching Car One. You see him?'

Frankie nodded. 'Got him. This isn't right Joe. Not for a night like this.'

Joe snorted. 'Agreed. You keep an eye on the woman and I'll watch the big lad here. Either of us sees anything strange, we lift, nice and casual until it kicks off. Got it?'

'Got it.'

Both men were silent as they observed their respective targets. Frankie was just about to mention that the woman was getting close when Joe's voice startled him.

'What the...?' Frankie turned to look at what had caught Joe's attention and his eyes widened as he saw a small red light being shone by the male pedestrian on to the pavement beside Car One. Joe spoke again, an urgent tone to his command. 'Frankie, lift off, lift off now. Nice and easy until we need to do otherwise, okay?'

Feeling his adrenaline building, Frankie started the engine and turned the lights and windscreen wipers on, the woman with the pram fully illuminated in the beams as she pushed the pram along the pavement. As the van pulled out of the parking space, Joe sent the transmission to the other callsigns.

'That's abort. All cars, that's abort. Travel together to the Glen Road then switch. All copy?'

The cars came back with their acknowledgements and their van passed the man who was walking into the estate. Joe observed him out of the corner of his eye and then through the wing mirror and gave a nod of satisfaction as he saw the man turn and pull his hood down, staring at the back of the van as it left the estate. As they passed the Red Sierra, Joe didn't give it so much as a look but watched the road in front of them closely, looking for any sign of the Police or Army. Frankie gave him a quick glance.

'Joe...What the fuck man?'

Joe snapped back at him. 'Just watch the fucken road. We're not out of this yet.'

Frankie merely nodded and did as ordered. Joe sighed and patted his shoulder by way of apology. 'Sorry, big lad. Didn't mean to bite your head off there, just got a shock that's all.'

Frankie shook his head. 'You and me both, brother. Don't worry about it Joe, I'll get us out of here. If they hit us, just stick to the plan; I'll draw them on while you disappear.'

'You're a good man Frankie Vallely and if only there was more like you. We need to be on our toes now though. After what we've just seen, I reckon we could be in a wee spot of bother.'

Frankie turned the van onto the main road and accelerated, changing up through the gears. He couldn't believe what he had just seen; a definite signal between the man walking into the estate and Kieran Mulgrew. He had no idea how Joe was going to deal with it but hoped they made it through the night to allow him to do so. Looking in the wing mirror he noticed headlights a little distance behind them.

'Joe. Might have a tail.'

Joe looked in his own mirror before speaking into the radio. 'Car One, what's your position?'

The reply was almost immediate. *Behind you, about two-hundred metres.*

Frankie relaxed a little, but he noticed Joe remained vigilant. He couldn't hold it in any longer. 'What was going on back there Joe?'

There was an uncomfortable silence for over a minute before Joe replied.

'It would appear, Frankie, that Denis O'Callaghan isn't the only one feeding information to the peelers.'

Frankie felt his mouth go dry at the thought they had just been set up by one of their own team. He'd never experienced this before and became hyper-vigilant, staring hard at the passing hedgerows and waiting for an SAS ambush team to leap out and take them on. Shaking his head, he tried to calm himself and concentrate on the road. As they left the streetlights of Lurgan behind them, he knew Joe's big brain would be ticking away over whatever they had seen earlier and how he was going to deal with it. The one thing that Frankie did know for sure, was that he was glad that it wasn't him that the dark thoughts were about.

CHAPTER 11

TCG, BELFAST

Colin was stood over the radio operator as he answered the net, the transmissions from all the callsigns on the ground coming through thick and fast. The Det's car teams wanted to pursue the van and the Sierra and the HMSU teams were asking what the fuck was going on. Colin pinched the bridge of his nose as he assessed the situation. *How the hell had they known? Had the foot callsigns highlighted themselves in some way*? In truth, it mattered very little. For whatever reason, the van and the Sierra had lifted off and were heading out of town. The HMSU wanted to steam in, conduct a hard-stop and arrest the occupants of the vehicles. Colin had vetoed this: There was no point. The IRA men had obviously identified the surveillance and aborted their operation. In all likelihood, they would have got rid of their weapons already, so there would be nothing incriminating found on them if they were stopped. Even if they hadn't tossed the guns yet, as soon as they saw anyone closing in on them, the weapons would be jettisoned into the dark fields and streams of which there were plenty. Yes, they would be found at some point, but by that time the retained republican solicitors would cry out that the weapons were probably planted by the Police in order to justify the harsh treatment of their clients. He let out a deep sigh and caught the eye of the Det Operations' Officer who met his gaze and shrugged his shoulders. Colin nodded and patted the radio operator on the shoulder. 'Call it, Steve and get everybody back to base.' He walked away from the desk as the transmission to end the operation and return to base was given. There would be some frustrated individuals looking for answers on their return, wondering why they hadn't just carried out the arrests of the IRA men.

But there would have been no point. With no weapons or activity carried out, a judge wouldn't give the case the light of day and Sinn Fein would crow about another victory against the biased State and its security forces. He walked into his office and sat down as he mentally prepared what to say to the Deputy Chief Constable. Colin wasn't overly concerned that the DCC would be anything other than relieved about the aborted operation; these days the RUC hierarchy seemed happier with no action over violent action. Arse-covering and political sensitivities taking precedence over robust leadership. Sighing to himself, he picked the receiver up and punched in the number. The conversation lasted only several minutes, and Colin could almost hear the relief in the senior officer's voice that there had been no shooting or violence. He terminated the call then made his way back into the Ops Room where he was informed that the Det and HMSU teams were heading back in for the debrief.

～

When the debrief had concluded, Colin turned down the offer of a few jars in The Det bar. With some paperwork still to finish, he wanted to get home at a reasonable hour for a change. He was sat at his desk when he heard someone clearing their throat and looked up. Colin tried not to grimace as he took in the smart suit, slicked back hair and perfect grooming of the individual stood in his doorway. Instead he smiled and stood.

'Jonathan, come in, come in. Take a pew.'

The individual entered his office and took the proffered seat, smoothing out the wrinkles on his trousers as he sat. Colin took his seat again and waited for the MI5 officer to speak.

'I won't keep you Colin, just wanted a quick update on tonight's activities.'

Colin nodded and gave a concise brief on the evening's operation and the non-event that it turned out to be. As he finished, he noted that his Security Service counterpart seemed satisfied with the result.

'Good. Very good. As I said before, it was imperative that RED LANCE be distanced from any exploitation that could be linked back to him, but thankfully we've taken care of that.'

'That's good news Jonathan. When we got your call that we could proceed with the Op we went in with the intention of arresting the PIRA team, but they got spooked and lifted off before committing anything.'

Jonathan Crowe watched the policeman for several moments before replying. 'Mm...bit of a shame that. Would have been nice to have removed a few players from the board. Any idea what made them so skittish?'

Colin shook his head. 'Nope. If I was to hazard a guess, I would say that they maybe got spooked by the presence of the foot teams in the estate.'

'Ah, I see. Still, we live to fight another day, eh? When can we expect to hear what the fallout is?'

'Well, SIG had an Agent on the job so I dare say they'll be the first to get the report back on why they took off, that is, unless RED LANCE can get it for you?'

The MI5 officer smiled. 'Alas, no. As I've said, we made sure that he was distanced from this operation to avoid having him compromised.' He looked down at his watch. 'Okay, would love to stay and chat but I have another meeting after this and need to get going or I'll be late.' He stood and extended his hand across the desk, shaking Colin's own hand with a warm and firm grip. 'Give me a call when the SIG report comes through and let's see if we can arrange for food and drinks at some point this week.'

'Sounds grand, Jonathan and I'll give you a bell as soon as we get the report.'

With that, the MI5 officer departed, and Colin sat back down behind his desk, thinking about his recent guest. While he didn't dislike Jonathan Crowe *per se*, Colin didn't trust the man. The Security Service were often found working to their own agenda with little thought or regard for the blowback or collateral when their operations went wrong. Jonathan was neither the best nor the worst that Colin had worked with, but he was one of the most experienced, having entered the Service after a brief stint in the Army. Slightly older than most of his contemporaries, he seemed to have a more measured approach to his dealings with TCG, realising correctly, that it was far better to have them onside and willing, than alienated and grudging. Colin wasn't sure how Jonathan had managed to distance RED LANCE from the operation, but it certainly made TCG's life a little easier as, even if the IRA team had tried to lift the informer, they would have felt the entire wrath of TCG's assets and would be either be looking at a significant stretch in jail or dead in the street. When RED LANCE had to be protected, Colin had recognised immediately that the life of the RUC informer would be in jeopardy as TCG couldn't react with a simple arrest Op.

He picked up the phone and dialled the SIG Operations Officer, informing him that as soon as their Agent reported in, Colin would require a verbal brief to keep him up to speed until the formal report was disseminated. Hanging up the call, Colin mused that he quite liked SIG. Their officers were always upfront with him and they didn't cause TCG many problems, seeming to take care of and clean up their own messes. Their Commanding Officer was a decent spud as well; a no-nonsense Scot who spoke plainly and liked a dram or two.

Looking at his watch, he saw that it was nearly midnight and let out a long sigh. *So much for the early night.* He stood and picked his jacket up from the seat back then turned his office lights off as he exited the room and closed the door behind him. He gave a wave to the collators still beavering away in the analyst's cell and made his way along the corridor, looking forward to some sleep. He would be back in the office before seven but at least he wouldn't have anything troubling his mind tonight, the earlier non-event leaving him without any anticipated fallout or negative PR with which to deal with in the morning. He opened the door and stepped into the stairwell, feeling the chill from the outside that was seeping in. Pulling his jacket tighter around him, he decided to put the day's activities behind him and pick them up again when he received the update from SIG.

CHAPTER 12

SIG, BELFAST

The Boss looked over the top of the piece of paper he was holding and held Marcus's gaze.

'That everything?'

Marcus nodded. 'That's all he gave me. Said he didn't have time for a longer call as he had to attend a meeting with Burns and Donnelly.'

'Okay, so he has no idea why Carluccio called the abort. They returned to Belfast, passed the weapons and comms to a courier arranged by Donnelly, ditched the vehicles at a pre-nominated location then went home to establish their alibis. That it?'

Marcus leaned forward. 'Yep. According to GRANITE nothing was said to explain why Carluccio called it off. He just heard the call on the radio then saw the van drive past him. He'd been briefed on the abort plan in advance, so he knew what he was doing, and this morning is the first opportunity he's had to ring in.'

'Okay. What about the meeting with Donnelly and Burns? Anything we need to be worried about?'

Marcus shook his head. 'I asked GRANITE, but he doesn't think there's any issues. He's probably just going to be told why the job was aborted and whether they plan to have another crack at it.'

He watched as the Boss made another couple of notes on his paper before looking back up. 'Okay Marcus, good work. I'll back-brief the Ops Officer as I know some of the higher-ups are keen to know what happened last night. If you crack on and get the formal report typed up, then give me a bell when it's good to go. Okay?'

Marcus stood and made his way down the corridor. He would make himself a coffee first then get to work on the report. It would be a fairly short one anyway, no real intelligence to report as yet, but it needed to be accurate as a lot of senior people would be reading it. As he made his coffee, he thought again how ballsy GRANITE was. Marcus was pretty sure that if he was in GRANITE's position being called to a meeting after a failed Op, he wouldn't be quite so confident. But that's what made GRANITE so good at what he did; that unique combination of courage and intelligence that every Handler wished their Agent possessed.

Marcus just hoped it would be enough.

CHAPTER 13

BOMBAY STREET, WEST BELFAST

As he sipped his tea, Kieran studied the dated wallpaper and kitsch ornaments displayed around the small room. In the old days they referred to these places as *call houses*; safe places where IRA members could meet or mount their operations from. They usually belonged to families that supported the movement but had never been in trouble with the police or the army, free from criminal connections and convictions. This house belonged to a widow, Mary McConville. She was a good Catholic who had lost her husband a couple of years ago and had never done anything illegal in her life. Hers was just one of many houses in the city that the Executive Ops Team utilised for meetings where they could talk freely without the risk of the property being bugged or monitored by the security forces. Mrs M was sat in the kitchen having a chat with Declan and Blackie and he could hear both men indulging in a bit of craic with the old dear. He looked up as the kitchen door opened and both men walked in.

Blackie Donnelly sat his bulky frame in the armchair and nodded to Kieran before clearing his throat and leaning forward. 'So, what the fuck happened out there, Kieran lad?'

Kieran frowned at the interrogatory nature of the question. He placed his cup and saucer on the small table beside him and leaned forward to respond. 'I think you need to talk to Joe about that. He's the one called it off and didn't tell us why.'

Blackie sat back and stroked his chin. 'Aye, that's what The Clap and Declan here said as well. Did you see or hear anything that you think might have spooked him?'

'No. Nothing. The place was dead. It was pissing down rain, dark as a witch's tit and feckin freezing. The only people I saw was a wee girl pushing a pram and some yoke walking home from the pub.'

Blackie looked over at Declan. 'You know anything about this?'

Kieran watched as Declan shook his head. 'No Blackie. First thing me and VD knew was the call from Joe to abort. No explanations or reasons from the big man.'

There was a moment's silence before Blackie continued. 'Kieran, these people you saw. Any chance they were Brits? SAS? Surveillance?'

He thought for a moment before replying. It was a good question and now he reflected on it, it *was* a little odd to have seen two people out at the same time on such a wild night.

'I wouldn't have thought so Blackie. I mean, if they *were* Brits, we wouldn't be sitting here eating jam rolls and sipping tea, would we?'

Blackie Donnelly nodded. 'Fair point Kieran, but just talk me through what you seen of these two people, how they were acting, what they were doing.'

Kieran shrugged and described the girl and the man he had seen entering the estate, remembering as best he could, their clothing and general details. When he'd finished, he took another sip of the hot, sweet tea and looked up. 'And that's it, mate. That's all I saw.'

Declan spoke. 'When are you talking to Joe, Blackie?'

'Later today. We're using a woman's funeral in Milltown to come together and have a chat about it. A kid came by and gave me the message earlier and that's all I've got at the moment.'

Kieran nodded, feeling the tension in his stomach ease somewhat. Even though he'd done nothing to compromise the operation, he was always aware of the possibility when called to one of these meetings that his role as an Agent had been discovered. On this occasion, however, it would appear that Joe got spooked by the presence of people in the estate and had decided to err on the side of caution. He raised his eyes as Blackie spoke again.

'Okay, and you're sure that's all you saw Kieran? These two didn't seem to be together or communicating with each other? No cars floating around that seemed suspicious?'

'Nope. Nothing like that. The pair of them seemed to be completely separate, were quite a bit apart as well and I didn't clock any cars that looked suspicious.'

There was a moment's silence before Blackie stood, sighing and running his fingers through his dark curly hair. 'Well, alright then. Sounds to me like big Joe got spooked by those people but I'm sure he'll let me know this afternoon. In the meantime, the pair of youse and VD just go about your daily business and I'll get back to you when I want to speak again.'

Kieran and Declan rose, and Kieran made his way to the front door. 'Okay boys, stay safe then and give me a wee bell when you want another word.'

Blackie patted him on the back as Kieran opened the door. 'You too big lad and I'll be in touch.'

Blackie closed the door behind Kieran and he and Declan peered through the net curtains as Kieran crossed the road and made his way down towards Clonard. The kitchen door opened behind them but neither man looked around, their focus solely on the receding figure in the distance. They maintained their vigil until Kieran had gone out of view. Without turning his head, Blackie spoke.

'Well Joe. What do you think?'

Joe Carluccio joined the pair as they watched Kieran Mulgrew turn a corner and disappear from view.

'What do I *think* Blackie? What do I *think*? I don't think, Blackie. I fucking *know*. I know what me and Frankie saw last night in that estate. I saw an undercover Brit give your man a wee signal with a torch as he entered that estate. Kieran didn't know that me and Frankie could see him from our position, but we caught him good. And he didn't mention a word about that signal.'

Blackie turned to face the IRA's most fearsome man, nervous about the question he was about to ask but needed to anyway.

'You're sure Joe? There's no doubt about what you saw?'

Blackie felt his mouth go dry as Big Joe Carluccio stared at him with his cold, dark eyes and blank expression.

'Oh, I'm sure Blackie. I'm very fucking sure. And you know what? I'll be even *more* sure in the next five minutes or so.'

Blackie looked at Declan who was clearly as puzzled as he was. The men stood in silence for several minutes and Blackie began to feel awkward and uncomfortable. He was about to ask Joe what he had meant when a knock on the door startled him and he jumped, making Joe grin as he reached for the doorknob.

'Relax Blackie. This is what I was telling ye about.' Joe opened the door to a young boy wearing a Gaelic football top and tracksuit trousers. The boy glanced at the two men stood behind Joe but spoke when Joe gave him the nod that it was fine to do so.

'He went along Kashmir down to Springfield then past the Citizen's Advice before cutting into the Blackstaff and making a call on the pay phone there.'

Joe rubbed the boy's head. 'Good lad, Niall. What'd he do after that?'

The youngster smiled, pleased with the attention from such a legend. 'He came back on himself, walked along Springfield Avenue then jumped on a bus on Cavendish.'

Joe patted the boy's shoulder. 'Grand job Niall. Keep this to yourself lad and say hi to your Ma and Da from me okay? Now, off you go wee man.'

The boy turned and sprinted down the street as Joe closed the door and looked at the other two men. Blackie's face had paled, and Declan was shaking his head. Blackie looked up and met Joe's gaze.

'Fuck me Joe, it looks like you were right. But *Kieran*? Of all people?' He sighed and slumped in the chair, watching as Joe sat on the sofa across from him. The IRA's Security Officer leaned forward and engaged Blackie once again with those terrible black eyes.

'Let me tell you something Blackie; it's *always* the ones you don't expect that are touts. That's why the Brits and the Peelers recruit them. Look at the evidence man: One, the Brits knew what we were up to last night. Two, one of the Brits gives your man a wee signal. Three, he's just left here, taken a very strange route to go and make a call on a public phone when he lives in the other direction. You fucking know rightly that I'm on the money here Blackie.'

'Yeah Joe. As sad as it makes me to say it, yeah, you're right. Only thing up for discussion now is what do we do about it?'

Joe Carluccio leaned back and flashed both men his predatory grin.

'Leave that to me boys. I've already got a plan and I'll need your help, but I'll let you know when the time is right. In the meantime, it's business as usual; Kieran can't suspect anything, or he'll tip off his handlers. So, this afternoon, give him a bell and get him up to The Slieve for a couple of jars. Tell him you met me, and I told you I wasn't happy with the two people in the estate, so I called the job off. Tell him it'll be back on, but you don't know when.'

Blackie nodded and looked at Declan, noting the tightness of the man's face as the full scope of Kieran's betrayal sank in. He turned his attention back to Joe as he spoke again.

'But whatever you do, don't worry about Kieran Mulgrew. I'll make sure a significant message is delivered to the Brits over this. *Very* significant.'

For the first time since learning of his friend's betrayal, Declan Burns spoke.

'Whatever message that is Joe, I want to be a part of it. A fucking *big* part of it. He has to pay hard for what he's done to us.'

Joe nodded. 'And you will Declan, you will. But for now, get your poker face on boy. Kieran can't be alerted to anything until we come for him, okay? Fuck this up for me Declan and I'll punish you the same way as him, got it?'

Declan felt a wave of anger surge through him but when

he looked at Joe's face, it dissipated immediately. 'Yes Joe, no dramas big man, I'll be a fucking Oscar award winner for as long as you need me to be.'

Joe Carluccio gave a rare laugh. 'Good man Declan, good man. Like I say, business as usual until I say otherwise and then we'll deal with the tout formerly known as Kieran Mulgrew in a manner befitting his crimes.'

Joe took the men's silence as assent and looked out the window as he thought about the next phase of his plan. He needed to act soon; the longer a tout was allowed to run free the higher the likelihood that he would become suspicious of those around him who were acting differently. Joe couldn't let that happen. He needed Kieran Mulgrew off the streets as soon as possible, into a van and then south for a few days of uncomfortable questions. Questions that the Provisional Army Council would want answered.

And Joe would be the one to get those answers.

CHAPTER 14

GROSVENOR ROAD, BELFAST CITY CENTRE

Marcus closed the newspaper and looked once again at the bus timetable in the shelter he was stood under. He glanced at his watch and shook his head, moving out of the bus shelter and walking along the road, playing the role of frustrated commuter to anyone interested enough to be watching. His earpiece buzzed with a transmission from Brian, letting him know he was in position and ready to look for GRANITE. Marcus acknowledged and crossed the road, heading towards the main shopping area. He paused to look in the window of a sports' shop, checking the reflection to see if anyone was following him. Content that he was clean, Marcus continued on his way.

It had been over a week since the operation to lift the informer had been aborted and Marcus had not met with GRANITE during that time, wanting to give the Agent a bit of space just in case there was any suspicion upon him. He'd rung Marcus a couple of times to let him know that everything was fine. Business as usual. It had turned out that

Big Joe had been spooked by a couple of people in the estate and called the Op off. Marcus wasn't privy to the details, but he'd assumed TCG had sent in a close surveillance team and they'd been rumbled. Still, no blame or harm seemed to have been attributed to anyone and they all lived to fight another day. That said, Marcus still wasn't taking any chances. Even though GRANITE had assured him every- thing was okay, Marcus was putting him through a Counter Surveillance route just to be sure.

Again, he'd put up with the comically exaggerated moans and groans when he'd briefed the team that morning that they'd be running a CS route in the city. And while it was done in good humour, Marcus could tell that his colleagues didn't share his opinion that it was necessary. But it was his call, not theirs. And the CS route stood.

As he made his way along May Street, he heard GRANITE had entered Royal Avenue, and Brian was looking for any indication that GRANITE was being tailed. Marcus listened as Brian stated that the road wasn't too busy, a handful of kids and a few mums pushing prams but that was it. Brian then stopped watching GRANITE, as Emma would pick him up from her position inside the shopping arcade. A few moments later, Marcus heard her call that GRANITE was walking through the shops and everything seemed okay. Marcus opened his stride, looking to join GRANITE once the Agent was through the arcade. They'd walk down to where Marcus had the car parked then head out of the city to the Safe House for the debrief.

Emma called GRANITE through the arcade and onto College Street. Marcus knew he would make it on time and slowed his pace a little, wanting to judge it so he appeared naturally at the Agent's side, just two acquaintances running into one another by chance.

Emma's commentary continued as she followed GRANITE through the crowds of shoppers. Marcus could see the area where GRANITE would enter the street and was happy that he would have a good view from his position. As he watched, Marcus saw GRANITE cross the road and leave the throng of shoppers behind him. The Agent wouldn't see Marcus from where he was but Marcus could see that there was nobody behind GRANITE except a couple of young boys who were fooling about, pushing one another and laughing. Marcus grinned as he envied the boys' carefree existence, their biggest worry probably making sure they were home in time for their tea. One of the boys was carrying a cuddly toy that he held up to his face. He looked a little old to have such a thing and Marcus mused that this was probably the source of the ribbing he was taking from his friend. He was about to step out onto the road and engineer his meeting with GRANITE when something warned him not to commit.

Marcus couldn't work out what it was but felt strongly that something was wrong. He looked up the road and saw GRANITE shambling along, the two boys a hundred feet or so behind him, and Emma about the same behind the boys. *What the hell is it?* He couldn't put his finger on it, but something wasn't right. His heart rate was climbing, and he could hear the blood rushing in his ears. Looking up the road again, he saw that GRANITE had seen him and continued to walk towards him. The boy with the toy brought it up to his face...*His face*. Marcus could now see the expression on the boy's face, and it was not that of a kid enjoying himself. It was a hard, focussed expression that was the opposite of the carefree behaviour that he and his friend were exhibiting. His earpiece buzzed as Emma asked him what was going on as she could also see Marcus from her position.

Just as he reached into his coat pocket for the radio pressel, GRANITE waved to him and began to cross the road. Marcus watched the kid raise the cuddly bear to his face again and saw his mouth moving. With cold clarity, Marcus understood what was happening.

He pressed the pressel and spoke. 'All callsigns, abort, abort, abort immediately. It's a set-up, I say again, it's a set-up.' He was about to turn and leave the area when he saw the boys stop suddenly then sprint back the way they'd come, almost knocking Emma over in their haste. GRANITE was now only twenty or so feet from him and was looking at Marcus with an expression of puzzlement on his face. Emma continued to walk along the road, completely ignoring Marcus and GRANITE as she had been briefed, making her way independently to her car. Marcus turned on his heel and was striding off when he heard the screech of tyres behind him. Spinning around, he

93

watched as a small car mounted the pavement and the passenger jumped out. The man was wearing a balaclava and pointing a rifle straight at Marcus.

Without any conscious thought process, Marcus dropped to one knee, drawing the MP5K from under his coat in a smooth, fluid movement as he did so. The sound of a bullet striking the brickwork of the wall above him was followed instantly by the loud retort of the rifle. Before the man knew he had missed, Marcus fired a burst from his own weapon and saw the individual slam back against the vehicle before dropping on to the pavement in a crumpled heap. The driver of the vehicle didn't exit, instead threw the car into reverse and was out of sight before Marcus could get a clear view of him. From the corner of his eye he saw Emma advancing down the street, her own MP5 up in aim and firing at the retreating vehicle. Marcus's ears were ringing from the shock of his own weapon being fired, and the sound of Emma's rounds reached him only as dull thuds. He shook his head in a vain attempt to clear them then joined Emma, chasing the small, red car as it reversed at speed along the street. Marcus could see that Emma had hit the windscreen with some of her shots, the shattered laminate testament to her accuracy. But whoever was driving the car was experienced. There was no tell-tale silhouette of a head behind the windscreen, meaning that the driver was keeping below the dashboard where the engine block in front of him offered the best cover from Marcus and Emma's bullets.

Marcus cursed as the car reached the bottom of the street and in one smooth manoeuvre, spun around and joined the flow of traffic, disappearing from view in a screech of tyres. He and Emma sprinted towards the junction in the hope that the red car would be caught up in traffic but even before they made it, Marcus could see that the traffic was moving freely. He lowered his gun, folding the stock back against the body of the weapon and slung it back under his armpit, looping the bungee-cord sling over his shoulder. Pulling his jacket over the weapon, he looked back up the street to where the body of the man he'd shot was laying.

Or should have been laying.

Marcus's mouth dropped open as he saw that not only was the body not there, but it was at the other end of the street, manhandling someone into a van. Screaming at the man to stop, Marcus drew his weapon out once again as he sprinted towards the top of the street. He knew in his heart he didn't have a hope in hell of making it and so skidded to a stop, dropped to one knee, and took careful aim at the van. Just as he was about to pull the trigger, it was gone. The van disappeared into the crowded road beyond, pedestrians scattering and turning their heads towards the speeding vehicle. Marcus stood and gave a breathless transmission just as Emma reached him.

'Zero, Delta, contact. Queen Street. Gunmen attacked team. Team all okay, gunmen escaped. Roger so far, Over?'

He waited for the reply and met Emma's wide-eyed stare before continuing. 'And gunmen have GRANITE. I say again, gunmen have GRANITE.' He felt pressure on his arm and looked up to see Emma had taken hold of him.

'C'mon Marcus, we need to get out of here. There's nothing we can do. Let's get to the vehicles and extract before the media arrive.'

Nodding, Marcus again stowed his weapon beneath his jacket and jogged behind Emma, aware of the stares and attention they were receiving from the shocked pedestrians they passed. As he turned on to Wellington Street, Marcus tried to work out what had just happened, but his brain was firing in all the wrong directions to come up with any kind of accurate assessment. The one thing he did know however, was that he was about to experience an Agent Handler's most dreaded nightmare:

Having his Agent captured by the enemy.

CHAPTER 15

WHITEROCK ROAD, WEST BELFAST

Frankie Vallely tore at the Velcro strips and ripped the body armour from his chest, pulling it over his head and tossing it into the back corner of the van. It clattered as the ballistic plates inside it hit the side of the van, but he was too concerned with checking his chest and abdomen for wounds to notice the noise. His hands frantically examined his stomach and sides beneath his shirt, and he started to calm down as he found no blood or wounds. Sighing with relief, he steadied himself as the van flew into a right turn and looked at Joe sitting near the rear of the van, busy placing restraints on the tout. He caught Joe's eye and the raised eyebrow.

'I'm good Joe. All good. The vest took the bullets, thank fuck. How's the tout?'

In answer, Joe Carluccio slapped the face of the prone man on the floor of the van and seeing no response looked back at Frankie. 'Sleeping like a baby. That stuffs knocked him out cold.'

Frankie grinned. The euphoria of a successful operation now replacing the adrenalin and excitement from before. 'Hell's teeth Joe but that was a good one, eh? Mind you, thought that Brit had me for sure.'

'Not a chance Frankie boy. *Fail to plan, plan to fail.* You know me by now big lad, I never leave anything to chance.'

Frankie had to give the big man credit; the lift had gone exactly as Joe had planned it. The use of the kids to tail the tout and keep them updated was good: Hiding a walkie-talkie in the body of a cuddly teddy-bear was genius. Joe had said that the Brits wouldn't suspect kids that young and this meant that the kids could be in constant contact with Joe and the team through the walkie-talkies. Frankie's diversion had pulled the Brits away, allowing Joe and Vincent Devine to scoop the tout as he tried to run. Exactly as Joe had said it would go. Frankie leaned back against the side of the van and closed his eyes with a big smile on his face. This was going to be the talk of the town tonight. *The lift of a tout in broad daylight in the city centre?* Front page news without a doubt. Of course, along with that would be the intense search and intelligence operations to find the tout. He turned to Joe.

'How far to the switch?'

Joe raised himself slightly so that he could see out of the window, then sat back down. 'One minute. We're coming up to the Upper Springfield now. C'mon, let's get ready. This needs to be slick.'

Frankie grabbed the large canvas holdall and began putting the rifles into it. He crawled along the length of the van, putting his hand out to balance himself as the speeding vehicle lurched from side to side. He retrieved the body armour and stowed it in the holdall along with the three hand-held radios, stun-gun, and the balaclavas. He looked up as Declan yelled over his shoulder.

'That's us boys. Blackie and the lads are here.'

Zipping the holdall up, Frankie looked at Joe and both men braced themselves as the van skidded to a halt. A split-second later daylight flooded the interior as the sliding door was hauled open and a pair of arms appeared. Without a word, Frankie placed the heavy holdall into the arms as Joe began dragging the unconscious form of Kieran Mulgrew. The holdall disappeared and Frankie grabbed the body by the shoulders, helping Joe to get him out quickly. Another face appeared at the door and Frankie gave a nod to Blackie Donnelly.

'Here, grab his shoulders and I'll jump out and get his feet.'

The pair ran with the slumped body between them to a filthy horsebox that was shackled to a Vauxhall estate with the engine running. A man that Frankie recognised as being from Pat McCusker's crew in Monaghan was stood on one side of the horsebox and a woman Frankie didn't know, on the other. As they approached with the body, the man and woman stooped and slid out a section from beneath the main body of the horsebox. Frankie and Blackie laid Kieran out carefully on the metal platform and stood back and watched as the man and woman pushed the tray-like platform back into the body of the horsebox. The secret compartment was just big enough to take the tout's prone form and once it was pushed home fully, they secured it with concealed bolts. The man and woman ran back to the front of the car and climbed in, closing the doors behind them. Blackie slapped the roof of the car and the driver took off, spraying gravel from the wheels as they accelerated away. Frankie took a second to catch his breath and looked around the deserted warehouse premises. A hand slapping his shoulder caught his attention and he began stripping off the overalls and gloves he had been wearing, using his teeth to tear at the masking tape he'd used to secure the gloves to the clothing. Frankie picked up the discarded items and threw them into a burning brazier, the flames leaping and licking as the clothing fed the fire. A few moments later Joe appeared carrying his clothing in a bundle in his arms and threw the entire heap into the brazier. He looked at Frankie and Blackie.

'Right; van's away to get burned out down in the quarry. The gear will sit at a temporary hide near Black Mountain until the heat dies down a wee bit. Frankie; me and thee need to get down to The Slieve and start getting hammered before the peelers lift us. Our alibis are good, so we won't be held and the solicitor's ramped up and ready. Blackie, I'll leave you to square your own boys away but from here on, no contact or communication between us until I give the go- ahead, alright?'

Both men nodded in reply, keen to move on as they knew the security forces would be tightening the net around the city. Joe took turns shaking each man's hand.

'Okay boys. Job well done. We're not home free just yet but one or two days and we will be. Frankie, there's a taxi outside for you and me so let's get going. Blackie, safe travels brother and I'll be in touch.'

Joe and Frankie jogged out of the warehouse and jumped in the taxi, the driver an older man but a trusted IRA Volunteer in his day. No words were necessary or spoken and Frankie leaned back in the seat as he relived the job in his head and how close he'd come to both killing a Brit and being killed by one. He smiled at the irony and imagined the tale being told in The Slieve for years to come, the story exaggerated and amplified to the point where it bore little resemblance to the facts but embedded itself in republican folklore. He looked out the corner of his eye and saw that Joe was engrossed in his own thoughts, staring out the window as they retraced the route they had just taken in the van. Frankie once again felt in awe of Joe's talent. From the moment they'd entered the deserted warehouse complex, to sitting in the taxi, less than three minutes had elapsed. Less than three minutes to switch cars, ditch the weapons and comms, burn clothing and have the tout on his way to the border. *Slick. Very slick.*

Joe's mind was racing as the urban boundaries of West Belfast passed by in a blur. The tout would be taken to a safe location in Monaghan where Pat and his boys would look after him until Joe managed to get there. It wouldn't be for a couple of days as he knew he'd be watched by the Brits. He wasn't too concerned about this. Pat and his crew were tried and tested and Aisling, Pat's niece would be on hand to monitor the effects of the anaesthetic on the tout and give him some more if he was a bit of a handful. His attention was brought back to the present as an RUC Land Rover sped past them travelling in the opposite direction. *Good.* The last thing the Brits and peelers would expect would be for them to be coming back into the city. It went against all common sense and that was precisely why Joe had planned it this way. He had no doubt that at some point later that evening his door would be booted in by a team of hard RUC men, his house torn apart and him taken to a cell. But again, he'd anticipated this, his alibi solid and the solicitor ready to go, so he didn't expect to be held for too long. Then he could get back to the business in hand.

The interrogation of the tout Kieran Mulgrew.

CHAPTER 15

SIG, BELFAST

Marcus downed the whisky in one go, and immediately poured another even as his throat burned and his eyes watered. Glancing at the clock on the wall, he saw that it was almost three in the morning. An hour ago, he had just finished his final interview with the RUC; a day of long interrogations and questioning finally over. What had helped though was the CCTV footage that showed Marcus and Emma's account of the incident to be accurate. The SOCO team on the ground had also given confirmation that the evidence they collected backed up the SIG Operators' stories. Marcus held no grudge against the investigators; Sinn Fein was already screaming about undercover British troops and shoot to kill policies in a busy city centre. He took a large gulp of the Macallan and leaned back in the chair, staring at the ceiling.

As soon as he'd made it back to his car, Marcus had tortured himself with the one question he still didn't know the answer to. *Was it my fault?* Had he done something that had compromised GRANITE? Fucked up during an operation and caused the Agent to be identified? He didn't think he had but it was a very real possibility. His Boss had deployed with the Ops Officer to TCG to help in any way they could with the search for GRANITE. The conventional thinking was that the Agent would be taken across the border as soon as possible for a lengthy interrogation. They knew from the previous IRA operation that the plan had been to take Denis O'Callaghan across the border at Monaghan, but TCG weren't sure that this would still be the case. The IRA, as a rule, always changed their *modus operandi* once an Op was compromised.

There had been brief spikes of hope that filtered through during the day: A burnt out van in the Upper Springfield Road area identified as the kidnap vehicle. A nearby search uncovered the charred remains of burned clothing in an abandoned warehouse complex. Two Belfast Brigade IRA members had already been caught trying to cross the border into Monaghan from Fermanagh and were now being questioned by the RUC. But this lead was starting to look like little more than coincidence, nothing in their car or on their persons to suggest any involvement. The Border Crossing Points all manned and every vehicle being searched. But still, nothing. Not a sighting of GRANITE or a report of unusual activity anywhere outside the city. TCG were ramping up for a series of raids on the properties of the key suspects; Joe Carluccio, Frankie Vallely, Blackie Donnelly and Declan Burns. The problem was that all these men had been in public places with plenty of eyewitnesses at the time of the abduction. Still, TCG were happy to authorise the arrests just to shake the tree and see what would fall out, if nothing else.

Marcus couldn't imagine what GRANITE would be going through. The Agent's terror magnified by the fact that he knew exactly what was going to happen to him. Tortured and maimed until he told his captors everything they wanted to know. And Marcus was under no illusions that GRANITE *would* talk. The Agent might be able to hold out for a while as he was a fairly tough individual, but in the end, it would come down to simple biology. The human mind and body can only tolerate so much before the defences get stripped away and the truth exposed. The inevitable death that followed far preferable to what the Agent would have endured in the final hours of his life. Sipping the whisky at a slower pace, Marcus thought about the day ahead of him. He had a sit-down with the CO, Ops Officer and his Boss just after lunch, which would constitute an informal investigation into any actions on Marcus's behalf that may have exposed the Agent. His Boss had told him that this was a formality rather than a witch-hunt and that Marcus should treat it as such. Before he'd left for TCG, Dom had patted him on the shoulder and ordered Marcus to stay in the base that night and rest up.

Pouring another whisky, Marcus looked around the room. Ostensibly a standard living room with the expected sofa, chairs, occasional tables and lamps, this was one of the debriefing suites where they would sometimes bring Agents. There was a comfortable bedroom next door where the Agents could spend the night if required although this was rarely the case. As if the thought of it triggered the reaction, Marcus realised how tired he was, the adrenalin he'd been running on since the incident now completely exhausted. He stood and taking the whisky with him, made his way to the bedroom. Turning the light on, he saw that the double bed was made up and ready to use. He downed his drink then undressed and climbed under the duvet.

Turning off the lights from a small switch above the head- board, he lay quietly in the darkness until a deep sleep over- took him.

~

Marcus reached out and shook the offered hand, the man's grip strong and confident. He'd only met the CO of the unit on a couple of brief occasions and knew more about the man from his reputation rather than personal exposure. The CO waved a hand.

'Sit, Marcus, please.' Marcus took a seat beside Dom and observed his Commanding Officer as he poured a glass of water. The Colonel was a tall, rangy Scot with a reputation for straight-talking and a no-nonsense approach to operations. From what Marcus had heard, the senior officer had been in the intelligence game for some time, cutting his teeth on operations in Northern Ireland in the bad old days of the seventies. The relationship between officers and other ranks in SIG was different to that in the conventional military. Other than the CO, everyone was referred to by name, and even the CO used the operators' names rather than ranks when addressing them. He caught Marcus looking at him and smiled.

'All right, I'm sure you're sat there shitting yourself that we're here to find some blame we can attach to you over this matter. Relax. Nothing could be further from the truth. You have a reputation as a very professional operator Marcus, and I have absolutely no doubt in my mind that there will be nothing we discuss today that will challenge that.'

Marcus nodded and looked at Dom. His Boss opened a file in front of him and began filling the CO in on the meetings and activities that Belfast Det had been engaged upon in the run up to the abduction of GRANITE. The CO listened for the main part, occasionally asking questions or wanting clarification. After an hour or so, Dom concluded his brief and the CO was quiet for a moment before addressing Marcus.

'Okay, your turn. Brief me on how, where and when you've been meeting GRANITE since taking him on.'

Marcus took a drink of water, then gave his Commanding Officer the information that he had asked for. The CO listened without interrupting, nodding now and then to show that he was still engaged, but remained silent until Marcus finished.

'Right. Number one; kudos on having the smarts to pump GRANITE through a CS route. There's a good chance if you hadn't, we might be looking at dead Handlers on the streets of the city. And two; there's nothing you've been doing that would have highlighted your Agent to his people. Whatever caused this was not yours, or the Detachment's fault. PIRA must have got wind of it themselves somehow. So, in the meantime, we carry on about our business. You and Emma will obviously need to look at a change of appearance when on the ground as the enemy know what you look like.' He paused and took a drink of water. 'If you have any leave to take, now might also be a good opportunity for that.'

Marcus shook his head. 'No sir. I want to be here till we get GRANITE back...however that may be.'

'Yes, I'd be exactly the same in your shoes Marcus. Alright, there's nothing much more we can do until TCG start generating some leads. Anything else?'

Marcus and Dom both shook their heads and stood, ready to leave, when the CO spoke again.

'Dominic, I'll catch up with you at the daily tomorrow. Marcus, if you've nothing pressing, do you mind staying for a bit?'

Marcus looked at Dom who gave him a nod before leaving and closing the door behind him. As he sat down again, Marcus watched as the CO opened a cabinet in the corner and removed two crystal glasses and a bottle of Balvenie. Without asking, he poured two generous measures before sliding a glass across the table to Marcus and seating himself. He raised his glass in Marcus's direction.

'Here's to GRANITE, wherever he is, and to the hope that he makes it back to us.'

Marcus raised his own glass to the toast and took a swig of the smooth single malt. The CO leaned back in his chair and smiled.

'Right Marcus, relax. I do this with the guys from time to time; a few drams and a bit of conversation. No bullshit, no agenda, just like getting to know my people. So, tell me how you came to join the unit? You were originally a Royal Marine, correct?'

Nodding, Marcus took a drink of the whisky before answering. 'Yes Sir. Was a Royal Marine for eleven years before I attempted the Selection Course.'

'And what drove you to arrive at the decision to try out for the Unit?'

'Well, to be honest Sir, the Corps wasn't really doing much in terms of deployments. We don't have the armoured capability of the army, so we weren't getting sent to the Balkans. I guess I just got a bit frustrated that I wasn't getting any operational experience.'

The CO nodded in sympathy. 'Yes, it's one thing to train men such as the Marines and maintain that physical and mental fortitude, but if they're not getting to deploy and use these skills, men tend to become bored very easily.'

'That's pretty much the size of it, Sir. I knew I didn't want to leave, thought I still had something to offer.'

'Well Marcus, the Royal Marines' loss is certainly SIG's gain. Cheers'

Marcus raised his glass in response to the toast. 'Cheers Sir.'

There was a comfortable pause before the Commanding Officer spoke again. 'So, what about family? Married?'

'No sir. Single for the time being. Haven't got around to finding the right girl just yet.'

The CO smiled. 'Time enough for that I'd imagine. What about your parents? You see much of them?'

Marcus took another drink before replying. 'No Sir. Both parents deceased.'

The CO shook his head. 'I'm very sorry Marcus, I had no idea.'

'No, that's fine Sir. It was a very long time ago.'

'Still, can't have been easy, particularly being young.'

Marcus ran his hand through his hair, feeling a little uncomfortable discussing the subject in any depth, but he could see the CO's intentions were good. 'No, it wasn't easy. Mum died first you see and Dad...well, Dad really never recovered from her death. Drank himself into the grave.'

The CO reached across and grabbed Marcus' glass then replenished their drinks with another hefty measure before passing the glass back. 'That's bloody terrible Marcus. Can't imagine what you must have gone through.'

Marcus felt his face flush at the sympathetic statement. 'Well, as tough as it was, I think I've come out of it all right.'

'Quite. Quite. And I take it there's no brothers or sisters?'

'No sir. Just me. Think my Mum wanted more but with her job and then passing so young it just didn't happen.'

'What was her job?'

Marcus smiled. 'Well, she was actually in the Army. Even got a British Empire Medal.'

The CO looked back at him in surprise. 'When was this?'

'Erm…must have been around 1973.'

'A woman earning a BEM back then was a very rare event. Do you know what she was awarded it for?'

'No. I think the citation must have got lost when I was a kid. I've just got the medal in its dusty old box as a keep-sake.' There was a quiet moment as the CO took a drink of his whisky. Marcus continued. 'Actually, this is where my Mum died; Belfast. A car accident somewhere in the city.' Marcus saw that the CO's demeanour had changed, and the man was staring at him fixedly.

'Your mother died *here*? In Belfast? When was this?'

'Same year as she got her medal Sir; 1973.'

The CO remained quiet and Marcus wondered if he'd made a mistake in being so open. Maybe his superior was now thinking that Marcus was carrying some issues probably best not dealt with in the city where his mother had been killed. Eventually, the CO met his eyes and spoke in a softer tone.

'What was your mother's name and regiment?'

Marcus raised his eyebrows in surprise. 'Corporal Julie Myers, Woman's Royal Army Corps, Sir.'

The quiet in the room was absolute as Marcus watched his CO deep in thought. He was about to say something to break the silence when a knock on the door startled them. The CO barked. 'Come.'

A young Lance-Corporal half-entered the room and addressed the Commanding Officer.

'Sorry Sir, but your transport's outside for the Officer's Mess function.'

Sighing, the CO downed the last of his drink before standing and offering out his hand to Marcus who also stood and shook hands with his superior.

'Marcus, good chat and I hope I wasn't too intrusive. Sorry I have to bugger off so suddenly, wouldn't have minded a bit more time. Might do this again if you've got no objections?'

Marcus was surprised by the offer but pleased he hadn't left the CO with a poor impression of himself. 'That would be fine Sir, especially if there's another couple of Balvenies on offer!'

The CO laughed and slapped Marcus' back as he made his way to the door.' Count on it, Marcus. Count on it. Until next time then.' With that, the CO left, and Marcus downed the last of his own drink. He was about to grab the glasses and give them a rinse out when the Lance-Corporal returned and beat him to it, tidying everything away. Marcus gave the young soldier a nod of thanks then made his way out of the Headquarters and back to the Detachment.

~

Colonel Stuart Coull leaned back in the leather seat, closed his eyes and thought back to the conversation he'd just had with Marcus. As the CO of a covert intelligence unit, it usually took a lot for something to surprise him, but Marcus' revelations had well and truly stunned him. Opening his eyes, he replayed the conversation in his mind, ensuring he'd heard correctly and gotten his facts right, but there was no real doubt.

Stuart hadn't heard the name Julie Myers for over twenty years. Hadn't wanted to. After the funeral The Boss's directive had been utterly clear; no one was to speak of Julie again if they wanted to remain with the Unit. No explanation was given, none needed. Back then you didn't question anything as you never knew everything that was going on. Only The Boss did. They'd mourned the loss of their guys of course; Julie, Frankie, George and Bill had been decent Operators. But they hadn't known each other personally, the Unit policy directing its Operators to keep their personal details secret, avoiding the threat of them becoming known to the enemy if an Operator was snatched and interrogated. So, Stuart and the others had no idea why any mention of Julie was forbidden but they'd just accepted it and moved on, too busy and probably too callous to really care.

He thought back to those days of the MRF; the gunfights in the back streets, breaking and entering into player's houses and planting listening devices, the targeted killings of key terrorists. The Laundry and Massage Parlour fronts that they'd used to get inside enemy territory and gain evidence of their crimes. His mind drifted back further to the day when they were given the news that four of their colleagues had been killed in a horrific car crash. They'd immediately asked if it was possible that PIRA had set the team up, but the answer had been definitive: *No*. A terrible accident involving a car carrying smuggled fuel hitting the laundry van at speed and both vehicles destroyed in a giant fireball. Absolutely bloody awful to think about. Stuart remembered the funerals and sat upright as it suddenly came to him that he must have met Marcus before. *Of course*. He would only have been around six years old at the time and a vague recollection of a shy kid clinging to his father's leg came to Stuart. He hadn't really noticed the kid that much, Julie's funeral being the last of the four and Stuart remembered being pretty numbed out by then.

As more details seemed to become unlocked, he also realised why Marcus' name didn't ring any bells whatsoever in Stuart's mind. Marcus's Mum *was* Julie Myers, but that was her married name. Her maiden name had been Vaughan, he remembered that now from the funeral and how he'd thought at the time how little the Operators actually knew about each other. And that was why Marcus's name hadn't even registered with him. The Marine had obviously reverted to his mother's maiden name at some point so rather than being Marcus Myers, he was Marcus Vaughan. And he clearly knew nothing about his mother's work in the MRF or what she'd been awarded her medal for. Which left Stuart with a dilemma; Should he tell Marcus about his mother and have the lad remember her for the hero she was? Or leave the situation as it was, with Marcus content with the information he'd been believing for all these years?

As his car turned into the sweeping gravel drive of the Officer's Mess, Stuart mused that the right thing to do would be to tell Marcus everything he knew about his mother. He'd have to leave out the specifics of their activities of course, that aspect was still heavily classified. But it felt right that the lad should be given the full story of his mother's bravery in fighting terrorism. As the car was slowing to a halt Stuart wondered why his usually decisive manner seemed to have abandoned him on this occasion. Why couldn't he just tell Marcus what he should know? As his door was opened for him by the driver, he stepped out and began walking up the steps when the realisation hit him. It was because, deep down inside, he'd never truly believed the Unit's explanation of the team's death. He didn't think any of them had. But things were done differently back then. There had been a lot of work carried out that wasn't entirely above board. There had even been whispers of a unit within a unit; a small, secret team carrying out some very dark work. He recalled that on occasion, they'd see strangers coming and going from the other wing of the building and be told that they were supporting troops, assisting with the MRF operation. He also recalled that these *supporting troops* were usually around when a lot of the heavy or strange stuff went down in the city.

And they'd been around when Julie's team had been killed in the crash.

CHAPTER 16

COUNTY MONAGHAN, REPUBLIC OF IRELAND

Kieran Mulgrew was cold. Cold, sore, and terrified. He could see nothing due to the blindfold but guessed he was in a farm shed or agricultural building by the smell of cow manure and silage. His head didn't feel right; heavy and sluggish whenever he moved it, and his tongue felt thick and dry in his mouth. His arms hurt and when he attempted to move them, he could feel that he was bound tightly to a chair. He moaned as the memory of being taken returned to him, the utter terror he had felt the moment before the stun gun had paralysed him with unbelievable agony. Kieran didn't really remember much after that, other than coming out of unconsciousness a couple of times only to fall back into it after a brief moment. Now however, he felt more aware, didn't think he would pass out again.

He listened but could only hear the wind outside as it whistled off the edges of the building. Kieran had no idea if there was anyone in this building with him, but he didn't really want to find out too quickly. He needed to get his shit together, get ready for some tough times. His knowledge of IRA security procedures told him that he was in deep trouble; the Nutting Squad never took a man away for questioning like this without good reason. And those men they did take never came back alive. Kieran's only hope was to keep himself alive long enough so that the police and army search that he knew would be underway, could find him.

He had no idea where he was. If pushed to hazard a guess, he would put his current location as somewhere in the Free State. Louth or maybe Monaghan. He moved slightly to alleviate the pressure on his arms and felt the coldness around his crotch as his clothing adjusted. The fact that he'd pissed himself added to his misery even though he couldn't actually remember doing it. *Fuck*! Real fear began gnawing at him now, the thought of the torture and pain to come causing his heart rate to rise and his breathing quicken. He wondered who would do it. *Joe*? *Frankie*? It didn't really matter when all was said and done, the result was going to be the same: Utter agony until he talked.

He chewed on the inside of his cheek as he wondered how they'd clocked him. He'd always been so careful whenever he went to meet Marcus, checked he wasn't being followed, looked for cars staying with him for too long on a road. *A chance sighting then*? Someone seeing him and Marcus together? Kieran hoped that was the case. He had any number of cover stories he could use to explain and buy some time. His greatest fear was that he'd done something stupid that had highlighted his role as an Agent to the IRA and that they'd confirmed it by following him. He still had no idea how the hell they had managed to ambush his meeting with Marcus when even he didn't know exactly where Marcus was going to bump him. A loud shrieking of metal on metal made him sit bolt upright, facing the direction that the noise had come from. A second later a large clang told him that it was a set of doors that had been opened and closed. He couldn't see anything through the blindfold but heard approaching steps and held his breath as he awaited his fate.

'Well, well, well. Looks like sleeping beauty's awake now. Did you have a nice wee doze there Kieran? All refreshed and keen to get on with things?' An unfamiliar man's voice that Kieran tried to place as his mystery captor chuckled before continuing. 'What's the matter? Cat got yer tongue, has it? Shame ye weren't a wee bit more tight-lipped to your British friends, eh?'

Kieran attempted to say something, but his mouth was too dry, and his tongue stuck to his palate.

'What? Ye have something to say to me? Probably best if ye hold that thought Kieran, leave it for the professionals, eh? I'm only the caretaker here, making sure you don't come to any harm before Joe and his boys can have a wee chat.'

There was some movement and Kieran gave an involuntary yell as his hair was yanked, and head pulled backward.

'Calm yerself down there, I'm only after giving you a wee drink of water. Not too much mind as our Aisling says it might make you sick.'

Kieran opened his mouth and was rewarded with a flood of cold, clean water. He swallowed quickly and opened his mouth for more, but the voice spoke again.

'No, that'll do ye now. I'll give you a wee bit more later and try you with some food. In the meantime, you just relax and make yourself comfortable. Oh, and don't bother shouting; there's a reason we didn't chuck a gag over yer pie-hole and that's 'cos nobody will hear you anyway. But if ye start, I'll stuff your mouth just on principle.'

Kieran heard the shriek of metal again as the doors were opened then closed. His head felt much better after the water, but his stomach felt queasy. He replayed the conversation in his head, seeking to identify who was holding him.

Aisling. The man had said '...*our Aisling.*' Although he didn't know the man personally, Kieran knew that Pat McCusker had a daughter called Aisling who was a nurse, had patched up many a wounded Volunteer over the years. So that's where he was; in Pat McCusker's farm in County Monaghan. This wasn't the best news: The IRA used Pat and his land for good reasons, chief among those the fact that McCusker had the local Garda in his pocket and could operate in the area with full impunity. There was nothing Kieran could do other than to run through some cover stories he could use to try and explain whatever evidence they threw at him, deny everything that they chucked at him until he couldn't. Then...well, then he'd have to come up with reasons they would either believe or have to check out. It was all about time. He had to buy himself time...

≈

Pat McCusker rubbed the head of the collie sat beside him, the dog's head warm in the glow of the fire. He sipped on his tea before placing his cup on the table and picking up the telephone receiver. Dialling a number from memory, he listened as it was answered almost instantly then spoke.

'Our guest is settling in well and seems in much better spirits. When do you think you'll be ready to visit?'

The person on the other end of the line hung up without another word and Pat did the same. The number he'd dialled was that of a public phone in Ballymurphy where a trusted *Fianna*, a young IRA supporter, hung around waiting for calls such as his. The teenager would relay Pat's message to Joe and get back to him as soon as possible. Pat stood and placed another cut of peat on the fire, enjoying the warmth on his face from the red embers. He took his seat and continued to drink his tea and got a small start when the telephone rang after only a few minutes.

'Hello? Is that right? Well that's grand, I'll be sure to tell him to be ready. All the best.'

He replaced the receiver on the cradle and stared into the fire. The messenger had told him, in veiled speech, that Joe expected to be down tomorrow night. That was fine with Pat, while he didn't mind the baby-sitting role, he was of the opinion that the quicker the situation was dealt with, the better. While he was reasonably confident that they wouldn't be disturbed without fair warning, it wasn't good practice to have a tortured tout stuck in your barn for any longer than was absolutely necessary. Being caught red-handed was something Pat had no intention of experiencing, but with Joe's arrival tomorrow night things should move on apace.

Pat had been very pleased with the result of the scoop. The tout lifted clean off the streets of Belfast, right from under the noses of his Brit handlers. This was a propaganda coup and no mistake. It was also going to bring a lot of heat down on the republican movement from the British Government and the military, but the Provisional IRA's Army Council was already working on a plausible deniability option aimed at blaming dissident republicans for the operation. Pat had been a sitting member of the PAC for over a year now and knew from first-hand experience how difficult it was to balance PIRA operations while telling the Brits you were committed to a ceasefire. But an operation to unmask and interrogate a tout would always be sanctioned, the damage they wreaked on PIRA the only justification that the PAC required to authorise such a high-risk job.

As he slurped his tea, Pat wondered if Kieran was *the one*. The tout that the PAC believed had given the Brits some of their biggest successes against the IRA. The arms shipment on The Eksund, The Gibraltar Martyrs, the Loughgall ambush, the decimation of East Tyrone Brigade, Dessie Grew and his boys, the underground cells in London. For some time now, the PAC had been convinced of a high-level informer giving the Brits information. And that this informer *had* to be at a very high level, or at least be close to a high-ranking member of the IRA. The operations that the Brits had intercepted had all been planned and executed by some of the IRA's top people and the details never divulged beyond those who needed to know.

Pat reflected on the damage that a tout wreaked upon the IRA: Mistrust, suspicion, paranoia, and fear. Fear that every time you picked up a gun or placed an explosive device, an SAS team was waiting to take you out. After the last arrests of the IRA's bombing team on the Mainland, the PAC held a meeting to address the matter: The tout had to be found. Big Gerry from South Armagh took the lead, telling the rest of the Council that he was only taking two more people on his crew to smoke out the informer. He had assured the Council that he did not suspect any of them in any way, shape or form, but things would have to be done that he couldn't hang around waiting to be sanctioned. Pat knew Gerry well and hadn't believed a word of it; Gerry, like him, *did* suspect someone at PAC level but could never state that publicly. He'd confided in Pat over a few jars one night that if he had to put money on it, he would point the finger at the one of the two *Shinners*; the members of the

Council who were now, to all intents and purposes, full time political representatives of Sinn Fein. While there was no doubt that, over the years, these men had earned their stripes as *bona fide* republicans, their recent public denials of being members of the IRA did not sit well with the movement.

Their defence was that of pragmatism; to be fully included in an establishment they were seeking to overthrow, they had to be as clean as any other politician. And that meant no proven links to violence. For men like Gerry and Pat who had dedicated their lives committed to such violence for their cause, the shinners' actions left a bitter taste in the mouth.

But if Kieran Mulgrew was their man...well, that would go a long way to healing some of the rifts that were opening up within the PAC. And Mulgrew certainly ticked a lot of the boxes. Apart from the fact he'd been lifted while meeting with his handlers, his pedigree as part of the IRA's Executive Ops team meant that he had access to high-level people and information. Pat wasn't sure that extended directly to operations like the Gibraltar Martyrs or the cells in London, but Kieran could have been told about these operations by someone who trusted him. When Gerry had approached Pat and asked him for his help, Pat had been only too happy to volunteer. When he'd asked who else would be working with him, he was told that only the head of the Nutting Squad, Joe Carluccio, would be involved. Joe would use his own crew for the heavy stuff while Pat was to be in charge of anything they needed in the South.

They thought they had their man with Denis O'Callaghan. The scoop ramped up and ready to go, team out, and Pat and his boys ready to take delivery. But then the real tout had been unmasked. When Joe aborted the operation to lift Doc, Pat and Gerry had been curious as to the big man's reasons. When they'd met shortly after and Joe had told them what he and Frankie had seen, the pieces began to fall into place. Gerry was convinced they'd found their tout and the planning began for the lift and interrogation of Kieran Mulgrew. Again, the division of labour was the same; Joe and his team do the scoop and Pat and his boys would get the tout over the border to a safe location where he could be held and interrogated.

And here they were. The collie groaned and Pat leaned over and stroked the animal's flank, smiling as it lay its head down on his feet. Stretching over to get the teapot, Pat felt a warm feeling of contentment as he realised that the hard work was done, that after Joe arrived tomorrow night it would almost all be over. They would have all the information they wanted and make an example of the filthy tout as a lesson to the rest of the Brit informers. As he poured the steaming tea into his mug, he wondered briefly how much heat was on Joe and his boys in the North.

CHAPTER 17

BALLYMURPHY, WEST BELFAST

As he scrunched up the greasy paper and tossed it in the bin, Joe turned and glanced at his reflection in the window of the fish and chip shop. He could see that, behind him at least, there was no sign of the car that had been tailing him for the last two days. *Good.* Hands in pockets he crossed the road and started walking down Glenalina Road, to all outward appearances taking no interest in his surroundings, head down and slouched, watching only the pavement in front of him. But he didn't need to watch; Joe had a small army of youngsters watching for him. Every junction, road, crescent and avenue had one of the *Fianna* on the lookout for any strange cars or people that were following Joe about. And here, in the 'Murph, in Joe's territory, the followers struggled to operate.

The day before, a few of these young toughs had identified an unfamiliar car with a man and a woman in it, driving around the areas near Joe's home for no apparent reason.

126

Joe had given the word and a mob of kids cornered the vehicle and blocked it in with a stolen car. When the occupants saw what was happening, they tried to escape from the trap carrying out defensive driving manoeuvres that marked them out immediately as undercover Police or Brits. The kids, led by the Fianna, had bricked and bottled the car then took to it with a couple of petrol bombs to try to force the people out of it. They heard the driver inside yelling for support and giving his location, presumably over a radio. He must have decided that they would never survive the wait and rammed the car that was blocking them in. They managed to shunt it out of the way just enough to get out of the estate. Flames licking at the bodywork and the screeching of parts being dragged along the road from when their car had rammed the blocker. The kids had been ecstatic and were rewarded with a fair chunk of cash for their efforts. That had been the last surveillance that had been reported and, although still wary, Joe was confident that close surveillance at least, had been pulled as a result of yesterday's compromise.

Even the raid and arrest he'd anticipated had come to nothing more than a damp squib. Rather than the door being booted in and getting dragged from his bed in the wee hours of the morning, a team of RUC had knocked on his door at a reasonable hour and showed him a search warrant. He'd allowed them access, slightly bemused that they weren't tearing the place apart and giving him a good hiding while they were at it. He'd called the solicitor immediately who had chuckled and told Joe that the RUC were on a very tight leash, Sinn Fein already busting their balls over undercover Brits shooting up pedestrians in Belfast City centre. After Joe had hung up, he noted the tight jaws of the police searchers, their rage and frustration barely restrained. They'd left after a couple of hours having done no damage whatsoever. He'd assumed they would have left a listening device of some sort but as Joe always assumed his house was bugged, this made no difference to him at all.

Crossing the road on to Divismore, he gave a casual look around him as though checking for traffic but again, saw nothing to indicate that he was being followed. He'd also heard no helicopters to suggest that aerial surveillance was being used against him. As he made his way down towards Springfield Road, he was almost certain he was clear, but almost didn't cut it in Joe's book; *almost* is what got you scooped or killed. If he had a pound for every IRA man he'd met who'd been arrested as a result of *almost*, well, he wouldn't be far shy of being a very rich man. As he was approaching the junction ahead, he saw the car parked up and waiting. A small Ford Fiesta belonging to a university student who'd loaned it to her boyfriend and who in turn, was loaning it to Joe. He needed a clean car to get him out of the city, one that would stand up to a plate check or a stop at a check point. The Police and Army would know who he was of course, but the boyfriend was primed to say he'd given Joe a loan of the car. Apparently as a favour for helping his girlfriend with her thesis on Irish Republicanism for the new millennium. *Whatever the fuck that means.*

Opening the car, he got into the driver's seat, closed the door behind him and opened the glove compartment where he found the keys. He grinned as the thought came to him that, while one of the most violent cities in Europe, in Belfast, an IRA man could leave an unlocked car on a busy road and it would never be touched. He started the engine, pulled out and began making his way to his switch point. He wanted to get to Monaghan and start his work as soon as possible but knew he needed to be cautious. His plan was to get down to Armagh and leave the car in Keady with a family who were going to provide him with an alibi for the next few days. One of Gerry's boys would then drive him to Tynan, down near the Monaghan border. He'd be met there by Pat McCusker's nephew who would get him over by using an old crossing point that had been cratered and blocked off with boulders. If all went well, he'd be at Pat's before nightfall. Pat would already have the Dictaphone, micro-cassettes and spare batteries that Joe would need to document the interrogation with. This evidence would be presented to the PAC who would in turn, produce a statement on behalf of PIRA regarding the issue. Sinn Fein would also use the death of the tout to attack the British Government for sanctioning the blackmail of citizens to coerce them to spy on their friends and neighbours and then getting them killed.

Sticking to the back roads as much as he could to avoid the risk of encountering a checkpoint, Joe knew it was taking him longer than he would have liked. But if he could get to Keady without being stopped, his alibi would hold up well if he was ever questioned about his absence from Belfast at a later date. It also meant he could be reasonably confident that he wasn't being followed and could make his way to Pat's safe in the knowledge that he was clean. He drove through Armagh without any problems and was soon on the small, country roads leading him towards Keady, driving through staunch republican territory. Once, he passed a military patrol, the bored, blank faces of the soldiers showing him no interest whatsoever as they clambered over a barbed-wire fence and crossed a field.

As he entered Keady, he remembered the address and how to get there from memory. Gerry's man would be waiting for him; no need to go in the house or speak to the family. His car would be parked outside, ready for his return in a couple of days and the family briefed once again on what to say if anyone came asking questions. He saw the sign for the Primary School and took the next turning, leading him into a small estate. Peering out at the house numbers, Joe continued along the road until he found the one he was looking for. Pulling over, he undid his seat belt, turned off the engine and stepped out onto the pavement. Locking the car, Joe looked up when he heard a noise behind him and saw a tall, thin man closing a front door then walk past Joe without saying a word. As he'd previously been briefed, Joe followed the man at a short distance as he made his way to another street around the corner. The man stopped at a red Ford Escort, opened it and climbed in. Joe made his way to the passenger side and followed suit as the man started the engine. They drove out of the estate in silence and Joe noted with satisfaction that the man was constantly glancing at his mirrors, vigilant for any sign that they were being followed. As they gathered speed along Madden Road, the man stuck his hand across his body and spoke.

'Padraig.'

Joe shook the offered hand. 'Joe.'

'Good to meet you Joe. Won't be too long and we'll get you to Pat's boy. He's in place and waiting for you now.'

Joe nodded. 'That's grand work Padraig, grand work indeed.'

They continued on in silence, Joe glad of the fact that Padraig wasn't a chatterbox. The man was a thorough professional, always checking his mirrors, studying the occupants of any cars that passed them. The area around them became much quieter as they crossed the Monaghan Road and took tiny back roads that weaved through the undulating countryside, the rolling hills broken only by occasional copses and woods. Feeling lulled by the movement of the car and the peace and quiet, Joe almost jumped when Padraig broke the silence.

'Right Joe, see that clump of trees up there? That's where Pat's boy is waiting for you. I won't stay, I'll just pull in and drop you off then be on my way, okay?'

'Good for me Padraig, and thanks for the help brother.'

'Don't mention it, *mo chara*, we've all to do our bit, eh?'

True to his word, Padraig pulled the vehicle into the side of a clearing leading to a forestry road. Joe saw a young man sitting on a dirt bike, smoking a cigarette. Joe got out of the car and Padraig was gone the instant the door was closed. Walking up the road, Joe watched as the young man stepped off the bike and stubbed out the cigarette on the ground. As he approached, Joe could smell the tobacco over the aroma of the pine trees. The young man held out his hand.

'Joe, I'm Connor, Pat's nephew.'

Joe shook his hand and indicated with his head towards the motor bike. 'We going on that?'

'Aye, it'll get us between the boulders and craters. They stopped watching this point years ago 'cos they think the boulders do the job for them, but it's good for us.' He gave Joe a grin. 'You wouldn't be the first man from the North we've had to bring through this way.'

Joe returned the grin. 'Okay, let's get this done then, shall we?'

They made their way to the bike as Connor talked about the route they would take. There were no police or military in the area and the crossing point was clear. As he handed Joe a crash-helmet, he told him that it would be a comfortable ride as he didn't speed in order not to draw attention to himself. If, for whatever reason, they were cornered, he had a pistol and would use it to distract the security forces while they went their separate ways and made a run for the border. Happy with the brief and actions for eventualities, Joe climbed on to the pillion seat after Connor, pulled on the crash-helmet and patted the younger man's back to let him know he was ready. Connor started the engine and Joe took a mouthful of four-stroke, a not entirely unpleasant sensation that took him back to the time when he was a teenager, stealing mopeds from commuters in the city centre. Before his nostalgia took hold, they were off and he pulled his feet up from the road and put them on the foot-pegs, relaxing into the ride.

CHAPTER 16

SIG SOUTH DET, BESSBROOK MILL, SOUTH ARMAGH

As the analyst concluded the brief, Marcus thanked her and stood, rubbing his eyes and stretching. He decided he needed a coffee to waken up a bit and made his way to the kitchen. It had surprised him when he'd first entered the Bessbrook Detachment that the layout was identical to Belfast, but he'd been informed by the South guys that all the Detachments were built to the same template. It felt slightly strange to Marcus, being in a completely different location but with all the rooms and offices in exactly the same places. It even *smelled* the same; an odd combination of cleaning materials and cooking food.

Dom had recommended that Marcus and Emma get themselves out of the city for a while until things cooled down and Marcus had at least the showings of a beard. Emma had already cut her hair shorter and dyed it dark, in complete contrast to her previous look. They'd accepted the Boss's suggestion that they head down to South for a week and familiarise themselves with the main players and activities in the region. They were to look out for anything that indicated PIRA were trying to get GRANITE across the border and into the Republic. TCG's theory was that GRANITE was being held in a rural area near the border and that PIRA was waiting for the military's alert status to ease off before trying to smuggle the Agent across. Box had apparently heard whispers that GRANITE was being kept in a farm somewhere in South Armagh although no further details had been provided regarding this.

To that end, Marcus had thrown himself at the task of getting up to speed as quickly as possible, spending the whole night trawling the databases and files, trying to identify likely candidates who would be involved in the movement of GRANITE. He'd started with what GRANITE had told them about the planned abduction of Denis O'Callaghan and the intention to get him over the border to Monaghan. With nothing better to go on, Marcus decided he would start with PIRA members from Monaghan who were likely to be included on such an operation, then work back from there, looking for links to the South Armagh and Belfast Brigades. While he'd been busy on that front, he had the analysts putting together a presentation on the movements of key personalities and vehicles linked to them over the past three days. Emma was across with the analysts at TCG South, some of the finest in the country, to see if their consolidated knowledge could throw anything up that would help them.

Disappointingly, Marcus had very little to show for his efforts other than the images of senior South Armagh PIRA members burned into his memory from his overnight cramming. He had however, found one small link that he was currently exploring; an old Military Intelligence Report highlighting an association between PAC member Gerry Trainor and Patrick McCusker, a recent addition to the PAC last year and who lived in County Monaghan. The analyst had just confirmed that Gerry's car had been triggered by cameras heading towards Armagh several days ago but returning back a few hours later. Trainor was apparently well-known for his reluctance to leave the local area and any such departure was noted for its rarity. Marcus had thought he'd struck gold when he saw that a horse-box registered to McCusker was triggered going through a Border Crossing Point two days after Trainor's trip, but when he checked the report, the vehicle had been driven by Aisling, McCusker's daughter, and the car and trailer searched with nothing found. Another senior PIRA man, Padraig McMullen had been sighted by a plainclothes RUC patrol car leaving Keady and heading west with an unidentified passenger. The car was not one currently associated to McMullen and had raised the RUC's suspicion. They'd turned around and tried to catch up but lost him in the maze of small country lanes in the area. While slim on details, Marcus would take whatever he could at the moment. He wandered over to a whiteboard and began plotting a timeline of events starting from Trainor's journey, through GRANITE's abduction, and slotting in the movements and sightings of McMullen. Standing back and observing his handiwork he realised that he was looking at *the square root of fuck-all*, as his troop corporal at Lympstone had been fond of saying.

Sipping on his coffee, he looked at the timeline again and ran it through his head. The abduction of GRANITE would have to have been authorised and planned in advance. Marcus had witnessed first-hand just how effective that planning had been. So, that would mean PAC approval. Then there would be the who; Who would be tasked to carry this out? That would be Joe Carluccio and his team, with maybe some help from the Executive Ops boys. But that was okay while the operation was running in the North. Marcus knew that PIRA liked to maintain operational borders between the northern and southern elements of its organisations. Yes, they worked together on many occasions, but operationally at least, anything happening in the Republic would be run by the PIRA members responsible for that area. Those with the ground and operational knowledge of their patch.

He walked back to the whiteboard and sketched out a rough hierarchy, highlighting Joe, Frankie Vallely, Blackie Donnelly and Declan Burns in one box, Gerry Trainor and Padraig McMullen in another box, and Patrick McCusker in the third box. *Would that be right?* He chewed on his lower lip as he thought through his reasoning. The Nutting Squad and Executive Ops team lift GRANITE and get him out of the city. The South Armagh boys take GRANITE and secure him somewhere safe in their patch until some of the heat dies down. Then Pat McCusker and his crew take charge of getting GRANITE across the border and into a location where he'd be held and interrogated until he died. In his mind, it was a very simple picture for Marcus to envisage but in reality, it was all just conjecture. But what else did he have?

He was still sure that Joe would be the one to carry out the interrogation, but all surveillance had been pulled when The Det team had been attacked in the Ballymurphy Estate. The listening device placed in Joe's home only told them that he wasn't there, but again, no one had any idea where the head of the Nutting Squad was. TCG's theory was that he had headed out of the city for a couple of weeks until things died down a little; a familiar pattern among senior IRA men looking to avoid being hassled by security forces every time they left their homes. Marcus, however, wasn't so sure about this. The 'Murph was Joe's territory, an area where he was revered as well as feared. In Marcus's opinion, Joe wasn't the type to slink away from his fiefdom just because things were getting a little rough. That would send a very different message to the residents of the 'Murph; that Joe was just as bad as the other higher-ups, turning tail when things got hard. *No.* As far as Marcus was concerned if Joe had left the area, he was definitely engaged on PIRA business. And the only PIRA business at the moment that was on a clock, was that of dealing with GRANITE.

Marcus felt a jolt of adrenaline as he consolidated his thoughts. *I'm right*! He knew if they could find Joe, or track his movements at least, they would get a strong lead on the whereabouts of GRANITE. The problem was, he had nothing more to go on. Joe had literally disappeared from the 'Murph with no sightings reported anywhere. But if he *was* heading to GRANITE, which way would he come? Marcus thought through his theory one more time then wandered over to the large-scale map of Northern Ireland that covered an entire wall. He located the Ballymurphy area first then using his finger, traced the main roads that someone could take to get into South Armagh. But would Joe use the main roads? Risk being stopped at checkpoints? Marcus thought this unlikely. Grabbing a chinagraph pen, he began highlighting the back roads Joe could have used to get him out of Belfast and into South Armagh. There were quite a few of these because, as Marcus had no idea where Joe's final destination was, he couldn't narrow them down any further. He then traced a couple of routes between Trainor's home and the camera he'd been triggered by in Armagh. This didn't really help Marcus due to the difference in dates, but it was aiding his mind in forming a picture of the movements. He stood back and stared at his work, desperately seeking inspiration, but there were no conclusions to be drawn. Sighing, he was just about to rub the markings off the Perspex covering when he remembered something and checked his notebook.

He walked back to the map and marked the location where Padraig McMullen had been spotted by the plain-clothes RUC patrol. North and West of Keady with an unidentified passenger. *What were you up to McMullen*? Marcus couldn't shake the feeling that he was on to something but just couldn't see what it was. His gut told him that he was definitely getting somewhere but it just wasn't obvious where that was. The confluence of movements, timings and personalities all made sense to him but didn't quite connect...yet. He needed to clear his head. Leaving his handiwork on the map, he headed upstairs to the bunk room where he was staying and changed into his PT kit. He'd noticed a decent punchbag in the gym, one of his favourite means of working out while trying to sort through problems. Even if he couldn't work out this particular problem, the phys would do him some good. He started off with a basic warm-up of boxing combinations before moving onto kicks and knee strikes. He'd built up a sweat and was well into his rounds when the door to the gym burst open. Looking around he saw Emma standing there holding a sheet of paper. He stepped back from the bag and wiped the sweat from his brow as she addressed him.

'I've just seen your squiggles on the map board and, if they're what I think they are, I might have something to help us.'

Marcus wasted no time, yanking his gloves off as he followed Emma back to the briefing room. He watched as she walked over to his map and looked down at the sheet of paper in her hand before studying the traces Marcus had drawn earlier.

'Right. This *here*, I take it is where the plainclothes RUC saw McMullen and the unidentified passenger?'

Marcus nodded, still catching his breath. Emma continued.

'Okay, as you know I've just been with the analysts at TCG and they are a bloody impressive bunch. There's nothing they don't know about their patch down here. So, while I was there a report came through from a military Observation Post based somewhere up here...' Marcus watched as she indicated a spot on the map near where his trace for Padraig McMullen ended. '...giving a sighting of the car that McMullen was driving coming *back* towards Keady.'

Marcus felt his breathing quicken. 'Time?'

Emma smiled and Marcus could see her cheeks flushing. 'Way ahead of you. Literally minutes after the RUC sighting. And the best part? McMullen was alone, Marcus. He was alone.'

Marcus nodded his understanding. 'It was a drop off. He was using a clean car to go and drop someone off there.' He walked over to the map and drew a ring around an area. 'Okay, speed, time and distance calculation mean that he had to drop his passenger somewhere *here*. But what's there? Looks really rural to me. The woods? A farmhouse? Maybe somewhere they're holding GRANITE?'

Emma shook her head. 'I don't think so. They won't want to risk drawing attention to somewhere like that by running around in strange vehicles and dropping people off.'

Marcus knew that Emma was right; PIRA wouldn't risk arousing local people's suspicions by trampling around an area where they were hiding an informer. But what else could it mean? Studying the map closely he jabbed at a point with his finger.

'What's this?'

Emma leaned in closer and studied the area where he was indicating. 'It's a closed BCP, sealed and unusable.'

Marcus nodded. 'Yeah it is. But look how close it is to where McMullen dropped his passenger off.' He let Emma digest the information for several moments before he jabbed his finger on another point, this time in the Republic of Ireland.

'Want to know what else it's really close to?' Without waiting for a reply, he slapped the Perspex hard, making Emma start. 'Patrick McCusker's farm. Pat McCusker of the Provisional Army Council, associate of Gerry Trainor, Padraig McMullen and our very own Joe Carluccio.' He paused and stared back at the map, translating the contour lines and symbols into a topographical image in his head.

'And *that* is where my Agent is currently being tortured and interrogated.'

CHAPTER 17

COUNTY MONAGHAN, REPUBLIC OF IRELAND

Kieran screwed his eyes shut as the blindfold was ripped from his face and the light blinded him. He could hear his breathing, quick and shallow, in the silence of the barn. A little at a time, he opened his eyes and saw someone moving around in front of him. As his focus adjusted, he could see it was Big Joe Carluccio. Joe was taking items from a bag and placing them on a table, to all intents and purposes ignoring his captive. Kieran's mouth was dry again as his focus returned and he could finally see what Joe was putting on the table. Hammers, a power drill, pliers, a blowtorch, some towels, bottles of water, a filleting knife, and a voice recorder with spare batteries and cassettes. His bowels felt loose and watery as he watched, with rapt fascination, his torturer laying out the tools of his trade. Kieran licked his lips and spoke, his voice croaky and dry from lack of use.

'What about ye, Joe? How's life?'

Joe did not acknowledge him in the slightest, just carried on laying out his macabre inventory. Kieran tried again.

'Here Joe, come on. You gonna tell me what the fuck I'm doing here?'

Once again, it was a though he wasn't there. The head of the Nutting Squad continued to calmly arrange his implements on the trestle table. Despite himself, Kieran felt a surge of rage well up inside him and screamed at his captor.

'I'M FUCKING TALKING TO YOU, YOU IGNORANT PRICK! LOOK AT ME!'

Joe picked up the empty bag and walked back out of the doors at the end of the barn without even a glance back at his prisoner, slamming them behind him as he disappeared from view. Kieran's head flopped on his chest and he let out a moan. Though it was the last thing he wanted to do, he lifted his head and studied the neat rows of implements paraded on the table awaiting their grisly employment. He'd never carried out, or even assisted in the torture of a tout, but he'd seen the bodies and witnessed the awful wounds and injuries that desecrated them. Most of them inflicted by Joe himself. As head of the Nutting Squad, Joe took the lead on interrogations, usually assisted by Frankie Vallely or wee Brendan Carragher. Kieran's mind raced as he attempted to stem the panic flooding it by rehearsing what he was going to say.

He'd start by denying he was a tout; he'd have to. Then, depending on how much pain he could endure, he'd eventually pretend to break and admit he'd been approached by the Brits. He'd explain that they were threatening to blackmail him because he was having an affair with the IRA Quartermaster General's wife. The affair was true, and he knew that Joe would have that checked out, giving Kieran a bit of time to string out his survival. He'd tell Joe that when he'd been scooped, that had been the first meeting that had been arranged and he'd only turned up at it to learn how the Brits did things so he could report it to the Army Council and set the Brits up for ambush. Kieran knew that Joe wouldn't swallow this but if he could remain convincing enough, he'd continue to buy time in the knowledge that a rescue must be getting closer. The one thing he remembered from his training with his handlers through the years regarding interrogations was that he must never, *never*, admit to having passed them any information. No matter how tempting, how much agony he was in, how confused or exhausted. Once that admission had passed his lips, he was a dead man, the remaining torture after that point used only to qualify what information he'd already passed. He threw his head back and felt a tear run down his cheek as he struggled with his emotions. *Come on you fucking eejit, you can do this. You can do this Kieran lad. You're tougher than any big bastard from the fucking 'Murph. Get it together man, come on.*

❧

Through a small gap between the doors, Joe Carluccio watched Kieran trying to prepare himself for what was to come. From experience, he recognised the stages that his captive was going through; the terror, the helplessness, the rage, the hope, the plan being formed in his head. It mattered little. They all broke. A human being could only stand so much pain. Anyone could get a prisoner to talk by applying violence and pain, but the real skill was in getting *all* the relevant information. All those details that would be used to put together intelligence that PIRA could use against the Brits. And recognising when the information was true: A man in agony would tell you what he thought you wanted to hear to stop the pain and there was a real skill in being able to separate fact from fiction.

As he watched Kieran struggle with his internal conflicts, Joe knew that the man would put up a tough defence. Kieran Mulgrew had a reputation as a hard man among hard men and could take a good beating as well as dishing one out. Joe remembered an occasion some years ago when Belfast Brigade had been crippled by the Brits intercepting their operations, the prevailing theory being that a tout was giving up information. A few suspects, Mulgrew amongst them, had been fingered as possible informers. The Brigade had decided to carry out informal interviews with the suspects prior to handing over a short-list to the Nutting Squad. The guys who had accused and tried to question Kieran however, got the tripe kicked out of them, despite being three against one. So, Joe knew Kieran would put up a strong fight. Regardless, the man was a tout. Caught red-handed on his way to meet with the Brits, so Joe wasn't concerned about the burden of proof. What he needed to concentrate on was getting the details of the information and getting it on record without killing him first. And that was Joe's only real concern. He'd had it before, where a tout had died while undergoing questioning and gone to the grave with whatever secrets he'd passed to the Brits. Joe was determined not to let that happen again.

He pushed himself away from the doors and made his way up to the farmhouse, rubbing his hands in the evening chill. Entering the kitchen, he immediately felt the warmth from the big range and held his hands out over the cooker. Pat walked over and handed him a mug of tea which he accepted gratefully.

How's the guest Joe?'

Joe took a few sips of the hot brew before replying. 'He's fine Pat. Just letting him stew a while before I go back in. He'll be trying to square himself away with a wee plan at the moment, so I'll give him some time to do that. Then I'll go back in and completely fuck that up for him.'

Pat chuckled. 'Ye think he even knows how bad this is going to be for him?'

Joe shook his head. 'They all *know* Pat, but their brain can't accept that fact. It's a survival mechanism built into us; keep fighting till you get out of this. For touts though, the only way out is the bullet. Kieran Mulgrew will know this better than most, but his head won't let him come to terms with that...yet.'

As Pat busied himself at the sink, Joe mentally rehearsed his plan. He intended starting with a completely formal approach, giving the impression that Kieran's guilt was a done deal and that all he wanted to know was what had been passed to the Brits. He'd also give Kieran a one-time offer; that if Kieran told him everything he'd done, Joe would record it and the evidence given to Sinn Fein who would use it to discredit the Brits and their dirty tricks campaign. He would put it to Kieran that he must be willing to appear in public, giving statements about how the Brits had blackmailed him into being an informer, threatened his life and that of his family. Although, as Joe recalled, Kieran didn't have any close family, being a widower, whose parents had also passed some time ago. There was a sister somewhere down in Kerry, Joe seemed to remember. That might be useful leverage if Kieran remained, as Joe anticipated he would, stubborn. The offer was, of course, a hollow one. Ceasefire or no ceasefire, the rule for touts remained as it had stood since time immemorial; torture then death. But sometimes the drowning man will clutch at anything to keep his head above water.

Joe was also well aware that he was on the clock with this one. The Brits would still be looking for Kieran, but Joe knew they couldn't operate across the border and Pat's pet Garda would make sure they got advance notice of any interest in them from the Republic's authorities. No, Joe knew that the longer he stayed away from Belfast, the harder it would be to hold down his alibi. He needed to get this done as quickly as he could. Get back in the North and watch the news reporters' solemn faces as they stood under umbrellas on a damp rural road reporting the find of a maimed body believed to be the suspected informer Kieran Mulgrew. He took his watch out of his pocket, looked at the time then put it away again. It was an old trick he'd learned, not giving the tout any indication of how long he was being held, tortured or rested between sessions. With the tout's fear and exhaustion adding to the stresses of their pain, it soon became difficult for them to keep track of time, the captor's comings and goings seemingly random and unpredictable.

Joe swigged the last of the tea and rinsed the mug in the soapy contents of the sink. Looking out of the window he saw night was fast approaching, the last of the light shrinking away in the west. He dried his hands and headed outside, bracing himself against the chill of the wind as he walked towards the large barn. As he hauled the doors open, he wondered if he should have worn a jacket as it was getting very cold, but he knew this first session would be a short one, plenty of time to get his coat later. He watched as Kieran's head jerked up, could see the whites of the tout's eyes as the fear took hold but Joe continued as though Kieran wasn't there. He walked over to his table and made a show of placing the batteries and cassette into the Dictaphone before testing it by clicking his fingers and listening back to the recording. Satisfied, he pulled a chair away from the table and dragged it to a spot several feet in front of the tout, still without making eye contact with Kieran. He sat in the chair, pressed the record button on the Dictaphone and looked Kieran in the eye for the first time.

'Kieran Mulgrew, you are hereby formally charged by the leadership of the Provisional Irish Republican Army with the offence of treason by betraying your oath as sworn on your acceptance into the organisation and providing intelligence to the enemy, namely the British Security Forces. You will now be formally questioned where all of your answers will be recorded and examined and used to determine your level of cooperation. You are ordered to provide an honest and open account of your activities and answer all questions to the best of your abilities. It is important that you understand this is a formal proceeding and that there are serious repercussions and penalties that will apply for anything less than truthful and honest cooperation. Do you understand?'

Kieran shook his head and began to speak but Joe shut him down, screaming into his face.

'IT'S A SIMPLE FUCKING YES OR NO YOU CUNT!'

Kieran recoiled from the unexpected lunge, could feel Joe's spittle on his face, and nodded vigorously.

'Yes. Yes, I understand.'

Joe relaxed back in the chair, appearing as though nothing had happened.

'Excellent, that's a grand start Kieran. Now, from the top, how long have you been a tout?'

CHAPTER 18

SIG SOUTH DET, BESSBROOK MILL

Marcus stared in disbelief at his Operations' Officer. 'What the hell do you mean *they won't act on it?*'

The Ops Officer laid a hand on Marcus's shoulder. 'Look, it's another country with their own laws and statutes and yes, we cooperate from time to time, but the Republic of Ireland won't be seen to be dancing to the UK's tune. Box have reached out some feelers but have advised us not to engage with the Irish law enforcement organisations as they are not interested. On top of which we really don't have any evidence to substantiate your theory.'

Marcus shrugged off the hand, his anger apparent. 'You must be kidding? We've worked it out Boss. McCusker's farm is *the* most likely spot for GRANITE to be held at. But he won't be there for much longer; Carluccio's been AWOL for two days now and you and I both know he's not been on a knitting retreat to occupy his time!'

The officer frowned at Marcus's sarcasm but held up a placatory hand. 'Marcus, I sympathise with your position, I

152

truly do. But the fact remains we have no *evidence*; informed guesswork, yes, but no evidence to put to the Garda Siochana to justify them raiding one of their citizen's properties.'

Marcus thought for a moment. 'What about a covert Special Forces' Op? In and out before anyone knew they were there?'

The Ops Officer snorted his derision. 'Absolutely out of the question. If caught, it's tantamount to conducting military operations in violation of a nation's laws, statutes and sovereignty. In short, serious jail time for everyone involved and ministerial level resignations.' He sighed and ran his hand through his hair. 'Sorry Marcus, it's a bloody good theory but in truth, that's all it is: A theory. I have to get back but keep me informed if you come up with anything new.'

With that, the Ops Officer patted Marcus's back as he passed him and let himself out of the briefing room. Marcus's head drooped on to his chest as he was over-whelmed by a feeling of helplessness. His frustration was returning as he thought about how ludicrous the situation was: His Agent was being tortured and interrogated less than forty kilometres from where he was standing, and nobody would do anything about it. He could understand the political sensitivities and restrictions, but he'd thought the Special Forces angle would have been worth considering. Depending where an SF team crossed over the border, they could literally run back across if things went wrong and have plausible deniability; say they got lost while conducting an operation and strayed over the border where it was unmarked. This used to happen all the time to regular military units when patrolling the border area. Nothing different to define the country to the South from the bogs and hillocks the soldiers manoeuvred around in the North.

He stretched and walked over to the map, leaning against the large-scale chart with both hands, eyes closed and concentrating. The Ops Officer would only act if Marcus could provide more accurate information, but there was no more information to find. He and Emma had exhausted every avenue of possibility, talking to TCG, and the local contingent of the Royal Irish Regiment, desperately looking for any other scrap of intelligence that could help them. But there had been nothing. Marcus's frustration was turning to anger as he imagined the agony that GRANITE was currently experiencing. All as a result of working for Military Intelligence, an organisation that had practically accepted the Agent's grisly fate as inevitable. He opened his eyes and stared at the spot where they had identified McMullen dropping his mystery passenger, assumed to be Carluccio, off by the woods. Marcus shook his head in frustration. *It can't be more than four kilometres from there to McCusker's farm. Four fucking klicks! You could literally run there and back in...*

Marcus straightened as he allowed the thought to run to its conclusion: A man could easily cover four kilometres in and back quickly. Very quickly indeed. Especially if no one was looking for him. He leaned back into the map and studied the area of the sealed Border Crossing Point closely. Adrenalin coursed through his body, the coppery taste in his mouth the confirmation that he was actually considering this. He knew it would require a bit of subterfuge on his part; getting his car and weapons out of the compound without alerting the Duty Operator that he was up to something. *But it could be done.* And in a flash of inspiration, he knew exactly how he would do it.

～

An hour later, Marcus took the turning towards the disused BCP and cut back on his speed, looking for somewhere he could park his car so that it wouldn't be seen by anyone passing. Though, looking at the grass growing in the middle of the road, it didn't seem like anyone used it that much anyway. His headlights picked out a small clearing ahead of him and as he pulled into it, he saw that it was perfect for his purposes; a wide cutting that led to a forest track beyond. He turned the car around so that it was facing back the way he'd come, ready for a quick extraction on his return. He turned the engine off and was stunned by how dark it was, no ambient light whatsoever. This was good for his purposes and he took several minutes to allow his eyes to adjust to the darkness before grabbing his rucksack and weapons and exiting the vehicle. He rammed the Sig Sauer into his waistband and looped the sling of the G3 over his shoulder. With a last look at his car, Marcus stepped onto the road and began jogging towards the crossing point.

He'd told the Duty Op at Bessbrook that he was heading back up to Belfast as there was nothing more to be gained from staying at South. This allowed him a reason to be leaving with his car and weapons. He'd stopped just outside Madden and called the Duty Op, telling him that he had arrived in Belfast, covering his back on the off chance that the Duty Op rang Belfast to make sure Marcus had got there in one piece. He had time now. Time to do what was right and to try to save a man who'd given his best years to stopping murders and killings. And *try* was the key word. Marcus was under no illusion that he might already be too late to save GRANITE, but he would never be able to look himself in the eye again if he didn't at least try to do the right thing.

The night was silent around him, the cold breeze his only companion on his nocturnal venture. His heart was racing, and he felt light-headed, but he knew this was just a result of the illicit nature of his actions. He didn't expect to get away with this, whether he managed to rescue GRANITE or not. The way he saw it there were several possible outcomes: GRANITE was not at the farm and Marcus made good his escape back to the North. GRANITE was not there but Marcus got caught and arrested. GRANITE was there, Marcus rescued him and got him back into the North. GRANITE was there but he and Marcus got killed by the PIRA team holding GRANITE. He shook his head in an attempt to dispel the negativity that was eroding his confidence. *Too late now conscience, you had your chance...*

He slowed and walked between two huge boulders that acted as an effective blockade for vehicles. This far from civilisation, there had been no need to consider pedestrians, so the restriction probably worked okay. And with that, Marcus found himself armed and operating completely without remit in the Republic of Ireland. He stepped off the disused road and conducted a check of his map, careful to shield the small pinprick of red light emanating from his torch. He set a bearing on his compass, checked it, then headed off across the boggy moor, going as fast as he dared over the rough ground.

Despite his good boots, his feet were soon wet, but he refused to allow the discomfort to distract him. He took another couple of map checks to confirm he was still on track then dropped to one knee as he ascended a small rise. The lights to his front were only a matter of three hundred metres away at the most and he stayed still, eyes scanning the dwellings for any sign of movement. The cold wind buffeted Marcus and made his eyes water, but he maintained his vigil for several minutes before standing up and advancing over the rough ground, towards McCusker's farm. The buildings were lit up by a couple of bright, exterior lights that seemed to be used to illuminate the areas between the main farmhouse and some large barns. The farm was on the top of a rise, giving it excellent fore-warning of any vehicles approaching. Marcus had identified this from his studies of the map back at Bessbrook and this had been the rationale for his approach on foot.

He made his way up the small hill, using the darkest area of the farm complex for his approach. The only noise he could hear was that of the wind moving the bracken and heather around him. As he got closer to the house he paused again, took a knee and studied the dwelling for several moments. A man came into view through one of the windows that was illuminated from within, and Marcus was close enough to recognise him as Pat McCusker. He watched as Pat poured a drink of some sort before returning back the way he had come. Marcus gave him another minute to settle then carefully made his way around the perimeter of the farmhouse and towards the barns at the rear.

Sticking to the shadows and grateful again for the dark night, Marcus advanced towards the smaller of the two barns and could smell cow manure emanating from it. A brief moment later he heard the lowing of cattle from inside and paused. It would be unlikely that PIRA would be interrogating someone in a building where their screams and cries would upset the animals and make it all but impossible to hear. He turned his face towards the second barn and noticed, now that he was closer, the slivers of light emanating from the gaps in the doors. His mouth flooded with the metallic taste of adrenalin and he moved towards the rear doors, slowly, legs bent and in the classic heel-toe gait of the covert approach.

As he reached the doors, Marcus slung the G3 around his side and drew his Sig, bringing the pistol up close to his chest, ready to be punched out and engage anyone who challenged him. He leaned into the metal wall of the barn and placed his eye up against a small gap between the door and the wall. His breath caught as he immediately identified the familiar shape of the man sat with his back to him.

GRANITE.

CHAPTER 19

COUNTY MONAGHAN, REPUBLIC OF IRELAND

Joe clicked the button to the off position and studied Kieran's face. Between the gashes, swelling and blood, it was now almost impossible for Joe to read his captive's demeanour. Kieran's head was drooped onto his chest and his breathing came in loud, wet rasps. Blood and spittle flecking his chin every time he exhaled. Joe wondered if he had enough with which to call it a day. He thought he did but there was no room for error on this one; he needed to be sure he'd got everything to take back to the PAC.

While he continued to study the broken specimen before him, Joe stretched back in his chair. True to form, Kieran had withstood a fearsome amount of pain, more than anyone else Joe had ever seen. The initial beatings had practically no effect other than to get Joe warmed up a little. The three fingernails he'd ripped out with the pliers had started the ball rolling with Kieran admitting he'd been approached by the Brits. But it had taken the combination of the drill into the back of Kieran's hand, then the blowtorch to cauterise the wound for him to start responding to the specifics.

Joe wrinkled his nose at the smells coming from his captive. The strong body odour magnified by pain and terror. The stench of urine, the recent incontinence adding to the older stink. The bad breath puffing in and out of Kieran's mouth, his nose crushed and unable to perform any function whatsoever. Joe sighed and stood, walked back to the table and placed the Dictaphone on it as he grabbed a towel and began wiping his hands clean. He ignored the ingrained blood stains to be dealt with later with some hot water and washing-up liquid. He glanced back at Kieran and noted the man hadn't moved position at all. Joe wasn't convinced Kieran had broken, at least not completely, but he was pretty sure that his recorder had all the information he needed. Even allowing for the odd break in proceedings, Kieran Mulgrew had taken four hours to break, and that was with Joe going straight into the beating. Usually, he would start with a bit of psychology; some mind games to throw the captive off-balance and open him up a bit before becoming physical. But with Kieran, Joe didn't have the luxury of time. He needed to get to the specifics as soon as possible, get them on record and back to the PAC. And he was pretty sure he'd achieved his aim. *Pretty* sure. With a nod of affirmation, Joe picked up the Dictaphone and walked towards the doors, deciding to go over the recordings in the warmth and privacy of the farmhouse. He didn't bother saying anything to Kieran as, next time he came into the barn, it would be to kill the tout and move the body into the North. Closing the large doors behind him, Joe braced himself against the cold wind and jogged across the concreted yard and into the warmth of the farmhouse.

~

Kieran waited for several minutes before slowly opening a swollen eyelid and looking at the doors. He struggled to focus and shook his head several times in a vain attempt to clear his vision. He could see that he was alone in the barn once again but knew from experience that Joe could return in a minute or half an hour. His torturer had done this throughout the duration, keeping Kieran off- guard and denying him any sense of routine or timings from which to prepare himself. He yelled as a bolt of pain shot up his arm and jerked forward as far as he could, vomit ejecting from his split and swollen mouth. He spat the detritus out and felt his entire body convulse, the shock of the torture now kicking in fully.

Kieran was under no illusions that he was probably breathing the last breaths he would take, the finality in Joe's demeanour telling him as much. He guessed that Joe would now be going over the recordings to check that he had everything he needed. The best that Kieran could hope for would be another visit from Joe to clarify some information. He gave a demented giggle. *The best I can hope for is more torture? Who would have thought it?* He stifled the laugh immediately, not convinced he wasn't being monitored and not really wanting to attract further agony.

Despite the pain he was enduring, Kieran could feel his head drooping back onto his chest and his eyes closing. He recognised this as his body starting to shut down, prioritising dealing with the injuries and wounds he had suffered. And he surrendered to it, relaxing completely as his breathing slowed and deepened, and his mind drifted off into a troubled dream.

He woke with a start and recoiled from the shape of the figure in front of him, opening his mouth to protest, to tell Joe that he'd given him everything, just to kill him and be done with it, but...it wasn't Joe. As his consciousness returned, Kieran could make out the blurred features of Marcus kneeling in front of him. He tried to smile, recognising that he was hallucinating, but his grin split his swollen lips further and he grunted in pain. And the hallucination didn't go away. His pulse began to race as he considered...*no, impossible surely*? But it wasn't impossible; Marcus was here and saying something to him. 'Kieran, c'mon Kieran. Look at me mate.'

Marcus kept his voice as low as he could, unaware of how much time he had and wanting to make sure he didn't give Joe the upper hand on his return. He took in his Agent's battered features, the face swollen and grotesque, painted with rivulets of dried and fresh blood. He'd noticed the hands immediately; the missing fingernails and the burnt crater on the back. He shook Kieran's shoulder again and this time was gratified to see a spark of recognition through the slit of the eye his Agent had managed to open. He leaned forward as Kieran mouthed something.

'Took...bloody...time didn't...you?'

Despite himself, Marcus gave a small laugh and gripped Kieran's shoulder, leaning in further to be sure his whisper was heard. 'Okay, we don't know how long we've got so I'm going to cut you free and get us the fuck out of here. Can you walk?'

Kieran nodded. 'I think so, he didn't bother with my legs. Didn't need to. Where's everybody else?'

'I'm it my friend. No time to explain now though. Let me get you out of here.'

Marcus took a small knife from the pocket of his cargo trousers. He cut the plastic zip-ties binding the Agent's arms to the chair then walked behind Kieran and slashed the cords holding him to the back of the seat. Grabbing his pistol once again, he put his hand under Kieran's armpit and helped his Agent get up out of the seat. Kieran collapsed immediately, thumping down hard into the chair. He let out a deep groan but sat forward again and tried to push up on his weakened legs. With Marcus's help, he managed to remain in a standing position even as his legs trembled beneath him. Marcus gave a raise of his eyebrows and Kieran nodded, shuffling his feet as Marcus supported his weight and led him towards the rear of the barn. When they reached the doors, Marcus let go of Kieran and pulled them open, leading the Agent outside before turning and closing them behind him. Taking control of Kieran with his free hand once again, Marcus led his Agent away from the barn and into the blackness of the night.

～

Joe Carluccio sipped at the tea and listened to the strained voice of Kieran Mulgrew through the tinny speaker of the voice recorder. He nodded, happy with the clarity and the information that was coming through. He stopped the tape occasionally, rewinding it to listen to again, satisfying himself with the quality of the recording before moving on. When the tape came to an end, Joe reached into the bag at his feet and brought out a second Dictaphone and cassette. He loaded the second recorder with the tape then checked the recording function. Satisfied that it was all in working order, he set about making a copy from the original.

It took Joe some time to accomplish, but these things couldn't be rushed; the PAC would scrutinise the tape for the evidence it provided so he took great care to make the recording the best he could. When he'd finished, he removed the cassettes and placed each recorder in a separate plastic bag before putting them into his large sports holdall. The cassettes he also separated in the same way but kept these on his person. This was usually never done, no PIRA man worth his salt stupid enough to risk being caught with a dead tout's confession on him, but this situation was different. While he could give the cassette to Pat and have him deliver it to the PAC, Joe wanted to make sure that *this* recording went straight to the man to whom it mattered most; Colm Murphy, Officer Commanding Northern Command: The entire IRA in Northern Ireland and the adjoining counties.

While PIRA had its own Chief of Staff, he had become seriously ill and was now really Chief in name only. Colm spoke with more authority than any other delegate, representing, as he did, the fighting men of the IRA. Colm had been born into republicanism and escalated his politics to the physical fight at the tender age of fourteen when he killed his first policeman in Whiterock. From that day forward, Colm Murphy became one of the most effective killers within the IRA. Initially a Belfast-based Volunteer, Colm's skill and courage were soon in demand all over the North and he planned, led and took part in the biggest successes in PIRA's history. His legend status was already on the rise when he escaped from the Maze prison with a handful of other IRA men. It was cemented further when he was one of only two men to escape the Loughgall ambush where eight of his fellow Volunteers were killed by the SAS. Murphy was lauded even more when he planned and executed the bombing of a busload of British soldiers at Ballygawley, killing eight and wounding twenty-eight in direct revenge for Loughgall. He had been promoted to OC Northern Command at a relatively young age but had shown himself to be competent and effective despite this.

From his own dealings with the PAC, Joe could see the divisions beginning to widen. On the one hand was Colm, Gerry and Pat; men who had carried out the physical struggle for over thirty years, done their time in the Kesh, been wounded and injured on operations. On the other side were those now representing the nationalist community as representatives of Sinn Fein, legitimate politicians in their own right. While they had also carried out operations in their day, these men had ceased the physical struggle a long time ago, promoting the use of the ballot box over the bombings. They had become very cautious in the past year, stamping out any suggestions of operations likely to attract negative attention to the republican movement. This caused friction between the two groupings, with Colm and the other hawks railing against this policy.

But there was another reason that Joe wanted Colm to be the recipient of the cassettes, and that was a personal one. Colm had been very close friends with the Savage family and had taken Sean Savage under his wing for quite some time as the younger man made his way up through the IRA. When Savage was killed by the SAS in Gibraltar, Murphy had been badly affected. His rage had been a terrible thing and he'd asserted from that point onwards, that there was a high-level tout within PIRA that was giving up operations to the Brits. He'd also vowed to spend the rest of his life finding out who that tout was. And now Joe could give that to him. The recorded confession of Kieran Mulgrew. Colm would be ecstatic and probably demand that he kill Mulgrew himself, but Joe couldn't risk that. They'd held the tout for longer than he was comfortable with and he had everything he needed from him. Time to finish this and get the recording to Colm.

From the quiet in the house, Joe assumed Pat had gone to bed and realised that it was well into the early hours of the morning. He eased the front door closed behind him and walked over to the barn, pulling his jacket collar up against the freezing wind. He opened the doors, wincing at the screeching metal then stopped dead, mouth open as he looked inside.

Mulgrew was gone.

～

Kieran tripped again and wailed as he broke his fall on his wounded hand. Marcus helped him to his feet, and they continued making their way through the small gully. Marcus wanted them to stay as low as they could, knowing that once Joe discovered that Kieran was missing, they would be out looking for him and Marcus didn't intend giving Joe any help in this regard. Staying off the higher ground minimised the risk that they could be spotted from a distance. While there was no ambient light, Marcus couldn't be sure that Joe wouldn't have access to any night-vision devices so was erring on the side of caution. Beside him, Kieran's laboured breathing was loud, even above the gusting wind. His Agent was hurt badly but despite this, Marcus knew they were making better time than he'd hoped, Kieran's toughness and determination pushing his pain aside for the time being.

By his reckoning, Marcus assessed that the border was less than a kilometre away. While he knew that this fact wouldn't stop Joe from pursuing them, he would feel much better about their chances in the North where his car and the possibility of support were in their favour. He heard his Agent talking to him. 'What? I can't hear you Kieran, you'll need to speak up.'

'I said, he was asking me about a lot of stuff I knew nothing about.'

Marcus helped steady the Agent as he stumbled on the rough ground. 'What do you mean?'

'Well, I was expecting him to grill me over how long I'd been working with the Brits, what I'd told them and how I met them and all that, but he was going on and on about loads of other shite.'

Marcus frowned. 'Like what?'

Kieran spat a glob of blood and phlegm to clear his throat. 'Like the Gibraltar Martyrs. Went on about them for fuckin ages. The Loughgall boys. The London cells. Stuff I knew fuck all about.'

'Yeah, he'll have been fishing, hoping it was you that had given them up.'

Kieran was silent as Marcus steered him to alter their course, then pointed with the pistol.

'There we go Kieran, the border's only about another half a klick. We're almost there mate, almost there.' He glanced back over his shoulder, but the farmhouse was well out of sight. From memory, he remembered that a road ran east of their current location and continued to check the area as they staggered northwards, for any signs that vehicles were on the move. He could hear that Kieran was struggling to breath, the Agent taking huge gulps of air and almost hyperventilating in an attempt to get the oxygen flowing to his lactic-heavy limbs. Marcus moved closer and threw Kieran's arm over his shoulders, propping his Agent up and taking most of the weight. They stumbled for several metres in their awkward embrace until they coordinated their steps in a steady rhythm. Marcus looked up and could just make out a darker blot ahead of them and realised with a start that this was the woods that marked the Border Crossing Point and his car. He yelled into Kieran's ear.

'We've made it mate. That's the border up ahead and my car's just the other side.'

He was waiting for Kieran's response when something caught his attention and turning towards the distraction, his heart sank when he saw the headlights of a vehicle speeding along the easterly road. He grabbed Kieran tighter. 'C'mon, we've got to move. Hurry.' He could feel that the Agent had given his all and Marcus found himself practically dragging Kieran as he tried to make it to his car before the other vehicle caught them up.

'I don't see fuck all Pat.'

Pat McCusker was silent for a second as he changed gear and threw the car into a tight corner. 'He'll have made a run for the border Joe. My moneys on him heading straight north. He'll think he's safe when he's on the other side but it's still my people over there. He's got nowhere to hide.'

Joe shook his head. 'I hope to fuck you're right Pat or the Council's gonna have my head for this.'

Pat McCusker offered Joe no solace or crumb of comfort because the big man was right: If they didn't find the tout, the PAC would punish Joe's failure with his execution. And Pat, for one, would be more than happy to pull the trigger on the big bollox. If the tout made it to safety, he would be able to finger Pat, Aisling and Connor in his abduction as well as the Belfast boys who'd lifted him. All thanks to Joe's fucking stupidity. When Joe had burst into Pat's bedroom screaming his head off, Pat had thought the SAS had hit the property. When Joe explained about the tout escaping and then said that someone must have helped him, Pat had shut him down. Why the hell would someone sneak into the barn, release the tout, then sneak out? Where were the Garda? The SAS? No, in Pat's mind the story was simple; Joe had fucked up and somehow or other the tout had managed to cut himself loose. And now here they were, tearing along a single-track road in the small hours of the morning hunting an escaped tout who should, by rights, be dead by now.

Joe stared out of the window but could see nothing beyond the limits of the car headlights. *Mulgrew could be anywhere, even made it over by now.* He didn't share Pat's faith that the tout could still be brought to heel even if he'd made it into the North. All Kieran needed was a phone, and the Army and RUC would swoop in from the nearest barracks to collect their pet. He risked a cautious glance at Pat, the man's face giving nothing away in the dim light of the car's interior. But he knew that Pat would place the blame firmly on Joe's shoulders, which was unfair as Joe knew beyond the shadow of doubt, that Kieran had been helped in his escape. The way the ties and rope had been cut told him as much. But Pat wasn't interested. Didn't believe that there was some mystery accomplice who'd snuck in, freed the tout, then snuck back out again. But Joe knew. And knew for sure. He looked up as Pat slowed the vehicle and brought it to a halt, turning the engine off and sitting silently for a few moments before turning to Joe.

'Come on. We go on foot from here.'

Joe shielded his eyes as the interior light came on, then followed Pat, closing the door behind him. He kept close to Pat as he was led along a small track that skirted the edge of a wood-line, listening over the sound of the wind for any signs of their quarry. Pat stopped and Joe caught up with him.

'What's up?'

'This is pointless. Look at it; it's as black as a gorilla's arsehole, Joe and we can't hear a thing over this damned wind.' Pat turned and faced him. 'Let's give it up. We'll head on over to Tynan and wake my cousins up. Get some phone calls made and see if we can get a few men out on the ground while we're about it.'

Without waiting for a reply, the older man strode past Joe and was heading back to the car. He paused when he realised Joe wasn't following him and turned to see what the problem was. He couldn't make out the shape of the pistol in the darkness and had been shot three times before his body spun and tumbled backwards into the bracken.

Joe lowered the pistol and shook his head in a vain attempt to stop the ringing in his ears. He advanced towards the prone figure of Pat McCusker, keeping the pistol trained on the body. As he stood above Pat, Joe could see that one of his shots had gone through the right eye and knew from this that the man was very definitely dead. Joe felt no remorse; if he was to survive this thing, he had to own the narrative and he couldn't very well do that with Patrick McCusker telling all and sundry that it was Joe's fault. No, far better that Pat went out to check on Mulgrew while Joe was resting and Mulgrew got the better of him. When Joe found the barn empty, he jumped in Pat's car and began searching, eventually finding Pat's body on the road near the border, killed by Kieran Mulgrew who continued to make good his escape. Yes, that was a far healthier version of events as far as Joe Carluccio was concerned. He put the pistol away and dragged Pat's body closer to the car then fished around in the dead man's pockets until he found the car keys. Taking these, he made his way back to the vehicle, opened it, then manhandled Pat's body into the rear seat. He got into the driver's seat, started the engine, turned the car around and began driving back to Pat's house. He would call Colm directly and give him a heads-up on Pat's error of judgement and subsequent passing. He would also let Colm know his hunt for the big tout was over. *You can do this, Joe. Just remain calm and talk your way through it.* By the time he had reached the long farm track leading to Pat's, Joe was confident he could get himself out of the situation without any blame attached.

∾

Marcus followed the retreating vehicle with his rifle lined up on the body of the car. Once it disappeared from view, he continued to monitor its progress by the position of its lights until, finally, it was gone from his view.

The gunshots had startled them. He'd pushed Kieran down into a bush while he'd taken cover behind a small mound, training his G3 in the direction from where the shots had come. He'd seen nothing other than the car turning around and racing back the way it came. Marcus still didn't know what to make of it. Maybe it had been a couple of rounds fired with the aim of drawing him out, getting him to fire back so that they could pinpoint his position. But it hadn't been repeated and the car had left so soon after the shots that Marcus discounted this notion. Still none the wiser, he knew that they needed to get moving immediately, as someone might report the shots and have the place flooded with Garda and RUC officers. He stood and jogged over to Kieran, helping the panting man to his feet before half-dragging the Agent to the car. Marcus opened the door and assisted Kieran in getting into the passenger seat. He closed Kieran's door, threw the rucksack and G3 into the back, covered them with a blanket, then jumped into the driver's seat and started the car.

Kieran could feel his eye closing, his body warming rapidly now that they were out of the biting wind. He noticed that Marcus hadn't put his lights on but realised this was deliberate, not wanting to give the hunters any advantage in locating them. His hand felt like it was immersed in molten wax and his head ached with a deep, pulsating throb. But he was alive, and bloody grateful to be so. He looked through his good eye at Marcus who was hunched forward in his seat, staring at the darkness ahead of them as they crawled along the narrow lane. His eyes watered with emotion as the thought struck him that Marcus had come alone. There was no rescue party. No British Military unit scouring the border looking for him. Just Marcus. Which meant that he was conducting this rescue mission completely off the books. Kieran didn't know much about how the army operated but had enough of a layman's knowledge to realise that Marcus would probably be kicked out of the military for this. He laid his head back as he tried to think about how they could get out of this together.

Marcus almost passed the junction before he saw it but braked just in time to take it. Once on the wider road, he turned on his headlights and increased their speed. He had no idea where he was going to take GRANITE, probably into the base at Keady. Marcus's ID card ensured him entry into any Security Forces' base in the country with no questions asked or encouraged. That would help protect Kieran's identity as GRANITE, get him the medical treatment he required and then let the grown-ups sort the rest out. Marcus would be interviewed and charged with any number of offences, but he felt remarkably calm about this. Confirmation, if any were needed, that he had done the right thing. He felt some sadness; he'd loved his military career and was really just getting stuck into the world of covert operations, but he had done what was needed. As he crossed another junction, he accelerated then heard Kieran clearing his throat to talk. Marcus eased off on the speed and looked at his Agent.

'You okay, Kieran?'

Kieran nodded and tried to moisten his lips with his tongue. 'Listen, I think...I think I might have a plan...for... get out.'

Marcus opened his mouth, but the Agent held up his hand and continued to speak with difficulty, but the words and the meaning becoming clearer as Marcus listened.

CHAPTER 20

COUNTY LOUTH, REPUBLIC OF IRELAND

Colm Murphy placed the empty mug on the table and stared at the man across from him. He'd never had a problem with Joe Carluccio, recognised that the man's talents and diligence in his work were essential to IRA security and integrity. But he'd never *liked* what Joe did: the tortures, interrogations, killings of bound and hooded men. Again, while he knew it was necessary, Colm had always felt a little revulsed by Joe and the role he played. Joe had never spent much time as a *soldier*, a Volunteer taking the fight to the Brits with all the odds stacked against you. Had never known the terror and adrenaline of being overwhelmed in a firefight by a platoon of Paras, escaping an SAS ambush as the rest of your team were slaughtered. But regardless of what Colm thought, Joe was good at his work. To Colm's knowledge, the cooling body of Pat McCusker currently lying under a tarpaulin in the barn was the first instance of one of Joe's operations going wrong.

When Joe had contacted Colm and passed the signal for an immediate meeting, Colm knew there had to be serious trouble. After a series of telephone calls from safe lines, he'd had the whole sorry tale related to him, and decided to head down to Louth in person. The door of the old cottage had been opened for him by a pale, grim-faced Joe and again, Colm knew the situation was serious. He'd asked to see the body for himself and had been taken to a barn where Joe pulled back the tarp and the ashen-faced, open mouth of a very dead Pat McCusker had looked back at him. Joe explained that he'd decided to get away from Monaghan as Pat's place would soon be flooded with Garda. He'd cleaned the place down before leaving, making sure there was no trace of him or what he'd been doing there.

Back in the warmth of the cottage, Colm had listened as Joe went over the incident in detail, hearing the anger in the man's voice as he relayed finding both Pat and the tout gone from the barn. Neither man could fathom how Pat had given the tout the opportunity to overwhelm him and make good his escape. Like Joe, Colm suspected that the tout had managed to goad Pat into coming close enough to attack him and get a hold of Pat's pistol. In truth, it mattered very little how Mulgrew had managed it, what mattered now was damage limitation. The tout would have made his way to a Security Force base in the North and be telling his whole sorry tale, implicating everyone involved in his abduction and interrogation. Joe had already warned off the rest of his boys and the Executive Ops team that the peelers would soon be coming for them, so at least they had a bit of a head start on getting over the border.

The Louth cottage was one of several PIRA safe houses that were retained and maintained throughout the County for emergency situations. Louth, and the Dundalk area had long been the first port of safety for IRA men fleeing the North, even referred to jokingly as *El Paso*, and there was a long history and network of support for the republican movement. Colm was satisfied that this was as good a place as any for Joe to go to ground until they worked out how they were going to handle things. He sighed as he contemplated the trouble coming their way. Once the tout talked, the raids and arrests would begin. Even those who had managed to escape would be of little use to PIRA as they would not be able to show their faces north of the border again, declared arrest on sight by the peelers. The tout would be spirited away by Special Branch to go and start his new life under a new name in another country and the RUC would leak the details of some of the big successes their tout had given them over the years. This was standard practice but still sowed the seeds of distrust and paranoia within the republican movement, playing right into the hands of the RUC and the Brits. Colm looked up as these thoughts dominated his thinking.

'Did we get much from the tout before he escaped?'

Joe paused for a moment then nodded. 'Actually Colm, I was done with the interrogation. Got everything he had to give us.'

Colm was surprised by this as he'd assumed the tout had escaped before talking. He listened with interest as Joe continued.

'And that's why I called you first Colm. There's a lot of things he's given to the Brits over the years, but there's a couple I think you'd be better off hearing about for yourself.'

Colm raised his eyebrows as Joe pulled out a small voice recorder and placed it on the table. He pressed the play button and Colm leaned in as the tinny voice emanated from the device.

'...*Kieran Mulgrew, you are hereby formally charged by the leadership of the Provisional Irish Republican Army with the offence of treason by betraying your oath as sworn on your acceptance into the organisation and providing intelligence to the enemy, namely the British Security Forces...*'

Joe studied Colm's face as the other man's entire attention was invested in listening to the recording. He watched as the nostrils flared and the mouth tightened in anger as the voice of Kieran Mulgrew spoke about the Loughgall Ambush and the Gibraltar Martyrs. When the tape came to an end, the device shut off with a click that was loud in the confines of the silent kitchen. Joe waited for Colm to speak and watched as he sat upright, shaking his head before meeting Joe's eyes.

'It's *him*, isn't it? He's the one. He's the one I've always said must have been feeding the Brits all our top-drawer stuff. *Fuck*. Kieran Mulgrew. He's done more damage to the organisation than anyone else I can think of.'

'Yeah, he has Colm. Now, I've obviously told no one about any of this. I would have let Pat hear it if he hadn't been murdered by the tout bastard, but I figured you'd want to hear it first-hand, both as a OC Northern Command and 'cos I know how close you were to Sean and his family and how bad the Gibraltar killings hit you.'

Colm nodded, his shoulders sagging as he lowered his head. 'It's still a big blow to think about it all these years later.' He stabbed a finger at the Dictaphone. 'And then to hear that dirty bastard talk about it as if it was nothing, as if...he was just talking about a game of football or something. Unbelievable.'

'Yeah, it's sometimes like that Colm. They fight and fight and then when they break, it's almost a relief for them to be able to get it off their chest. All these secrets they've been carrying around over the years.'

Colm looked back at him. 'We can't let it out that someone in one of our top teams gave up all these brave boys Joe. The movement would be in uproar and they'd have no confidence in our leadership. We'd shatter into pieces and that's just what the Brits want. I'm going to have to talk to the shinners on the Council, get them to come up with some spin to counter this.' The corner of his mouth raised in a sneer as he spoke. 'At least that's *something* they're fucking good for.'

Joe shook his head. 'I know Colm, it's a terrible situation right enough, but we'll get through it. We always do. And you're right; give this to the shinners and let them do all that political shit they're always going on about, help us army yokes out for a change.'

Colm placed his hand on Joe's. 'You're a good man Joe Carluccio. I might not like what you do but fair play to you, you're the only man for the job and I'm grateful you thought of me on this one.'

Joe felt the colour rise to his cheeks at the unexpected praise. 'I've always hated touts Colm, so for me it's not just a job. I take it very personal. We all swore our oaths when we were Green Booked, and we know the price for breaking them.'

Colm patted Joe's hand and stood, indicating with his head towards the living room. 'The line here still solid?'

Joe nodded. 'Yeah, it's fine Colm. Engineer cleared it not long after I got here.'

'Good. Look, make us another cup of tea would ye? I'll make a few calls and get the ball rolling on this. I'll arrange a Council meeting for somewhere down here but the lads in the North might find moving about a bit tight once the tout talks.'

Joe began filling the kettle and listened as Colm started making his telephone calls. The Telecom Eireann engineer that the IRA had on their books had given the line an all clear when Joe had said he needed to use the Safe House. He put the kettle on the cooker and lit the gas ring. Joe returned to the sink and looked out of the window at the fields beyond, his mind finally beginning to relax now that the story was out there being disseminated to the PIRA leadership by Colm Murphy himself. He allowed himself a small smile as he considered this, but it disappeared the instant that the thought of Kieran Mulgrew spilling his guts in an RUC station entered his head.

CHAPTER 21

HQNI, LISBURN, NORTHERN IRELAND

Colin Woods took a seat next to the CO of SIG and offered the man a smile.

'Morning Stuart. Bit of a result for you boys today, eh?'

Stuart Coull returned the smile with a small shake of his head. 'Well, obviously we're glad our Agent is safe but apparently there's some questions to be answered about the whole affair.' He leaned in closer to the Police Officer and lowered his voice. 'Box aren't happy. Have been on my case all bloody morning.'

Colin chuckled in sympathy. 'When *are* they happy Stuart? Probably wanted to find your man for themselves, bask in the glory so to speak.'

The pair were interrupted when the door opened and Marcus entered, looking ill at ease in his suit and tie. He'd been requested to attend this meeting to discuss the whole GRANITE affair even though he had given his version of events during a formal interview earlier that morning. He nodded to his CO and shook the offered hand.

'Marcus, this is Colin Woods from TCG. He'll be interested in chatting to you about anything GRANITE has said that might not have made it into the formal report. Oh, and despite the fact that he's a policeman, he's actually not a bad person.'

Colin laughed and extended his own hand over the table. 'Ignore this old bastard Marcus, all that whisky has gone to his head.'

Marcus was about to reply when the door opened behind him and he saw both men's expressions become serious. Turning around, he saw a tall, lean man in an immaculate suit enter. The man nodded to everyone then sat down, opening a briefcase before saying a word. Marcus took his own seat and waited expectantly for the individual to introduce himself. After an uncomfortable, silent minute of paper shuffling and getting a notebook and pens arranged on the table in front of him, the man looked over at Marcus.

'We haven't met before. I'm Jonathan, Security Service and you're Marcus Vaughan, handler of GRANITE, yes?'

Marcus nodded, 'Yes sir, I'm...'

'No need for the *sir*. I'm not a knight of the realm. Jonathan will suffice.'

Marcus felt his cheeks redden at the man's curt interruption but was saved from responding as the MI5 officer continued.

'Okay, start to finish, all the details regarding how your Agent escaped and then managed to get in touch with you.

Leave nothing out and I'll ask questions as and when.' He gave Marcus a hard stare. 'Begin.'

Marcus caught his CO's eye and the senior officer gave a discreet nod of encouragement. Marcus turned back to face Jonathan and began relating the tale that he and GRANITE had concocted to explain the Agent's escape from the Nutting Squad.

It had been GRANITE's idea. Marcus was more than prepared to face whatever disciplinary measures the military threw at him, but the Agent was adamant that Marcus walk away from the situation unscathed. GRANITE had then briefed Marcus on a plan where the Agent would walk into the base at Keady and demand medical attention. He would tell the RUC and the soldiers that he'd just escaped a PIRA hit-team and needed sanctuary. Tell them outright that he had been an Agent for the British Army, knowing that he would be taken in, searched and his identity confirmed. He would insist that he be allowed to call Marcus, or at least nominate Marcus as the point of contact to be called first. Marcus saw immediately that this plan could work but that he would need to get himself back to Belfast. Between them, they worked out rough timings of how long it would take Marcus to get back to the Detachment, at which point GRANITE would initiate his 'walk-in'.

And it had worked. Marcus had just got under the duvet in the debriefing suite when he was roused by the Duty Operator hammering on the bedroom door and demanding he get up immediately. Marcus had rushed to the Ops

Room where he took a call from an Army Captain in Keady who was clearly confused over the whole situation. He informed Marcus that a man claiming to be a British Agent had just turned up at the base with terrible injuries consistent with having been tortured. He would give no other details other than his name, a telephone number he'd memorised, and the name of his Handler. Marcus played his part in the charade, acting stunned then demanding to speak to the Agent. GRANITE had come on the line and the pair continued to maintain their act, becoming emotional before getting down to the business of formal arrangements for GRANITE's medical treatment and security.

Marcus had called Dom and the Ops Officer, informing the sleepy individuals of the fortuitous turn of events. Both men had appeared in the Detachment within the hour, demanding a full explanation of the circumstances. The three had then travelled to Keady and were escorted to a room where a couple of medics were cleaning and dressing GRANITE's injuries. Marcus and GRANITE had hugged each other, real emotion now replacing the staged performances from earlier. The medics had informed the SIG team that their Agent needed immediate hospital attention as they were limited with what they could achieve with their resources. GRANITE was then provided with a military security team who had taken him to Musgrave Park Hospital in Belfast where the Agent was currently being treated for his wounds.

As he finished his fictional recollection of the incident, Marcus looked at the Security Service officer who took several more notes then turned to face him.

'And that's it? Nothing more to add?'

Marcus shook his head. 'No, that's it. All a bit of a blur to be honest and completely unexpected.'

He watched as the man pursed his lips and Marcus knew immediately that he hadn't believed a word of his account.

'Tell me Marcus, what do you know about Patrick McCusker?'

Marcus frowned, wondering where this line of questioning was going. 'Well, I know he's Provisional Army Council and has a farm complex across in Monaghan where I suspected GRANITE might have been taken to for interrogation.'

'Which would, according to your Agent's story, be correct, yes?'

Marcus noted the MI5 officer's use of the word *story* when he referred to the Agent's account of events. 'Yes, apparently that's where GRANITE was being held.'

There was a moment's silence before the officer spoke again. 'Mmm. It's just that according to my sources across the border, Mr McCusker might have encountered a bit of a problem last night. A very *fatal* problem, if you get my drift.'

Marcus didn't have to feign the puzzlement on his face. 'I don't *get your drift*. From what GRANITE said, he managed to overpower McCusker, grab hold of one of

Carluccio's knives, then forced McCusker to drive him to the nearest base in the North that GRANITE knew; Keady. When he jumped out of the car, McCusker couldn't get away fast enough. That's the last GRANITE saw of McCusker.'

He could see the MI5 officer studying his face and Marcus was grateful for the fact that he had actually been telling the truth about McCusker's death. He looked at his CO and the TCG policeman and could see that this was the first time either man had heard this information. The policeman leaned forward with a frown on his face.

'Sorry Jonathan, but just to be clear here, are you saying that Pat McCusker has been killed?'

'I don't have full corroboration yet but yes, that would appear to be the case.'

Marcus interrupted. 'Look, this is the first time I've heard anything about this but if GRANITE had killed McCusker, he'd have admitted it. There wouldn't be any reason to lie as he would have been fighting for his life.'

The Security Service officer turned his focus back to Marcus with a smile that had no warmth in it. 'Quite. Which begs the question; why didn't he tell you?'

Marcus shook his head. 'Because he didn't do it. It's probably the case that the 'RA punished their own man for allowing their prisoner to escape.'

'No. Not a PAC-level player. Rank and file foot-soldiers perhaps, but even then, only after a court-martial, however brief.'

Marcus looked up as his CO weighed in on the subject. 'I agree with Marcus. If GRANITE had killed McCusker he would have no reason to lie about it. In fact, he'd probably have been quite proud of himself.'

There was silence in the room for several moments then the MI5 officer turned his attention back to Marcus. 'What did GRANITE say he'd given up?'

Marcus didn't hesitate. 'Everything. Once Joe drilled his hand and took the blowtorch to it, he broke and told Carluccio everything he asked.' He watched as the man annotated his notes before continuing. 'He did say that Carluccio was focussed on a lot of stuff that had nothing to do with GRANITE; Loughgall, The Gibraltar Three, The London Cells. He found that a bit...' He was cut off by the MI5 officer waving his hand.

'Yes, yes, very good but I'm not the least bit interested in listening to what Carluccio *wanted* to know, only in what he *does* know after interrogating your Agent.'

Marcus's dislike of this individual was growing. The man's dismissive responses, his superiority complex and lack of interest in anything other than his own agenda were starting to grate. He caught himself before his temper got the better of him, remembering that he had a lot to lose if the story of GRANITE's escape was examined *too* closely. Marcus gave a brief summary of the information that GRANITE had given to Joe and concluded with what was currently being done to ensure that the tactics and techniques GRANITE had given up could not be used to identify other Agents. Again, the man was quiet, jotting down his notes before closing the notebook and looking up.

'Well, if that's it?'

Marcus nodded.

'Very well. Can't say I for one believe this fairy tale but you've got your Agent back and I'm sure the killing of a PAC member during this incident is a bonus to the military.'

Marcus bristled. 'I've just told you GRANITE had nothing to do with that. Something wrong with your ears?'

Stuart Coull held up a placatory hand. 'Gentlemen, gentlemen, let's keep this civil, shall we? It's been a stressful time but it's over now.'

Marcus nodded but saw that the MI5 officer's expression hadn't changed. Eventually, the man nodded.

'Okay then, that's everything from me.' He looked across the table. 'Colin, if you get anything on the situation regarding McCusker, I'll need it ASAP thank you.' Without further ado, Jonathan stood, closed his briefcase and held up his hand. 'Gentlemen, thank you for your time and patience. I'll see myself out.'

Marcus watched the door close behind the departing MI5 officer and shook his head at the man's rudeness. He turned back to catch Colin looking at him with a smile on his face.

'Bit of a prick, eh Marcus?'

Marcus laughed. 'I'd have to disagree with you there Colin; the man's a *lot* of a prick!'

Stuart nodded his agreement. 'And to think he used to be one of us.' Seeing Marcus's questioning look, he elaborated. 'A soldier. He started his career in the army. Actually seen him a few times back in the very old days.'

Marcus was surprised. The man's demeanour and attitude giving no hint of commonality with those around the table. 'When was that sir?'

'Back in the bad old days of the seventies Marcus. Think he went over to Box sometime after that.'

Colin Woods looked at his watch. 'Right gents, it's been a pleasure as usual. Marcus, nice to meet you and don't take Jonathan too seriously; all these Box people are cut from the same cloth. They've never *fought* the war here so it's only a concept to them, not real.'

All three stood and exchanged handshakes then Colin left the room. Marcus was just about to go when his CO placed a hand on his arm.

'Marcus, you got an hour or so you could spare me?'

Marcus nodded. 'Sure Sir. No problem'

'Good, let's have a spot of lunch while I chat to you about something.'

Marcus followed his CO out of the room and prepared himself to have the story of GRANITE's escape dissected by his superior. He'd resigned himself to this happening at some point and decided not to lie to the man. If the CO challenged him on it, Marcus would tell him the entire truth and let the cards fall where they may. He remained happy with his decision to rescue GRANITE when no one else would lift a finger and intended leaving the Unit with his honour intact. As they left the building and walked towards the CO's car, Marcus thought that, at the very least, he knew exactly how he was going to handle this meeting.

As it turned out, nothing could have been farther from the truth.

CHAPTER 22

PALACE BARRACKS, HOLYWOOD

Jonathan Crowe screwed his eyes shut, pinched the bridge of his nose, and let out a sigh of exasperation. Opening them, he saw the curious look Charles shot him from the other side of the office and waved his colleague's concern away with a shake of his head. Looking back at his computer screen, he marvelled at the military's ability to always be exactly where they weren't wanted. His operation had been running perfectly until SIG and their bloody GRANITE had decided to stray from the template. Now Jonathan had been boxed into a corner that he was finding it difficult to fight his way out from.

The report on his screen was from the Garda Emergency Response Unit, the ERU, and did not bring Jonathan any good news. From their own agents, the unit had learned of the death of Pat McCusker and the escape of Kieran Mulgrew. They were already reaching out across the border to the Security Service for any details that they might have. And they were not happy at having been kept in the dark over the fact that an agent in the employ of the British state had been kidnapped, brought into Ireland, killed a senior terrorist and then escaped. Jonathan understood the ire but smirked at the thought of full cooperation with the Garda Siochana. *More heavily infiltrated than PIRA for goodness sake.* Still, he could see the complaint escalating until it was dealt with and the last thing he needed was London poking its nose in on his affairs. He sighed again and picked up the phone on his desk, dialled a number and was answered almost immediately.

Jonathan kept the conversation to a minimum, wanting only to arrange the meeting that would allow him to smooth the waters somewhat before the situation got out of hand. Michael Healy, Jonathan's counterpart at G2 in Dublin was a safe pair of hands and could be relied upon to keep a lid on the situation until Jonathan had decided on how he was going to proceed. With the meeting arranged, he leaned back in his chair and put his hands behind his head as he contemplated his options. For the military, the work in Northern Ireland was a fairly basic task of keeping the peace by stopping each side from annihilating the other. For the Security Service however, strategic aims that would facilitate the end of British involvement in the conflict were the priority. A very difficult balancing act but an essential one; the British Government having neither the appetite nor the budget to continue their interventions in the divided province indefinitely.

But Jonathan was close to a succeeding in a major achievement that would bring this goal closer than it had ever been. *Very* close. Over his years working in Northern Ireland he'd gained probably the most in-depth knowledge of PIRA, its leadership, and their methodology than anyone else in the Service. He'd recruited some of the best agents that his organisation had and indeed, still had in the form of RED LANCE. Jonathan had also recognised early on in his experiences that this was a long game. The military mindset operated in short-term blocks, with most battalions running through a six-month cycle before returning home for tea and medals. For Jonathan and the other MI5 officers in Northern Ireland, they worked in a more linear timeline that dealt in years rather than months.

One of Jonathan's key successes had been the manipulation of the IRA's Provisional Army Council. When he'd first joined the Security Service, the PAC had been entirely populated by the soldiers; the fighters and officers of the IRA now commanding the direction of the war through their seniority and consolidated experience. Jonathan had recognised that if there was to be any forward progress in getting the IRA to put away their arms, it would have to come from dialogue and there would never be any constructive dialogue while the hawks were running the show. Over the years he had managed to elevate the status of some of the more politically leaning, senior PIRA members to positions where they had influence. This included the PAC. It had not been easy and had taken a lot of hard work, recruitments, disinformation campaigns, selective arrests, scandal exposures, and every other strategy that was at Jonathan's disposal. But he was almost there.

With several Sinn Fein representatives and backers on the PAC, there had already been a marked difference in the direction the Council was taking the IRA. Every suggestion of military action was examined and assessed for its necessity and justification with the shinners having a lot of success in closing down many of these operations before they came to fruition. There were of course, divisions between the shinners and the soldiers, but this was exactly what Jonathan wanted: If he could engineer a *complete* divide within the PAC, he could wield the power of his Service to completely discredit the hawks and marginalise them to the point where they were regarded as little more than bitter old has-beens. And he was nearly there. The incident with GRANITE however, had set his plan back somewhat.

When Jonathan had learned that GRANITE had escaped and Pat McCusker was dead, he knew instantly that there would be repercussions. McCusker was well-respected among PIRA and the PAC and the demand for retribution would be immediate. With GRANITE in the safe custody of the RUC while receiving medical treatment, there wasn't much that PIRA could do to avenge McCusker's death. The problem was, if they couldn't get to GRANITE, they were more likely to carry out a *spectacular*; a high-profile operation guaranteed to receive maximum publicity from the media. Another bomb in London, the assassination of a prominent politician with ties to Northern Ireland, a large- scale attack on a military base. The possibilities were many. But no matter which target they chose, any such attack would set back the progress Jonathan and MI5 were making by years. And he wasn't going to just sit back and allow this to happen.

He needed to talk to RED LANCE.

CHAPTER 23

COUNTY LOUTH, REPUBLIC OF IRELAND

Colm banged the cup on the table to get everyone's attention. He waited for complete silence until he spoke. 'First thing's first. Pat's family have collected the body. They're obviously in a real bad way so I've had Barry McKevitt take care of the authorities down here so the McCuskers can bury their Da in peace. Barry's told me that the cause of death will be listed as cardiac arrest and the funeral plan is already under way. I've authorised the money for this as our supposedly friendly Garda wanted a big old chunk of cash to make this happen.' There was a ripple of approving murmurs from the men sat around the small table and Colm let it subside before continuing. 'I've also sworn on my word to Aisling and Connor that we will not sit on our hands with this one; we will avenge Pat's death no matter what it takes.'

Someone to his left cleared their throat and Colm stared hard at the man, Peter Devlin, former PIRA fundraiser now the Sinn Fein representative for Fermanagh and South

Tyrone. Colm knew what was coming; another carefully worded suggestion that they stay their hand until the Council had looked at everything from all the angles. He could feel his temper rising but gritted his teeth and indicated that the man should talk.

Peter Devlin licked his lips and looked around the table at his fellow PAC members.

'Gentlemen, I am in complete agreement with our OC Northern Command that we must be seen to have retribution for the killing of Pat McCusker by the tout Kieran Mulgrew. Of that there can be no doubt.' He cleared his throat again, already seeing the frown deepen on Colm's face. 'But...this is not an action that we should rush into. We must think carefully about the options available to us and, more importantly, their impact on the republican movement as a whole.'

Colm snorted then sneered at the man. 'Fuck's sake. Pat McCusker's not even in the ground and you're already shitting yourself that there'll be some impact on your *political progress.*'

The assembled voices began chiming in, some irate, others conciliatory but Colm stilled them by banging the table with his fist. He leaned forward and thrust his finger at Devlin.

'I'll tell you something now: There *will* be retribution for the murder of Pat McCusker and that retribution will be both revenge and warning: Revenge for the murder of a great man and a warning to any other touts or people thinking about becoming touts that the Provisional IRA will *always* hunt them down.' He saw Devlin pale as the aggression in his tone hit home. 'So, we *will* consider all the options but at the end of the day, they will only come down to two; the death of Kieran Mulgrew or a hard hit against the Brits. And that's it.'

There was a moment's silence as the Council took in Colm's words. Seamus Keenan spoke up, his soft Derry brogue a contrast to the man's reputation for unbridled violence.

'I'm with Colm. Once word gets out that Pat was killed by a tout, our boys will want to know what's being done. And they're not going to accept any half-measures on this one. Pat's a well-respected soldier, even up our way.' He paused and nodded towards Devlin and the other Sinn Fein representatives. 'And no harm to your suggestion Peter, but we're all struggling to keep control of the hot heads and hold this ceasefire. One cock-up from us and they'll slip the leash. Take matters into their own hands.'

Colm nodded his agreement. 'Aye, we've already had a couple of yokes from the Short Strand we had to clip last month for giving details of a weapons hide to their Dissident pals. So, let's not forget that if we don't act, those clowns will also make a lot of capital out of this.' He could see the consternation on the faces of the political element but also knew that they would recognise the validity of his words. The Continuity IRA, CIRA, or the Dissidents as they were sometimes called, were working hard to discredit

PIRA and recruit from their ranks. With every passing week of the ceasefire and political deadlock, PIRA were finding it harder to control those members keen to continue with the armed struggle.

Looking at the grave expressions around him, Colm knew there was nothing to be gained from holding on to the rest of the information he had. He gave Joe Carluccio a brief nod to indicate he should speak. Joe returned his nod and opened up a small notebook that he laid on the table in front of him.

'Friends, it gives me no pleasure at all to be telling you this, but you need to know what Kieran Mulgrew has given the Brits over the years. There's a fair bit here so if you let me get through it all then I'll answer any questions at the end.' When there was silence, Joe read from his notebook, briefing the men on the information that he had extracted from his interrogation of Kieran Mulgrew. Other than the occasional profanity in response to a key betrayal, the Council remained silent until Joe concluded his account. He closed the notebook and looked up at the circle of pale, tight faces. Seamus Keenan spoke first.

'Hell's teeth but that bastard's done us a fearsome amount of damage in his time, eh? I had no idea he even had access to the level of information on those operations that he's given up. Loughgall? Gibraltar? London? How did he get all this info? I know he wasn't part of the operations' teams.'

Joe nodded. 'I didn't get as much of *that* aspect as I would have liked Seamus. That was planned for the next round of questioning. But some of it I know was from loose talk. Let's not forget that until he was blown, Kieran Mulgrew was a well-trusted member of our organisation and mixed with republicans at all levels.'

Seamus spoke again. 'I get that, Joe, I really do. But the information the Brits must have had to take out our martyrs at Loughgall and Gibraltar was very accurate. How the hell could someone outside of the planning or the Ops team have gotten all of that?'

Joe shrugged his shoulders. 'I'd be lying if I said I had all the answers Seamus. As I said, where he got his information from was my next round of questions, but the fucker escaped before I got the chance. Remember as well, he was Executive Ops, so a lot of the boys trusted him with a bit more stuff than they would normally.'

There was silence as the men around the table digested this information until Colm spoke again. 'All right. Now we all know where we are, let's move on to what we do next. Joe, you want to brief the Council on what we were discussing earlier?'

Joe nodded. 'Right. From my experiences over the years as Head of Internal Security, I've learned a lot about the process the Brits follow when their touts are blown. We saw this after they got McGartland out. They refer to it as *resettlement*. It starts with getting the tout into an army base or big RUC station where they can debrief him on everything that's happened to him. Then MI5 take over and get the tout to the mainland where they stick them in a safe house somewhere and get them new identities and paperwork. MI5 are then responsible for the tout's safety and wellbeing.' He paused and took a drink of his tea before continuing. 'In Mulgrew's case, he's injured so will be getting medical treatment here before they move him to the mainland. It so happens that I've followed up on this and have got confirmation where the tout is being treated.' He paused for effect while he enjoyed the satisfaction of the open-mouthed astonishment around the table. He hadn't even told Colm this part, wanting to surprise the man along with the other members of the PAC.

'Kieran Mulgrew is being treated in the Military Wing of Musgrave Park Hospital, Belfast.'

As Joe observed them, he noted how the faces around the table portrayed the various individuals' responses to this information in accordance with their stance. The hardliners exchanged jubilant grins while the shinners could not hide their disappointment that, now there was both a target and a location, a military operation was inevitable. His attention was caught as the OC Southern Command, Bernie O'Connell addressed him.

'Didn't you mad bastards bomb that place already?'

Joe laughed. 'Yeah, we hit the Military Wing back in '91. Got a couple of Brits with the bang.'

Peter Devlin interrupted. 'Which means that the security is going be a helluva lot harder to break, won't it?'

Joe raised a hand to hush the frustrated tuts from the hardliners. 'Absolutely true Peter. Absolutely true. Which is why I've got my own wee tout at the hospital who's going to tell us exactly when Kieran Mulgrew is going to be moved.'

After a moment of astonished silence, there was an eruption of cheering and yelling and Joe threw his hands up in a mock defence as his back was pounded with congratulatory slaps. As the noise subsided, he looked up and met Colm Murphy's eyes, the OC Northern Command making no attempt to conceal his emotions. Colm's voice was husky as he spoke.

'That's some bloody good work and no mistake Joe Carluccio. I thought for a while there we'd have to hit the Brits and give the tout a pass until we could hunt him down. But this, *this*, is fantastic news.' Colm looked at his fellow Council members before continuing.

'So, only question now is; how do we do this?'

CHAPTER 24

OFFICERS' MESS, HQNI, LISBURN

It was the first time that Marcus had been in an Officers' Mess but he didn't find it all that different from the Sergeants' Mess he was accustomed to. Similar interior décor; military pictures depicting historical battles and actions, dark wooden tables, decent food. He had been surprised when the CO had told him that they would be eating there as he wasn't sure he would be allowed in. His CO had laughed and told him that if the Commanding Officer of a covert intelligence unit couldn't sneak someone into lunch, he was in the wrong job.

They'd chatted more about GRANITE and although he never stated it outright, Marcus was sure his CO suspected that the Agent's escape didn't happen quite the way that it was being portrayed. While nothing overt was spoken of, Marcus seemed to pick up that his CO had a grudging respect for...whatever he thought Marcus had done. They'd finished their lunch and were enjoying coffee in the conservatory, which was empty but for them, most people back to their offices after the lunch break. Marcus felt like the CO was stringing the lunch out but couldn't understand why. He was undoubtedly a very busy man for whom a two-hour lunch was probably a huge luxury. He watched as his superior put his cup and saucer on the table and met his eyes.

'Marcus, I have something to tell you that has been bothering me ever since our last chat. No please, don't be worried, it has absolutely nothing to do with your work or performance.'

Marcus nodded his understanding but was unaware of what else it could be that his CO would possibly want to talk about. He could see that, whatever it was, his Colonel was not his usual, confident self.

'Marcus, there's no way other way to say this so I'm just going to blurt it out: I knew your mother.'

For a moment, Marcus thought he'd misheard. 'Sorry sir. Say again?'

Stuart Coull gave a rueful grin. 'I knew your mother, Julie. Worked with her actually. Back in the old days.'

Marcus could hear the blood rushing in his ears and his face flushing. 'You...worked with my mother? *Here*?'

The CO leaned forward. 'Yes. Here, in Belfast. I can see this is a bit of a shock to you and completely understand why. You're probably wondering why I didn't tell you sooner, but the truth is, I only just worked it out after our chat the other afternoon.'

Marcus could feel his mouth drying up and took a swig of the tepid coffee. 'How...?'

'I was MRF. Military Reaction Force? Our Unit's predecessors back in the seventies. We were only operational for a few years when it was a bit like the wild west here. But your mother was one of us. One of the very few women in the Force actually. That was what she was awarded her BEM for. I don't recall the specific action but she was operating, like the rest of us, under Natural Cover in republican West Belfast.'

Marcus shook his head. 'Why have I never heard this before? Did my Dad know?'

'Probably not. None of us told our partners what we were really doing out here. We couldn't; Official Secrets Act and all that. I told my girlfriend that I was a courier, delivering documents between bases in civilian cars and that's why I had long hair and an earring. I imagine your mother probably told your father a similar cover story.'

Marcus felt a bizarre sensation of detachment as he listened to his CO talking about his mother as an undercover intelligence officer. *This can't be right.* 'Sir, you're sure it's *my* mum, Julie Myers, Women's Royal Army Corps?'

'Marcus, you won't remember it, but we've met before; I was at your mum's funeral in Watford. You couldn't have been more than what? Five? Six? I would have been in uniform and had a haircut and a shave so probably just looked like every other soldier who was there.'

Marcus sank back in the chair. 'Bloody hell sir...I can't believe this. This is the first time that...' he felt his throat tighten as the emotions kicked in. He cleared his throat and collected his thoughts. 'Please sir, go on.'

The CO nodded and smiled. 'Your mother was highly thought of you know. Very talented operator and in fact, still credited with being the reason our laundry operation was so fully accepted in the republican estates.' He saw Marcus frown in confusion. 'Ah, I see you're not familiar with the work of the MRF. Again, it was all very tightly controlled for obvious reasons but let me run you through some of our operations, so you get an idea of the incredible work your mother was carrying out.'

For the next half hour, Marcus listened in silence as his CO briefed him on the work that his mum had been involved in. He was stunned to learn that she played a key role in the deployment of the Four-Square Laundry; an intelligence front that collected dirty laundry from households and analysed the clothing for traces of weapons or explosives before returning them cleaned and pressed to the unsuspecting customer. He learned that she'd been very proficient at CME; Covert Methods of Entry, or lock-picking to the layman. She had gained access to the hardest republican areas by walking straight past armed IRA checkpoints pushing a pram and smoking a cigarette as she stomped by, the perfect picture of the harassed new mother. The CO paused and looked at Marcus intently.

'There's more if you think you're up to it, or I'm happy to stop and answer any questions?'

'No, please, go on Sir?'

You're sure?'

'Positive.'

'Very well. Your mother wasn't just natural cover and surveillance Marcus; she was also an effective soldier. Another, even less publicised role of the MRF was to shoot on sight terrorists that were cleared targets. Fighting them the way they fought us. Killing them in their own territory where they felt untouchable. And your mother was good at this too. Didn't flinch or shy away from the dark work. I worked with her personally on several of these operations and I know for a fact she'd already had a couple of kills under her belt by that time.'

Marcus reeled from the revelations. 'My mother did this? She took out terrorists on the street?'

The CO nodded. 'You have to understand Marcus, it was a completely different war back then. The streets here were brutal and there was no quarter asked or given on either side. The violence was horrific and getting worse. The MRF was created to do what conventional means had failed to; disrupt the IRA and stop the violence by taking the war to them in their own territory.'

Marcus could not reconcile the image of the cheerful, bubbly blonde and the cold-blooded killer to whom his CO referred. *My mum*? He leaned forward in the chair and put his head in his hands, letting out a deep breath. He lifted his head back up and met the gaze of his CO. 'Were you there when she died, sir?'

The CO shook his head. 'No Marcus, I wasn't. My team was on a foot-follow in the city centre that day.'

'Is there anyone you know who was with her?'

'No. Everyone on the laundry Op that day was killed in the crash unfortunately. We couldn't take it in; four of our unit wiped out in a bloody accident? Unbelievable.'

'Why was I never told any of this?'

'The MRF was disbanded officially at the end of seventy-three Marcus. It was reconfigured into the Special Reconnaissance Unit and the Force Research Unit and given far more direction and accountability. The MRF archives will never be released into the public domain to protect the sensitivity of the work and the people who carried it out. That includes the senior officers and ministers who signed off on it at the time. Although in fairness, a lot of these people have passed on as time catches up with us.' He paused and studied Marcus's reaction before standing up. 'Stay there, I'm going to get us a drink. I think we could both use one.'

When he returned, he placed a glass in front of Marcus with a generous measure of whisky before taking his seat.

He raised his glass. 'To your mother, Julie Myers. One hell of an Operator.'

Marcus lifted his own glass. 'To mum.'

Both men were quiet for several moments before Marcus spoke.

'This feels...surreal sir. Like the woman I've carried around in my head for all these years isn't the same woman you're talking about. I know she *is*, that much is obvious, but it's just...incredible really.'

'I can't imagine what you must be feeling Marcus, but I felt obligated to tell you what I knew. There's less and less of us old MRF hands as the years go by and someday, not too far from now, there will be none of us left who were there. That's why I wanted you to know that your mother was an exceptional woman Marcus. Very exceptional.'

'Are you the only one left who's still serving sir?'

The CO shook his head. 'Not exactly. Our friend from the Security Service, Jonathan, was with the MRF for a while, but he worked in a different team and we never really saw much of each other. He's never seen fit to mention it, so I've never bothered. He probably wants to keep it quiet from his elders and betters, strikes me as not too keen to be associated with his military background. Prick.'

Marcus laughed at the unexpected profanity and took a sip of the whisky. 'Yeah, he didn't come across as a fan of ours.'

'Convert turned zealot Marcus. All too common I'm afraid to say.' He looked at his watch. 'Right, I've pushed a lot of commitments to the side today, so I need to get back to work and back on track.' He stood and extended his hand. 'I'm glad I did this Marcus. I feel much better just knowing you're aware of the crucial role your mother played here.'

Marcus shook the Colonel's hand. 'I'm glad too sir. Stunned, if I'm honest, but still glad.'

The CO turned to leave but paused, facing Marcus once again. 'Look, Marcus, if you're interested and give me your word that you'll be discreet, I might be able to get you access to some of the MRF archives. It would be read-only of course, no note-taking or photocopying, but you might find some specific reports regarding your mother's operations and actions.'

'Bloody hell sir, that would be brilliant.'

'Okay, leave it with me. I need to speak to a man who owes me a favour or two. In fact, you've met him; Colin Woods, TCG?' Marcus nodded. 'He can access the archives at Palace Barracks, so I'll give him a call and set it up.'

With that, his CO departed and Marcus sat down again, picking up his glass and sipping at the whisky as he came to terms with the knowledge that his mother had been a completely different woman from the one he'd remembered. Mixed emotions of pride in her accomplishments, and sorrow that he would never be able to share this with her, flooded him and he felt his eyes well up with tears. Rubbing them with his sleeve, he downed the whisky and stood, looking around the deserted Mess and wondering what the hell to do with himself now.

CHAPTER 25

DUNDALK HARBOUR, COUNTY LOUTH, REPUBLIC OF IRELAND

The sea was slight, which as far as Joe was concerned, was a bonus. He'd never spent much time near the water and couldn't really see the attraction. As the trawler sailed past the headland, he sipped on his coffee as he contemplated what the next few days held in store for him. He hadn't dared try the usual routes back into the North; had no doubt that after Mulgrew's escape and debrief by the security forces, even the unused Border Crossing Points would be covered.

The maritime option was something that PIRA used on rare occasions and was only ever sanctioned at PAC level in order to retain the capability without compromising it. The last time it had been used was the year before when the PAC had deployed several individuals to the mainland of Britain to set up another bombing cell in London. Joe knew that Kieran Mulgrew had no knowledge of the shipping connection as it had never been made public to anyone outside the PAC or the London team. And even if the tout had overheard it at some point, it would be very difficult for anyone to pinpoint the exact ship and timings that PIRA would be using. Joe had shaved, cut his hair, and was also wearing glasses in an attempt to match the photograph on his false documentation that showed him as being a Daniel McLaughlin from County Kildare.

He would be taken ashore on a small inflatable just north of Donaghadee, where a pick-up had been arranged. Joe knew the risks in returning to the North, but his alibi could be checked and would hold, the family back in Keady well-briefed in what to say in the event that Joe was lifted for questioning regarding his absence. He would, of course, be held due to Kieran Mulgrew's testimony, but proving Joe's involvement was another matter entirely. That said, he had no intention of getting caught and was confident that if he could make it to the pick-up point, he would be safe. He'd thought about remaining in the South and trying to plan the killing of the tout from the relative safety of the Republic, but he knew that his presence in the North was expected. Demanded even.

As the trawler turned its bow to change course, Joe thought about how close he was to finishing Mulgrew and bringing the operation to an end. He needed to do this. Needed to see it through to the death of Kieran Mulgrew. Once that had been achieved, the PAC and GHQ could get back to business as usual. This high-level tout that Colm had been obsessing over would finally be dealt with and

PIRA could move on. He tightened the collar of his heavy jacket around his neck as the chill of the wind started to bite. One of the deckhands walked past and gave him a brief nod, uninterested in who Joe was or what his business involved. This was a tried and tested crew with a strong allegiance to the IRA but also paid very well for their assistance and their silence. He looked at his watch and decided to head below for a couple of hours kip before the pick-up.

～

The small outboard motor made very little sound as the inflatable boat carried Joe through the darkness and towards the shore. He couldn't see any sign of life on the beach as they approached and he wondered for a brief moment if they had landed in the right spot. He turned to the crew member at the stern and was about to ask as much when the man pointed with his finger. Joe turned back and scanned the foreshore where he saw a small red circle of light moving around. He recognised this as the signal he'd been told to look for and turned back to the crew member and gave him the thumbs-up to show he was happy to proceed. As the boat made its way into the shallows, Joe grabbed his false documents from the jacket pocket and held them in his hands. While he was reasonably sure everything was going to plan, he couldn't risk being caught with false identity papers if his pick-up had somehow been compromised. He grabbed the small rope to his front as the boat suddenly accelerated and rode up the beach, the bottom scraping along the sand. The crew member was occupied holding the engine out of the shallow water and it was left to Joe to decide if he was happy to commit. Straining his eyes to see in the gloom, he watched as a figure approached, preceded by a small red disc of light on the sand in front of them. A lean individual with long hair and a beard approached the boat, shone the red torch just short of the bow, and flicked the light on and off three times. Joe turned to the crew member behind him.

'Okay, we're good here *mo chara*. Thanks again for all the help.' The man didn't reply, and Joe stepped out of the boat and on to the sand where the individual stood. He was about to say something when the man indicated with his head that Joe should follow him. They walked along the sand for a few minutes then the man led them through a small path between the dunes and out into a gravel car park where a van was waiting with the engine running. The man reached the van first and pulled the side door open, stepping to one side and waiting for Joe. Without hesitation, Joe climbed into the dark, cavernous space and took a seat as the door closed behind him, leaving him in total darkness. He felt the weight of the van change as the man got into the front, closed the door and then they were moving, the crunch of gravel under the tyres the only real sound that Joe could hear. He lay his head back on the seat and closed his eyes. He just wanted this whole situation to be over so that he could go back to business as usual without having to have eyes in the back of his head every time he went anywhere. And it would be over soon, of that he had no doubt. While he might feel safe and sound in the military wing of a hospital, Kieran Mulgrew was a dead man walking; he just didn't know it yet. And with the team, planning, and support that was going in against him, Mulgrew would probably *never* know. He'd just be dead.

The van's movement beneath him changed and he could feel the vehicle accelerating and realised they must now be on a main road. Joe thought about the next meeting he would have, where the details of the plan would be discussed, examined and assessed to be as good as they could be. There was no margin for error on this one. The plan was sound and had the added bonus of knowing Mulgrew's movements in advance, which was going to be a key factor in the success of the operation. The Brits wouldn't be expecting PIRA to carry out a hit on a tout that was being moved, wouldn't believe that they could get such protected information. And that was the ace up Joe's sleeve. The last card he would play in this deadly game of cat and mouse with Mulgrew and the security forces.

The last card he *could* play.

CHAPTER 26

PALACE BARRACKS, HOLYWOOD

Marcus tossed the magazine back on to the pile on the coffee table and looked at his watch. Colin had arranged to meet him here ten minutes ago but still there was no sign of the policeman. He was about to get up and grab another plastic cup of what was criminally mislabelled as coffee when the door opened and Colin walked in, an apologetic smile greeting Marcus.

'Marcus, very, very sorry my man. Got a phone call I had to take just as I was leaving there.' He extended his hand and they shook.

'No worries Colin, I know how it goes.'

The policeman nodded and opened a door behind Marcus. 'Shall we?'

Marcus walked alongside Colin through a corridor, the walls adorned with military plaques and paintings. They came to another door with a restricted access sign on it and Colin used his badge to swipe them in. After they descended a staircase, Colin stopped at another door and picked up a telephone handset that was mounted on the wall. He gave his name over the line and an instant later a buzzing noise sounded, and Colin pushed the door open. When he followed him in, Marcus saw Colin writing on a booking-in sheet just as he was approached by an older man from behind the mesh grille.

'Colin Woods. Not often we see your uneducated arse in these parts. Didn't even know you could read.'

Marcus watched as the door was opened. Colin laughed and shook hands with the man. 'Billy Boy, how the devil?'

The other man replied in his deep voice and Fermanagh accent. 'All good mate, all good. What can I do you for today?'

Colin explained that Marcus needed to have a trawl through some archived files but didn't have the clearance himself, so Colin had signed him in to facilitate this. The man nodded and turned a key in a second large, mesh door and pulled it open, looking at Marcus.

'Well, don't stand on ceremony young 'un. In ye come.' When Marcus entered, the door was closed behind him. Colin addressed the other policeman.

'Billy, I've got some people to see here so I'm around for a couple of hours. If you page me when Marcus is done, I'll come back down and sign him out mate.'

'No problem Colin, I'll do just that.'

Marcus raised a hand and returned the policeman's wave as Colin turned to leave.

'Marcus, hope you find what you're after and don't

rush. Like I said, I've got a couple of hours here.'

As Colin left, Marcus turned and saw the other man holding out his hand. 'Marcus, I'm Billy Smith and I run the archives here after a wee blast from our Provo friends saw me pensioned out a couple of years back.'

Marcus now saw that the man favoured the right side of his body as he moved. Conscious of staring, he looked up and met Billy's gaze. 'Nice to meet you Billy. Look, I'm interested in anything you have from the MRF, but in particular, whatever MRF documents you know of relating to 1973?'

The policeman raised his eyebrows. 'Now *that's* going back a wee while. We definitely have MRF reports but as for the year, I couldn't tell you. There's been a lot of interest in these recently from Sinn Fein, but we've managed to keep their snouts out of it for the time being. Come on, I'll show you where they are.' Marcus followed the policeman as he limped between rows of filing cabinets and computer desks until they reached a small room at the end. Billy opened it and as Marcus entered, he saw a dozen or so tall filing cabinets stacked against the walls. Billy proceeded to unlock several of these and remove the locking bars which he placed to one side. Once done, he turned back to Marcus.

'That's all the MRF files in these three cabinets. If you need anything just come and find me but otherwise make yourself at home.'

Marcus nodded his thanks and turned back to the cabinets as he heard Billy close the door behind him. Taking off his jacket, he draped it over one of the chairs beside a large desk. He could feel a sense of excitement building at the thought of actually reading about his mother's intelligence operations back in the seventies. It still struck him as surreal to be thinking about his mum as a special operations' soldier working undercover in the back streets of republican Belfast. Realising he was wasting precious time, he turned his attention back to the cabinets and, with no other means of prioritising them, chose the one farthest to his left. Opening the top drawer, he was presented with bundles of paper folders marked with months and dates. These began in 1971, so he closed this drawer and moved on to the third cabinet, opening the top drawer and letting out a small exclamation of triumph as his hunch proved correct.

This drawer contained files from January to March 1973 and he removed the first folder and carried it over to the desk where he sat down, undid the flap and pulled out the first document. It was an old intelligence report, the paper slightly yellowed with age and clearly produced on a typewriter, giving details about the shooting of a Kevin Dwyer in Whiterock. The report indicated that Dwyer had been identified by MRF officers, who were named on the report by their initials, challenged and shot when they believed he had been reaching for a weapon. The report was very short, blunt in its language and straight to the point. Putting it to one side, Marcus picked up the next report and opened it, noting the same typewritten format. This one concerned an MRF operator being compromised outside the Rock Bar and battering a couple of locals with his pistol until another team swooped in with a vehicle to extract him. Marcus raised his eyebrows as he noted the initials of the operator concerned: SC. *Stuart Coull?* Could it have been his CO, back in the days when, in his own words, it had been like the wild west? Marcus replaced this report and took the next one behind it.

He was well into the thick folder of reports when he encountered the first record of his mother's activities. Halfway through the January 1973 archives, he found a report regarding a bugging operation that had been compromised when a neighbour heard the MRF team inserting into the target house. A hostile crowd had gathered outside the house, blocking the MRF operators inside until an IRA gun team arrived. The IRA men turned up and ordered the MRF team to come out of the building and surrender their weapons. The team inside could not get any communications with their Headquarters and were running out of options. Operator *JM*, face covered by a balaclava to protect her identity, walked out of the front door with her Sterling held out to one side. She was ordered to drop the gun and advance forward. As she neared the gunmen, she threw herself to one side, drew her pistol and engaged. She killed two gunmen immediately and the distraction allowed the team inside to extract from the building. Operator *JM* had then chased down and killed a third gunman and recovered his weapon from the street.

On her return to the target house, the team had established communications with Headquarters and a QRF was deployed to assist in their extraction from the scene. There was an annex attached to this document and Marcus gave a grunt of surprise when he recognised what it was. A citation for a British Empire Medal. The official write-up for a bravery award for the courage and heroism of Operator *JM*. He had just read the reason for the faded photograph of a happy family standing outside Buckingham Palace in 1973. Mixed emotions of pride, respect, and loss surged through him as he came to terms with the person his mother really was.

Marcus pored over the documents, oblivious to time, as he devoured each and every report that mentioned his mother. Some were mundane, a brief note that she had been part of a team operating in an area, while others were more detailed. From what he could see from the reports, his mother had taken a lead role in the laundry operation in early '73 as well as carrying out her other duties. As he trawled through the documents, Marcus was impressed by the results that the maverick unit his mother belonged to had achieved. Their methods were a combination of creative and aggressive policies with no idea seeming to be too whacky or lethal. He reflected that, back then, the MRF was probably just making it up as they went along, with no formal guidance or templates to follow in their intelligence collection efforts.

It still surprised him however, when he encountered reports mentioning the shooting of IRA men on the streets of Belfast by the MRF. The language in these reports was reduced to nothing more than a factual record of the incident with no mention of fallout, public perception or negative consequences. As he progressed through the year's reports, Marcus noted an increase in these shootings and wondered what the reason for that could be. Once he'd finished with the intelligence reports from 1973, he replaced them in the cabinet and was about to tell Billy he'd finished when he decided to look at what was in the last drawer of the MRF archives. He accessed the drawer and pulled out the first folder, opening it up and grunting with surprise as he took in the contents: MRF Personnel files.

He was looking at an old file of an individual named Robert Sneddon, a soldier from the Royal Scots. The small, passport-sized, black and white photograph stapled to the corner of the document showed a long-haired, taciturn-looking individual. It was a typical soldier's file, not dissimilar to the ones currently used and a smile came to Marcus's face as he thought how little some things had changed. The smile dropped when he realised that there would be a file in here with his mother's details. He replaced Sneddon's documents and began rifling through the other folders, eventually finding what he was searching for. He took the file to the desk, sat down and stared at the small monochrome image for several minutes.

She looked very serious in the photograph; no smile or levity of any sort apparent. But then, he supposed that was always the way of it when you were photographed for an official purpose. His eyes watered as memories came to him of her laugh and sense of humour and he wondered if she'd had to curb these tendencies for the photograph to be taken. Reluctant to do so, but well aware that time was running out, he tore his eyes away from the image and began reading his mother's file. She was a Corporal in the WRAC when she joined MRF in early 1972 and had passed the selection course with excellent results *for a member of the fairer sex*. Marcus shook his head at the outdated language but felt a small burst of pride at her accomplishments. She was reported as having particularly good surveillance and shooting skills and had been recommended for immediate deployment in the field.

There was then a summary of the operations she had been engaged upon and her roles within them, including the action where she'd been awarded her BEM. Turning the pages on the report, he found himself looking at the professional development section where her performance was documented in a series of notes covering three-month periods. Again, these were all exemplary and she had been recommended for promotion to Sergeant when operational commitments allowed her to return to England to attend the course. As he turned to the last page, Marcus saw that a further sheet of paper was stapled to this and he read it through, struggling to understand what it meant.

It was dated November 1973 and covered a personal interview with her Commanding Officer. The prose that the document was written in seemed strange in comparison to the other reports he'd read. Gone was the straightforward, factual language to be replaced by ambiguous terms and generalisations. From what he could retrieve from the garbled narrative, his mother had sought a private interview as she had concerns regarding an operational matter. It appeared that she had witnessed something she felt was wrong and felt obligated to report it. Her Commanding Officer's comment stated that ...*JM believes she observed unsanctioned operational activities. JM misunderstood situation and realises error. JC made aware and will move WHIPLASH to alternative locstat.*

Marcus stopped reading and tried to work out what was being said here. *What was WHIPLASH?* Taking an educated guess, he assumed it was the name of an operation, the capitalised emphasis still used today for formal operational naming conventions. And who was *JC*? To Marcus, the CO's comments seemed to contradict one another in that, his mother had made a mistake about what she'd seen but an operation was being moved because of this? It made no sense. He read the document again but gained no further information. Inspiration struck and he went back to the personnel files and looked for anybody with the initials JC. *Nothing.* Maybe JC wasn't a part of MRF, could have been from another section of the military. He chewed on his lip as the puzzle bothered him further. He stooped and opened the bottom drawer and was rewarded with a series of folders squashed together with tags attached for easy identification. Marcus smiled as he took in the untidy documents crammed into the drawer, each little tag identifying it by the pre-fix that told him he'd found what he was looking for: Op; Operation.

There were a lot of them, probably covering the MRF's entire operational history in the three years that it functioned. Again, conscious of the time, he rifled through the folders' contents, looking for the one he wanted, but found no *Op WHIPLASH*. Sighing, he then went to the front of the drawer and began pulling out every folder, opening them up and examining the reports within for any mention of *WHIPLASH*. Some of the folders were in poor condition through age and the fact that they'd been rammed together in the small drawer and as he pulled them out, the tags would fall off or photographs would spill out. His motivation started to wane by the time he was two-thirds of the way through the drawer, but he carried on, determined to search every folder. He'd just pulled out another folder to check when the name tag fell from it and into the bottom of the drawer. Muttering a curse, he placed the folder on the floor beside the others he'd checked and went back into the drawer to fish out the name tag. He noticed there were half a dozen or so tags in the bottom of the drawer along with the one he'd just dropped. He scooped them out and examined each one in turn. Three of them matched with folders he'd already looked at and remembered the operational name from and one didn't. He was unaware that he'd been holding his breath until he exhaled a loud expulsion of air as he continued to stare at the small, hand-written label in his hand.

Op WHIPLASH.

CHAPTER 26

MUSGRAVE PARK HOSPITAL, BELFAST

Kieran Mulgrew pushed the empty plate away on the small table that the nurses had placed over his bed. He winced at the pain in his bandaged hand as he moved and reminded himself that he'd need to ask for some more painkillers. The doctors had told him that he'd never regain full use of his hand due to the trauma that had been inflicted on the nerves and tendons. That had come as no real surprise to him, the excruciating agony that he'd endured during and after the torture to his hand a clear enough indicator.

He hadn't seen Marcus since their escape from Pat McCusker's farm but knew that he would be up at some point to visit him. Kieran shook his head slightly and a small smile came to him as he thought back to Marcus's one-man rescue operation. *Ballsy bastard*. He'd been worried that their story wouldn't hold up, but it seemed that they'd succeeded in having their version of events accepted. Earlier that morning, Kieran had been visited by a British Military

Intelligence officer and a man called Roger from the Security Service; MI5.

The army man had told Kieran that, obviously, he would no longer be working as an agent and therefore decisions had to be made regarding his future and safety. He explained that this was now out of the military's hands and rested with MI5. Roger had taken over the conversation and explained what he called the Resettlement process. Kieran had assumed that something like this would happen as he couldn't very well be released back on to the streets of Belfast and expect to live beyond twenty-four hours. Roger briefed Kieran on how the Resettlement process worked and what he could expect from it. As the MI5 officer was filling him on the details, Kieran had felt a flutter of panic at the thought of leaving his home, and West Belfast, forever. The city was his life. He'd only ever ventured away from it for the odd holiday but even at that, couldn't wait to get back and catch up with the *craic* that he'd missed while away. The idea came to him that he could approach the IRA and bluff his way out, tell them that he'd just been approached by the Bits but had given them nothing and that under Joe's torture, he'd made up stuff just to make the pain stop. He knew of course, how ridiculous this notion was and soon discounted it, the realisation finally sinking in that he would never see Belfast again.

Roger told Kieran that he'd be resettled in England, in a city where his presence wouldn't be of any note. He'd be set up with a house that was purchased for him and a lump sum of money to get him started. He went on to explain that the Security Service would monitor him and be in regular contact over the first few months to make sure he was doing okay. Roger cautioned Kieran that he wouldn't find it easy. In his experience, former IRA men struggled to cope with the vast number of issues suddenly thrust upon them. Anonymity and loss of status apparently, were issues that took some time to adjust to. As Roger pointed out, Kieran had been known and respected as a veteran member of the IRA for over twenty years but now would be just another bloke in the street. No more walking into The Slieve and having your back slapped by the men you passed, a pint of the black already waiting for you on the bar. No respect from neighbours other than that given for remembering to put your bins out on the right day.

There would be the temptation to come back, or at least call people back home and ask how things were going. Roger emphasised that Kieran could never do this. He mentioned the Frank Hegarty case which Kieran was familiar with. Poor old Franco; lured back home by the false promises of the PIRA leadership only to wind up brutally tortured and killed. No, there was no coming back from this. Roger also told him that he would struggle to find, and keep, gainful employment. Most resettled agents found this difficult. He asked Kieran when the last time was that he'd held down a full-time job, and Kieran had to think hard, laughing when the answer came to him. It had been over twenty years before in a butcher's shop. Roger had nodded and told him that slotting back into the nine to five grind would be a difficult obstacle to overcome. He'd gone on to say that the money would go a long way to helping with this.

Because of the length of time he'd worked as an agent, he would be paid a considerable sum of money, close to two hundred thousand pounds. As his accommodation would be bought outright for him, this meant that he only need concern himself with living expenses. He was cautioned however, that some people struggled to cope with such vast sums of money and frittered the payment away through frivolous purchases, high-living and gambling.

The MI5 officer had then covered the security issues. He was blunt in this, informing Kieran that PIRA would actively look for him for a long time. He reassured Kieran that they had never found a resettled agent but there had been occasions where these agents had compromised their locations through breaking the rules, calling home when drunk or lonely. Roger put it to Kieran that as long as he exercised common sense and didn't draw attention to himself, there was no reason why he couldn't enjoy a comfortable and peaceful life.

Kieran had asked where they would resettle him, and Roger had informed him that a team on the mainland was looking at options now and he would be informed in due course. He'd also asked when he would be moved across and was told that, because of his injuries, it would be a couple of days before they were happy to move him from the hospital. They informed Kieran that he would have ongoing treatment and physiotherapy for his hand at a secure location in the UK, so he shouldn't worry about that too much. It was a good point; Kieran hadn't even thought about the ongoing treatment for his injuries. Now that the subject had been broached however, he was glad that the MI5 officer was already on top of it. Kieran knew that as soon as he was off the scene, the IRA would send word to its members, supporters and associates on the mainland to watch for anyone matching Kieran's injuries turning up at hospitals or clinics.

With that, the men had wrapped up the meeting, promising to be in touch soon. Roger had informed Kieran that his next move would be in a couple of days when he would be taken to a secure military barracks in preparation for his journey to the mainland. He'd be there for a couple of days while a lot of the administrative details were put in place. This would also give Kieran some time to recover outside of the hospital environment and come to terms with his new circumstances. The military officer wished Kieran the best and told him that Marcus would be visiting at some point, which gave Kieran a small lift in his spirits after the sombre nature of the meeting. The men had said their final goodbyes and left him to his thoughts.

Kieran picked up the small plastic tumbler and took a drink of the tepid water, thinking about how he was going to adjust to a new life, alone and in a strange city. He had no doubts that he would find it difficult. West Belfast had been his life. It was strange the way the place and its people got their hooks into you. Kieran didn't know anyone who wanted to leave the area. Even those PIRA members who were OTR, On The Run in the South, usually risked everything just to get back to Belfast at some point. He supposed it was a legacy of the siege mentality, all nationalists rallying together to defend their homes against the loyalists and then their streets against the Brits. His eyes began to water as the realisation hit home that it was over for him. Everything he had ever known was now history. He didn't want to live in some big English city, another anonymous face in the crowd. No friends, no social life, suspicious of everyone asking you about yourself. But he didn't want to be lying dead, naked and bound on a wet road in South Armagh either.

He looked up as an orderly walked into the room to clear his tray away. The man smiled and Kieran returned it although he felt that the man could use a bloody good haircut and a shave. The man whistled as he worked and loaded Kieran's tray onto a trolley and as he bent to close the trolley door, Kieran noticed a small earring and frowned with distaste. It seemed to him that standards everywhere were slipping. Surely in a hospital, particularly a military hospital, someone should have gotten a grip of a lad like this turning up scruffy and unkempt? *Mind you, he is only the cleaner. Not like he's going to be operating on anybody.* As the man wheeled the trolley from the room, Kieran let out a sigh as the thought struck him that he was in no position to dictate standards to anyone and would have to rein these impulses in if he didn't want to draw attention to himself. He picked up the bed control handle and lowered himself slightly, feeling a wave of tiredness overwhelm him. As sleep came quickly, his last thoughts centred around the new life he could expect. He tried to find the positives that would outweigh the reality of looking over his shoulder for the rest of his life. But as he dozed off, he came to the conclusion that these were very hard to find.

CHAPTER 27

SESKINORE FOREST, COUNTY TYRONE, NORTHERN IRELAND

The two men grunted with effort as they removed the large plastic barrel from the hole in the earth. The third man turned around and cautioned them to keep the noise down, nervously fingering the trigger guard of the AR15 as he did so. He turned his attention back to the darkness between the trees, vigilant for any sign of movement or strange noises. The luminous green view provided by his night vision goggles highlighted the forest around him and comforted him that, should anyone come into the area, he would see them well before they reached the hide. He glanced at his watch and saw that they were making good time. They only needed the four rifles from this hide, and they were all in the same barrel so they would be reasonably quick in getting them out and re-sealing the cache.

The occasional sound came from behind him as the men removed the weapons from the plastic barrel and wrapped them in blankets to muffle any noises during the future transit. He recognised the sound of the barrel being returned to the hole and the pallet and cover replaced. The soft scrape of the shovels told him that the loose earth was being layered back on top in preparation for the turfs that would cover and conceal the hide location. After some time, he heard movement and felt a tap on his arm. Without turning around, he brought the rifle up into his shoulder and began moving forward, leading the pair through the maze of conifers towards the track, all highlighted in the green luminescence of his NVGs. The men stayed close; their vision practically useless now they were under the canopy of the trees.

He'd been surprised to get the call and the tasking for the weapons. With the ceasefire in place less than a year, he couldn't imagine what these guns were going to be used for. Whatever it was, he knew that it was important. As Quartermaster for PIRA's East Tyrone Brigade, he had been contacted by the Army Council directly and ordered to get the weapons out of the hides and moved to a forward position. Tonight's operation was just one of three currently happening. He had a team lifting the big Barrett sniper rifle from its hide in a farmhouse in the Sperrins, and another getting the RPGs from the cache in Pomeroy. Usually a coordinated lift like this would be preceded by a fair amount of warning to allow the QM to plan the weapons' removals, but not this time. He'd been given a day to get his shit together and get back to the PAC with his answer. Which, of course, had been yes. He knew he had a reputation as one of the IRA's most effective Quartermasters and thought that this was probably the reason that the PAC had approached him. He also knew that whatever the weapons were for, it wasn't going to be happening in Tyrone or Fermanagh, as they were heading east once they left his care.

He stepped out of the cover of the forest and on to a track. Scanning the pathway in both directions, he satisfied himself that it was clear, then led the two men down the small incline. Ahead of him he could make out the shape of the vehicle, and studied it closely as they approached, weapon up and on aim, ready to deal with any problems. But there were none. He opened the driver's door and relaxed, climbing in and starting the engine as the men behind him secured the rifles into the hidden compartment. The boot was closed softly and the two men climbed into the back seat and fastened the seat belts. He put the vehicle in gear and crept along the track, using his night-vision goggles to navigate them through the dark. After several minutes the forest track ended and joined a tarmac road. The QM stopped the vehicle, removed the goggles and turned on the car headlights. He put the vehicle back into gear and moved off, picking up speed and heading south towards Ballygawley where he would hook-up with the scout car for the journey east. His passengers were silent as he navigated through the small, winding roads and he thought once again about what target could be so important that PIRA would risk breaking the ceasefire for. In truth, the Quartermaster didn't care; he'd never supported the current path to peace, like many from East Tyrone preferring to bomb the Brits out of the country rather than negotiate with them. He hoped that, whatever was happening with these weapons, it would bring the conflict back to a war footing. He and his boys would be happy with that. *More* than happy.

CHAPTER 28

TCG, BELFAST

Colin Woods pointed to the large-scale map in front of him. 'So, that's our operational remit, Marcus, but, as with most things, we overlap quite a lot with other regions.' Marcus nodded, interested to learn how the various intelligence agencies were tasked and coordinated throughout greater Belfast. He and Colin had got on well since their visit to Palace Barracks. Colin had been stunned when Marcus filled him in on the information he'd found out about his mother. He'd asked Marcus a lot of questions and been genuinely interested in the situation. Like Marcus, he had been puzzled by the fact that the *Op WHIPLASH* file had been missing but couldn't really offer any new ideas as to what may have happened to it. He'd taken Marcus to lunch at a country pub in Hillsborough and continued the discussion there. As they were leaving, he'd invited Marcus to accompany him back to TCG where he would get the analysts to have a dig around their own archives to see if there was anything relating to *WHIPLASH*. Marcus had been surprised but grateful for the offer and found himself warming even more to the policeman.

A young Police Analyst entered the operations room and handed Colin a piece of paper. He read it, shrugged, thanked the analyst and sent them away. Turning to Marcus, he gave a shake of his head.

'Sorry Marcus. All *WHIPLASH* files were retained years ago by the Security Service and have been secured away under Crown Privilege so they're unlikely to see the light of day for another fifty years or so. Sorry mate.'

'Don't worry about it, Colin. Didn't really have my hopes up as it was so long ago now.'

The policeman sighed and nodded his agreement. 'Yeah, unfortunately it's quite common with a lot of sensitive operations and actions; don't want the general public knowing all the skulduggery that went on until the people that carried it out are all dead and gone.'

Marcus smiled at the humour and followed Colin as he continued with his tour of the building, introducing him to various personalities as they passed in corridors or the open doors of offices. As they walked along a ground floor passage, Marcus could see some activity going on around a room at the end. Colin caught his look.

'Weekly meeting of the grown-ups. Sometimes here, other times Knock or Palace. All the adults together, working out how PIRA's going to wrong foot them this week and what they can do about it.'

As they approached the room, a familiar face entered the corridor from the external door and glanced at both men before smiling.

'Colin. And...Marcus, isn't it? How are you both?' The MI5 officer extended his hand and shook both men's.

Colin replied that they were well, and he was just giving Marcus a tour of the building while he was there. Marcus watched Jonathan nod and give a quick glance at his watch before speaking again.

'Good, good. Look, don't have time to dilly dally I'm afraid, but wouldn't mind five minutes of your time after this to bend your ear about something one of our Sources has given us recently.'

Colin nodded. 'Just give me a wee bell, Jonathan. I'm in all day today.'

With that the MI5 officer patted Colin's shoulder, smiled at Marcus then walked into the conference room, greeting several of the senior police officers inside. Colin indicated for Marcus to follow him and they took the stairs, heading on to the first floor and the smell of fresh coffee brewing. They entered a canteen area and Colin headed for a row of coffee percolators, grabbing a couple of mugs from the side and filling them up with the dark brew. He nodded towards a table and Marcus took a seat as Colin joined him. Both men were quiet for several moments before Colin spoke.

'You know, that time when your mum was with the MRF was a crazy time out here. There were a lot of shenanigans going on as we were all finding our feet on how to fight this war.'

'Yeah, my CO told me as much. He referred to it as the wild west.'

Colin laughed. 'Not a bad way of putting it at all. I was a young constable back then, just getting into covert operations and I'll tell you, it was mad some days. Even on the other side, the 'RA were getting to grips with who *they* were and what kind of war they wanted to fight.'

Marcus sipped at his coffee as the policeman continued. 'Did you ever hear of Operation DEMETRIUS Marcus?'

Marcus shook his head.

'Code name for internment. 1971. Where we rounded up anybody we thought was a bad apple and put them in jail. At the time, we thought it was a great initiative but now, I think that was one of the worst mistakes we made. We didn't have the intelligence back then, you see? We were putting away old men, young men, the entire male complement of families. The guilty and the innocent.' He paused and sipped at his coffee. 'I saw a big change in the IRA after that. Effectively, we radicalised the nationalist community through our grand scheme. Did the Provo's work for them. That's why we needed the MRF and the like to get *accurate* intelligence on the real bad guys in the community.'

Marcus cleared his throat. 'From what I hear though, MRF overstepped its boundaries, didn't they? Went beyond intelligence collection and were carrying out killings.'

Colin sighed. 'Yes, that's true. But it's important to remember that their activities were sanctioned Marcus, as incredible as that might seem to us today. But as I say, it was a different time back then, a bloodier war and we were all just trying to determine how we were going to fight it.'

There was a moment's quiet as each man reflected on his own thoughts. Marcus tried to imagine the world in which his mother had been operating in and respected her even more. A slight, English soldier conducting clandestine operations at the height of an insurgency against a formidable enemy. He still found it incredible. He was also disappointed that he hadn't managed to get his hands on whatever *Op WHIPLASH* was. He had a feeling it was quite important although he couldn't really say why. The thought crossed his mind that he could approach Jonathan from the Security Service and ask him what the chances were that he'd let Marcus access the file, but he discounted this almost immediately. He could see that Jonathan was a career civil servant and wouldn't go out of his way to assist the poorer cousins in the military unless it suited him. He sighed and drank more of his coffee as he decided to put the whole *WHIPLASH* issue to bed.

Colin looked at his watch. 'Here, Marcus. I've got to head off now mucker, there's an Op on tonight and I want a quick heads-up from the Det Boss before the guys arrive. Come on and I'll walk you out.'

Marcus took a final swig of his coffee and followed Colin out of the canteen and back down the stairs. As they entered the bottom corridor, he could see that the meeting had finished, and the senior officers were making their way outside. He saw Jonathan walking across the car park, stop and speak with a tall, long-haired, scruffy individual for a couple of moments. Jonathan then patted the man's shoulder and the man made his way towards the building as Jonathan continued walking over to the row of parked cars. Colin led Marcus to the side of the compound where Marcus had parked his own vehicle.

'What's the plans for the rest of the week Marcus? Got much on?'

'Bits and bobs, Colin. Still waiting to see if the Unit's going to keep me at Belfast or send me off to one of the other locations. Oh, and I'm off up to see GRANITE in the next couple of days as he's getting moved, so just want to say my goodbyes before he disappears.'

Colin nodded sympathetically. 'Aye, he seemed like one of the good ones. A real shame what he went through but he's getting out, and that's the important thing to remember here.'

They'd reached Marcus's car and shook hands with a commitment to make the next meeting a more social affair. As he drove out of the compound, Marcus realised that he'd quite enjoyed Colin's company. The policeman was very down to earth for someone of his rank and had a good sense of humour. He could see why his CO liked him. He was looking forward to sharing a few drinks with Colin and getting some stories from the bad old days of policing in

Northern Ireland. Exiting the main gate, Marcus immediately switched on, scanning the area around him for dickers; watchers who would note his car details and pass them on to the IRA or, even worse, be setting him up for an attack right now. He noted the vehicles on the road behind him and took a convoluted route to get him back on the main road. Satisfied that there was nobody following him, he relaxed a little and tuned into a local radio station as he made his way back to the Detachment. As he drove, he thought about the meeting he would have with GRANITE and felt a little sad at the prospect. He knew, of course, that Agents were merely assets; another tool for gathering intelligence, but GRANITE had been a loyal and trusted Agent for many years. Marcus had also liked the guy and could only imagine how difficult the next phase of GRANITE's life was going to be. But Colin was right; at least GRANITE would be out of the life and safe. And that's what Marcus had to remember. That, for the first time in all those years of working for Military Intelligence, GRANITE would be safe.

CHAPTER 28

MUSGRAVE PARK HOSPITAL, BELFAST

Kieran Mulgrew belched contentedly. His final breakfast in the hospital and not a bad one at that. The bacon especially, had been very good. He washed the greasy fare down with a large mug of sweet tea and thought about the day ahead. A big day for him as he was being moved to a safe house in a barracks somewhere. The RUC officer in charge had been in the day before and given him a quick chat about the move although it sounded simple enough. A team of specialist police officers would get him into an armoured Land Rover, and he'd be escorted safely down to wherever they were taking him. He'd asked where but the officer hadn't told him, citing security as his reason for not doing so. Kieran had been surprised at this, being in the Military Wing of the hospital but he supposed that you couldn't be too careful. Wouldn't be the first time PIRA had surprised the security forces by having someone on the inside.

And Marcus was coming up today to see him before he left. He'd miss Marcus and still felt emotional when he thought about the risk the soldier had taken at McCusker's farm that night. Kieran's eyes watered and he felt a wave of panic rising within him as the realisation that he would never see Belfast again sank in. It was all he'd ever really known, this dirty, damp, deranged city but it was in his veins, like all West Belfast men. When you'd come through the hell of the 1970s, survived the loyalist murder squads, gone to funeral after funeral of friends and neighbours, the city was *in* you. There was a real camaraderie among the people of West Belfast, born of adversity and suffering with a coping mechanism of black humour and banter. And he would miss it. *Badly*. He wiped his eyes with the sleeve of his gown as he heard a knock on the door and a female orderly came in to take his tray away. She gave him a quick smile which he returned, feigning happiness. She stepped back into the corridor and he heard her say something just as Marcus walked in.

Kieran smiled, a genuine grin this time and Marcus walked over to the bed and hugged his former Agent. As they separated, Marcus indicated with his head towards the departing orderly.

'Wasn't interrupting anything was I?'

Kieran laughed. 'Ha! Chance would be a fine thing Marcus. How are you, big man?'

Marcus took a seat beside the bed. 'I'm good, Kieran. All good. What about you? You ready for today?'

'Yeah. Bricking it a bit if I'm honest. Trying to tell myself it's all going to be okay.'

Marcus sat forward and looked him in the eye. 'Hey, it's *already* okay mate. Yeah? You're alive and about to start a new life where you'll be safe. Where the animals who tried to tear you apart in Monaghan will never find you. It's already okay.'

Kieran sighed. 'I know, I know. It's just that...you've no idea what it's like to think about turning your back on everything you've ever known and disappearing onto the mainland for the rest of your natural.'

Marcus nodded. 'That's true. I don't know what it's like. What I do know is that you've got a chance mate; a chance to start a new life. Have a go at something you've always wanted to do. There's not many of us get that opportunity and if I was you, I'd grab it by the balls.'

Kieran laughed. 'Yeah, I'll just have to keep telling myself that. *Grab it by the balls Kieran*! You're right Marcus, I've got to look at this as a new chance at a completely different life. Make the most of it.'

Marcus nodded and the pair were silent for several moments until Kieran spoke again.

'Why did you come back for me that night? I mean, you knew the odds were well against you and at best, you were giving up your career but more likely your life. So, why?'

Marcus answered with no hesitation. 'Because it was *right* Kieran. It was the right thing to do. I couldn't sit back, knowing where you were and what was happening to you because it was too *politically unacceptable* for us to mount an official rescue attempt. I couldn't have faced myself again if I hadn't at least tried.'

Kieran nodded. 'I'll never forget that Marcus. Never.'

Marcus laughed, lightening the mood. 'Neither will I! And I promise you this; that's the first and last time I'll try something as crazy as that!'

Kieran laughed and both men looked up as a uniformed RUC officer stood in the doorway. The man entered and explained he was the officer in charge of the move and that it was time for Kieran to get ready and collect up his belongings. Marcus stood and pushed the chair away from the bed to give Kieran some room. He moved towards the door and nodded at an orderly he recognised and felt a hand on his shoulder. Turning, he saw that the RUC officer was addressing him.

'You coming with us? Only I don't have you down on the flap-sheet.'

Kieran had gone into the small bathroom to change as Marcus answered. 'No, I was just up visiting. I'm Marcus, his Handler...well, former Handler now I suppose. Where are you taking him?'

'We're getting him down to Palace where he'll be for the next few days. I don't know what the plan is after that as Box will direct his movements from that point on.'

Marcus nodded. 'That's fine. I'll say cheerio when he comes out and I'll see if I can visit him while he's at Palace.'

The RUC officer nodded his agreement and spoke into his radio, letting someone know that he would be ready in five minutes. Marcus looked up as Kieran came back into the room, dressed in jacket and jeans with a small plastic bag. For a moment, Marcus felt emotional at the sad sight of his former agent leaving the only life he had ever known with a faded plastic bag containing a couple of toiletries and a dog-eared paperback. He walked over and embraced Kieran, feeling the man's emotions in the tightness with which he returned it. When they separated, Marcus held Kieran by the shoulders.

'Look mate, they've told me where you're going so I'll make some calls and get permission to come and see you over the next couple of days, okay?'

'That would be grand Marcus. I'd really like that pal.'

Marcus nodded. 'Okay. Look, relax, you're in good hands now. Enjoy your taxi ride and I'll catch up with you soonest. Promise.'

He could see the trepidation in the Agent's eyes and again, his heart went out to the man who'd devoted over twenty years of his life to saving others and was now reduced to a hunched form nervously clutching a supermarket carrier bag. Giving him a huge smile to cover his emotions, Marcus left the room and walked down the corridor towards the main entrance. When he opened the door of the ward, a team of burly, uniformed RUC officers looked up before going back to the magazines they were reading. Marcus signed out and walked out of the main entrance, taking a deep breath of the fresh air as he made his way towards the car park. There was a convoy of three

RUC Hotspurs; the armoured Land Rovers that the police used to patrol the streets of the city and Marcus realised that this was Kieran's transport. He unlocked his own car and got in, locking the doors automatically before turning on his covert radio and calling in to the Detachment. Marcus asked Zero if there were any changes to the morning's intelligence brief and was informed that everything remained the same. Content that he could drive the route that he'd chosen previously, Marcus started the car and eased out of the parking bay and towards the exit checkpoint.

CHAPTER 29

STOCKMAN'S LANE, BELFAST

The sniper crept forward and adjusted the length of the bipod legs before settling back behind the scope and focusing the sight. Joe Carluccio raised the binoculars and moved the focus ring until the junction of the road in the distance came into sharp relief. He lowered the binoculars and looked at the gunman lying on the table and covering the view from the window.

'How we doing?'

The man answered quietly, not moving from his position. 'Good. It's an easy shot. The AP will go right through it.'

Joe nodded and picked up the hand-held radio, checking the dials to see that it was still on the correct channel and setting. There was silence in the room, the only sounds coming from the busy traffic on their road and Boucher Road behind them as it filtered through the half-open window. He picked up the binoculars again and stared at the junction of Stockman's Lane and Musgrave Park Court.

He didn't need to, knew that he would get the call as soon as the vehicles approached the junction, but he had to do something to occupy his hands. Looking back down at the prone gunman, he ran through the plan once again, trying to identify any weaknesses or problems that he hadn't already foreseen.

The sniper would disable the first Hotspur with an Armour-Piercing round, an AP, from the Barrett .50 cal straight through the engine. The second team at Weston Drive would hit the rear vehicle of the convoy, taking out the front wheel with an RPG. The middle vehicle would have no choice but to drive through the ambush in order to escape and it would then be taken out by a coordinated assault from the third team and the sniper. The sniper would wait until the middle vehicle was in the killing ground then he would take out the engine before killing the RUC men in the front. They knew that there were two more RUC officers in the back with the tout so the RPG team would hit the Hotspur with a couple of warheads while the sniper fired through the weakened armour. Nobody was going to survive that. He jumped slightly as a voice came out of the radio.

One hundred to.

Joe grabbed the radio and pressed the transmit button. 'All teams, that's one hundred to junction. One hundred to.'

The responses were instant. *Team 2, copy that. Team 3, copy.* He looked down at the sniper.

'Any second now Fergal.'

The man grunted in response, his body remaining completely still. Joe's mouth was dry as he raised the binoculars once more and studied the junction in the distance. The traffic was busy, the early afternoon school runs and shoppers trying to get ahead of the evening rush hour. The radio squawked again.

Junction.

The teams acknowledged and Joe could hear the tension in their replies even through the squelch of static. The sniper spoke.

'First vehicle through...second vehicle through...and third. That's the packet through the junction and towards us.'

Joe transmitted. 'Packet through. That is a go. That is a go.'

He lowered the radio and was lifting the binoculars up when the sniper spoke again.

'Ears.'

Joe quickly donned the ear defenders they'd brought as the sniper put his own ones on. A brief moment later the sniper spoke again.

'Standby for shot.'

Joe heard the metallic click of the safety catch being disengaged and watched as Fergal readjusted his position slightly. There was a second's silence then a huge boom sounded, filling the room with its invasive percussion and the shock wave striking Joe's chest. Joe's heart was racing as he picked up the binoculars and looked down the road.

The first Hotspur was belching smoke from the front end and was rolling to a stop. Some way behind it, a streak of movement flashed across the road and there was an immediate explosion and a cloud of debris and smoke billowed into the air. The rear Hotspur now disabled, Joe turned his attention to the middle vehicle which had stopped in the centre of the road when the front Hotspur had been hit. As he watched, he saw the vehicle start speeding forward, the driver obviously now aware they were in an ambush. The Hotspur careered between other vehicles on the road that had pulled over or crashed into each other at the beginning of the attack. He observed the Hotspur clear a couple of vans that had blocked part of the road then the room was rocked by another boom as the sniper fired the big rifle again. Looking through the binoculars Joe gave a yell of triumph as he watched the smoke and fluids explode from the engine area of the vehicle. His heart racing with excitement, Joe could hardly believe that they were carrying out one of the most audacious operations in IRA history.

And it was working.

Marcus heard the explosion and braked hard to avoid hitting the vehicle in front. A plume of smoke billowed above the trees that bordered Stockman's Lane and he wondered for a brief second if the convoy had been involved in an accident. Stuck in the static traffic, he opened his door and stepped out just as a loud shot rang out. There was no mistaking what was happening now. *Fuck*! He grabbed his radio mic and informed Zero that an RUC convoy was being ambushed on Stockman's Lane and that he was going to assist. Dropping the mic, he grabbed his gun bag from the passenger footwell and pulled out the G3, cocking the weapon and making it ready. He slammed his door shut and locked the car before sprinting into the playing fields that bordered the road. The bag bounced on his back as he ran across the field, cutting the corner that would take him straight on to Stockman's Lane.

He couldn't believe it: The IRA taking on an armoured RUC convoy, broad daylight, on a bustling Belfast thoroughfare. It was only luck that he had been travelling the same direction as the convoy. He'd smiled in surprise when it had overtaken him on Musgrave Park Court, the thought that his Agent was, once again, mere metres from him but wouldn't know it. He heard another loud shot and wondered what the hell they were firing. *A 7.62? Bigger?* As he reached the trees, a man stepped out, holding something in his hand. Marcus recognised him from somewhere but couldn't place where. The man's eyes widened as he saw Marcus in full flight, big rifle in one arm as he pumped with the other, trying to run as fast as he could. The man dropped to the ground and Marcus ignored him as, across the road, he saw three men in balaclavas taking aim at a crippled Hotspur. Skidding to a stop, he dropped to one knee, brought the G3 up on aim, released the safety and engaged them, the rifle kicking hard against his shoulder with the recoil of the shots.

Joe Carluccio turned the binoculars towards the park and lifted up one side of his ear defenders. 'What the fuck is that?'

Fergal lifted his head from behind the weapon sight. 'Looked like a tracer round being fired from across the road. I can't see. Trees are covering whoever it is doing the shooting.'

A burst of gunfire came from the direction of the park and a loud, panicked voice came over the radio.

'WE'RE HIT! WE'RE HIT! TWO MEN DOWN! WE'RE PULLING OUT NOW!'

Joe cursed and grabbed the radio. 'No. You will NOT pull out. Team 3 can you support Team 2?'

'Team 3...we'll try.'

Joe dropped the radio and studied the park area again, but whoever was shooting at the other team was still in the cover of the trees. 'What do you reckon Fergal?'

'Might just be bad luck Joe. Might just be we've a tout fingered us for it. All I know for sure is we're on a clock here. We need to be moving if we're going to keep the big fella safe.'

Joe knew the sniper was right. There was a priority on getting the big .50 cal to safety as soon as its role was complete. The Barrett was a premium weapon in the IRA arsenal and treated as such by the leadership. But Joe needed the operation to be concluded before he was ready to give the call to extract. He saw Fergal looking up at him.

'Well?'

Joe shook his head. 'Not yet. Look, can you get a couple of rounds into the back of the wagon at least? Surely one of them will hit the tout.'

Fergal raised an eyebrow and lifted up the right ear defender.

'Joe man, we can't be scooped with the big gun. You *know* that.'

'Do as I fucking tell you Fergal! Get the rounds down.'

He watched as the sniper made no attempt to disguise his contempt at the order but turned back to his weapon, getting his sight picture once again before firing another shot. Joe looked through the binoculars, scanning between the Hotspur, the park and the other IRA team that should have been moving up the road to help their colleagues.

Marcus ducked behind a large tree and changed magazines just as another shot rang out down the street, the loud crack and the thump as it hit the Hotspur echoing above the noise of screaming commuters. He also knew what he was dealing with now; a .50 cal. A bloody big weapon. That must have been how they disabled the first Hotspur. He took a second to gather his thoughts and try and calm his erratic breathing. He knew he'd dropped two of the terrorists across the street and saw the third run away between a couple of industrial units. The shots sounded like they were coming from further up Stockman's Lane, which would make sense, having the bigger gun in a stand-off capacity. He raised the rifle once more and edged around the side of the tree, studying the crippled Hotspurs and the road beside them. Drivers were abandoning their cars and running in all directions, making it difficult for him to identify anything unusual, but a dark blur caught his attention and he saw it bobbing up and down between the static vehicles in the road. *A balaclava.* Marcus took aim at the last point where he'd seen the figure moving and was rewarded a split-second later when it came back into view. It was an armed man with a balaclava, and he was showing more of his body as he raised himself from behind the cover of a blue car. Marcus realised that the man was looking for him, his entire attention on the area of the trees where Marcus had just been. Taking aim at the centre of the man's body, Marcus fired a bust of three shots and saw the man snatched away as if yanked by an invisible rope. *Good hit.* Not wanting to be pinned down by anyone who had seen him shoot, Marcus slung his bag over his shoulder and sprinted along the tree line, taking up a position further along the road. Glancing back at where he had just shot the terrorist, he saw two more men in balaclavas running away in the opposite direction. He looked up the road, the visibility limited in the smoke and steam coming from the Hotspurs. Straining his eyes, he saw a bright flash from the first-floor window of an industrial unit, followed by the loud crack and the thump as the huge bullet thudded into the flank of a crippled Hotspur. Without pausing for thought, Marcus stepped out into the open, lined up his sights on the window and opened fire.

Fergal reached into the bag lying next to him on the table. 'Changing mags.'

Joe looked down at the sniper and was just about to say something when he was punched back against the wall. He screamed in agony as his shoulder hit the wall and he collapsed on the floor. The window frame continued to splinter as bullets shredded into it and Joe screamed at Fergal that he was hit, and they needed to extract. Hearing nothing, he looked up, eyes wild with pain, breathing rapidly, and saw that Fergal wouldn't be going anywhere. A large flap of hair and scalp dangled from the back of the South Armagh man's head and thick blood was already pooling and dripping off the table. Joe attempted to stand but found his arm wasn't responding to his commands and looked down at it. His shoulder was torn open and blood was running freely down his sleeve. He moaned in fear and lifted his good hand up, placing pressure on the shattered joint then screamed as the pain kicked in. Trying to control his panic, he began taking big, deep breaths, struggling to his knees and dragging himself away from the line of sight of the windows. The shooting seemed to have stopped but he knew that if he didn't get out of the building now, he never would. Taking a last look at the dead body of his comrade and the rifle that was too much for him to carry, Joe raised himself to his feet, clutched at his shoulder and stumbled out of the room and into the stairwell. If the extraction team had held their nerve, he had a chance. If they'd run however, he was fucked. Well and truly fucked.

Sprinting across the road, Marcus spun around when he heard a noise behind him. A uniformed RUC officer staggered out of the crippled Hotspur and seeing the gun pointed at him raised his hands. Marcus yelled at him.

'ARMY, ARMY, ARMY. DO YOU UNDERSTAND?'

Even before he replied, Marcus could see from the relief on the policeman's face that he had. Marcus pointed at the two Hotspurs behind.

'You need to get to your lads and see they're okay. Radio for help. I'm Hot Pursuit. Got it?'

The policeman nodded and reached into his own vehicle, bringing out a rifle then following Marcus's directive and walking back towards the other Hotspurs. Marcus turned and ran towards the house where the big gun had been fired from. Since he'd put the bursts through the window there had been no more from the rifle and he assumed the team had withdrawn from the position and were making good their escape. He knew that they wouldn't leave a .50 cal behind and that meant that their extraction team were somewhere close by as they couldn't run very far due to the size of the weapon. Sirens were sounding from all directions and pierced through the cries and shouts of fear from the pedestrians huddled behind cars and any cover that they could find. Some screamed as Marcus ran past, but he had no time to spend comforting and reassuring them. The gun team would be well on their way to their extraction and he couldn't allow that to happen. He reached the door of the unit and looked up at the window that he'd fired upon less than a minute before. There were no sounds and he took a deep breath, aimed the weapon in front of him and with his free hand, swung the entrance door wide open.

Joe heard the front door of the unit crash open and slam against the wall. He staggered under the stairwell and held his breath as he heard someone pounding up the stairs, the metal steps clanging under the feet. As soon as he dared, he stepped out from his hiding place and crept towards the rear entrance, careful not to make any unnecessary noise. His breathing sounded incredibly loud to him and he was beginning to feel light-headed, the blood loss from his shoulder starting to tell. When he reached the door, he swore under his breath as he saw it was an emergency exit, guaranteed to make a racket the moment he slammed down on the bar. But there was nothing else for it; the extraction team for him and Fergal would be...*should* be, waiting with the car running in the Carpetright car park ready to get them away across the M1 and into the west where they could scatter before the raids began. He laid his good hand on the metal release bar and waited a couple of beats, his mind conjuring up a team of SAS waiting on the other side of the door ready to cut him down. He gave a small chuckle. *So what? It's either a team of SAS outside or the SAS guy upstairs.* He shook his head, confused as to why he would think something so dangerous was so funny. *Come on, keep it together Joey boy, keep it together.* With a deep breath, he leaned down on the metal bar and as softly as he could manage, pushed down to release the door mechanism.

Marcus saw there was no need to check if the shooter was dead. The big flap of scalp dangling from the back of the head and the viscous pool of blood on the table under the face telling him as much. The sniper's weapon, a big Barrett .50 cal, lay in the position it had been fired from, to all intents and purposes just waiting for the shooter to put the weapon back in his shoulder. Lowering his rifle, Marcus felt his legs shaking a little as he relaxed for the first time since the incident had begun. He felt light-headed and his ears were ringing from the aural assault of the G3's retorts. Marcus knew his adrenaline was wearing off quickly, but it didn't bother him as it was over. The sniper was dead, and the big gun was here, which would be a huge blow to PIRA. He looked out of the shattered window and watched as

RUC and Military vehicles arrived on the scene and uniformed men began running towards the smoking Hotspurs. He rested the butt of the G3 on the ground as he leaned his head against the window frame. He focused on the Hotspurs as the security forces helped with the wounded and kept watching as he needed to know. Needed to see for himself that this all hadn't been in vain. That GRANITE had made it. His attention was drawn to the back doors of the first Hotspur where a uniformed man stumbled out and steadied himself against the vehicle. He reached back in and a moment later another person exited, this one dressed in civilian clothes, taking the arm of the policeman for support. Marcus almost laughed with relief. *GRANITE*. He shook his head at the thought of the Agent cheating death on two occasions and felt a strong surge of joy at the thought that the IRA had failed once again, to kill a good man. A noise from downstairs drew his attention and he turned towards the doorway, assuming it was the Police or the Army and not wanting to be shot by accident by them. He was laying the G3 on the table next to the dead sniper when his eyes were drawn towards something on the floor beside the door. Frowning, he picked his rifle back up and walked over to investigate. His eyes widened as he realised what he was looking at. Saw now what he had missed on his way in: A blood trail. He threw himself through the door and bounded down the stairs, taking them three at a time. On the ground floor he turned and ran towards the direction where he had just heard the noise from. Seeing an open door swinging in the wind, Marcus cursed. There was a second shooter.

And he was getting away.

Joe bellowed in agony as he tripped on a kerb stone and jolted his shoulder. His breathing was ragged, and waves of dizziness assailed him as he stumbled across the carriageway towards the car park. He had forgotten where the extraction team had said the car would be, panic and fear dulling his memory. As he reached the car park, he swore at the number of vehicles present and could see people were stopping and staring at him, connecting the deranged and wounded man before them with the shootings and explosions around the corner. Joe knew he had to act fast; he was fading. His strength and energy sapping as quick as the blood streaming from his shoulder. *Where the fuck's the team?* Looking around wildly, he saw no sign of any car coming towards him. Pulling his pistol from his waist- band, he staggered towards a family who were rushing to get into their car. He raised the pistol, aiming it at them and was about to yell at them to give him their car when he tripped on something and crashed to the ground, dropping his weapon as his wounded shoulder smashed into the wet tarmac. He screamed and gagged, turning his head to one side as a stream of vomit erupted from his mouth. He retched several more times and was aware of a car moving past him at speed, the tyres screeching as it turned a corner behind him. *Well, there goes that fucking plan.* He rolled on to his good side and spat the remains of the sick from his mouth then dragged himself to his feet. Taking a deep breath, he looked around the car park again in the forlorn hope that the extraction team had seen him and were coming to get him. But they weren't.

He bent down to pick up the pistol but straightened up as he heard screams and shouts. Following the direction of the noise his eyes widened as he watched an armed man sprinting across the carriageway towards the car park, a large rifle slung by his side. Joe was about to reach back down for the pistol when the man caught sight of him and stopped running, lifted the rifle up and took aim. Joe bent down and scurried between the parked cars, keeping them between him and his pursuer. His wounded arm was now limp at his side and would occasionally bang against a car as he staggered past, sending a river of agony through his entire body.

He looked up from between two cars and saw that his hunter was stalking him, weapon in the shoulder and advancing through the rows of vehicles. Joe turned his head, frantically looking for a way out but saw none. Wounded and with no extraction plan, no weapon and no support, he was out of options. And his pursuer was gaining. He hauled himself to his feet and, grabbing his wounded shoulder, began running as fast as he could towards the entrance of the carpet superstore. He tried to keep below the line of the car roofs, but the stress of this position was burning his thighs and his breathing struggled as the exhaustion kicked in. Looking up, he gave a small shout of triumph as he saw the store entrance was just beyond a final stretch of road. He flinched as a loud shot rang out and a chunk of stone façade shattered in front of him. Staggering and off-balance, he threw his good arm out as he tripped over the threshold of the store and slammed into the carpeted floor. He screamed again as his wounded shoulder struck the floor and his face burned with friction as he slid to a halt.

Marcus lowered the rifle and began running towards the store entrance. *Missed the bastard.* But he'd seen that the man was wounded and moving with difficulty. Marcus wanted to get into the store fast, before the terrorist could take a hostage and as he sprinted through the large entrance, he grunted when he saw the wounded man attempting to get to his feet but fail. Marcus brought the weapon up on aim and advanced towards the man who was now on his knees, cradling a wounded arm, head back and drawing in deep breaths. Around him, Marcus could see shoppers and staff hugging the walls of the store as they tried to get away from the incident. He ignored them and continued to move towards the kneeling man. With a jolt, Marcus realised it was Big Joe Carluccio he was looking at. The head of the Nutting Squad was in a bad way, hair plastered to his forehead with sweat, his face a pale, waxy consistency and the clothing on his left arm saturated with blood. Marcus circled until he was in front of Joe and yelled.

'ARMY, ARMY, ARMY. DROP ANY WEAPONS YOU HAVE AND LIE FLAT ON THE FLOOR.'

When Joe didn't respond, Marcus repeated the command. This time, Joe opened his eyes and looked at him. The IRA man didn't say anything, just continued to suck in deep breaths of air. Marcus took a quick glance around him. He couldn't see anyone nearby. He didn't think that the store would have CCTV, not as if you would expect shoplifters in a carpet store. His mind was made up: Here was the IRA's most evil bastard, a man who had now tried to kill Marcus's Agent twice. Marcus had heard rumours that there were already discussions underway at the highest level to negotiate pardons for IRA prisoners in return for a commitment to peace. In all likelihood, and despite his dozens of murders over the years, Joe Carluccio would never receive anything close to the punishment that he deserved. Placing his finger on the trigger of the G3, Marcus spoke quietly.

'I want you to reach into your pocket and pull it out, showing me there's nothing in it.' He watched as Joe cocked his head to one side. Marcus couldn't be sure there weren't any cameras, but if there were, they would record Joe reaching for something in a pocket that Marcus could easily justify as his reason for shooting. But Joe didn't move.

'I said, reach into your fucking pocket and show me that it's empty. Now.'

He watched in disbelief as Joe shook his head and gave a small laugh. Sirens were sounding outside, and Marcus knew it was only a matter of time before the police or the military entered the store. *Fuck it*. He dropped his head behind the rear sight and applied pressure to the trigger just as Joe spoke.

'You can't...can't shoot...'

Marcus raised his head. 'Why not? Isn't as if anyone's going to question it, you miserable piece of shit.'

Joe laughed again then grunted, grabbing at his wounded shoulder.

'No...you don't get it. I...I work for you. I work for you guys...'

Marcus frowned as he tried to understand Joe's words. 'What the hell are you on about?'

Joe opened his eyes and locked his gaze on Marcus's face.

'I work for *you*. For the Brits.'

Marcus watched as Joe dropped his head, took another deep breath, then met Marcus's eyes once again.

'I'm RED LANCE.'

CHAPTER 30

PALACE BARRACKS, HOLYWOOD

The tremors in the hand showed the strains that the brave smile and false bonhomie were hiding. Marcus saw Kieran lower his cup back on to the table, glancing up to see if Marcus had noticed the shaking. Marcus quickly turned his attention to a picture on the wall above his former Agent to spare the proud man any perceived indignity. He looked back as Kieran spoke.

'I tell you Marcus, I thought I was done for back there when they came for us.'

Marcus nodded. 'I'm not surprised mate. That was a well-coordinated attack.'

Kieran grinned. 'And once again I've got you to thank for my life. This is getting to be a habit between us.'

Marcus smiled, happy to keep the conversation light. 'Well, if it's all the same to you Kieran, if I don't have to do it ever again, that'll be fine by me.'

Kieran laughed then picked up his coffee. Marcus noticed that the tremors had subsided and was pleased. He looked at his watch.

'Kieran, the Doc is going to be here to give you the once over any minute now, and I've got to go and give a formal statement. I'll be back as soon as I can and see if I can't get a hold of something a little stronger than instant coffee to toast our good fortune.'

'I'm all for that Marcus. Think we're entitled to a couple of jars after today's shenanigans.'

Marcus was about to reply when there was a knock on the door and an RUC officer poked his head in.

'The Doctor's here to see the patient now if you're ready gents?'

Marcus stood. 'That's fine, just send him in.' As the doctor entered, Marcus patted Kieran on the shoulder. 'Right Kieran, be good for the Doc and I'll see you later tonight.'

Kieran patted his former Handler's hand and felt a surge of affection for the man who had saved his life on two occasions. 'No problem Marcus. See you soon.'

Marcus closed the door behind him and made his way to the main exit which was guarded by an imposing RUC officer in plain clothes. The policeman cleared his throat and addressed Marcus in a deep baritone.

'Just like to say bloody well done today. Those were some of my friends whose lives you saved. We're very grateful and won't forget it.'

Marcus blushed at the unexpected praise, nodded to the man and signed out on the booking register before exiting the suite and entering the corridor. As he walked past the closed doors and nondescript offices of the Security Service element, he felt tiredness creeping in, the comedown from the huge adrenalin rush he'd experienced earlier that day. He was still reeling from Joe Carluccio's claim that he was an agent. *RED LANCE? What the hell is RED LANCE?* Marcus had still been tempted to pull the trigger, but a team of armed RUC had entered the carpet store and he'd been more concerned with identifying himself in order not to get shot. He had no idea what the hell was going on. If Carluccio was an agent, then he would have to belong to the RUC, MI5 or the Garda Siochana, because he certainly wasn't one of SIG's. But whoever was running him would now be in a world of hurt, their agent effectively complicit in the attack and attempted murder of policemen as well as a Military Intelligence Agent.

Making his way up the stairs to the first floor, he wasn't looking forward to another round of interviews, however at least this time he wasn't trying to conceal anything. He'd already given an initial statement at the scene but told the policemen that he had to get off the streets before the media arrived in numbers and his identity was compromised. He hadn't mentioned anything about Carluccio's claim to be an agent as the IRA man had collapsed and two of the police officers had begun rendering first aid until the medics could arrive. Marcus had directed the other RUC officers to get

Kieran to Palace Barracks as soon as possible and that he would go directly there himself and be available for a formal interview. He'd called Dom as soon as he'd arrived at Palace and apprised him of the situation, his boss staggered by Marcus's account of the ambush. The CO and Ops Officer were on their way, but Marcus was keen to get the interview done and get back to Kieran. As much as the former Agent was putting on a brave face, Marcus knew that he was probably still in a state of shock. Feeling drained and a little out of sorts himself, Marcus wanted nothing more than the anaesthetising effects of a good bottle of single malt.

He reached the office he had been looking for and knocked on the door. A yell from inside told him to enter and as he opened the door, he was confronted by a group of individuals who stood up and gave him a round of applause. Taken off-guard, he froze for a second before taking in some familiar faces; Dom, his CO, the Ops Officer, Colin Woods. There were several others, including a very senior police officer, the peak of his cap rimmed with silver garlands. This man walked over to Marcus and held out his hand.

'Marcus, on behalf of a very grateful Royal Ulster Constabulary, may I be the first to offer my respect for your courage and determination that saved the lives of a lot of our people today. Thank you, Sergeant Vaughan. Thank you.'

Marcus shook the offered hand and the man patted his shoulder as he departed with another two uniformed officers who gave Marcus a hearty slap on the back and a whispered '*good work son*', as they followed their boss. When the door closed again, Marcus's colleagues closed in around him, shaking his hand and showering him with praise for his actions. The last to approach was Colin Woods and Marcus saw that the policeman seemed to be struggling to express himself as he took Marcus's hand.

'You won't know it Marcus, but one of the boys in the middle Hotspur was my nephew, Leslie. A cracking lad with a wife and two wee daughters. And thanks to you, he's going to be able to go home to them again. Thanks son, thank you so much.'

Marcus shook his head. 'Colin, I only did what any one of us would have done if they'd been in the same situation mate. That's all.'

'The difference is Marcus, that we weren't; *you* were. Unbelievable bravery, Marcus, unbelievable.'

Dom patted Marcus on the back and told him that he had to leave as the guys were on a big job later that night. He promised to catch up with Marcus properly once everything had settled down, said his goodbyes and left.

Marcus's attention was drawn to the sound of a bottle top cracking open and he watched as his CO poured generous measures of Macallan into several glasses, passing them around before addressing the small group.

'Gentlemen, a toast. To the courage and tenacity of Royal Marine Sergeant Marcus Vaughan that has saved the lives of eight RUC officers and a former Agent. To Marcus.'

The men raised their glasses and echoed the host before drinking their whisky. The Ops Officer nodded at Marcus.

'And not only that but the capture of Joe Carluccio and the big Barrett. All in all, a bloody good day Marcus.'

Marcus lowered his head. He'd never been good at accepting compliments and was starting to feel uncomfortable so decided to change the subject.

'What's happened to my formal interview? I thought that's what I was here for.'

Colin nodded. 'We've got your initial statement Marcus and I've told the higher-ups that I'll have a chat with you tonight to see if there's anything else you remember or want to add. All very informal and we'll do it now if that works, as your head-shed want to hear the whole tale in all its glory.'

Marcus was surprised but happy that he could just run over what he'd already given while enjoying a few drams. The whisky was relaxing him, and he took a seat in a comfortable armchair before recounting his actions of earlier that day. The others remained quiet, allowing him to get the details out. He had just finished talking about his initial firefight on the street when Colin interjected.

'Sorry Marcus, but you say you thought you recognised the individual who came out of the treeline carrying something? A player?'

Marcus thought back to the incident. 'I really couldn't say, Colin. I've definitely seen him somewhere before but... nope, just can't place him. He was carrying something dark and rectangular but that's all I noticed. I know I've seen him before though.'

'Okay mate, but if anything does come back to you, let me know ASAP.'

Marcus carried on with his account but paused when the Ops Officer held up his hand.

'Just to let everyone know, the Barrett that we recovered is *the* Barrett.'

There was silence as the men in the room assimilated this information. The big rifle had killed several policemen and soldiers over the past three years and was a fearsome weapon, the heavy calibre round tearing through the protective Kevlar and armour of the security forces. The propaganda alone in capturing this weapon would be a huge blow to the IRA and a massive success for the security forces. The Ops Officer continued.

'Not only that, but the dead sniper was none other than Fergal McCabe himself, taking a rare trip out of South Armagh. A one-way trip as it turned out.' He raised his glass in Marcus's direction. 'Another feather in your cap from today.'

Colin leaned forward in his chair. 'This was a big Op, gents and must have come straight from Army Council. No way this was handled by anything lower. We've got South Armagh snipers firing weapons from East Tyrone, Belfast toe-rags on the RPGs and Big Joe Carluccio risking arrest to be on the ground here? This has the big boys' dabs all over it.'

Stuart Coull stood and began pouring refills into the glasses as he walked around the room. 'HMG are spitting feathers apparently. Huge outcry at the fact the republican movement has been playing a double game regarding the ceasefire. Nice to see Sinn Fein on the other side of the beating for a change. Marcus, please continue.'

Marcus carried on with his recollection, explaining how he'd heard the noise downstairs and followed the blood trail that eventually led him to the sight of Joe Carluccio stumbling across a car park. He recounted his missed shot and how he'd eventually secured the head of the Nutting Squad beside a roll of Axminster deep pile. Leaning forward in his chair, Marcus made eye contact with Colin.

'There is one thing I left out of my initial statement. When I was stood in front of Carluccio, and I'll be honest here, I was going to slot him. Had that in my head and was actually putting first pressure on the trigger.' He could see his CO and Ops Officer share a quick look of concern at Marcus's admission. 'But before I could, he told me that I couldn't kill him because he worked for us.'

Colin Woods put down his pen and frowned. 'What do you mean?'

'Well, I asked him just that and he repeated it; *I work for you. I work for the Brits.*'

Colin leaned back in his chair, his face showing the puzzlement he was feeling.

'What, you mean as an *agent*? Joe Carluccio told you he was an agent?'

Marcus nodded. 'Not only that, but he told me his code name.'

Colin gave a wide grin and picked up his pen again.

'Brilliant: Big Bad Joe saying anything to save his skin. Go on then, what did he say his code name was?'

'RED LANCE. He said his code name was RED LANCE.'

Marcus immediately noticed two things. First, the absolute silence in the room and second, that Colin Woods wasn't smiling anymore.

CHAPTER 31

PALACE BARRACKS, HOLYWOOD

The silence in the room lasted for almost a minute before Colin spoke.

'*RED LANCE*? You're absolutely positive he said *RED LANCE*?'

Marcus nodded, noting that his CO and Ops Officer were staring at him. 'Er...yes. *RED LANCE*. No way I'd forget it.' He looked over at his CO as the man swore but turned back to Colin and noticed how pale the policeman's face had become. 'Gents, who the hell is RED LANCE?'

There was another moment of quiet before Colin spoke.

'Marcus, RED LANCE is not something for discussion at your level of clearance. I only know of the existence of RED LANCE, no more details than that.' He paused before seeming to come to a decision. 'But in light of what you've done today, I'll bring you in on what I know. RED LANCE is the code name for a high-level agent being run by the

Security Service. He's been running, at least to my knowledge, for over twenty years now.'

Marcus shook his head. 'Okay, but RED LANCE can't be Joe, can he? Joe's a murderer many times over. Hell, if I hadn't stopped him today, he'd have added another nine to his count.'

Colin rubbed his face, suddenly feeling nauseous at the implications they were facing. 'No, Big Joe can't be RED LANCE because that would mean that the Security Service were allowing their agent to torture and kill people. Many people.'

Marcus nodded. 'Including my fucking agent.'

Stuart Coull held up his hand. 'Gentlemen, we're getting a little ahead of ourselves here. All we have is Carluccio's *claim* that he is RED LANCE. Probably just a ploy to stop Marcus shooting him. Buy some time.'

Marcus shook his head. 'No. He could have said anything. Why say he was an agent and then *name* a high-level agent by code-name? A code-name that I didn't even know? And why the hell would he even know a code name? Our agents are never told theirs.'

Stuart leaned forward in his chair. 'Marcus, the implications of Joe Carluccio being RED LANCE are appalling. The head of the Nutting Squad employed as an agent for the Crown? Unthinkable.'

Colin spoke again, his voice quieter. 'Maybe not *that* unthinkable Stuart. Look at what RED LANCE has given up over the years; The Gib Three, The London Cells, The

Loughgall Team, The East Tyrone Crew. That's all top-drawer stuff, had to come from a top-drawer Provo.'

Stuart shook his head. 'No way, Colin, could Joe Carluccio have been an agent for over twenty years. The torture and murders that he's committed would mean that if anyone found out, his handlers would be implicated in his crimes and be charged and incarcerated.'

Colin met his eyes. '*If* anybody found out...'

Marcus cleared his throat. 'Wait a second...something just clicked.'

He stood and picked up the bottle of Macallan and walked around the room, replenishing the glasses before continuing. 'GRANITE said that during his interrogation, Joe kept asking him about a lot of stuff he didn't know. Focused on it was his exact term.' He pointed at Colin. 'Those operations you just mentioned were what Joe was concentrating on when he was torturing GRANITE.'

Colin pursed his lips. 'Okay, but he was bound to ask about them; they're some of the worst defeats that the IRA has suffered.'

'Yeah, but GRANITE had already broken, given him everything. So, he was surprised that when he denied knowing about these other operations, Joe kept at him. Never mentioned the stuff GRANITE had given up, not even to check out the details.'

Colin nodded slowly. 'Yeah, that's not right. I know from experience that touts are made to give a long account of everything they've given, how they're met, what their Handlers look like, how much they're paid.'

'Exactly! But once GRANITE broke, Joe wasn't all that interested in what he'd said, just kept going over all that other stuff you just mentioned.'

The Ops Officer looked at Marcus. 'Do you think Joe was trying to force GRANITE to take the rap for those operations?'

Marcus shook his head. 'I don't know, but it sounded really strange to me at the time and even stranger to GRANITE.'

Colin leaned back in his seat and took a large swig of his whisky. 'This is insane. The Provisional IRA's top murderer an MI5 agent? But it also makes sense; I mean, why would he be so personally invested in taking out GRANITE? There has to be a reason why he risked everything to come back to Belfast to take out a tout.'

Marcus turned as his Commanding Officer spoke. 'Unfinished business perhaps? Or maybe just professional pride?'

Colin shook his head. 'Nope. Big Joe was safe as houses in the South. The PAC must have had good reason to allow him to be a part of it as well knowing how risky it would be to have him back in the North. He's not just any old scruffy bastard whose arrest wouldn't make the middle pages of the Belfast Telegraph.'

Marcus stared at Colin as something the policeman had said triggered a memory. He screwed his eyes shut to concentrate better. *What the hell was it?* He ran through Colin's statement in his head, attempting to identify what had sparked in his brain. *What was it?...* '*Scruffy Bastard*'...*that was it!* He opened his eyes and looked at the policeman who was staring at him with a concerned look on his face.

'You okay Marcus? Thought you'd left us there for a wee minute.'

Marcus nodded. 'You told me if I remembered any details about the man I recognised in the park today, I should tell you ASAP.'

Colin reached for his notebook and pen and nodded for Marcus to continue.

'It was your term *scruffy bastard*. I'd seen that scruffy bastard from the park somewhere else recently and it's only now I remember where.'

Colin looked up. 'Well, don't keep us in suspense man; where did you know him from?'

Marcus pointed to the window. 'A couple of days ago, in the car park of this building.' He paused and took in the stunned expressions around the room. 'Talking to Jonathan from MI5.'

CHAPTER 32

MUSGRAVE PARK HOSPITAL, BELFAST

He supposed the drugs were keeping the worst of the pain away, but still, his shoulder felt like it had been hit by a sledgehammer. Joe Carluccio twisted his head to attempt to look at his injury but grimaced in pain as even this minor movement irritated his shoulder. He lay back against his pillows and sighed, his eyes drawn to the handcuffs that shackled him to the hospital bed. The irony hadn't escaped him that only earlier that day he had ambushed an RUC convoy that had just left this very hospital. And now here he was, recovering from an operation on his shoulder where the Brit had wounded him.

A movement through the glass pane in his door drew his eye and he caught sight of one of the RUC guards staring at him. As Joe watched, the man gave him a huge grin and waved. Joe turned his head away from the jubilant sentry. The RUC had taunted him constantly since his capture. They'd managed to land a few digs into him as they'd helped the medics move him, once even smashing his shoulder with a rifle butt and causing him to pass out for a few minutes. Safe to say there was no love lost there.

He hadn't said anything to the peelers about who he worked for. Didn't trust them not to feed the information straight back to the street or the press. Joe wasn't sure how long he'd been in the hospital but was beginning to wonder why Jonathan hadn't come for him yet. He would have known about Joe's capture very soon after the event and even if he was back on the mainland, surely he would jump on the next flight across and come and get his man? The longer he waited for this to happen, the more uneasy Joe became. He tried to put the negative thoughts to one side as he reminded himself of how much he'd done for Jonathan over the twenty-three years they had been working together. Jonathan had always treated him fair, particularly when the IRA were getting close to identifying the informer in their high echelons. Jonathan had no qualms about sacrificing a smaller player in the game to take the fall and allow Joe to continue working as an agent. Until Kieran Mulgrew.

Joe sighed and rubbed at his forehead, becoming irritated at the thought of how close they had come to finishing the whole thing but for Mulgrew and that bloody Brit. By now Mulgrew would have told the Brits about Joe's role in torturing him. And then to be nabbed on the job today? Joe knew that if Jonathan didn't go to bat for him, he was going away for a very long time. But where the hell *was* Jonathan? Surely all the years Joe had given the man would count in his favour. Maybe they would resettle him, somewhere anonymous on the mainland. That could work. Joe wasn't like most people he knew; he could turn his back on Belfast in a heartbeat and never look back. Especially if it meant staying out of prison.

The longer that he waited for Jonathan the more concerned he became at the prospect of being abandoned. Maybe Jonathan had thrown him to the wolves, leaving him to take the rap for everything and denying that Joe had ever worked for the Brits. If that was the case, Joe could pretty much guarantee that he would see out the end of his days in prison. Mulgrew's torture, then being lifted during an operation where peelers had been hit with RPGs, rifles, and the big Barrett. As well as that, they would have recovered Joe's pistol from the road outside the carpet store and while he had no idea what the history of that weapon might be, knew that he would be in the frame for all of its previous misdeeds. The loss of the Barrett would be a big blow to the movement. Not only that, but because Joe had been caught running from that building, he would also be linked to the previous killings that the rifle had been used for. *Shite*! Where the hell was Jonathan? Self-pity, an emotion Joe was very unfamiliar with, began to seep into his brain and he thought back to what had landed him in this mess in the first place.

❧

The year 1972 had been an important one for Joe; It marked both his eighteenth birthday and the year in which he was recruited by the Brits as an informer. He'd been an active IRA volunteer for three years already and been lucky enough to have escaped the dragnet of internment, his name not yet known well enough to justify an arrest. He'd kept up the fight and was soon making a name for himself as an aggressive hard-man, happy to take the war to the Brits. He'd been part of the original hard-core element that had driven the split from the Official IRA, the 'stickies', and as such, was trusted implicitly from the beginning of PIRA's formation. But he'd also been young, and a good-looking lad into the bargain. This combined with his growing reputation, made him very attractive to the opposite sex. And that's where the young Joe Carluccio became the architect of his own demise.

Bernadette McMahon was one of the McMahons of Ardoyne and an absolute stunner. Jet-black hair and ice-blue eyes and a figure that was the envy of the girls in the city, shown off to great effect in the mini-skirts she liked to wear. At the dances and bars around West Belfast she would draw the discreet glances of any red-blooded male. Discreet because she was married to Frankie Mac; OC D Company, Belfast Brigade PIRA. D Company, or 'the dogs' as they liked to refer to themselves, were a force to be reckoned with in the early seventies and Frankie Mac was the man who drove that force. Frankie was a legend in the IRA, a cold man and an efficient killer with a true gift for tactical command. His operations back then were daily: Bombings, shootings, kidnap, robberies. Back then, Frankie Mac *was* the IRA. Until he was arrested.

With Frankie in the can, Bernadette wasn't seen as often around the social scene and Joe couldn't quite remember where he'd first bumped into her while Frankie was inside. He recalled seeing her on several occasions and engaging in conversation as part of a group, but the first time he saw her alone had been when he'd seen her getting on a bus to Carnlough. Weeks later, there had been a function in The Slieve and he'd gone out the back for a bit of air and she followed him out, sitting on a keg and lighting up a cigarette, crossing her long legs as she leaned back and looked at him. He'd mentioned that he'd seen her get on the Carnlough bus and she explained that she did this once a week, just to give her head peace from the kids. Her ma would look after them for the day while she went up to Carnlough for a wee bit of quiet, enjoy a day by the sea. She'd asked him if he'd ever been and he told her that he hadn't. She'd looked at him with those stunning blue eyes of hers and told him he should really make an effort to see it sometime. And that Wednesdays were good days. It had taken a second or two for the penny to drop, by which time Bernadette stood up and smoothed the creases in her mini- skirt. She gave him a coy smile and as she walked past, brushed the back of his hand with her own. He remembered that the touch had felt electric and his state of arousal and excitement at what had just happened.

They began their affair the very next week, initially grabbing brief moments together in Carnlough but soon realising that this wasn't enough and found ways of seeing each other more regularly in the city. Joe knew that what he was doing was, after being a tout, the worst crime an IRA man could carry out: Sleeping with the wife of a prisoner. The IRA prisoners were lauded and respected for their sacrifices to the cause and their women were completely off-limits. But Joe couldn't help himself; he was smitten by this stunning, funny and intelligent woman. He knew well enough the penalty for his transgressions; a couple of bullets to the back of his knees, a cripple for life. But this just added to the intensity of their experience. They were careful, ignoring each other at public events and making sure when they came together it was almost like an IRA operation; checking to see if they were followed, switching buses, meeting in predominately mixed or even protestant areas outside the city. But it could never have lasted.

Joe had been having a drink in The Crown in the city centre. Rare for him to socialise there but he had just carried out the recce for a bombing target and had fancied a quick pint before the bus home. He'd been stood on his own when a man in a suit had sidled up next to him and asked Joe if he would join him for a drink in one of the booths. His English accent surprised Joe and he assumed he was a Brit soldier. Joe had grasped his pint with the intention of ramming the glass into the man's face when the man had told him to calm down, that he just wanted to talk about Bernadette. And that's how it had started.

In the privacy of the booth, the man explained that he was Military Intelligence and that he needed Joe's help with a couple of small things. Joe had resisted, denying he was in the IRA and didn't know what the man was talking about. The man produced some photographs. Some of Joe on his own, some of Joe with other IRA men, some of Bernadette on her own, some of Bernadette and Joe, and some of Bernadette having sex with Joe. And then a photo of Frankie Mac, the big bastard looking as hard and as mean as Joe had ever seen him. The man explained that, should Joe refuse his offer, he had a car waiting and would go directly to the Kesh and give the photographs to Frankie Mac. Joe remembered that he had been reeling from the fact that the Brits had these photographs and that the answer for him was to run. Almost as if reading his mind, the intelligence officer had leaned forward and explained that, should Joe suddenly disappear, the photos would go to Frankie Mac anyway. Then it would only then be a matter of time until the beautiful Bernadette McMahon was tarred, feathered and shackled to a lamp post in the middle of West Belfast in the time-honoured, traditional punishment for this transgression. And the man was right; this horrific punitive measure was the standard punishment for a woman who had been unfaithful while her man was inside. It was particularly brutal for the women as they never recovered from it, either mentally or physically, the hospital procedures limited in what they could achieve to minimise the damage from tar embedded in the scalp and skin of the victim. Joe could never have let that happen to Bernadette and so he'd taken the devil's deal and become a tout for the Brits.

He closed his eyes at the memory of that day. The shame, the fear, the helplessness he'd felt. Twenty-three years ago. He and Jonathan had done a lot of work together since that day. *A lot*. Jonathan was a very clever man who, even back in the early days of their partnership, had viewed the war as a long game and played it as such. And Joe had been the key to much of that success. He began to feel angry about the no-show from Jonathan and opened his eyes, staring at the door, willing his handler to walk through it.

Where the hell are you Jonathan?

∽

Constable Davy McCullough smiled at the nurse as she approached and told him that there was a phone call for them. He turned to Sam, who nodded, and Davy followed the nurse to the desk where he was handed the receiver by another nurse. He answered the phone then listened, ending the call with a single *yes* before handing the phone back and returning along the corridor to join his partner outside Joe Carluccio's room. Sam looked at him and raised an eyebrow. Davy nodded.

'That was Colin Woods. From him, nobody, absolutely *nobody* goes into that room unless it's a doctor or a nurse. Anybody else tries, no matter who, and we are to use any means necessary to stop them. Closed ranks. You good with all that?'

Sam Ferris, a man of very few words, nodded his understanding and resumed his sentinel stance, leaning against the wall, thumbs looped under his Kevlar vest. Like Davy, he'd worked with Colin Woods in the HMSU and had nothing but respect for the man; a copper's copper if ever there was one. And if Colin Woods was telling them not to let anyone in, that was just fine with Sam. Closed ranks was a seldom-used term by the RUC but every policeman and woman on the force knew exactly what it meant; no outsiders. In the murky world of counterterrorism, intelligence agencies and operations, the RUC had sometimes found itself carrying the can for situations not of their making. A closed ranks call from a senior officer usually meant that someone would be trying to pass the buck of whatever shite they had stirred up on to the RUC. *Well, not this time.*

The two men returned to their silent vigils, relaxed but alert and quietly determined that no one would be getting anywhere near the vile piece of IRA scum that was resting in the bed in the room behind them. No one.

CHAPTER 33

PALACE BARRACKS, HOLYWOOD

Colin Woods replaced the telephone receiver on its cradle and looked over at Marcus who was studying a series of photographs. Marcus looked up and caught Colin's eye. Colin gave him a thumbs-up.

'Right, we've bought some time. The guards at MPH are old workmates of mine and won't let anyone into Joe's room without my say-so. *Anyone*. You still sure?'

Marcus nodded slowly as he studied the photos once again. 'I can't believe it. It's definitely him. I was as close to him in the park as you and I are now. Shit! He was dressed as an orderly at the Hospital; I saw him go past GRANITE's room and thought I recognised him then. No mistaking him with that scruffy appearance and earring.'

Colin nodded. 'I believe you Marcus. It also fits in with something else that had troubled me at the time, but I couldn't quite put my finger on.' Colin gave Marcus, the CO and Ops Officer a quick synopsis of his suspicions when the new SAS soldier had joined the Det team on the

295

operation to stop the abduction of Denis O'Callaghan. The same SAS soldier that Marcus had identified in the park was now the subject of the photographs taken from the barrack's CCTV recordings. And Colin had seen this soldier talking with Jonathan on a separate occasion himself. He turned as Stuart Coull began to speak.

'Colin, I think what we have here is a very...sensitive operation. It sounds like MI5 have been running one of PIRA's most prolific killers and doing anything to keep him in play. We have to be very, very careful how we proceed from this point on.'

Colin's anger was immediate. '*Sensitive*? Try fucking outright illegal Stuart.' He stabbed his finger in the direction of the window. 'That was my nephew that was nearly killed yesterday as a result of this *sensitive* operation. Call it what it is, Stuart; illegal.'

The Ops Officer leaned forward in his chair. 'So, what do we do now?'

Colin leaned back and took another drink of whisky. 'If I'm right, Jonathan will want to take custody of Carluccio as soon as the hospital will allow. My guys will deny him access, no matter what piece of paper he flashes at them. He'll then kick it up the chain and I can expect a call from my Chief Constable ordering me to release Joe.'

Marcus nodded. 'Yep; we can't let Box anywhere near Carluccio or they'll give him a cover story to feed to the police until they can secure his release. But they'll get their way in the end I'm guessing.'

Colin steepled his fingers as he mulled over Marcus's statement. 'Maybe not Marcus. Maybe not.'

The CO of SIG smiled at his police counterpart. 'You look like you've got a plan forming in that big brain of yours Colin.'

'I've got a bit of a plan Stuart. A bit of a plan. It's messy, and there's a lot of moving parts, but I reckon the idea is sound.'

The Ops Officer placed his glass on the table beside him. 'Care to share?'

Colin smiled. 'Probably better if I don't. *To know is to be responsible.* And believe me gentlemen, neither you nor your unit want to be responsible for anything I'm going to be putting into effect.'

There was a moment's silence before Stuart cleared his throat and spoke quietly. 'Understood Colin. But is there anything we can do...discreetly, to assist?'

'No, Stuart. Appreciate the offer but this is going to take a few favours that I've been keeping in the bank for a special occasion and I'm pretty sure that this qualifies.'

The CO of SIG nodded then looked at his Operations Officer. 'I think Simon, that we should head back and prepare an update for MoD.'

The Ops Officer nodded and stood as did Marcus. Colin walked around from behind the desk and shook each of them by the hand.

'Gents, once again my thanks for your efforts. And Marcus, the RUC owes you a large one after today mate so don't be shy in coming forward if there's anything you think we can do for you.'

Again, Marcus felt the flush of embarrassment on his neck and cheeks, enhanced by the large whiskies he'd consumed. 'Colin, thanks for everything and good luck with...whatever it is you're planning and don't hesitate to get in touch if you think there's anything I can do.'

The three men left and made their way towards the exit. As they signed out, Marcus realised he had probably drunk too much to be driving but was saved from mentioning this when the CO's car pulled up and the driver opened the doors as Stuart Coull indicated that Marcus should get in.

'Give your keys to Corporal Youngs and he'll have someone collect your car and drop it off at the Detachment for you.'

As Marcus reached the car, the smartly attired driver was already holding out his hand for Marcus's keys. He handed the keys over and climbed into the front seat, allowing the CO and Ops Officer to talk over matters together in the rear. As they pulled away from the building, Marcus wondered what Colin Woods' plan was but knew enough about the policeman to be confident that it would be a good one.

Colin Woods refilled his glass, took a swig then began listing the phone calls that he would make. He had to be careful;

this wasn't just career-ending stuff; it could also mean serious jail time. But things needed to be put right. What was the point of being a policeman if you didn't do the right thing at least most of the time? Yes, the intelligence war against the IRA was a dirty one with all manner of misdeeds carried out on both sides, but there was a line, a definitive line that shouldn't be crossed. And in the case of MI5 running Joe Carluccio, that line wasn't just *crossed*; it was so far behind them it was in another universe. For over twenty years Box had been directing Joe's ascension through the ranks of PIRA, privy to every kidnap, torture and murder that their agent had been involved in. And it looked like they hadn't been shy in giving up other organisations' agents to cover up the information Joe had been giving them. Colin doubted that the Kieran Mulgrew case was the first of its kind and he thought back to some of the informers that PIRA, *Joe*, had tortured and killed over the years. How many of these were deliberately sacrificed to keep Joe Carluccio in the game?

He had to hand it to the Security Service. It was pretty impressive when you thought about it: That the man responsible for the interrogation of suspected informers was the most important informer within the entire republican movement. A man who could report back to the PAC with whatever he needed to keep himself safe. And but for the actions of a SIG Operator, would have survived to carry on with his activities. *Well, no more.* He downed the remnants of the whisky and picked up the phone, making his first call of many.

CHAPTER 34

MUSGRAVE PARK HOSPITAL, BELFAST

Jonathan paused at the door and took a deep breath before entering. He made his way to the main reception and smiled as he produced his credentials to the security officer. He asked where he could find Joe Carluccio and was given the location and directions on how to get there. After he'd been booked in, he thanked the officer and made his way along the anonymous magnolia corridor, wrinkling his nose in distaste at the antiseptic smell that pervaded the building. As he walked, he thought about the options open to him in dealing with RED LANCE.

His initial response on hearing that RED LANCE had been arrested at the scene had been one of anger. He'd been back at Thames House for a conference and had felt a tug on his sleeve during a coffee break. Evelyn from the Northern Ireland Desk had pulled him to one side and informed him that a large PIRA operation in Belfast had been thwarted by the Security Forces and that word was seeping out that Joe Carluccio may have been captured.

He'd left immediately, getting on the first flight back to Belfast, his mind racing as he considered what actions were open to him. He realised much of it depended on what Joe had told his captors. If he'd kept his mouth shut, Jonathan had some wiggle room. If he'd blabbed about who he was and who he was working with, there would be a lot of political fallout coming Jonathan's way. He'd gone straight to the office and began ringing anyone he could think of who could give him an update on the Carluccio situation but had learned that Joe had been in surgery most of the afternoon so hadn't spoken to anyone. This gave Jonathan some optimism that he could recover the situation before anything further happened, and his mood was lifted somewhat.

He rang the buzzer on the door of the secure unit and a nurse studied his Warrant Card through the glass panel before letting him in. He signed in at the desk then made his way along the corridor to the room where he'd been told that Joe was being held. Turning the corner, he frowned as he saw the bulky figures of the RUC constables stationed outside of the door, their weapons, body armour and equipment adding to their intimidating presence. Jonathan smiled as he approached them and held up his Warrant Card.

'Good evening gentlemen, just need a few minutes with our friend inside.'

He frowned as he saw the first constable hold up his hand.

'No visitors.'

Jonathan laughed. 'As you can plainly see, I am not a visitor. I am here in my official capacity and demand that you stand aside and grant me entry.'

The police officer continued to regard him with a fixed stare, devoid of emotion.

'No visitors.'

Jonathan lowered his Warrant Card and turned towards the other policeman.

'Is your friend retarded? Let me speak to the prisoner immediately.'

There was a brief pause before this officer replied. 'No visitors.'

Jonathan swore in exasperation. 'Right, you can clearly see I'm an officer with the Security Service and I have official business with Joe Carluccio. I recommend that if you both want to have a job tomorrow morning, you let me in that fucking room now.'

The police officers glanced at each other before the first one turned back to Jonathan.

'No visitors.'

Jonathan felt the rage welling up within him at the thought of being denied access by a couple of street plods. *Fuck this*! He stepped forward, thrust his arm out and attempted to push the first officer aside. He didn't even see the blow to his solar plexus that propelled him across the corridor where he smashed against the wall and collapsed, gasping for air. One of the policemen leaned over him and spoke as though addressing a small child.

'No. Visitors. Sir.'

Jonathan's eyes were bulging, and his mouth stretched as wide as possible as he gulped for air that seemed to be a long time coming. Slowly, his breathing returned, and he struggled into a sitting position, back against the wall. He was in shock. It had been many years since he'd been involved in any kind of physical altercation and even then, it had consisted of a bit of pushing and shoving. He stared at the two policemen who were watching him struggle, faces blank and non-emotional. The anger came again, and he stood up on unsteady legs, pointing his finger at the RUC men.

'Well, you've done it now haven't you? You stupid bastards. You've just assaulted a Crown servant and obstructed him in the course of his duties. Say goodbye to your jobs and your pensions gents, it's all over for you now.' He turned and began walking down the corridor, needing a phone and needing it quickly. He couldn't understand the policemen's stance; his Warrant Card was the key to the kingdom, access all areas. Yet here were two basic plods not just denying him entry but *assaulting* him. Without the slightest concern for consequences. But he'd make them pay for that. Make them pay *dearly*.

He reached the reception desk and was about to ask for a telephone when the door buzzed, and he turned to see Colin Woods and another man walk in. Colin saw Jonathan but completely blanked him as he signed the booking's sheet. The two men then ignored Jonathan and started walking towards Carluccio's room. Jonathan's mouth dropped open in astonishment. *What the hell is going on here tonight?* He jogged after the pair and reached them just as they were approaching Carluccio's door.

'COLIN, COLIN. WAIT.'

He was gratified to see that his shouts had stopped the pair and the TCG Officer turned to face him. Jonathan marched straight up to him and began prodding the policeman's chest.

'I don't know what the hell you plods think you're playing at but two things are going to happen now: One, I am getting a private interview with Joe Carluccio and two, you are going to dismiss these two fucking morons who just assaulted me.'

He watched as Colin stared down at the finger prodding his chest until Jonathan withdrew it. The TCG officer then turned to the constables.

'Is that true? Did you assault this good Servant of the Crown?'

The first constable spoke. 'Ah, to be fair, I just gave him a wee poke in his belly there.'

Jonathan stepped forward and thrust his finger in the constable's face. 'You bloody well attacked me. Don't try and weasel out of it now.' He turned back to Colin. 'And as for you, if *you* want to have a job by this time tomorrow, get rid of your goons and get your Chief Constable to schedule me in for a meeting immediately after this. NOW!'

He watched as Colin Woods recoiled slightly from his yell then shook his head.

'Jonathan, I'm very sorry if you feel that Davy here assaulted you. Back in our MSU days, we'd refer to what he done as a *Johnny Adair*; a wee prod!'

Jonathan was staggered that the TCG officer belittled his experience with levity and was about to say something when Colin stepped closer to him and spoke quietly.

'This however, now *this* is assault.'

Jonathan was unconscious from Colin's uppercut before his body even hit the floor, collapsing in a crumpled heap. Davy and Sam grabbed an arm each and dragged Jonathan's body to one side, placing it in the recovery position before reclaiming their spots back at the door. Colin gave them a nod as he opened the door and ushered the other man inside.

'Anybody asks, he fainted. If he comes to while we're still in here, just tell him to piss off and give me a knock.'

With that, he entered the room and closed the door behind him.

Davy McCullough looked at the prone body across the corridor, mouth open and dribbling saliva down the chin, to all intents and purposes a drunk sleeping off a night on the tiles. He chuckled to himself.

'Say what you like Sam, but Colin Woods hasn't changed a bit.'

There was a moment's silence before his colleague replied.

'I don't know Davy. Looked to me like he's had a new haircut.'

Davy burst out laughing. He had to hand it to Sam; the man didn't say much but when he did, it was pure gold. His laughter subsided as he considered the fallout that was coming someone's way; you didn't just knock out a member of MI5 and walk away scot-free. Still, he'd follow Colin's direction on this, no matter what. *Closed Ranks*, that's what the call had been, and Closed Ranks was what it would remain.

CHAPTER 35

SIG, BELFAST

The calls had started coming through even before Marcus had made it into work. He'd been roused from the bedroom of the debriefing suite by the shrill ringing of the bedside phone and only two words from the Duty Operator: *Get in*.

Every TV and radio in the Detachment were turned on, with either a collator or a Handler sitting close by with a notepad scribbling furiously. There was a rush of activity as the guys driving in from the Safe Houses brought piles of newspapers and dumped them on the Ops Room desk where they were squabbled over, everyone wanting to see first-hand, that the rumours were true.

And it seemed they were.

Front page of the Belfast Newsletter and The Irish News. Lead articles in The Times, The Telegraph and The Guardian. On the television, the BBC and Sky news were leading with the story and the shocking revelations falling out of it.

The secure phones were busy too, as the Ops Officer and Company Commander sought any updates that the Handlers were getting. Several of the agents had also rung in, asking if it was true, and if so, what were the implications for them.

Marcus stared at the wall-mounted TV screen, still stunned to see, above the red logo of the BBC, the forlorn face of Big Joe Carluccio looking down on him. The banner beneath the picture screaming the headline that was the focus of the frenetic activity within SIG:

IRA murderer works for MI5.

The commentators were all talking about an unprecedented public confession from the head of the so-called *Nutting Squad*, that he had been working for MI5 for over twenty years under the code name *RED LANCE*. Photographs of Joe Carluccio propped up in his hospital bed covered the front pages of the tabloids along with a raft of headlines that ran from the succinct to the lurid. The Northern Ireland edition of The Sun falling into the latter category with the leading line of *Tout killer is IRA's biggest Tout!* Marcus reached for the volume control as a reporter from Sky News began airing a piece as she stood outside Musgrave Park Hospital.

The reporter introduced the story, taking the viewer back to the events of the day before where the IRA broke the ceasefire in a failed attack against an RUC convoy. Joe Carluccio had been part of that attack and had been wounded and captured at the scene after a dramatic gun battle. Last night, Joe Carluccio had been interviewed by a reporter from the Belfast Telegraph while he was recovering in hospital. In an incredible turn of events, Joe wanted his whole story on record; that for over twenty years he had been an agent for the British Security Service; MI5. The reporter looked down at her notes and read from them to the camera. When asked during the interview whether MI5 were aware of his torturing and killing activities, Joe had not only said that they were, but had actually *directed* many of these operations.

Marcus gave a low whistle. This was going to hurt the Security Service badly. Public and Government confidence in MI5 had not been particularly high in recent years but this was going to set that back even further. And whoever was currently handling RED LANCE could stand by for a legal investigation into what they had been asking their agent to do. Marcus still couldn't work out how the hell a journalist had got into Joe's room, would have thought it impossible for someone to get through all that security *and* the RUC officers at the door. He also wondered why Joe was doing this. He thought that Joe's best course of action would have been to sit tight until MI5 got to him and squirrelled him away into the Resettlement Program. The RUC would have cried foul over that, but MI5 would simply have ignored any objections and done what they wanted anyway. *So why? Why had Joe thought it necessary to go public?*

The Agent phones were ringing constantly as they sought reassurance or reported information that they were picking up on the street even at this early hour. Already, intelligence was coming in suggesting high-level IRA and Sinn Fein meetings had been scheduled. IRA security teams and drivers from various parts of the city were being roused from their beds and told to be ready. Marcus could only imagine the chaos and disarray that the republican movement was experiencing this morning. One of their top operators, a man who knows all the secrets, revealed to be the most important agent in the history of the Troubles. Marcus rubbed his eyes. He needed coffee.

Sitting at the desk sipping his brew, Marcus turned to the double centre-page spread of the Belfast Telegraph and raised his eyebrows in surprise. The reporter had put together a very comprehensive piece, supported by photographs of The Gibraltar Three, the site of the Lough-gall ambush and a scene of devastation in London. Three of some of the major operations that Joe claimed to have given to MI5 over the years. Joe told the reporter that he had been recruited in the early seventies, when MI5 had used something Joe had done in his private life to blackmail him with. He went on to say that over the years, PIRA had come close to identifying him as the high-level informer but that his handler had always managed to find another agent to take the fall for him. And as Joe was the interrogator for these unfortunates, he would feed the Army Council whatever information his handler told him to. In this way, whenever there was a risk of compromise, Joe Carluccio would always be the last person that PIRA suspected. He spoke about the previous day's attack against the convoy as an example of this. Joe stated that his MI5 handler had directed him to come back north and take out another tout that MI5 wanted to be blamed for all the information Joe had given up. He told the reporter that this tout had escaped the interrogation session and that his MI5 handler had been angry and ordered Joe to finish what he'd started. Joe claimed that it was the MI5 officer who had given him the details of when the tout was to be moved from MPH. He'd also provided PIRA with a spotter for the convoy ambush, calling Joe on the radio with a countdown as the convoy reached the road junction.

Marcus swore as the memory of the scruffy SAS soldier at the park came back to him. Suddenly, the rectangular object he'd seen in the man's hand made sense; a radio. Shaking his head, Marcus was staggered by the level that Box had gone to in order to keep Joe Carluccio, RED LANCE, running as an agent. *Willing to kill police officers and a SIG Agent?* Utterly insane. The RUC would be demanding some very serious answers this morning. The repercussions for this would be felt all the way to the door of Ten Downing Street. Marcus looked up as a familiar face entered the room and gave the man a smile.

'Good morning Colin. You look knackered.' As he watched, the RUC man merely nodded and as he stepped into the room, Marcus saw that he was followed by Stuart Coull, the Colonel's expression as sombre as Marcus had seen. He stood up from the desk.

'And morning to you too Sir.'

The CO nodded and indicated with his head towards the far end of the building.

'Marcus, good morning. Look, we need to have a very discreet chat, so I've commandeered the DSM's office for the next hour or so.'

With that, the CO left the room followed by Colin and Marcus as they made their way along the corridor. They entered the DSM's room as a collator walked out, leaving a tray of coffee and biscuits behind on the small table. Marcus closed the door and sat down in one of the armchairs. There was silence in the room as the CO poured the coffees and passed them around before taking a seat himself. Marcus was curious as to why he'd been called to such a meeting and couldn't hold his tongue any longer.

'Has something happened to GRANITE sir?'

The CO looked almost distracted. 'Has something...no Marcus, GRANITE is fine. This is...well, this is another matter entirely.'

Marcus nodded. 'Okay...'

Colin Woods took a loud slurp of his coffee then looked at Marcus.

'Right Marcus. I spent over four hours with Big Joe last night. I took in a reporter from the Belfast Telegraph because I knew that Box would try and get their man away and deny any involvement in yesterday's ambush.' He shook his head, his eyes hard and piercing as they held Marcus's. 'And I wasn't having that.'

Marcus listened as Colin recounted the whole situation, his coffee going cold as he focused on the incredible information that the TCG officer was sharing. Colin had taken the drastic measure of smuggling the reporter into Joe's room because he needed Joe to go public with his story. By keeping MI5 away from Joe, he'd been able to convince Joe that they had abandoned him and were letting him take the fall for the ambush and the killings linked to the big Barrett rifle. Colin had told Joe that he, better than anyone, should know that the best Joe could now hope for was a bullet in the back from a mystery assassin. That there was no way MI5 were going to allow him to go to trial and prison with all the dirty secrets he had about them. His only choice was to go public. That way, there would be no option but to have him transferred to a secure custodial location or, depending on his level of cooperation, the Resettlement Program where MI5 would have no choice but to leave Joe alone. Any retribution after that, far too obvious. Apparently, it had taken Joe some time to assimilate all this, but in the end, he had seen the wisdom behind Colin's words. And he'd talked.

Colin explained that Joe had been recruited back in the early seventies through blackmail by a member of Military Intelligence. He worked with this individual for a couple of years carrying out some seriously illegal operations. Colin hesitated, glanced at Stuart, then back to Marcus before saying that he would talk more in depth about that period later. Marcus nodded, curious but fascinated by the revelations the TCG officer was providing.

According to Joe, his first Handler left Northern Ireland for a year then returned, but this time as a Case Officer with MI5. The Case Officer had explained to Joe that the British Government were keen to get out of the quagmire that was the Northern Ireland conflict, but didn't have anyone credible within the republican movement with which to engage. Over the years, this Case Officer helped Joe to rise through the ranks of PIRA until he was in a position of absolute trust with GHQ, the Army Executive and the Army Council. Through selective arrests, killings and the identification of informers through the years, Joe and his Case Officer managed to get the personalities that the Case Officer wanted into positions of authority. Joe had given Colin the names of these people, mostly Sinn Fein representatives or more political leaning than military. It was the Case Officer's stated aim to eventually have the PAC and the IRA leader- ship as a whole, heavily weighted towards political personalities. And it was working.

According to Joe, the only problem had been when the London bombing cells had been arrested, the PAC knew that the informer was someone at their level or very close to it. Colm Murphy, PIRA's *de facto* Chief of Staff had put the call out that everyone was a suspect and that everyone should expect to be investigated. He had a special team that no one was told about, snooping around and gathering intelligence on all the PAC members. When Joe had told his

Case Officer about this, he'd been told that the matter was already in hand and just to wait for direction. Joe explained that he'd then had a meeting with his Case Officer where he'd been told that Kieran Mulgrew of the Executive Ops team was a Military Intelligence agent. Joe had been surprised but his Case Officer told him that this meant Mulgrew was the perfect candidate to take the fall for being the high-level informer that Colm was hunting.

Joe had seen immediately that Mulgrew was a good fit for this. The man's pedigree and access to high-level PIRA personalities could easily be used to point the finger at him as the mole. Unfortunately, for Joe at least, it hadn't worked out that way. The other problem that Joe and his handler faced was the fact that Joe had made two tapes of Mulgrew's 'confession'; the original one and then a second, where he'd copied elements of the first tape across but edited it in such a manner Mulgrew would be heard confessing to the major PIRA operations that Joe had given up. Joe, and MI5's concern, was that with Mulgrew alive and talking, the RUC would soon put the pieces together and identify Joe's own role as an agent. And with the amount of RUC officers killed over the years, it would only be a matter of time before Joe's role as a tout would be leaked to PIRA as retribution. The Resettlement Program had apparently been discussed, but according to Joe, his handler was sure that by taking Kieran out in the ambush, Joe would be seen by PIRA as an even more committed republican and well above suspicion. PIRA would have their tout and Joe would be a hero. But, of course, it hadn't worked out that way.

Colin sipped at his coffee before continuing. He'd asked Joe why his handler was so willing to risk so much to keep Joe in the game. Joe had replied that he'd not been told the details but had been made aware that an important development between the British Government and PIRA was very close. Colin went on to say that Joe had been very forthcoming, hadn't hesitated once he'd begun talking. He'd provided lots of details about PIRA operations that Colin and the RUC had been missing as well as names of those involved. PIRA sympathisers and contacts within government departments and agencies including the RUC, Military, and Garda Siochana. Colin sighed and explained that, four hours might sound a lot but when there was so much information, by his own admission, he'd only really skimmed the surface of Joe's knowledge. He paused and gave Stuart Coull a meaningful look that, again, had Marcus wondering what else was going on. He didn't have long to wait as his CO sighed, leaned forward across the desk and looked Marcus in the eyes.

'Marcus, what we're going to show you now is...is going to be very difficult for you. We talked long and hard about whether or not to give it to you in the first place but, and I know Colin is in complete agreement with me here, I think it's the right thing to do.' He held his hand up to stop Marcus from speaking. 'I'm not going to say any more and Colin and I will leave the room and allow you some privacy while you read, then we'll return and see how you're doing.' With that, the CO stood, and Colin handed Marcus a thin file, as he too, stood up and walked towards the door. The TCG policeman pointed at the slim document.

'That's something I had pulled from the transcript of my wee chat with Joe at the hospital. There's obviously a lot more detail to be got on that Marcus but, as I said, I only had four hours to cover everything. I've had it cleaned up a bit and typed out so it's easier to read than my handwriting.' He laid his hand on Marcus's shoulder as he passed. 'Good luck son and we'll see you in a bit.' With that, both men exited the room and closed the door behind them. Marcus could feel his heart rate climbing and his face flushing with heat. *What the hell is in this? Why have they given it to me?* With a slight trembling in his hand, he opened the cover page of the folder, looked down at a thick block of text and began to read.

The IRA first started putting the bombs into the cities in 72, maybe early 73. I think Big Colm was OC around then and the bombing campaign was working really well. My handler told me that this was a big problem for the Brits as their plan was to bring the war to an end sooner rather than later. Internment had taken a lot of good IRA men off the street and I was telling my handler who he needed to help bump up the ladder to keep the IRA weak and in poor operational condition. And though that was working, my handler told me that we needed another strategy to run beside this, something that would help turn the people against the IRA and make it harder for them to get support from within their own communities. That's where Operation WHIPLASH came in.

As part of the Military Reaction Force, MRF, I was smuggled into Palace Barracks in a van and met a team of undercover Army intelligence officers that I'd be working with. They used to call me a 'Fred'; their name for someone who they turned, but to be fair, they always treated me right. These were some pretty tough boys, not shy of getting their hands dirty and they certainly weren't playing by the Army's rules. I was told that Operation WHIPLASH was only known to the men in that room, of which I was one and that it would always stay that way. My handler was in charge of it and I was introduced to the team as the man on the inside who would make a lot of the operation happen. Basically, it was this; the IRA would put together a bomb to be placed in the City Centre or near a barracks or Police Station. I'd learn when and where the bomb would be then the Op WHIPLASH team would make another device, get it to me, and I'd put it either with the bomb itself or very close to it. This combined device would be fucking massive and destroy an awful lot more than the IRA intended. Local businesses and the community would go mental, stirring up a lot of bad feeling towards the IRA, and because we had some real idiots running the show at the time, it wasn't being handled the best.

This was working really well for the MRF. There was pressure from the IRA leadership in Dublin to stop the bombs as public opinion in the South was turning against The Provisionals and this violent strategy. In Belfast, a lot of people were asking what the hell the IRA was up to, bombing their own the way they were. The IRA leadership were also confused; they couldn't work out why these bombs were causing the damage they were. But the campaign went on. PIRA put their bombs out and me and the WHIPLASH team added our bangs to the mix. But then there was a big problem.

My handler told me that someone had learned about WHIPLASH and was going to blab about it, killing the operation before it was the success it had a chance to be. Not only that, but the WHIPLASH team could end up in serious trouble as this was an MRF-sanctioned operation and not cleared through the proper channels. My handler told me that we needed to act fast to stop this, as he wasn't ready to go to jail for doing his job and we needed to make sure WHIPLASH could run its course. In Belfast at the time there was a business called the Four-Square Laundry. It was pretty popular with the families in West Belfast, picking up and dropping off washing every other day. What I didn't know until my handler told me, was that the laundry was a front for a military intelligence operation. Apparently, they tested all the washing they collected for traces of weapons and explosives and used that to arrest or kill the person associated to that clothing. And it was this team that had learned about WHIPLASH and were going to shoot their mouths off about it. So, my handler put together a plan.

He got the laundry van's routes and timings and told us that the easiest way to do this would be to ambush it in one of the estates. We had to be careful though; these were very well-trained undercover soldiers who were armed and would fight back. I got the WHIPLASH team the weapons; RPGs and Armalites, and they got the cars. We decided to hit them in Bombay Street as we could close them down really well there. On the day, I called old Bobby

McFarlane, a veteran IRA man from the fifties, and told him I was an officer in Belfast Brigade Provisional IRA and to get everyone off the street. That an official IRA operation was about to take place with a lot of bullets and bombs flying about. This wasn't unusual back then, and I knew he'd follow my directive and we'd have the street clear of witnesses.

We had one of the team follow the van that day and he counted it down to the RPG boy. He took out the van then the shooters went in to finish the soldiers inside. But it didn't work out that way. First thing we heard from the RPG fella was that two of our team had been shot and killed by someone from the van. My handler was going ballistic at this and told another one of the team to get in there and fucking finish them off.

Next thing we know, this guys on the radio telling us that one of the soldiers from the van has escaped and is running towards the cars we'd used to block the road. I was in a car with my handler, just around the corner in Clonard Gardens, and he put his foot down and drove straight there. I couldn't believe it when we turned the corner and here was this girl, a wee blondie carrying a sub-machine gun. She jumped into one of the cars and started it up, but my handler rammed her hard and she stalled. I got out and looked up the road, saw two bodies and someone who was obviously wounded being helped by the RPG fella. I was thinking that this had gone really wrong when my handler fired a shot. I looked around and seen him pointing his rifle at the blonde girl. She'd been blown back out of the car and was lying on the road beside it...

Marcus stood and backed away from the table and the vile document, his face pale and eyes wide, shaking his head to dispel the haunting images playing in his head of his mother's death. He let out a shaky breath as tears rolled down his face and clenched his fists, the knuckles white under the strain. Closing his eyes, he felt a wave of nausea and inhaled deeply to counter it. Raising a hand to wipe his eyes, he saw the tremors from the emotions he was feeling and started to walk out of the room. He reached for the door before pausing and looking back at the open folder and the testimony of Joe Carluccio. The last thing Marcus wanted to do was read any more of the horrific narrative but he knew he had no choice. He needed to know everything, no matter how painful. He owed it to her memory, to his father, and to himself to know every detail of the death of his mother. Head drooped in resignation at the daunting task ahead of him, he sat down, took a deep breath and continued to read.

...I didn't really know what to do but my handler just told me to get to the fucking van and finish off the driver and the camera boys then torch the whole thing, as we only had a couple of minutes until the military responded. I was going to take the fuel cans with me but thought I better finish off the soldiers first in case they came out shooting like blondie had. When I passed the RPG man, he told me he'd come back with the fuel and help me finish the job. When I got to the van, the driver was already dead. He'd taken a few to the body and his throat had been shot out. There was another two in the back. The first boy was still breathing but he was fucked; he'd taken a couple in his guts and was unconscious. I put one through his head then looked for the last soldier. He had been covered up by some bags of washing, but

he was dead already, a big gash in his head. When I came out of the van, the RPG boy was running up with the fuel cans and my handler came up to help us. He told us to soak the van thoroughly but leave enough for another vehicle. While we did this, he drove one of the cars up, put the bodies of our guys into it and drove it back to the bottom of the street. We'd just finished when he came up the road in another car with the body of the blonde woman inside. I saw she was dead, a big old hole in her chest and covered in blood. The RPG fella helped my handler carry blondie's body into the van before he drove the car into the side of it, jumped out and poured the rest of the fuel into this car. We had one last look around the street to make sure we hadn't forgotten anything then we ran back to the other motors while my handler set fire to the fuel then ran down to join us.

We went back to Palace, but it wasn't like before. We didn't share beers or have a laugh about stuff that went wrong. It didn't sit right with me that we'd shot and burned a woman. Don't ask me why, I've done much worse in my time, I know. I don't think the others were very happy either. They'd lost two of their mates and another one was wounded pretty bad. My handler warned us that we could never speak of the incident again. He told us that, as far as the military was concerned, this was a horrific crash; nothing more, and he'd make sure that this was the party line they followed. That our dead would be accounted for in a firefight in Newry later tonight. The next day we were back to business as usual, building and placing bombs alongside those that the IRA were putting out. But something was different; there was never that feeling of being in a team that we used to have. We stopped sharing beers after jobs, the banter dried up, we got a couple of new lads in who were good boys, but we had to watch what we said *around them. There was a lot of confusion within Belfast Brigade PIRA about what the fuck had happened in Bombay Street. Old Bobby McFarlane told the IRA that he had been called and ordered to tell the residents to get away into their back rooms and ignore everything they heard or saw. That it was an official IRA operation and there might be a bit of a rattle and a bang. After the security forces had dealt with the burning vehicles, PIRA started their own investigation, but nobody knew a thing. They were puzzled by the reports of explosions and gunfire but who had done it? And what had they done? No one knew. The incident was soon put to the back of the agenda as the IRA continued to fight on two fronts against ongoing internment and the increasing British military presence.*

The bombing campaign pretty much stopped in late '73, early '74 so Operation WHIPLASH worked. In early '74, my handler told me that our little unit was being closed down as the military couldn't understand why we operated the way we did and wouldn't sanction it anymore. He was going away for a bit but said I'd be working with another Military Intelligence officer. I wasn't happy with this, but he told me not to worry, he'd be back in a while and we'd pick up where we left off. And that's what happened. About a year after he left, I got a call from him asking to meet up. We met down in Bangor and he told me that he'd left the military and was now working for MI5. We started working together again and he began feeding me information that helped me get up to higher positions in the IRA. He'd also pass me personal stuff MI5 knew about some of the 'RA that I could feed into the leadership to have these boys discredited or removed from their positions. We also had a decent relationship, enjoyed a few good nights on the tear with one another. I remember we were having a drink one time when he laughed and asked me to guess what my code name was. I told him I didn't even know I had a code name and he told me it was RED LANCE; the Red Indian chief from my favourite western movie I'd loved as a kid. He said I was like a lance into the heart of the IRA that would eventually destroy the organisation. Over the years I've given him good info that's stopped a lot of IRA attacks and also engineered getting the people he wanted into positions of authority.

He's close now, to pulling off something big between the Brit government and the IRA but I don't know what it is. All I know is that he keeps saying that this is what we've been working towards all these years. Like I say, I don't know what it is, but I know it's big.

What's that?

His name?

Jonathan.

I don't know his last name, but I've always called him

Jonathan. His last name begins with C though, that much I do know as he always called me JC and joked that we had the same initials.

CHAPTER 36

PALACE BARRACKS, HOLYWOOD, 1973

Julie pulled her holster and magazines from her waistband and stowed them in the metal locker. She smiled, picked up the photograph of Marcus and Alan, and gave it a light kiss before returning it to the shelf. Stripping off her jeans and heavy clothing, she changed into a tracksuit and donned her plimsolls. From the bottom of the locker she retrieved some leather bag mitts then closed the door and secured it with the padlock.

As she walked towards the gym she smiled and nodded to the familiar faces as they passed her in the corridor. She was looking forward to a good workout, having spent much of the day in and out the van as they'd done the laundry collections and got them in for testing. She moved her head from side to side as she walked, loosening the neck muscles in preparation for the workout ahead. At the end of the corridor, she pushed open the exit door, stepping out into a cold, breezy late afternoon.

Julie pulled the zipper of her top all the way up and jogged across the courtyard, keen to be out of the wind. As she turned the corner towards the gym she drew to a halt when she saw a mob of uniformed individuals stood outside the door, hunched figures smoking cigarettes and rubbing their hands in the cold air. She tutted in disappointment, realising that the gym was being used again as overspill accommodation for arriving soldiers. Turning around, she remembered that there were a couple of punch-bags in a room in the other wing. As there were no ablutions or even electricity in that part of the building, it was usually empty. She resumed her jogging and made her way to the other side of the square, opened the side door of the building and entered.

The building was as empty as she'd hoped, and she could hear no sign of any activity. There was enough light for her to see where she was going, and she turned down a deserted corridor heading towards the punchbag room. Ahead of her, she noticed a yellow glow in the corridor and frowned, wondering if they'd finally put electricity into this wing. She reached the door of the room she was looking for and was reaching for the handle when she heard voices and some laughter. She recognised one of the voices but struggled to put a name to it. Without really knowing why, she turned away from the door and headed towards the sounds. As she got closer, she saw that the yellow glow was coming from a light in the same room as the voices. She also noticed that this room had a very secure door in relation to all the other decrepit, paint-flaked entrances along the corridor. The door was slightly ajar and as she reached to push it open a deep Irish voice inside stopped her.

'It's about five hundred pounds and young Sean Murray is the driver. He'll park it just *there*, then head to the phone box *here*, and call in the warning.'

Julie frowned as she wondered if she'd inadvertently stumbled upon a debrief with a *Fred* and waited to see if a Handler began asking questions. She nodded as an English voice spoke up.

'Good stuff JC. Okay, as usual we'll give that a bit of help with a big old lump of our own which should produce a pretty healthy bang.'

Julie shook her head as she listened to several people chuckling. *What the hell is this guy talking about?* She leaned closer to the door, needing to know what was being discussed. The Irish voice was speaking again and Julie could tell from his words that he was briefing from a map.

'That's what I thought. So, if you get the Semtex to me *here* at half-one, I'll make my way down to the van and get it planted while Sean's tearing away out of the area. Don't be fucking late though; I don't trust those bloody timers and want a decent window to get to the van and well away before it blows.'

'Come on JC, you know me. I've never let you down yet and don't intend to start now. Okay, let's leave that to one side, we've got plenty of time before that happens. Next item, technical stuff. Take a look at this, gents; with this bit of kit we can override their timers and set our own. That way we can blow the fuckers up on the way to dropping the bombs off. Will look like an accident or a faulty mechanism.'

Julie held her breath as she listened to the sounds of chair legs scraping on a floor. Her heart beating loudly in her ears, she took a half step forward and edged the side of her face into the gap between the door and the frame. She saw four men standing around a table covered in maps, looking at an object they were picking up and examining. With her limited viewpoint, it looked to Julie just like a timer control for a car bomb and coupled with what she'd just heard the English voice saying, she guessed that this was the override timing mechanism he'd mentioned. One of the men stood back from the table and lit a cigarette as the others continued to study the device.

Julie recognised this man. *Joe? Jack? John?* She knew it was something like that. She also knew he was MRF but in a different department, something to do with support she seemed to remember. One of the other men at the table straightened up and also lit a cigarette, turning his head towards Julie as he blew the smoke away from the two men still hunched over the table. Julie's eyes widened as she could now attribute a name to the Irish voice she had heard: Joe Carluccio. *What the hell is going on here?* She pulled her head back and listened but there were no sounds to indicate she'd been seen. Her heart was racing now, and she knew she'd been witness to something terrible. She couldn't quite join all the dots yet but the main picture in her head was clear:

MRF were using IRA members to make IRA car bombs bigger and more deadly.

She couldn't understand why this would be happening, but she knew she had to tell someone. While all she wanted to do was sprint as fast as she could away from the door, Julie backed up in tiny steps, rolling her feet to avoid compromising herself with a clumsy foot fall. She continued to back away from the door in this manner, expecting at any second, one of the men to burst out and catch her in the act. When she was far enough away, she widened her stride, still walking backwards until she reached the end of the corridor then, with a final wide-eyed look towards the room, turned and ran out of the building.

Taking the stairs two at a time, she made her way to the head-shed's offices. Her mind was made up; as much as she'd tried to convince herself that what she'd witnessed could have a benign explanation, her experience and her gut told her otherwise. Julie was far from squeamish, had put down her share of PIRA killers but what she'd just listened to told her that MRF was conducting some serious black operations that certainly her squad at least, knew nothing about. She yanked on the door of the first floor and strode quickly along the corridor until she reached the office she was looking for. Taking a deep breath, and before her confidence wavered, she knocked hard and was responded to almost immediately, the CO's voice booming through the door.

ENTER.

Pulling her shoulders back and thrusting her chin forward, Julie opened the door and entered her Colonel's office, portraying a picture of confidence and determination that she didn't really feel.

~

As the door closed behind Corporal Myers, Colonel Richard Knight picked up the telephone and dialled an extension. When he was answered his clipped, estuary English barked down the line.

'Get word to Lieutenant Crowe. He's in The Wing. Tell him to call me immediately.'

He replaced the phone in its cradle and turned back to the paperwork he'd been completing before Corporal Myers' unexpected visit. Her interruption had been of the most unwelcome sort; more bloody trouble that he didn't need. He'd told her she had probably misunderstood what she'd heard but that he would discreetly investigate and get back to her by the end of the week. The phone rang, shattering the quiet of the office and he picked it up.

'Jonathan? It's Richard. You've got a problem. A fucking *big* problem.'

He summarised the information that Corporal Myers had supplied and answered a couple of questions until there was a brief pause on the line. 'Jonathan? Please ensure WHIPLASH is not compromised in any way, shape or form and that I am never surprised in this manner again. I sanctioned WHIPLASH because I believe in its effectiveness but I am not going to the wall if Corporal fucking Myers takes her information outside my command. Sort this and sort it soon. Understood? Good. Proceed as you need to. Goodbye.'

He returned to his paperwork satisfied that the situation was resolved. Richard didn't want to know what Jonathan would do to take care of the issue but what he did know was that Jonathan *would* take care of it. He and his crew were very reliable in that regard and Jonathan had a real talent for unconventional thinking that had led to some of the less advertised, but most successful operations that MRF conducted. Richard sighed as he authorised a surveillance request form for a target in Divis and thought about Corporal Myers for a brief moment. He'd thought it was a clear rule, unspoken but understood, that one didn't run around listening to conversations that didn't concern you and then blab about them. Plenty of places in the regular Army if that was your bag but not here in MRF. You could get hurt playing at that game.

Badly hurt.

CHAPTER 37

HILLSBOROUGH CASTLE, NORTHERN IRELAND, 1995

Jonathan Crowe attempted to steady his nerves, the jiggling of his leg and drumming fingers on the arm of the chair attracting irritated glances from the secretary. It wasn't the first time he'd been to the Castle or indeed, been requested to meet with the Secretary of State for Northern Ireland, or SOSNI as he was referred to. But Jonathan knew that this would be no standard chat regarding the strategic aims of the Provisional IRA. No, this would be an altogether different conversation. This SOSNI was renowned for making individuals accountable for their actions rather than the organisation to which they belonged, and Jonathan was under no illusion that this was exactly why he was here.

He'd known it wasn't going to be good when the Service's Director and Coordinator of Intelligence, effectively Jonathan's boss, had told him that he wouldn't be at the meeting. For the DCI not to attend meant that he was making himself scarce, having thrown Jonathan under the bus for the current domination of the media's reporting on Joe Carluccio and MI5's involvement in the matter. The DCI's representative at RUC HQ in Knock had been politely asked to leave the building, the rank and file policemen disgusted that the Security Service had been running an agent while turning a blind eye to his links to the deaths of some of their friends and colleagues.

In fairness to the DCI, he *had* been recalled to London to explain the situation, but he could easily have waited until the meeting with SOSNI had been concluded. Supported Jonathan by presenting a unified front. But he hadn't, and Jonathan was long enough in the tooth to recognise when he was being thrown to the wolves.

When he'd returned to his Safe House after being assaulted in the hospital, he'd taken a couple of painkillers and gone straight to bed with a crippling headache and a determination to crucify Colin Woods and the other RUC monkeys who'd hit him. What he'd woken to in the morning however, had been a different world entirely. The recognition of the severity of the situation was instant, and he was on the phones as soon as he could, demanding meetings with anyone he felt could assist in reining this in. But no one was taking his calls. Even walking around the offices in Palace Barracks, he saw the stares and discreet shakes of heads as he passed and had felt the alienation expanding around him. Nobody wanting to be associated with the condemned man.

He knew that he wouldn't be *severely* punished. They couldn't. Any formal measures such as being charged or putting him under official investigation would bring the Security Service and its operations in Northern Ireland under a very uncomfortable spotlight. As well as being an obvious admission that they were conducting some legally questionable operations. And his Service wouldn't want that. Couldn't have it. So, Jonathan knew that whatever punitive measures were being considered, they would be administrative in the main. But extremely disabling to his career prospects.

He assumed the DCI had painted Jonathan's actions as those of a rogue Case Officer who meant well but had gotten a little carried away in the execution of his duties. This would give the DCI and the Service as a whole, some plausible deniability in that they could claim to have had no knowledge of Jonathan's activities. *But they've been bloody happy to take the credit for my results.* And he'd been close. *Really close.* Jonathan knew his work was appreciated and that the Cabinet had been following the progress he was making, even though it was disclosed as a collaborative Service operation. The DCI had hinted that even though the Prime Minister was not a particularly effusive individual, he was very passionate when discussing the momentum being made through Jonathan's efforts. Suggested that a decoration was a certainty given the current optimism for the next leap in progressing the initiative.

The Belfast Agreement. The secret name for the classified initiative of bringing PIRA to a formal agreement to put violence behind them and embrace the political path. The full extent of the details known only to those within the inner circle: The Prime Minister and a couple of his most trusted advisors, SOSNI, the DCI. And Jonathan. Because Jonathan had made a lot of it possible. From back in the mid-seventies when he'd begun identifying suitable candidates and, with Joe's help, getting them into positions of influence within PIRA, to stopping the big attacks that would make dialogue with the IRA a difficult sell to the Great British public. Jonathan knew PIRA and Sinn Fein better than anyone in the Security Service and his superiors had exploited this, allowing him his roving role, responsible to the DCI in name only. No questions asked as long as he was producing the goods. Which he had.

But that was all gone now, thanks to Joe Carluccio and Colin Woods. The cat was well and truly out of the bag. Even from initial reports back at the office, Jonathan had picked up on the rage from the general public that a violent killer such as Carluccio had been an MI5 agent for over twenty years. From the republican side there had been no public announcements yet as they came to grips with one of their most trusted, higher-echelon operators having been exposed as the worst of their traitors. No doubt there would also be howls from the opposition party in Westminster later this afternoon about their beloved republican brethren being subjected to dirty tricks by the Security Service. His train of thought was interrupted by the secretary telling him that he could go through. He gave the man a weak smile, stood and smoothed the creases out on his suit, then made his way to the large oak doors.

CHAPTER 38

SIX MONTHS LATER

SIG, BELFAST

Marcus unzipped the large holdall and began removing the items from his locker. He packed the bigger items first, the boots, shoes, heavy jackets. Then the clothing, some books, several CDs. The last item he removed from the metal locker was the picture. He was taken back instantly to when he'd first arrived in SIG and had been unpacking and looking at the same picture in the same manner as he was now. Except now he knew his mother hadn't died in a crash. She'd been murdered.

He sat heavily on the bench and his eyes watered as he took in her smile, the happiness in her eyes, in *all* of their eyes. He looked at the image of his father with a very different viewpoint now. Sympathy and anger replacing the hollow emptiness he'd held onto for most of his adult life. The murder of his mother had also been the death of his father, the man never recovering from the heartbreak he'd experienced.

Marcus sniffed and rubbed his eyes with his sleeves, wiping the tears away. He looked around the changing room and knew he'd miss the place, the people, the work. His final day as a covert intelligence operator. He lowered his head as he struggled with the mixed emotions he was feeling. Finding out, after over twenty years, that his mother had been murdered still staggered Marcus. That she was murdered by another soldier had been almost too much to take in. That the killer had then become an MI5 officer running an agent who had also been involved in his mother's death was equally unbelievable. That when the Carluccio case came to light and the same MI5 officer was punished only by being reassigned in the UK, was impossible for Marcus to accept.

The Security Service managed to get much of the media reporting on Carluccio toned down by the issuing of a DA Notice as a measure to protect national security interests. SIG and the RUC had been told that Jonathan Crowe had received the most severe of punishments that the Security Service could award. However, when Stuart Coull had looked into what this entailed, it appeared to be nothing more than having Crowe reassigned to a department on the mainland, away from the mess he'd left behind in Northern Ireland.

Marcus had raged at the injustice. Demanded that Joe's testimony to Colin Woods be used to have Jonathan charged with the murder of his mother and the other MRF operators. Both his CO and Colin had agreed, getting the ball rolling by engaging the appropriate personalities within the RUC and the Security Service.

But they were too late.

No paper trail for Operation WHIPLASH could be found to identify where and when it had existed. No record that the death of the MRF operators was anything other than the accident that had been the official line for over twenty years. The archives at Palace Barracks had been accessed by persons unknown and all the references to WHIPLASH that Marcus had seen with his own eyes disappeared overnight. Joe Carluccio couldn't be touched, protected by his status within the Resettlement Program. A ghost in all but name.

Marcus had learned that the Security Service had tried to have Colin Woods and Stuart Coull removed from post due to their involvement in the exposure of RED LANCE. They hadn't counted on the rage extending to the top of both the RUC and the Army and had been told in no uncertain terms to back off or face the prospect of zero future cooperation. Calls had been made to the Secretary of State and Number Ten, making it clear that if Box persisted with their efforts to remove the men, there would be a public show of solidarity from the RUC and Army leaderships. *Very* public. And Box really didn't need another media circus on their hands. So, the matter was dropped, and Colin and Stuart retained their positions, both men angry but relieved.

But Marcus wasn't relieved. Marcus was raging. The angriest he'd ever been in his life. He thought about engaging a private prosecution. Getting his mother's body exhumed and examined. Sure that, even after being burned, bullet wounds and perhaps even the rounds themselves, might still be present in the bones of her body. His CO had cautioned him against this, pointing out that as soon as the Security Service got wind of what he was up to, he could count on being shut down or his mother's body disappearing from the cemetery one night. Or that any coroner taking the case would easily be browbeaten by the power of MI5 to deliver the findings that suited their purpose.

The cocktail of rage, frustration, grief and injustice tore Marcus apart. He hit the drink and lashed out at anyone attempting to console or support him. With no way of getting to the guilty parties to vent this rage, he took it out on those closest to him. A fistfight in the Detachment bar with an operator from West Det had been the tipping point for Dom. The next morning he'd called Marcus in for a private meeting and told him that he couldn't carry on drinking and taking out his frustrations on the people around him. Marcus had agreed and stunned his Boss by telling him that he was leaving. Dom had told him not to be rash, to take a couple of weeks' leave, have a think about it. But Marcus was adamant: He was done.

He knew that by staying in Northern Ireland he would never lose the anger and sense of injustice that burned inside him. That every time he was walking or driving through Belfast, he would only ever think of the city as the place where his mother had been murdered by the British Army. That the Security Service's first instinct on learning that one of their Case Officers was a murderer was not that of justice, but of arse-covering and career protection.

But first and foremost, that his mother's killers would never face the justice they deserved.

Looking down at the photograph once again, he sighed, placed it carefully into the holdall and zipped the bag up. He gave the locker a final glance to confirm it was empty, then grabbed the bag and headed out of the changing rooms. As he walked into the bar area, Marcus smiled when he saw the CO and Colin Woods standing with Dom, the three men drinking coffee and talking quietly. Marcus placed his holdall beside his other luggage and walked over to the men as they looked up. The CO smiled at him and put his coffee down on the bar.

'Nearly set for the off then Marcus?'

'Yes sir. Transport should be downstairs waiting.'

Stuart Coull nodded, his face now serious. 'Not too late to change your mind, you know. You're a bloody good operator and we're gutted to be losing you.'

Marcus shook his head. 'No sir. Appreciate the offer, but this is the right thing for me.'

Stuart Coull held out his hand. 'I know we've been over this before but let me say once again how devastated I am that this whole situation unfolded the way it did and that, if there was anything more in my power that I could have done, I would have.'

Marcus shook the hand. 'I know sir, and I really appreciate everything you've done.'

Dom patted Marcus on the back. 'Been a pleasure Marcus. Gutted it had to end like this but I guess we'd all be the same in your shoes.'

Marcus shook his Boss's hand and smiled. 'Thanks Boss, you've been brilliant throughout my whole time here. I'm going to miss this place.'

He turned to Colin Woods and was about to offer his hand when the RUC man nodded towards the door.

'Here, I'll give you a hand with your bags down to the car. Don't want one of your Army colleagues here straining themselves, do we?'

The men laughed and Marcus raised his hand in a final goodbye that the CO and Dom returned. He and Colin picked up the luggage and made their way downstairs. The collators and clerks stepped out of their offices and wished him good luck and Marcus thanked them as he made his way to the car park. He spotted the driver at the same time he saw Marcus and stepped out of the car and opened the boot. Colin and Marcus made their way over and loaded the luggage, closing the boot when they'd done. Marcus smiled and held out his hand to Colin and was surprised when, instead of shaking it, the RUC officer placed something in it. Marcus looked at the object and saw that it was a small card with a telephone number on it. Puzzled, he looked up at Colin as the policeman stepped closer and lowered his voice.

'Marcus, that's my private home telephone number. I don't care when or what it is, but you ever need anything, you come to me first, understand? We owe you a lot mate and we'll never forget that. *Never*. And Marcus? I really mean *anything*.' The policeman's eyes took on an intensity Marcus hadn't seen before as he emphasised his point. Marcus nodded and shook Colin's hand.

'Thanks Colin. Thanks for all you've done and tried to do. You've been a true friend.'

The policeman grinned. 'Well, you're not too bad a chap yourself...for a Royal Marine!'

Marcus laughed as Colin continued. 'What's your plans now?'

'Well, I'm in my late twenties but still fit and wanting to push myself so I'm seriously considering selection.'

Colin whistled. 'SAS? Tough gig that mate.'

Marcus nodded. 'Yeah it is but I've still got something inside me that's not quite satisfied yet. There's a good chance I won't pass it, but I know I need to try. Will give me something to focus on as well.'

The policeman nodded and patted Marcus on the shoulder. 'You'll pass mate. I can see it in you. Good luck to you Marcus and remember; anything, okay? *Anything*.' With that, Colin walked away, heading back to the building and Marcus got into the car, fastening the seat belt as the driver put the car in gear and headed out of the compound.

As they weaved their way through the outskirts of Belfast, Marcus felt a sadness wash over him at the thought of leaving the city where his mother had been killed without having seen anyone held accountable for it. The sadness was replaced by the preferable presence of anger at this injustice, that those responsible were living new lives, unconcerned and untouchable. As he tried to push the negativity out of his thoughts, Marcus recalled the emphasis and intensity of Colin Woods's last word to him:

Anything.

CHAPTER 39

NOVEMBER 1999

DUNDEE, SCOTLAND

Brendan Molloy nodded at the barmaid as she pointed to his empty glass. He watched as she grabbed a clean one and began pouring the Guinness, the churning brown mess soon settling into the velvet-black liquid he was looking forward to drinking. A familiar voice drew Brendan's attention back to the television set up in the corner and he grimaced, shaking his head slightly. The voice cut through the conversations around the bar and became the only thing that Brendan could hear. The voice remained calm, smug even as it informed the reporters that, according to the *agreement*, this man was no longer being sought by the British police and as such, was well within his rights to be released. The voice was replaced by the appearance of the news anchor, summarising the story of an IRA man that the police had arrested in the UK for the City of London bombings but then had to release under the terms of the Good Friday Agreement. Brendan looked up as the barmaid placed his pint in front of him and he fished out the pound coins to pay her, indicating she keep the change. She flashed him a flirtatious smile and swayed her hips as she walked back to the bar, knowing full well he'd be watching. He picked up his Guinness and took a sip of the creamy brew, wiping the pale moustache from his lips as he placed the glass back down.

Brendan shook his head at the memory of the news report. *The Agreement.* Unbelievable. IRA prisoners released from jail and now even the OTRs, those IRA men On The Run from the Brits, getting off the hook because of The Agreement. The Good Friday Agreement. Brendan never thought he'd live to see the day. And now senior IRA men were even taking up positions as members of government, legitimised by the Brits themselves. He shook his head again in wonder then took a large swig of his drink. Belfast today was a far cry from the Belfast that he remembered, as was the republican movement. Sinn Fein sitting down and trying to govern alongside the Unionist parties. *Incredible.*

He glanced at his watch and thought about making a move. He'd grab a pizza on the way home and get his feet up in front of the telly for a couple of hours before bed. He downed the last of his pint, stood and put on his coat, scarf and cap before giving a wave to the barmaid as he turned to the doors. A few of the older men sat around the tables gave him a nod or a smile which he returned as he passed. He stepped out into the freezing evening, a thick sea mist, or *haar* as the locals called it, adding to the frigid atmosphere. Grimacing as a dull, aching throb settled in his shoulder, he cursed the damp and the arthritic pain it brought with it. Pulling his jacket tighter around him, he hunched his chin down into his scarf, denying the cold any opening through which to invade. He walked downhill towards Mario's, one of the best pizza take-aways in the city and could hear his stomach growling in anticipation. Brendan hadn't bothered with lunch today, the shop being quite busy, and he'd finished a bit later, locking up just after seven before heading to Trades for his customary couple of pints before home. The streets were quiet, all sensible people either warm in their homes or enjoying the toasty fire of a nearby pub. Not to worry, he'd be home himself soon and sat in front of his own fire. He looked up as he reached Mario's and smiled when he saw the shop was empty. *No queues, I'm on a roll tonight!* He pushed open the door and savoured both the warmth and the welcoming aroma of freshly baked pizza.

≈

Brendan increased his pace as he crossed the main road and headed towards the quayside, wanting to get home and out of the cold before his pizza cooled. He could barely see the building through the dense sea fog, the softened orbs of the sodium streetlights lacking any detail or providing even an adequate light. As he reached the cobbled road that led towards the apartment block, Brendan reflected on how good life was. His shop was doing well, the appetite for high-end home furnishings pretty much a recession-proof concept. People with money tended not to be too affected by minor irritants like financial crashes. And he loved his flat, with its views over the River Tay and across to Newport, liked nothing better than a quiet Sunday on the balcony with his coffee and newspapers. All in all, life wasn't too shabby for Brendan Molloy.

He turned down the road towards his building and smelled the sea, now that he was walking directly alongside the quay, the water below him and off to his left. He could hear a gentle lapping of waves and knew that it must be high tide but again, couldn't see the water due to the thick *haar*. He jumped backwards and let out an exclamation of surprise as a dark figure loomed directly in front of him.

'Hell's teeth man! Scared the tripe out of me there.' He gave a chuckle as he made to walk around the figure, but the person mirrored him and blocked Brendan's path. The Irishman stopped and took a step backwards to create some distance. He stared at the person's face and was about to say something when the person moved closer and lowered their hood. Brendan blinked rapidly as he tried to recall where he knew the face from. Although the memory wouldn't return to him, his heart was racing and small beads of sweat broke out on his forehead as the person smiled at him and spoke.

'Hello Joe.'

The pizza box fell from his hands and scattered its contents on to the slippery black cobbles. Brendan Molloy took another step backwards, his mouth opening and closing without any words coming out, his face draining of colour and eyes widening. As the shock of hearing his real name assailed him, he was struck by a deeper dread when he remembered the identity of the dark figure in front of him. A low moaning noise that he was unaware he was making came out of his mouth as he continued to stagger backwards on unsteady legs. He held his hands up in front of him.

'Wait...wait. Please. Look, we can talk about this yeah? I'm not who...'

He screamed as the knife sliced through skin, veins, and tendons, blood spraying from the obscene gashes that opened up across his wrists. His breathing became frantic as he stared at the wounds, unable to comprehend what he was looking at. The person moved closer and to one side of him and Joe stepped back faster.

'Please, don't do this. I'm not Joe anymore. PLEASE.'

But the silent knifeman was relentless. There was a blur of movement and Joe Carluccio screamed again as a lance of agony burned the side of his face. He could feel the blood flowing down his cheek. He tried to lift his hand to his face just as the attacker slashed the other side. Joe threw both hands up and screamed again, stumbling backwards as he did so. In a sudden blur of motion, the knifeman was right next to Joe and he felt two blows, on the inside thigh of each leg. It took a couple of seconds for him to register the hot blood pouring down his inner thighs and the realisation that his attacker had just severed Joe's femoral arteries. He looked up and shivered, the cold now joining the assault on his weakened body. The knifeman's eyes were calm and focused as they held Joe's own and the Irishman started to sway as the blood loss began to take its toll. He opened his eyes again as he heard his attacker move closer and felt the man's breath on his face. Joe stared into the piercing blue eyes and nodded. It was time.

The knifeman placed a hand on Joe's chest and leaned in, his lips almost touching Joe's ear, and whispered.

This is for my mother.

The shove sent Joe tumbling backwards and into the frigid waters below. The impact knocked the air from his lungs then the cold water shocked him, panic and terror fuelling his survival instinct. He began fighting to reach the glow of light on the surface above him but tired quickly and soon lacked the strength. His clothing became heavier and the thrashing of his limbs slowed to a halt. He could hear the noises he was making as he strained to keep his mouth shut and felt his chest bucking wildly as his lungs demanded oxygen. No longer able to control himself Joe's mouth opened, and the freezing saltwater poured in, filling every void with its lethality. Joe Carluccio's body convulsed and spasmed as the last vestiges of life were extinguished until there was no fight left within him. His last conscious act was to raise his head and watch the diminishing glow of light on the surface as his body sank in a slow, graceful descent into the pitch darkness below.

CHAPTER 40

NOVEMBER 1999

UPPER LOUGH ERNE, NORTHERN IRELAND

Jonathan Crowe hummed as he loaded more wood into the opening of the log-burner then closed the hatch. He settled back down on the small sofa and picked up his book, returning to the page he was reading. Out on the water the plaintive cry of a curlew pierced the silence of the night and Jonathan looked out of the window in the direction of the sound. He could only see his own reflection, the dark outside an almost complete blackness. A slight rocking motion moved beneath him as a small swell passed under the hull, a legacy of yesterday's winds.

He should have done this years ago. The houseboat was his saviour. The peace and solitude that his mooring on Lough Erne provided was Jonathan's escape. His only regret was not doing it sooner. All those years of grim Belfast Safe Houses, Police Stations and Army Barracks and he could have been here, with only the dark water and birds for company.

Jonathan hadn't expected to be asked to return to Northern Ireland, but with the devastation caused by the Omagh Bomb and the subsequent realisation that it could happen again, old quarrels were put to one side. His experience was still recognised and valued but he was on a tighter leash, had been told as much back in London when he'd been asked if he was willing to pitch in again. In the four years since he'd been away, a lot had changed in the Northern Irish political landscape. Jonathan had been given little to no credit for the years of work he'd put into getting the pieces in place for what was now called The Good Friday Agreement. It rankled with him still, that none of it could have happened without his foresight and planning that had gotten the key IRA players into the positions of influence where MI5 could steer the movement. No invitation to any of Tony and Cherie's soirees at Number Ten. No informal coffee with his own Director General. No medal as a formal recognition, although his former DCI had been awarded the OBE for the department's role in assisting the Agreement. Jonathan sipped at his merlot and smiled as he recalled his Service's alternative expansion of the abbreviation OBE; *Other Bugger's Efforts*. Based upon the cynical assertion that the gongs were always awarded to the people higher up the chain rather than the worker bees that carried out the hard graft. *Oh well, life goes on...*

He turned back to his book, wanting to take his mind away from his bitter musings. It was an entertaining biography about a German prisoner of war who escaped a

Soviet gulag by walking all the way from Siberia to Europe. As he sipped his wine, Jonathan began to lose himself in the book, accompanying the protagonist through his incredible journey. At some point he looked up, frowning as he attempted to identify what had interrupted his concentration. He heard it again; a slight thump as though something was banging against the hull. He listened closely for several minutes and identified that it was coming from the stern. He needed to check what it was in the event that it might damage his hull. Probably something cast adrift in yesterday's winds. A branch or log maybe. Still, better to make sure.

He stood and walked to the door where he donned a heavy waterproof jacket and grabbed the torch from its mount. Opening the door, he saw his breath mist in the frigid air. He gave an involuntary shiver then set out along the deck, the boat moving slightly beneath him. When he reached the stern, he saw an object bobbing on the wavelets below and smiled as his theory was proven true. An orange and white fender was bumping the hull as it was lifted and dropped by the small swells. He lay down on the deck, stretched his arm down and grabbed the fender by its rope-hold, hauling it out of the water. He stood and took the item to a storage bin and placed it inside before closing the bin again and heading back to the cabin. He paused for several moments and looked out towards the dark waters and islands of Lower Lough Erne. Another cry from a curlew made him shiver and he headed back to the warmth of his log burner. Stepping back inside, he replaced the torch and took off his jacket before heading back to his book. He walked towards the sofa but stopped and let out a yell of surprise.

There was a man sitting on the sofa looking at his book.

The man looked up as he heard Jonathan's yell. He stared at the MI5 officer for a moment before putting the book back on the cushion.

'Hello Jonathan.'

Jonathan felt his mouth become dry and the room seem very hot. He tried to speak but nothing intelligible came out. He licked his lips and tried again.

'Who are you and what do you want?'

The man smiled and leaned forward, elbows on his knees as he studied Jonathan's face.

'You don't remember me, do you?'

Jonathan frowned. There *was* something familiar about the man, but he couldn't quite place what it was. The black wavy hair and piercing blue eyes triggering something in the dim recesses of Jonathan's memory. Regardless, he needed to get to his pistol which was in the drawer of the table that the man was sitting beside. To his relief, the man patted the sofa beside the book.

'Jonathan, come. Take a seat.'

Feigning indifference, Jonathan shrugged. 'Okay, but you still haven't told me who you are or why you're here.' He walked around the table and lowered himself on to the sofa, the two men now only a couple of feet apart. Jonathan stretched out his arm slowly as though picking up his wine, then yanked the drawer open and reached for his pistol. His hand scrabbled around, and he looked down in confusion to see that the drawer was empty. Looking up, he saw the stranger pointing Jonathan's Sig Sauer at his stomach. He felt faint and there was an odd buzzing sensation in his ears as he held his hands up and shuffled as far back in the sofa as he could. His mind raced as he struggled to identify how he was going to get out of this. There was no panic button on the houseboat with which to alert anyone. The stranger had his only weapon. And Jonathan didn't know if the man had come alone.

Dialogue; that was all Jonathan had in his bag. He'd have to talk his way out of it or at least talk his way to the point where he could overpower or hoodwink the man.

Why is he here? Robbery? But he knows my name. The thought came to Jonathan that it might be more serious than a robbery when he remembered he'd gone out to see what was banging on the side of his boat. Whoever this stranger was, he'd managed to get into the main cabin while Jonathan was preoccupied and without causing the boat to shift under his weight. The implication being that the man had planned this and staged the distraction. Which in turn probably meant he was a professional. *But professional what?* He opened his arms in an attempt to convey his willingness to cooperate.

'Look, I don't know who you are or what you want but why don't we put the gun down, eh? Tell me why it is you're here and let's see if I can do something about it.'

The shot was deafening in the small confines of the cabin and Jonathan's mouth dropped open in shock a split second before he was aware of the blow to his leg. Looking down, he saw that his kneecap was shattered with small pieces of white bone showing through the mess of blood, tissue and tendons. He gave a scream and was reaching towards the hideous wound when the stranger leaned forward and smashed the butt of the pistol into the bridge of his nose. Jonathan screamed again and collapsed backwards, bringing his hands up to his broken face. He opened his mouth to breath as the blood gushed from the gash on his nose and the crushed cartilage inside. Eyes open wide, he stared at his assailant.

The stranger shuffled closer along the sofa and leaned in towards Jonathan.

'You probably *don't* remember me, but you will remember my mum.'

Even with the agony he was feeling, Jonathan's face portrayed the confusion he was experiencing. The stranger sighed and with little more than a casual glance towards it, shot Jonathan in his other kneecap.

Jonathan's scream pierced the air for almost a minute and as it dissipated, he began to hyper-ventilate, making loud moans as real shock kicked in. A hard slap on his cheek made him open his eyes and the stranger's face was close to his, staring at him with those cold blue eyes.

'Oh no you don't. Not yet.'

The stranger stood and walked out of the room and Jonathan heard the door open. He dared to hope. *Has he gone? Can I get to my mobile phone? Can I get a signal?* He looked down at his shattered kneecaps and started to cry. He wasn't going anywhere on these legs. Bubbles of bloodied mucus grew from his nose as the pain started to become overwhelming. His vision was blurry but the movement of the boat beneath him told him what he didn't need his eyes to confirm: The stranger had returned. Jonathan started sobbing.

'What do you want? Take it! Take anything.'

The stranger put down whatever it was he was carrying and looked at Jonathan.

'Oh, don't worry. I *am* taking it.'

Feeling faint, Jonathan sank back further into the sofa and allowed his eyes to close as he fought waves of nausea. He could hear the stranger moving around and figured that he was searching for valuables. But even through the fog of pain and suffering, the noises sounded odd to Jonathan. And the smell...

His eyes opened wide as he realised what the overpowering stench in the small room was; Petrol. He watched as the stranger splashed the liquid from a large canister, dousing the carpets and curtains as he went.

Jonathan felt his heart hammering in his chest and tried to get himself off the sofa.

'No, no, no. please, PLEASE!'

The stranger stopped and tossed the empty jerry can into the corner. He stood still, looking at Jonathan for several moments before speaking.

'I'm going to give you a chance here Jonathan. Does that sound fair?'

Jonathan nodded and sobbed at the thought of getting out of the situation.

The man smiled. 'Yes. I like to think I'm a fair man and it's only fair to give you the same chance that you gave my mother.'

Jonathan frowned as he tried to understand what the man was talking about. Seeing his confusion, the stranger elaborated.

'My mother? Corporal Julie Myers? Belfast 1973?'

Jonathan felt as though his heart had stopped as the significance of the stranger's visit took hold.

'You're Sergeant...Marcus...her son...'

The man nodded. 'Almost. It's actually Trooper Vaughan now. Boat Troop, D Squadron, 22 SAS. But yes, I'm Marcus, Julie Myers' son.'

The tears started to roll down Jonathan's face and he began shaking his head.

'Please, Marcus...that was a different time...things were done that...'

'Shut up. I told you I'd give you the same chance she got and I'm a man of my word.'

Jonathan watched as Marcus took several steps backward until he was at the door. He reached into his pocket and pulled out a small object that glinted in the light. There was a clicking of metal on metal and a flame shot up from the object.

'So, here's your chance Jonathan. You shot my mother then placed her in a van that you set on fire. I'm giving you the same chance you gave her. Good luck.'

Jonathan threw his body forward as the zippo lighter spun through the air, the blue and yellow flame sputtering as it arced through its descent. Marcus hurled himself out the door and leaped from the deck onto the wharf below just as a giant whoosh blew out the windows of the boat behind him and the hot overpressure of the blast shoved him to the ground. He rolled over several times before getting to his feet and checking himself quickly for any burning embers. Shielding his eyes as the fire on the boat raced through the varnished wood and furnishings, he walked backwards to get away from the intense heat being emitted. Pulling the Sig from his pocket, he hurled it into the darkness of the Lough and with a last look at the floating inferno, turned away and walked back towards the woods. Picking up the path he'd used for his infil, Marcus made his way through the trees, the light from the burning boat highlighting the forest before him in a sea of dancing shadows.

CHAPTER 41

DECEMBER 1999

WATFORD, ENGLAND

Stuart Coull laid the small bunch of flowers on the grass and stood up, brushing the knees of his trousers. He looked at Marcus, the younger man giving him a soft smile as he stepped forward and placed his own floral arrangement on each of the graves. Behind them, Colin Woods stood looking awkward and a little self-conscious. Marcus rose from his kneeling position and stood with his hands clasped in front of him, quietly studying the headstones.

He had managed to get his dad to be buried alongside his mum after a lot of bureaucratic wrangling. But it had been the right thing to do. And today's small ceremony was his way of acknowledging that fact. Ever since he'd learned the truth about his mother's death, he hadn't been able to hold on to the antipathy he'd previously held for his father. He remembered the love that his dad had for both of them before his mum's death and knew that the end of that love was not his father's fault but that of the men who killed his mother. But those men were gone now. Gone for good.

Stuart could see that Marcus had filled out since the time he had been his CO at SIG. Even under the winter jacket, the muscular physique was apparent. Three years in the SAS. Stuart still struggled to believe so much time had passed so quickly. When he'd received Marcus's call the previous week, he'd been surprised, then touched to be invited to the small ceremony. Marcus must have worked very hard to get his father's remains moved here but had clearly been determined to do so. Stuart couldn't help but notice how much more at peace with himself Marcus seemed to be.

Stuart had heard of course, about the murders of Joe Carluccio and Jonathan Crowe. As head of Defence HUMINT Operations, Stuart liaised a great deal with his counterparts at the Security Service. MI5 were still reeling from the fact that in one year, two of their resettled agents had been found and attacked by PIRA, and although Martin McGartland had survived, it had been touch and go for some time. Joe's body had washed up on the shores of Broughty Ferry near Dundee where he had been living under the name of Brendan Molloy. Stuart had been told that the former head of the Nutting Squad had been mutilated before he drowned and would have been under intense pain and suffering. To add to MI5's problems, Jonathan Crowe was murdered around the same time as Big

Joe. According to the autopsy he'd been kneecapped before being burned alive.

The current thinking from Box was that Jonathan had been compromised and a special PIRA team assembled to torture and interrogate him before killing him. Stuart had heard that MI5 had subsequently stopped meeting agents and had moved out of their Safe Houses until they could identify what information Jonathan had given up. There was real fear regarding the threat from a secret PIRA hit-squad that hunted down and killed resettled agents and MI5 officers with such utter ruthlessness. Looking at Marcus now, he didn't think the SAS Trooper would be shedding a tear over the death of either the former head of the Nutting Squad or the rogue MI5 Case Officer.

Marcus turned around and caught Stuart looking at him and flashed his old CO a smile. Walking forward to the headstones, he kissed the tips of his fingers then touched each stone in turn. He straightened up and began walking back towards the path, grinning at the policeman standing awkwardly by the large yew tree.

'Come on Colin, I'll put you out of your misery and get you that pint I promised!'

Colin Woods smiled and joined Marcus and Stuart as they walked across the grass towards the car park. He looked back over his shoulder at the two headstones with the fresh flowers at their base and felt a small lump in his throat. He could imagine that Marcus was finally able to put a lot of the ghosts of the past to rest and move on with his life. Crunching along the gravel path, Colin reflected that he was glad he'd been able to help.

Glad that, when he'd received a telephone call nearly a year ago from a young man calling in a debt, he hadn't hesitated. Had said yes, despite the obvious implications of the request. Had called in favours of his own from men and women he trusted to never breathe a word of his requests. Obligated to repay a debt that he'd promised to a young Royal Marine in a car park in Belfast four years before. Determined to find out the whereabouts of a resettled IRA killer and a murderer protected by the badge of the Security Service.

Because when the telephone rang on a wild January night and the caller only spoke one word, one question, Colin had known from that question the exact path that he was embarking on. But he always repaid a debt. Especially a debt of honour. So, when the question had come, he'd listened.

Anything?

And answered.

Yes. Anything.

Because that's what he'd promised.

THE END

AFTERWORD

The conflict in Northern Ireland is often referred to as 'The Dirty War'; a nod to the nefarious actions and activities conducted by all sides. As incredible as it may seem, the story in Chapter One where an undercover intelligence operation is ambushed, actually happened. In my novel I have altered the outcome slightly but the MRF, the Four-Square Laundry and many of the other activities I mention in this book are drawn from real events. For the 30-plus years of violence in Northern Ireland, spooks, soldiers, policemen and terrorists fought and vied for victory in any way they could.

Observers of the Troubles will obviously spot strong similarities between Big Joe Carluccio and the real-life circumstances of STAKEKNIFE, aka Freddie Scappaticci, an IRA mole-hunter turned Military Intelligence spy. STAKENIFE's identity was 'blown' around 2001 and rocked both the Provisional IRA and the general public alike. The IRA due to the damage STAKEKNIFE's work had inflicted upon them over the years and the general public who were stunned that a cold-blooded killer could be in the employ of the state.

Northern Ireland provided the British Military and Security services with the ultimate platform with which to test and hone counter-insurgency tactics and practices. All the way from internment without trial in the early 1970s to the hacking of telephones and computers in more modern times. 30 years of lessons that would be adapted and applied in the killing fields of Afghanistan and Iraq in later years. The legacy of this covert war remains today as Freedom of Information requests and relaxation of statutes means that more and more initiatives like the Four-Square Laundry are brought to light.

But clearly, there are operations and information that will never be released to the general public for reasons of National Security or political sensitivity. And I believe that this is the reason that the fascination with the covert war in Northern Ireland remains. That so much more happened which has been left unexplained and consequently fuels the conspiracy theories and accusations of deep state skulduggery. Of course, the sad, and often overlooked aspect is that of the suffering from all sides. The victims and families of victims from both sides of the sectarian divide and the security forces. To those people, the legacy of this violence is heartbreak and loss. A personal connection to atrocities that many of us witnessed as disinterested bystanders as we watched our national news bulletins, far removed from the battleground of the Divided Province.

Sins of the Fathers is a work of fiction that draws on the history of covert operations in Northern Ireland and, hopefully, entertains rather than acts as social commentary. That was never my intention nor my place to do so. That right rests solely with the people of Northern Ireland. Those who lived through and experienced the darkest 30-odd years that their small corner of the world is likely to endure.

Thank you for reading and I truly hope you enjoyed this book. Please, if you have enjoyed it, take the time to leave a review and let others know how much you liked it. Thank you once again.

James

ALSO, BY JAMES E MACK:

ONLY THE DEAD

'*Only the dead have seen the end of war*'

In war-torn Libya, veteran Commando Finn Douglas is forced to commit an appalling act in order to save the lives of his men. Haunted by his actions, he suffers a further blow when he learns that his family has been killed in a terrorist attack in London. Numb with grief and trauma, Finn turns his back on the world of war and killing and flees to an island wilderness to escape his demons.

A team of Military Police are tasked with bringing Finn to justice. But for one of the policemen, the manhunt is a more personal issue; a chance for revenge to right a wrong suffered years before.

When Finn intervenes in a life and death situation, his sanctuary is shattered, and the net tightens. The manhunt becomes a race against time between the forces of law and order and a psychotic mercenary determined to exact his revenge on Finn for thwarting his plans.

For Finn, the world of killing and conflict returns with a vengeance on the blizzard-swept mountains of the island. Only this time there is nowhere left to run.

Only The Dead is a thriller in the tradition of Gerald Seymour and a standout debut from a new British author.

FEAR OF THE DARK

An idyllic Scottish village...

A small team of rural Police Officers...

A man who won't talk...

When a violent stranger is arrested and refuses to give his name, it is only the beginning. Digging further into the background of their mysterious prisoner, Police Constable Tess Cameron finds that he is a disgraced former Special Forces soldier with a chequered past.

As the worst storm of winter hits the village and communications and electricity are cut, the severe weather is blamed. Tess, however, feels that something more sinister may be responsible for their isolation.

Because the stranger has friends.

And they want him back.

Whatever it takes.

In the darkest night of winter, Tess and her fellow police officers find themselves facing an elite team of killers determined to rescue their leader. And Tess knows that if they are to survive the night, they have only one choice:

Fight.

First Blood meets *The Bill* in this exciting new thriller from the author of Only the Dead.

THE KILLING AGENT

London. Cardiff. Edinburgh.

The worst terrorist attacks that the UK has seen.

A country in turmoil, a government in disarray.

Lovat Reid, a veteran covert operator with the Special Intelligence Group, is tasked to help track down the mastermind behind the attacks. With his partner Nadia, an officer from the Special Reconnaissance Regiment, they soon realise that they are dealing with an individual the likes of which they have not seen before.

When another atrocity is carried out, the entire weight of the Intelligence agencies and Special Forces is thrown behind the effort to find the terrorist responsible. But for Lovat, something isn't quite right. Suspecting a dangerous power-play between the agencies, Lovat digs a little deeper into the background of the terrorist suspect.

And is stunned by what he finds.

With a race against time to halt the next attack, Lovat and Nadia find themselves fighting a war on two fronts as they strive to uncover the depth of deception while hunting the master terrorist.

From the killing fields of Kandahar to the back streets of London, the consequences of a secret assassination program are brutally levelled against an unsuspecting British public.

LINKS

https://web.facebook.com/authorjamesemack

www.jamesemack.com

Printed in Great Britain
by Amazon